I0534933

To Capture a Unicorn

LAURIE SANFORD

RIVER LEAF PRESS

RIVER LEAF PRESS

To Capture a Unicorn

Published by River Leaf Press

To Capture a Unicorn is a work of fiction. All incidents, dialogue, and characters are products of the author's imagination and are not to be construed as real. Any resemblance to actual persons, living or dead, events, or locales is entirely coincidental.

Copyright © 2023 by Laurie Sanford

Cover Art by: Carpe Librum Book Design, carpelibrumbookdesign.com

All rights reserved. No part of this book may be reproduced or transmitted in any form or by any means, electronic or mechanical, including photocopying or recording, or by any information storage or retrieval system, without permission in writing from the publisher.

For more information, visit:

www.lauriesanfordbooks.com

www.facebook.com/lauriesanfordbooks

To Mark, my partner in life and my forever love. I wouldn't want to take this wild ride with anyone but you.

One

Forging one's own path is never an easy endeavor. Her grandmother's words tolled through her mind as Jane stepped down from her carriage and settled her hood over her blonde hair. The family matriarch was one of two souls who knew her decision that day, and the most vocal in opposition to it. But she would never try to stop her—not when her happiness teetered on the edge of destruction.

Trailing the masculine form of her companion, Jane weaved through tall grasses that tickled her stockings until they reached the shoreline. The dawning sun spilled over an endless panorama of sea and sand, its golden rays glimmering off a tall ship anchored just beyond the shallows. Her heart hammered against her ribcage. She was really here. The life she had always known was about to vanish forever.

"Well, here we are." Edward turned to her, concern tracing the lines of his shaven face. "The captain of this vessel is a good friend, and he will see you safely to Barbados. She is primarily a cargo vessel, but there are a number of passengers already on board." He attempted to smile, but his lips merely twitched before falling into a dismal line.

Jane nodded, taking a quivering breath. "I'll write to you as soon as I'm safely at the mission." The wind whipped down the grassy hills, flapping her hooded cape against her slender form and lifting stray locks of her hair.

"Are you sure you want to do this?" Edward asked. Jane looked up into eyes that implored her deepest parts. "I'm sure your father will alter his course if he knows you would sooner become a nun than marry the man of his choosing."

More likely he would lock her away until the day of her unwanted wedding. She recoiled at the thought, drawing her valise against her body. "He will never be happy with my decisions, whether I stay or go. Besides, it isn't just about escaping my betrothal to Davenport. I want to do good with my life. I want to serve the Lord."

Edward smiled sadly, his fingertips squeezing her upper arm through her cloak. "You're a fine woman, Jane Whitecliffe. Davenport could never hope to deserve you, even if he could see past his vanity to appreciate what was nearly his."

Cheeks warm, Jane diverted her gaze to the tossing waves littering the air with the scents of salt and algae. If only her father had considered someone like Edward to marry her. If only Edward had made an offer. They had never truly loved each other, but he would have made a kind and decent husband. She would much rather be married to a lifelong friend than a drunkard who scandalized women, leaving them behind like a trail of discarded trash.

The sun had risen into the open sky now, breaching the snowy clouds that parted to emit its rays across her skin. A rowboat glided through the water, ready to carry her away from England, away from the comforting shores of her homeland. The idea launched a shiver through her—both terrifying and thrilling at once. Books had provided the only picture she had of her future home—wild depictions of an untamed place so different from anything she knew. Perhaps she would hate it and long for the familiar. But she had forsaken that the day she'd decided to defy her father.

"Promise me you'll keep me abreast of my family's news," Jane said as they trekked across the uneven sand. "Especially my grand-mother." She was a spritely woman for her age, but a determined attitude couldn't keep her alive forever.

"I promise." Edward took her valise in one hand and held out the other to assist her.

With her skirts gathered in a fist, Jane grasped his hand and climbed into the rowboat now nested on shore. She could barely hear her thrashing heart over the rush of blood in her ears. Edward gave her one last worried look before settling her bag beside her and standing back with his hands in his pockets. He'd already tried to talk her out of her harebrained scheme several times since she'd first told him of her plans. He could do nothing now but watch her go.

Every thrust of the rowboat's oars tugged her farther from her beloved friend and the home of her childhood. Jane held her head high, reminding herself again why she'd chosen this path. She would not be trapped in a loveless marriage, the victim of a husband's depraved whims and abuses. She would not die inside of herself every day, bringing children into a life she hated.

The Church stood inside a halo of light in her mind's eye, untouched and brilliant in its radiance. Surely, God would fulfill her every need. His love would far outweigh any earthly affection she'd ever longed for from a man. Jane gazed up at the imposing ship they neared, resolute in her heart. She would take her vows and don the cloth of sisterhood, devoting her life to a cause so much greater than herself. Romantic love would just have to lay its sights on another woman.

C hristophe Roux hardly heard the gentle lapping of the waves and the cry of the gulls overhead as they swooped through the misty air. His eyes swept the beach, roving over the large assembly of men just waiting for his word. Behind him, two ships sat side by side beyond the clear blue shallows, waiting to transport human life from Traitor Isle for good.

The briny sea air clung to his skin and fluttered his white linen shirt as Christophe planted his boots in the sand before a group clustered on the ground, their hands bound with ropes. Some of them shot him looks of contempt, but most only appeared tired, hungry—just how he wanted them.

"I feel for you men," he said in broken Italian, expertly ensuring his eyes met every pair staring back. "You were simply doing your duty. You were simply earning a living to keep your families alive. It is not your fault that your leader was a tyrant"—he glanced through the trees toward the tent Stefano Cavaretta's body still lay within—"a dead tyrant now."

Diego Vivianno swore and spat at the ground. His narrowed eyes trailed Christophe's steps, his clenched fists promising to end him if ever given the chance.

"Now, *most* of you have a choice in the matter at hand." The captain's mocking gaze slid over Vivianno before landing solemnly back on Cavaretta's men. "There are two ships behind me, either of which you might board to escape this godforsaken island once and for all."

Crossing his arms over his broad chest, Christophe flicked his blond head toward Auguste Bertrand. The man stood proudly in his loose ruffled shirt and leather pants, feigning the look of a seasoned captain despite his inexperience. A full crew waited at his back, ready to defend their leader if the need arose.

"Now, Captain Bertrand here has a cargo vessel," Christophe said. "If you leave with him, you will be safely carried back to the European continent to go about your life as you please. You might even join his crew if he approves." Several heads bobbed, seemingly pleased with the lenient avenue laid before them.

"Or you could come with me." Christophe gazed lovingly at his brigantine, dancing in the sloshing waves, a mermaid with flowing hair affixed to her bow. "The treasure you came here for is leaving aboard my ship, so if you still want to share in its rewards, I suggest you join my ranks."

He paused, considering his words carefully. He needed enough of Cavaretta's men to successfully sail his ship back to France after his numbers had been obliterated, but not so many that they caused trouble among his crew. These men had fought and killed each other. Too many on the decks of the *Sirene* would certainly stir up conflict, something he couldn't have with a priceless treasure hidden below his decks.

"If you vow to serve me faithfully on our journey back, you shall share in the Moon King's wealth." He watched anticipation spark on their faces as they glanced at one another. "However, I must warn you. We are a pirate band. A voyage with us will never be safe, nor easy. You will follow my instructions. You will earn your keep, working day and night. You will fight who I tell you to fight, or you will die. You will abide by our code of conduct."

Christophe squared his shoulders, his chest expanding as he stood boldly before them. "We are not the dictatorship you have served under thus far. We make decisions together. We elect our leaders. We share everything that comes our way. They say the age of the pirate is dead, but we continue to thrive because we refuse to break the rules that keep us united."

His eyes narrowed on the group listening with rapt attention. "If you come aboard my ship, you are subject to our laws. That means you will not hoard anything for yourself, no matter how you acquired it. You will not gamble for money. If a woman comes aboard this ship, you will not touch her." He paused, recalling how he'd broken his own command the night he'd kissed Madeleine. Shoving the painful memory aside, he glared down at them. "If I hear that any of you has taken a woman against her will, anywhere, I will drown you."

Standing back, Christophe signaled to his men with a nod. They spread around Cavaretta's surviving crew and started untying the ropes binding their wrists until only one remained confined, seething up at the captain with hatred swarming his dark gaze.

"It is time to make a choice, gentlemen." Christophe's arms spread wide. "You may stay here and die with Cavaretta, or you may come with one of us." He gestured toward Auguste, who straightened up like a toy soldier.

After mumbled discussion moved through the group, they began to break apart, one by one. Many ambled over to Auguste's crew, their weakened bodies and tired gaits bespeaking their desire to simply go home again. A handful of the men sauntered daringly toward Christophe, ambition alive in their eyes. Good. He needed deckhands ready to fight, as long as they didn't fight each other.

As the men began moving past him, bidding each other farewell and climbing into the rowboats sitting ashore, Christophe stepped to the man with arms still tethered behind his back. Vivianno refused to look at him, staring off at the rolling surf with bile raging on his clenched face.

Christophe's fingers coiled around the hilt of the pistol stationed on his hip. How badly he wanted to yank it free and end the miserable life sitting before him. When he remembered Vivianno's maniacal laughter, the way he'd held Madeleine and pierced her beautiful skin with his blade, his body trembled with rage. All that stopped him was his promise to the woman his heart remained loyal to. He would not kill Vivianno unless he had to.

"And what happens to me?" Vivianno asked, lips curling in disgust. "Will you leave me here to die slowly with my brother?"

"It is what you deserve—what both of you deserve."

Vivianno's venomous gaze swung up to meet Christophe's, his sorrow converting to stone.

The captain breathed, quelling his need for vengeance. "Because of the good woman you tried to kill, you will live. Only because of her." He laughed lightly at Vivianno's expanding eyes. "Your brother was a fool." Only an imbecile could possess her love and squander it.

Christophe's boot kicked at a pebble in the sand, dusting the breezy air. "You will ride back to Europe in the cell beneath my decks, locked away like you should be. When we reach France, I will dump you on the shore and be rid of you for good." Be rid of the treasure, of Madeleine, of everything keeping him from blasting into the endless ocean without a care. That's what he really wanted, wasn't it?

A gull flew over them, its guttural cry heralding the late hour. Vivianno's jaw tensed, but he said nothing. Though relief had subtly flooded his face, he still hadn't lost that malicious sneer. His dark eyes shifted past Christophe, landing on something behind him. Before he could turn to inspect it, a hand had fallen on Christophe's forearm.

His breath hardened at the face looking up into his. Her raven hair fell loosely around her face in a wild, captivating manner that she'd never be allowed to wear in France. Her gentle eyes looked through him, past his exterior to the vulnerable soul beneath. Christophe cursed his hammering heart, the tingles that rose on his skin at her touch. She belonged to someone else, and still his rebellious heart refused to believe it.

"Auguste says it's time for us to go," she said, a tender smile on her face. "I couldn't leave without wishing you well."

Uncomfortable, he turned away from Vivianno's wicked stare and led her by the hand a few steps away. His soul ached to let go of her hand and watch it fall limp at her side. How much he wanted to lace her fingers with his, to feel her within his arms again. But her husband's form waiting by the water brought reality crushingly back. Despite his appeals, she had made her choice.

Her eyes were soft as they latched with his. "You're sure about taking the treasure back to France for us? I know it's a dangerous endeavor that I ask of you."

He shrugged. "It presents no more danger than I regularly put myself in. I promised you I would deliver it to your priest, and I will." He would protect it with his life for her sake.

Madeleine nodded, then swept a hand up her arm. "I suppose we won't see much of each other again—unless you visit Avance someday. There will always be an open door for you."

Christophe forced his lips upward. How much it would pain him to see her in that role—the baroness of another man's estate. He shook his head. "It is dangerous for me to travel that far inland in case the authorities catch wind of my whereabouts. I'm a wanted man in France." He'd risked it before to bring her back with him—and to deceive her.

She nodded, sad resolution on her face. "Then this is goodbye." She inhaled the salty sea air, the breeze angelically lifting strands of her hair. "Fitting that it's in the same spot we met."

He remembered that day as if it had transpired only yesterday. How scared she'd appeared upon their first meeting, with dirt caking her skin and her gown torn. He'd realized the moment her skin had first warmed his that she would distract him from the task of finding Henri Clement's treasure. Yet he'd never expected his heart to utterly shatter for her.

Sunlight winked through the dancing leaves, shadows moving across her face. He allowed himself a moment to memorize her sparkling eyes, the delicate lines of her cheeks, the way her pink lips gently curved. Then his gaze plummeted to the sand. Looking at her only made their parting more difficult.

"I'm sorry for everything I've done," he said, eyes fixed to the black rocks jutting up from the beach. "You trusted me, and I chose to lie to you. I hope you know that I—" The words stuck in his dry throat, unwilling to dislodge.

"I do." The wind swept over them, tinged with hibiscus and guava. She said nothing more, only covered the distance between them and lovingly wrapped her arms around his large frame.

Christophe hesitantly returned her embrace, content to hold her even in the pure gesture of a friend.

"You're a good man, Christophe Roux," she said in his ear, "despite what you believe about yourself. You deserve a good life." Her eyes shimmered sweetly as she pulled away and squeezed his arm, giving him one last look before making her way across the sand.

The breath seized in Christophe's chest as he watched Madeleine take her husband's hand. The pair strode happily over the beach and climbed into a rowboat, eager to continue their lives together. The aching inside of him mingled with joy, knowing she'd be safe and loved, that she'd live a better life than she ever could have with him.

"You're a bigger fool than my brother ever was," a voice called from behind him. Christophe swiveled back to find Vivianno glaring mockingly back. "You let that temptress worm her way into your affections. Your crew is going to cannibalize you to get their hands on that treasure." His laughter lit the air with a mad, hollow sound.

Christophe clamped his lips shut and spun toward his ship, ready to issue commands and get his crew underway. Focusing on the work at hand, he ignored the emotions that pulled at him as Auguste Bertrand's ship sailed into the morning mist, carrying away the only woman he'd ever loved. He employed his strong hands to lift the anchor, unfurl the sails, pour himself into the only part of his life that now brought him joy.

As the ship he lovingly called *"The Lady of Many Faces"* drifted into the vast Atlantic, Christophe gazed one last time at the tiny spot of land that had brought Madeleine into his life. A priceless treasure rested beneath his feet, and he had one mission to fulfill now. He'd promised her. Resolute, he marched across the deck and squelched the lingering premonition that Vivianno was right—they would never reach Europe without Clement's treasure tearing them apart.

Two

A stubborn wind tossed Christophe's mighty ship around like a feather caught on the breeze. The vessel moaned, her bow rising and plummeting with the roiling sea. Despite his familiarity with the ocean's moods, Christophe's stomach churned with each roll of the creaking brigantine. Perhaps it was merely his encroaching fears that unsettled him.

Sleep that night swept in horrific memories—images he'd tried a thousand times to shake. He flipped over and again between his satin sheets, the sights and smells of his childhood haunting him. He saw his mother standing in the grassy yard of their country home, pinning up clothes on a wash line suspended from the cottage's edge. The warm breeze blew back strands of her wild red hair. She bent to collect more sopping laundry, "The Marseilles Hymn" whistling from her lips.

How old had he been as he watched her from the branches of a chestnut tree? Eight, perhaps? He distinctly recalled the way her skirt fluttered on the breeze and how the air smelled of peach blossoms. His brothers and sisters giggled as they flounced about the yard playing knights engaged in swordplay. Why hadn't he joined them? Why had he sat in the tree and tried to memorize everything about this moment? Did he sense their perfect life would be splintered forever?

His fair-haired father had crept up behind his mother, quiet despite his brawny form and gigantic feet. When he reached her, he threw his muscular arms around her torso and tickled her below the ribs. His mother yelped, dropping her soaking laundry in the grass. Her chortles filled the air with a magical sound as she struggled against him, her eyes alight with glee. Christophe leaned back against the tree's solid trunk, content in the knowledge that he had a good life, a family who loved one another.

Memories of the months that followed flashed in his mind. Compelling them back, Christophe scrunched himself into a ball on his bed. He saw the army marching down the Vendée's hills, their bayonets gleaming in the sun. The screams of his siblings still echoed in his ears, his mother's plea for them to run pumping blood into his pounding heart. Ripped mercifully from his dream, Christophe bolted up in bed. Breathless, he looked down at the sweat-covered chest of a man and realized where he was. That little boy had vanished long ago.

He threw back his blankets, his legs aching as they swung over his mattress. Setting his elbows on his knees, he ran his fingers through his loose hair and cradled his face in splayed hands. After almost twenty years, he still felt the pangs of that day as if he were that child again. His legs still burned at the thought of racing into the woods. His head ached to picture the blood that stained the streets of his village after the army marched through it and killed everyone he'd ever known.

Christophe pushed himself off the bed, his powerful frame shaking with grief and anger. He'd physically survived that day, but a part of him had died. That sweet, innocent boy who had watched his parents' joy had grown into a man wary of the world, suspicious of authority. Blast Napoleon and his dastardly army. The nation of France could drown for all he cared.

Attempting to steady his rapid breath, Christophe reached for the shirt he'd left hanging on a chair back. He pulled it over his shoulders in one motion, his skin still raised from remembering. Bending, he took a swig of the water jug sitting on the floor before swiping an arm over his mouth and starting for the door. No sense in trying to sleep now.

The deck above already thumped with his crew's scurrying boots, a sure indication that the morning shift had taken over. They would soon lift the sails and take advantage of the predawn winds, aiming the ship across the endless waters toward France. The very prospect of stepping upon those shores made his stomach sour.

Christophe emerged from the stairs to a deck scattered in sailors working beneath a black sky. Icy wind unsettled his hair and plastered his shirt to his chest. He ambled through the busy production, pausing to inspect his men as they climbed the rigging and adjusted the sails. A group had formed around the capstan, ready to propel it into motion.

With approval, he turned aside and approached the ship's side. Faint blue light spilled over the eastern horizon, where soon the sun would color the sky in dazzling yellows and pinks. He sighed, drinking in the briny air, savoring the chilling spray as it peppered his face. The pain of his past dissolved as he gazed into the Atlantic's stunning waves. Not only did he love the sea, but he needed her—to forget, and to keep going.

"You're up early," a friendly voice greeted him from behind.

The captain pivoted to find his quartermaster approaching from the forecastle. "Does a sailor ever truly sleep?" he asked with a chuckle.

Monsieur Simon grinned, joining him at the ship's side. "I fear we do not, especially on a mercenary ship like this one."

The words planted a peculiar ache in Christophe's chest. He recalled the look in Madeleine's eyes when she had discovered his true profession, the utter distrust and disappointment. Would his parents approve of the life he'd built for himself, making a living stealing from innocent people? Surely not, but what had integrity ever gotten his family but the sword?

Casting the agonizing notion aside, he swallowed. "Do you anticipate any trouble on the seas between here and Brest?" They had made the decision on Traitor Isle to point the ship northward rather than sail through the Strait of Gibraltar. With such precious cargo aboard, the open sea gave them the safest chance of reaching France undeterred.

"None that I foresee at this point." Monsieur Simon speared a finger eastward. "We should avoid the French coastal patrols going this way, and the Spanish don't sail beyond Biscay. Once we're close enough to land, we should be able to circumvent them."

"Good." The fewer people they encountered, the better. Christophe had long ago learned the art of disguise to conceal his motives and avoid unnecessary hostility, but he would rather not have the need for it.

"Have you heard much talk among the men?" he asked, lowering his voice. His quartermaster spent a considerably larger amount of time amongst them and usually provided what information failed to reach a captain's ears.

Monsieur Simon glanced furtively at the bustling crew before turning toward the sea. "If they are talking, they haven't allowed me to hear much. Every so often, though, I catch Blanc's grumblings when he thinks I'm not near enough to hear them."

Christophe's brows girded. "What does he say?"

"Much of the same he did on the island. He complains about the baroness. He says you broke our code when you brought her on board." His lips pursed tentatively. "Someone says they saw you kiss her, but I don't know who."

Fear budded in Christophe's center. How reckless of him to have let his emotions overtake him in front of his crew. Of course, many thought the two were intimate in the privacy of his cabin. His foolish kiss would only fan the flames of gossip.

He sighed, aware Monsieur Simon still gazed at him in question. He hadn't even revealed the fact to his closest comrade. "I did kiss her, Jacob. I'm sorry." His head shook. "It was a moment of weakness, and nothing more transpired."

A slight smile curled his quartermaster's lips. "I don't fault you for kissing a beautiful woman you love. It is nature, after all."

Christophe scoffed. "She did. I thought she would hop into the ocean and swim back to shore that night." He set his large hands atop the bulwark. "Anyway, I *did* break our code, and I shouldn't have. The men have every reason to question me, especially after all that transpired on Traitor Isle. I clearly chose her life over theirs."

Monsieur Simon considered his words a moment, his gray eyes scanning the ocean. "I do believe that most of the men still trust and revere you, but Blanc could be a dangerous influence if he isn't managed properly. Don't forget—a small portion of these men were your enemies only days ago."

"What do you suggest?"

The quartermaster's shoulders lifted. "It's your vessel and I dare not tell you how to run it. Just remember, talk like Blanc's is a slow cancer. It will spread until you can no longer contain it. I would make an example of him before it's too late."

Christophe reached for a rope above his head and anchored a fist there. "I don't punish men for talking. If he begins conspiring with Cavaretta's men, surely the loyal members of this crew will bring it to my attention." His gaze flitted around them at the sailors climbing the rigging. Didn't they share a degree of trust unlike any companionship one could find in regular life?

"I hope so, but Captain"—Monsieur Simon's lips pulled downward, his eyes searching for the right words—"there is an angered man below decks who wants nothing but to tear you apart. There is a treasure beyond anything these men have ever dreamed of possessing. *Anybody* might seize the opportunity to use Vivianno's hatred for their own gain."

Sighing, Christophe rubbed the back of his neck. Curse Vivianno. He should have left the scoundrel to die on Traitor Isle. He should have been sailing to a safe destination where his men could evenly split the treasure they'd so long sought. Instead, he'd let a woman draw the most dangerous possible path for him, then followed it like an eager puppy looking for approval. Sometimes he considered forgoing her wishes altogether and simply taking the treasure for themselves. How could she stop him?

He looked back at Monsieur Simon, casting his foolish notions aside. He could never betray Madeleine—not after he'd failed her so many times. He would prove himself a man of integrity for once in his life.

"We must inspire camaraderie among the men," Christophe said. "We must remind them why they're on this ship in the first place, why they chose a pirate's life. They're bound to come together if they are distracted enough."

Monsieur Simon's eyebrows quirked. "What lies below decks is quite a lot to distract one from."

Christophe nodded. "Aye, but we must. If they catch wind of my true intentions for that treasure—" The thought suspended about the misty air, unfinished and daunting.

"What do you plan to tell them?" Monsieur Simon asked.

The question had long weighed on Christophe's mind. What could he possibly say to assuage an entire boatload of men expecting to be rich by their journey's end? "I still don't know."

A grunt issued from his quartermaster's throat. "If they find out all that wealth will pass through their fingers, they won't need Blanc or Vivianno's help to kill us both."

Fingers blanching on the bulwark, Christophe dragged in the sea air and gazed into the fathomless ocean. He could almost forget his present troubles as he came home to it, watching how the waves frolicked over one another. The sun had risen by now, painting the horizon in sparkling colors, clouds roving its spectacular face. If only he could dwell here forever—live the uncomplicated life of a seaman who had yet to find his pot of gold. How had fulfilling his lifelong dream ripped the existence he'd known asunder?

As the clouds parted and more golden sunlight spilled across the heavens, a distant form caught his eye. Christophe frowned, his open palm seeking a spyglass from Monsieur Simon. Without needing a word, the quartermaster deposited the item into Christophe's hand and stepped closer. He peered over the captain's shoulder to get a better look as Christophe gripped the spyglass and brought it to one eye.

The world went black as he closed one eye and focused the other. Within the circle of light the spyglass provided, the vague outline he'd spotted sharpened into the silhouette of a ship sailing through the waters east of them. His heartbeat picked up speed, as it often did when he discovered the existence of another vessel nearby. This could be exactly the solution they needed.

"It's a merchant ship," Christophe said, focusing on the craft's construction. Three masts protruded into the air—broad, square sails unfurled in the wind. "She appears to be a barque. There's nothing threatening about her."

"French?" Monsieur Simon asked.

Christophe glanced up the tallest mast to the blue flag with red and white stripes proudly flapping in the breeze. "British. She's flying the Union Jack."

Ideas quickly materializing in his mind, Christophe keenly surveyed the vessel. It couldn't have that large of a crew, and certainly they wouldn't possess the fighting skills needed to confront his men. The gunports looked new, as if they'd never been opened. Their speed was sluggish, and he doubted they could increase it much if provoked. "We could easily overtake them," he said above his whirring thoughts.

"You can't possibly be entertaining the idea." The quartermaster's hand clapped his shoulder. "Didn't we agree to forgo pirating until after we leave France? We can't afford to draw unnecessary attention to ourselves with the fortune we're carrying."

Christophe could barely hear him over his own thumping heart. The ship in the distance taunted him like a prize to be won. With the thrill of finding the Moon King's bounty behind him, he needed *something* to help him forget all he'd left behind when he'd alighted from Traitor Island.

"There is wisdom in that route, but think about it." Christophe lowered his spyglass and looked toward Monsieur Simon. "This could be exactly what we need. Fellowship. Togetherness. The chance to overtake something together."

At Monsieur Simon's dubious expression, the captain laughed. "These men are pirates. If they don't have the chance to band together for a purpose, they will splinter apart. I need them to remember who they are."

His companion's brow hooked, his arms crossing over his chest. "What logic could you possibly conjure to incite these men to risk their lives in pursuit of this ship? They think that if they sail to France one last time, they'll never have to work another day. They expect to disperse into the world without another care."

Christophe's head wagged, his blond hair blowing back from his face. "A pirate would never be content with such a life, and you know it. They live for the thrill of the catch, not the money it brings." He stood tall, his plan coming full circle in his mind. "I will tell them we must maintain our reputation on the sea, that we must not appear as if we've fallen into oblivion."

Monsieur Simon's doubts still played on his face. "You're sure about this? It seems like an unnecessary risk to me."

Christophe had already begun signaling to his men, his mind made up. "I am certain. This is how we'll survive this journey, Jacob. Trust me. I know the words to convince them. They will listen to me."

Hot blood rushed through Christophe's veins as his crew began to gather near, their curiosity piqued. "Change out the masthead before we're spotted," he said to a boatswain. "The unicorn."

His directive sparked a stirring among the men, their whispers bounding nearly soundlessly about the ship. Christophe stepped forward, assuming the air of authority he needed to perform the task at hand. "Yes, gentleman. Today we are the *Licorne*, and we will fight." His glimmering eyes met each of theirs, casting his confidence into them. "Set our course toward the merchant ship on the horizon. When we are in range, we will raise the black."

Three

J ane woke to the subtle sounds of scuffling in her cabin, her
anxious dreams of Barbados melting away as the tiny space
came into focus. A single candle had been lit on the table, thin
rays of light beaming over the four wooden walls. Around it, two
sets of bunks were stationed perpendicular to one another. The
only other items in the room were the trunks they'd secured in one
corner.

Rubbing her eyes, Jane forced herself to sit up on the lower
bunk she occupied. The straw mattress and scratchy wool of her
blanket contrasted starkly to anything she'd experienced before.
Since infancy, her skin had never touched anything but the finest
silk sheets, her bed at home as warm and comfortable as sleeping
on a cloud. Grateful for the experience, she tossed back her blanket
and drew her knees to her chest. What might her bed at the mission
be like?

An older woman stood at the table, glancing at Jane with a
kind smile. She wore a cotton chemise and stays, a thick stack of
petticoats extending to her ankles. "Good morning, dear Jane," she
said, the genteel accent of a refined lady singing from her rosy lips.

"Good morning, Mrs. Byrd." Jane grinned as she swung her legs over the bed and set her bare feet on the chilly floor. "It seems I'm up late yet again."

"Aren't we all?" Mrs. Byrd looked to the maid kneeling before her trunk, selecting her clothing for the day. "I told Martha I'm going to develop bad habits down here with no sun to wake us in the morning. My timepiece says 8 o'clock."

"Oh, dear." Jane popped up from the bed and headed straight for her valise. "I hope they still have food in the mess for us." No wonder her stomach growled with such intensity.

"Not to worry. We paid for passage aboard this ship." Mrs. Byrd stretched her arms high as Martha returned with a damask-printed day dress and lifted it over her head. "The captain wouldn't allow ladies such as ourselves to go hungry. He is a decent man."

Hoping she was right, Jane unfolded one of the few simple day dresses she'd brought with her and began removing her night shift. The linen garment slid over her skin with ease, leaving Jane to grapple in the dim light for the basin and pitcher. At least she might wipe away her sweat from sleeping before donning her clothes for the day. Already, she missed her porcelain bathtub from home.

Now fully clothed and letting Martha adjust the back of her dress, Mrs. Byrd clicked her tongue. "I do wish you would allow my maid to dress you, dear. It doesn't seem fitting for a daughter of an earl to be fixing her own stays."

Jane laughed, her nimble fingers already growing used to the task. "It is nothing but a bit of a trick to learn." She reached for her calico dress. "Besides, I shall never have a maid again. What am I to do in Barbados if I can't even dress myself?"

Mrs. Byrd flattened a hand on her middle. "That's right, you are joining the order of Anglican nuns." She sighed listlessly. "What a pity. A beautiful young woman of breeding such as yourself would make such a fine wife for a gentleman. I know plenty who are searching for someone just like you."

"I suppose they will just have to keep looking," Jane said with a trite laugh. "My father found me nothing but a cad obsessed with gambling and bedding women. I would sooner join a hundred convents than strap myself to a libertine who will make my life utterly miserable." Reaching behind her, she seized the ribbons to tie at her back.

"You are wise to be prudent." A spark of mischief glinted in Mrs. Byrd's eye. "Although, perhaps I should take you by my son's office when we dock in Barbados. He is a good boy and rather handsome. You might change your mind about wedding yourself to God."

Jane sat to pull on her stockings as Martha knelt before Mrs. Byrd to help her do the same. "You are simply scheming to get your son back to England." Her boots came next, a practical alternative to the usual slippers she wore at her family's estate. "No, Mrs. Byrd, I don't care how handsome any man is. I have made up my mind. God is the only man who will captain my heart, no matter who comes my way."

Even as she said it with conviction, a small piece of her needed reminding. Hadn't she always dreamed of running a modest home with children skittering around her doorstep? Perhaps God put unfulfilled dreams in one's heart to help one appreciate those he chose to grant.

"It was at least worth an attempt." Mrs. Byrd shot Martha a playful wink as she rearranged her skirts and rose. For a woman in her fifties, she still appeared young and agile. Her graying hair was knotted beautifully, an elegant style that contrasted with Jane's simple bun as they exited the small cabin.

A series of dark hallways brought them to a mess that sat empty save for an old sailor carting dishes to the galley. A single lantern swung over the room, casting orange streams of light on the rows of tables secured to two long walls. The trio of women found a table on which the crew had indeed left them a large ship's biscuit and overripe fruit. Jane imagined what fresh delicacies the West

Indies might bring—surely food she'd never dreamed of. For now, she would have to settle for soggy peaches.

The women partook of their breakfast between chatting. Martha had stories of her childhood home in Ireland, while Mrs. Byrd bemoaned the necessity of entertaining the dullest of society that came her way. Jane's accounts of life on the Earl of Brambleshire's estate fascinated her companions, raising their eager questions one after the other. As much as she hated dwelling on the world she left behind, Jane was thankful for their company. How lonely might her journey have proved without them?

"I still can't believe you boarded a ship all by yourself," Mrs. Byrd said, wagging her head. "If only I had possessed such audacity in my youth, my life might have transpired in a completely different manner."

"Are you inferring you might have been a nun, mistress?" Martha asked.

"Good heavens, no." Mrs. Byrd's skin lit red with her chuckle. "But I might have run off with a criminally good-looking soldier I met on a trip to London. I don't even remember where he was from now, but I wouldn't have minded living on the dark side of the moon with a man like that."

Jane joined in their merry laughter. "Was your husband so bad, Mrs. Byrd?"

Taking a breath, Mrs. Byrd pursed her lips in a sad smile. "No, Gordon was quite a lovely man. I wouldn't change my life in the slightest. But sometimes I do wonder." Her thoughtful eyes drifted to Jane's collarbone. "My, that's a lovely pendant."

Pinching her necklace in her fingers, Jane raised it in the lamplight. "It was my grandmother's. She gave it to me when I told her of my plans to run away." The elegant ruby teardrop glimmered beneath her chin, a thin strand of diamonds attaching it to the silver chain around her neck.

"In hopes of bribing you to stay?" Martha asked, her eyes admiring the piece of jewelry from across the table.

"Surely not." Jane clamped her fingers around the bauble, aching at the very thought of parting with it. "From a young age, this was my favorite of my grandmother's collection. I would always ask her to put it on me, then I'd dance around and pretend to be queen. I felt free when I wore this necklace—like the world couldn't stop me." Her mouth dimpled in a poignant smile. "My grandmother gave it to me to remind me that I am. That I can do anything I set my mind to if I want it badly enough."

Mrs. Byrd covered Jane's other hand in her wrinkled one. "What a lovely idea. You must cherish your grandmother very much."

Eyelashes beating back her sudden tears, Jane nodded. "Sometimes I think we are two halves of the same soul. She understands me like nobody else in the world. When I told her I was fleeing to the West Indies, she didn't want me to go, but she didn't try to stop me." Her eyes slipped shut. "She told me to follow my heart wherever it led me."

How strongly her emotions pulled at her now, begging her to return to the old woman's side. A pain like no other sprouted in her heart to realize she'd never sit at her grandmother's feet again, never feel her warm touch or hear her melodious voice of calm in moments of distress. Blazing her own trail meant leaving so much behind. Sometimes the sting of it overwhelmed her into questioning her choices.

Running footsteps on the stairs outside the mess yanked her from her wandering thoughts. Jane's eyes flew open just as a figure rushed through the doorway. A high-ranking member of the crew stood before them, his chest heaving and skin flushed. Dread crept over Jane's body as his frantic eyes found them in the dim room.

"Get back to your cabin as quickly as you can," he said breathlessly. "Go now. We've just spotted a pirate ship approaching from the west, coming too quickly to outrun. Hide yourselves. We're under attack."

"Gentlemen, ahead of us is a prize to be had. She is a small prize, but she will serve us nicely." Christophe stood on the forecastle deck with hands planted firmly on his hips, looking down on the main deck, where his entire crew had assembled. The wind whipped around them, fanning their sails and propelling them closer to the vulnerable barque within their sights.

"You may wonder why we have need of taking another ship with immeasurable spoils already on board," Christophe said, inciting several heads to bob. His eyes narrowed, scanning them in challenge. "But I have piracy in my blood, and if you chose to step aboard my ship, you have it, too. We feel it in our bones."

Christophe stood tall to several hollers of approval. Blanc and his closest companions still looked dubious, eyeing each other in silence. "That ship on the horizon may not look like much, but it represents our way of life. If we simply sail back to Europe and collect our money, what have we left from our time on this earth? To fritter it away on wine and uncouth women?" The question launched a rumble of laughter and whistles through the crowd.

Joining in their mirth, the captain held up both hands. "All right, perhaps a little of that never hurt anyone." His head shook, his blond hair blowing on the wind. "If that is your pleasure, then you're welcome to it. But I will sail from those shores rejuvenated, ready to make my next kill. I will never stop searching for the next prize, and the next. I am a pirate at heart."

With one hand on the ropes, Christophe gazed at the barque they neared. "The *Licorne's* name is known all over these waters. The people on board that ship are quaking in fear at this moment. They're wondering what we will do to them, how much we will take, if we will slaughter them or have mercy."

His focused stare swung back on his men. "There is *power* in fear, gentleman, and that power far outweighs any earthly riches one might acquire." His words were working. He could see the fever beginning to build in their ruddy faces. Christophe clenched his fist around the rope, summoning his mightiest voice. "Let us seize that power. Let us make them tremble. Let their dreams be supplanted by nightmares of the day their worlds were shaken by the fierce band of men I call my brothers."

Christophe fairly shook with passion as a few scattered hollers swelled to a roar. The men shouted and pumped their fists in the air, jostling each other excitedly. Blanc still wore a pinched expression on his chubby face, but most of his closest associates had joined in the revelry. Even Cavaretta's men had begun to jump and cheer, mingling with Christophe's crew like natural members.

Monsieur Simon's knowing smile caught Christophe's eye, and he turned to give him a nod. His men needed this kill, small as it was. They needed to feel victorious again and again after the tragedy that had struck them on Traitor Isle. Too many brothers had been lost that day.

"Look!" one of his deckhands shouted, pointing toward the other vessel. "They're already surrendering."

Squinting, Christophe turned back to watch a white sail ascending one of the barque's masts. The thought both relieved and disappointed him. Their victory would be easy, but a battle always united them like nothing else. At least no more of his men would have to die that day.

Only a handful of sailors were sprinkled over the barque's decks as Christophe expertly guided his brigantine alongside them. His crew flung grappling hooks over the narrow space between them, hauling the ships closer until they rubbed against one another in the moving waves. Christophe couldn't miss the fear on the sailors' faces as he climbed over the bulwark and leaped onto their deck.

With anxious shouts, his men fanned around him like a flock of birds. Even with their diminished size, they still outnumbered the poor ship's crew perhaps four to one. The men in their refined outfits and polished boots trembled the nearer the *Licorne's* men approached, but they bravely stood their ground.

The obvious captain of the ship met them with a rod of iron through his back. A tall man in corduroy and gleaming gold buttons, his visage bespoke pride even in the face of defeat. He extended his ledgers to Christophe without a word, solemnity thick in his dark eyes.

Christophe accepted the book from him and flipped through the pages of neat, beautifully scrolled lines. "What are you transporting and where are you going?" he asked in English, his eyes rapidly scanning the book.

"Textiles, mainly. Iron, brick. Other building materials." The captain tipped his chin up. "We are en route to the Caribbean."

"Hmmm." Christophe sounded disinterested, even as his assessment of their inventory pleased him. It would easily replenish their dwindling supply of food.

Addressing his waiting men, Christophe flicked his head toward the passage leading below deck. "All right, gather everything but the iron and brick. I can't have us weighed down." Before they could disappear, he added, "Leave enough for the crew to survive passage to the Caribbean."

The ship's captain lifted one brow. "You're a pirate with a conscience, are you?" Despite the clear mockery in his words, genuine curiosity peered back at Christophe.

"I can have them take everything if you'd prefer," he said dryly, quieting the man. Christophe returned to the ledgers, his forehead wrinkling at the information scrawled there. "There are passengers aboard this ship."

"Aye." The captain nodded. "Five men and"—he hesitated briefly—"and three women."

Dread filled Christophe's chest. His men knew better than to lay their hands on a woman or try to take her by force. He'd nearly killed the last one who had attempted such a crime and left his beaten body ashore. But he couldn't yet trust Cavaretta's men to obey his orders.

Swallowing back his unpleasant memories, Christophe snapped the book shut and handed it back to the captain. "Very well. My men will gather their spoils and we'll be on our way. You have been wise in obliging us."

The captain studied him cautiously a moment before speaking. "It would have been utter foolishness to fight a larger crew with more experience in the art of war. I couldn't walk my men into certain death." He blinked, eyes examining Christophe's face. "Besides, you are Danglar, are you not? The fearsome Thief of the Atlantic."

The breath unexpectedly hitched in Christophe's chest. How long had it been since someone had addressed him by that name—the awe-inspiring pirate captain who planted fear in the hearts of seamen from Europe to the Americas? Had he been so absorbed with Clement's treasure and winning Madeleine that he'd forgotten this feeling? Warmth trickled down his extremities, the man's recognition carrying a surprising thrill.

"*Oui,* I am he." He could say no more. Once he had pillaged entire ships without a care in the world, but today strange guilt plagued him. Had his love for Madeleine softened him? He cursed the very idea.

"You are younger than I imagined for a man so feared," the captain said. "I had imagined a man well-versed in life."

Christophe's mouth lifted in a sardonic smile. "Yes, well I'm sure the years will quickly cure this fault in me." Indeed, the twenty-six years he'd already walked this earth had matured him well beyond most men of his age.

Before he could think on it further, a pair of pounding feet ripped Christophe's attention away. He reeled toward the sound, where one of his gunners appeared from the stairwell a moment later. "Captain, we have a situation you must attend to," he said, out of breath.

Christophe frowned in concern, his heart already battering. "What is it?"

The man bent over with his hands on his thighs. "In a cabin downstairs, there are—" he sputtered, desperate for air, "there are women. You must come quickly before it's too late."

With ice in his veins, Christophe thundered off in the direction his gunner pointed. Whatever he found below decks, he doubted he wanted to face.

Four

J ane stood within the narrow confines of her cabin aboard ship, her skin pink and her teeth gritted. When the officer had raced to warn them of impending attack, her heart dropped to her knees. She and her traveling companions couldn't scramble fast enough to the little room below decks, terrified of the group of pirates about to descend upon them.

It had felt like an eternity of waiting as she knelt with the two trembling women, clutching their hands and leading them in prayer. As strong as she had grown in her faith during her easy life in England, nothing had ever rattled her like this. Her quivering voice barely choked out the ancient prayers that normally flowed melodiously from her lips.

When the ships bumped and scraped against one another, she could only whisper. The thump of boots scattered over the deck above their heads. Jane wound her arms around Mrs. Byrd and Martha as the maid began sobbing in her fear. *Help us, Lord. Help us!* Her mind reeled when she tried to imagine what a band of pirates might do to three vulnerable women. Perhaps Edward and her grandmother had been right—this journey was far too dangerous for her to undertake alone.

It had taken only moments for footsteps to breach the silence outside their cabin and their door to punch inward. The sputtering candlelight revealed the face of a young man with long wavy hair and dark, glistening eyes. Jane could barely stand to look at him filling the doorway, surveying the three of them like they were livestock selling at market.

He advanced on them quickly, his confident strides jarring every muscle in Jane's body. Then he stopped short as if remembering something, his hands resting awkwardly on his waist, where she couldn't miss the sword and pistol gleaming from his belt.

"Get up," the man said in Italian.

Jane and Mrs. Byrd understood the directive, shakily pulling Martha up along with them. The poor maid wept harder and covered her face, inciting a laugh from the unwelcome pirate. His eyes swept Jane almost regretfully as he shoved past them and knelt before Mrs. Byrd's trunks.

Mrs. Byrd angrily exhaled but said nothing as the man dug through her belongings, tossing undergarments and dresses over his shoulder. When he found her trove of jewelry, he whistled and began tucking the precious pieces into a leather bag he'd brought with him. He briefly pawed through Jane and Martha's bags, but found nothing of interest and twisted back to the women.

As the man rose and ambled toward her, Jane forced her wobbly legs to stand firm. Sweat beaded her skin and her heart raced faster than she knew it could, but she would mask her fear. Maybe he'd leave if he thought his presence didn't disturb her. Maybe he would forgo the terrible actions her mind conjured.

His dark eyes descended her approvingly before shifting to Mrs. Byrd. "Your jewels," he said, extending his palm.

Mrs. Byrd pursed her lips, silently unlatching the diamond trinket around her neck and removing her matching earrings. Her wrinkled hand remained remarkably steady as she reluctantly plopped her ornaments into his waiting hand.

The pirate's eyes scampered over Martha and seemingly found nothing, Jane their next target. "You too," he said, his head indicating the ruby necklace she'd forgotten hung at her collarbone.

Jane stiffened, her blood going cold. Her juddering hand rose to shield the bauble in question, as if she could hide its existence now. Why hadn't she thought to hide it while they waited for the pirates' approach? Why had she worn it at all that day, knowing it could be stolen or lost to the sea?

Her fingers curled around the ruby's smooth surface. Her head shook. "No, signore." She couldn't give up the one piece of home she still possessed, the only token of her grandmother's memory she would likely ever see again. He would have to kill her before she parted with it.

The man's brows shot up on his forehead. "No?" He strode two steps closer, covering her in his menacing form. "I ask for your necklace and you tell me no?"

Steeling herself, Jane stood taller despite feeling like an ant about to be crushed. "Pardon me," she said in perfect Italian, "but this necklace has sentimental value to me. I cannot part with it. Take anything else you'd like."

"Jane," Mrs. Byrd's voice strained, her eyes round with disbelief.

The man's cheeks flushed with color, his jaw tensing. "You will give me that necklace before I gut you with my sword." His hand moved to cover the hilt of his weapon, renewing Martha's tears.

Her gut cowered in fear, but her spirit was resolute. Jane narrowed her eyes, forcing bravery into her quivering frame. "I will not." She lifted her chin determinedly, staring into the man's wild eyes.

He grunted, snatching her arm in his vise-like grip. "You will." His fingers constricted painfully against her skin, his face seething above her.

"Jane, I beg you," Mrs. Byrd said, one hand extending toward her. "Your grandmother would understand you giving the necklace up to save your life. She can always give you another."

Jane shook her head. "There is not another that could replace it." She glanced at Mrs. Byrd, who had tucked her crying maid into her embrace. If the pirate threatened to hurt them, she would have no choice, but she would sooner die than let her grandmother's memory slip so easily through her fingers.

Before she had time to ponder it further, the man's other hand clamped on her shoulder. He shook her with force, rattling her every anxious nerve. Jane held her breath as his unwashed smell showered her, his face coming so close to hers that drops of spittle sprinkled her skin.

From within the noxious cloud of his presence, she barely perceived that a new person had joined them. "What are you doing?" he asked, directing every eye but the incensed pirate's his way. "You know you're not supposed to touch them."

Jane barely glimpsed the wide-eyed sailor in the doorway before a large hand cracked across her face. She recoiled, her skin fiery and stinging. Every instinct told her to shield her injured face in her hand, but she couldn't move within the man's unyielding grasp.

"I'm teaching this one a lesson," the pirate snarled. "She thinks she's above following orders." He shook her again, so hard her hairpin loosened and sent her blonde tresses cascading over her shoulders.

"Leave her be," the sailor urged. "Roux will have you thrown to the sea."

"Blast Roux and his rules." The pirate's hand tightened around Jane's throat, wicked pleasure dancing in his eyes as panic overtook hers.

As the newcomer's retreating footsteps echoed off the walls, Jane perceived the reality she'd boxed herself in. Her denial of this man's authority had provoked him in a way that her necklace alone could never remedy. He could easily take it from her. The spite raging in his maniacal eyes told her he would not be satisfied until he punished her.

His fingers coiled around her throat, squeezing until she could barely breathe. Pleasure overtook his face at her gasping breaths. Her free hand clutched his sun-worn clothing, begging him to stop. But her silent protests only seemed to encourage him. The man drove her backward, colliding her floundering form with the wall, lifting her feet off the floor.

Jane could barely hear Mrs. Byrd's pleas over the rush of blood in her ears. She felt as if submerged under water, the candlelight blurring, the cabin drifting into a hazy cloud. The man's murderous laughter rang in her head, an incessant echo. She realized with dwindling vitality that her desperate need to hold onto her past would prove the death of her. The new life she'd planned was over nearly before it had begun.

Then, as if a torrent had blown through the cabin, a rush of banging noises blasted through it. The man released her, sending Jane to the floor in a heap. With hands over her aching throat, she peered up through her blurred vision at the colossal form of a man shoving her attacker against the opposing wall.

Chest heaving, Jane allowed Martha and Mrs. Byrd to help her up. She was still disoriented as she gazed through the candlelight at the arguing men. Her rescuer had the pirate pinned to the wall, his large hand clenching a fistful of his shirt. All of the rage and conceit had drained from the man, his head drooping as the newest man's words assaulted him.

"How dare you go against my commands in so flagrant a manner." Her rescuer seethed, his face red beneath disheveled blond hair falling into his eyes. "You boarded my ship on the condition that you would never touch a woman. Were my instructions not clear?"

"She refused to give me her necklace. I couldn't let her believe we are weak."

With an angered grunt, the blond man threw back his fist and drove it into the offender's face. "You *are* weak if you believe hurting a woman denotes power." He thrust the pirate back, letting him slump against the wall.

Fire still roared in his every motion as the man spun around and set his sights on Jane. She knotted her hands in front of her, anxious despite the conversation she'd just witnessed. The closer he came, the more his towering form bespoke the fact that he could snap her in half if he so desired. He slowed as he approached, his eyes briefly scouring the marks undoubtedly checking her throat before ascending to her face.

Jane tried to breathe but couldn't. She could barely see him before, but now the thin streams of candlelight revealed a man in his mid-twenties with hair the color of straw and blue eyes that blazed through her. He possessed a commanding presence, with wide shoulders and muscles that tautened with his every movement. He looked at her with a mingling of rage and compassion, conflict alive on every contour of his face.

"What is this stir you've caused among my crew?" he asked in English thick with a French accent.

Jane glanced at the pirate still laid out on the floor, his glaring eyes searing back at her. "I only wish to retain what is rightfully mine." She avoided the captain's gaze. He *was* the captain, wasn't he? She'd heard the crew shouting "Danglar" as she ran to safety, but the sailor before had called him Roux.

He was quiet for a moment, incredulously studying her face. "You do realize we are pirates, don't you? We *take* what is yours for ourselves."

Despite her trepidation, Jane squared her shoulders. "Not this, you won't. It is too precious. It was my grandmother's—"

The captain stomped toward her, silencing what was left of her sentence. Jane begged her body not to shiver as he stood a breath away from her, gazing down like a hawk eyeing its next meal. "I don't care about your grandmother," he said, voice gravelly. "I don't care about *you*. Give us what we ask for or we take it by force. Do you understand?"

His impassioned breath flooded her skin. Jane's gaze wandered from the dagger affixed to his hip up the length of his muscular arm to the eyes pinning her in place. No man had dared come so close to her before, let alone one so virile. His menacing expression told her he would tear her apart even as a rogue vein of curiosity flickered in his gaze.

"I understand perfectly, monsieur," she said in his native tongue, driving his thick brows upward. "Just as I understood what you said to your subordinate. How do you plan to take it from me without breaking your own rules? Surely you won't commit such a crime in front of your men." Already a crowd had gathered at the door, eager to watch how their captain might respond.

His bright eyes shifted over her face in disbelief, plummeting to the ruby teardrop beneath her chin and back up to her solemn stare. A low growl issued from his throat, yet he still made not a move to seize her as the other man had. Instead, he searched her face, his nostrils flared and strong jaw clenched.

"Mademoiselle, I warn you. Give me that pendant now, or you will *not* enjoy the repercussions that await you."

Jane swallowed, barely keeping her chin up in the face of his threats. What would he do? Kill her? Certainly not after what she'd witnessed moments before. This pirate captain had some sort of moral code that wouldn't allow him to. Her face converted to stone, determination gripping her. "I will never allow you to have it, sir. *Never.*"

The captain perused her face a moment longer before yanking his dagger from his belt. Jane's heart hammered, the scrape of steel meeting her ears before its metallic scent reached her. The blade rose before her face, glimmering in the soft light. The pulse in her throat thumped wildly as the dagger pointed its direction and came closer. Her breath stopped. Every thought halted as cold steel met her throat. The captain's unwavering stare drilled into her, delving beneath the layers she'd built in defense, his knife's tip pressing into her skin.

Then with a tug of his wrist, the weight around her neck released. The chain snapped below her hairline, releasing the treasured jewels into his waiting palm.

"No!" Jane lurched forward, desperately trying to snatch back the stolen item, but already he'd deposited it into a satchel slung around his shoulder.

Turning back to her, the captain eyed her almost mournfully. "I regret having to break your cherished necklace, mademoiselle, but you gave me no other choice."

Against her better judgment, she stood taller, her fists clenched. "You have no right to my grandmother's necklace. Give it back." No one had ever dared take such an audacious action against her before. Fire burned in her chest, engulfing the fear that had lived there only moments before.

The smallest of laughs bubbled on the captain's lips. "And how do you plan to take it from me?" Her own words mocked her, stabbing into a soul she'd thought she'd freed of pride.

The captain spun on his heel and addressed the gathering outside the little cabin. "Men, it's time to go now. We have what we came for."

The man who'd apparently snitched on his fellow sailor nodded toward the scoundrel still sitting on the floor. "What do you want done with this one?"

Silence pervaded the cabin a moment, the two men staring each other down. Finally, the captain sighed and started for the door. "Leave him here. I'm sure the captain will have a use for him."

"Captain, please." The man scrambled up, rushing past the women he'd assaulted earlier. "You can't leave me here. He'll kill me."

Fire erupted in the captain's eyes as his gaze snapped back on the man. "You should have thought of that when you disobeyed my orders. I don't tolerate insubordination on my ship. Not even once." His gaze flashed briefly back to Jane one last time before he turned and tramped into the hall. Two of his sailors grabbed the pirate by his upper arms and dragged his flailing form up the stairs.

"Wait!" Jane rushed to the door, shouting after him. "You can't take that necklace. I demand you come back here at once!" But the captain gave no heed, his retreating form disappearing onto the deck overhead.

Her limbs shaking, Jane paced the floor. The boards beneath her boots creaked as she laced her fingers into her loose hair. "What am I going to do? How do I get it back?"

"You *don't*, dear." Mrs. Byrd flashed her an irritated scowl as she settled her quietly sobbing maid on her bunk. "That was extremely foolish of you. We are fortunate to be alive after the selfish actions you took just to retain an expendable piece of jewelry."

Jane peered back at her, blinking. *Selfish?* She'd never been accused of such sin before. *Expendable?* How could anyone compare her last piece of her beloved grandmother to trash so easily dispensed of? Hard reality captured her as she looked into the unmoved expression on Mrs. Byrd's face. No one would ever care about that necklace as she did—not really. It would be sold to the highest bidder and tossed around as if it had never mattered to anyone. Perhaps she *was* selfish, believing anyone could salvage that necklace but her.

Breathless, Jane grabbed a handful of her skirt and jogged toward the door.

"What are you doing?" Mrs. Byrd asked from behind her.

"I'm not letting it go." Throwing all reason to the wind, Jane seized the rail on the wall and began to scamper up the stairs.

"Stop, Jane!" Mrs. Byrd called. "You're going to get yourself killed!"

But Jane could hardly hear her, the strained voice below fading beneath her clomping boots and her mad rush of blood. When she emerged on deck, she abandoned all fear for her own safety and sprinted toward the side with singular focus. She *had* to get that necklace back. She *had* to. Once the pirate ship pulled away from them, her chances of ever seeing it again would vanish. A sickening ache within said all memory of her grandmother would go with it.

The last of the pirate crew was climbing into their ship as Jane ran in their direction, her loose hair whipping backward. "What are you doing?" a voice behind her urged. "Stop." But Jane gave them no heed, seizing the moment when the pirate crew was still distracted. Trying not to think, she climbed atop the bulwark and stretched her foot across the narrow gap between the ships. Below her, an azure strip of ocean churned, knocking the ships together and yanking them apart.

A frenzied sensation had grabbed hold of her as Jane gripped the ropes and hauled herself onto the pirate ship. She could not think; she could barely breathe. Before anyone could spy her intrusion, she dropped low and crawled into a group of barrels huddled near the quarter deck. Pulling her skirts in, she tucked her knees beneath her chin and hugged her legs to her chest.

All around her, men worked and shouted. The captain's familiar voice hollered over the assembly, urging them to quickly unhinge their vessel from the one she'd escaped and set sail. Still elated from the thrill of her flight, she tried not to imagine what might happen if they caught her. Where she would go from here, she hadn't a clue.

Five

S lowly her nerves began to settle as Jane sat within her hideout of barrels, listening to the crew go about their work. The ship groaned as it sloshed through the cavorting waves, rocking beneath her aching feet. After some time in her crouched position, Jane realized she'd have to free herself. Already, her legs stung and her sore back begged for relief.

Peeking through the barrels, she made out a darkened alcove beyond them. Supposing it as good a spot as any to hide, Jane crawled between the barrels and crept soundlessly toward the hiding place. The air was cold within the ship's shadows, and she wrapped her arms around her quivering frame as she sank down against the wall.

Above her head, the quarterdeck resounded with life. Up and down the stairs on either side of the ship, boots stomped a frenzied rhythm. From her hidden alcove, Jane spied glimpses of the skull and crossbones being lowered from the sail, replaced by the French flag. Someone walked past toting the unicorn masthead she'd noticed while racing across the other ship.

She bit her lip. What a strange practice. This *was* the *Licorne* she'd read about in news articles, was it not? The golden age of piracy had died long ago, but there were still a few stragglers who refused to stop terrorizing the seas. The French government wanted this captain's head on a platter—that much was certain. From the stories she'd read, one would have imagined him the fiercest of criminals, an enemy of humanity intent on killing anyone who crossed his path.

But he wasn't. Jane could see the back of him now, his shoulder-length blond hair tossing in the wind as he issued commands with his finger pointed. Not only had he chosen to leave her unharmed when she defied him, he had saved her life. As hard as she looked, she could not find the man the papers called the terrible Thief of the Atlantic. He appeared hardened, surely, but not a murderer.

Her stomach roiled, for the ship's incessant rocking or her own fear, she couldn't be sure. What would happen now that she'd hastily climbed aboard his ship? She had no food or water. Even if she could stay hidden in this alcove forever, she would die without sustenance. And what purpose would her bravery serve if she didn't go after that necklace?

A plan gradually took shape as Jane watched the captain turn and stare after the ship he'd just robbed. She would wait until nightfall, then sneak below decks. It couldn't be difficult to locate the captain's quarters on a ship like this—they always claimed the beautiful space with windows flanking the wall. She would find where he stowed the necklace and whatever other items she needed to keep her alive before burrowing in some forgotten corner of the ship to wait out the journey's end.

As confidence began to thaw her doubt, two whispered voices touched her ears. Jane went rigid, their proximity chilling her. How had she not perceived their approach? The two men must have stood but two feet in front of her, yet the dark obscured their presence. Jane pressed herself to the wall, whispering a silent prayer.

"Did you see what he did to that Italian fellow?" one whispered passionately. "Despicable. How can we call him 'captain' when he treats his men like that?" Jane made out the vague shape of a rotund belly as he spoke.

"I thought you didn't approve of the Italians sailing with us," the other said.

"I don't, but they're part of our crew now. We should treat them like it." Breath blew heavily from his nostrils. "Roux cares for no man but himself. It's clear how fast he'll turn on any of us if we break one of his archaic rules."

The second man shifted. "Perrone said he was trying to kill her."

"He should have, from what I gather." The chubby one grunted. "Or at least been allowed to have his way with her after what she said to him."

Nausea brewed in Jane's stomach, her entire body recoiling. She had never heard such talk, especially directed toward her. Of course, she had considered the possibility of rape while traveling alone, but she'd always supposed any would-be attacker would see her station and think better of it.

"There were *women* aboard that ship," he continued, slicing through her thoughts. "She was a fine one, at that. Do you know how long it's been since I've had a woman?" He thumped a fist on the low ceiling above their heads. "We must be the only pirate ship in the world whose captain has a conscience. It's growing tiresome."

"Especially after he had the baroness to warm his bed every night while he commanded us not to come near her."

He growled in agreement. "Her husband effectively remedied that problem, didn't he?"

"Well, what do you want to do about it?" his companion asked.

The man was quiet a prolonged moment, considering. Then his voice came, low and menacing. "Nothing—for now. We'll bide our time. We'll get as many men on our side as we can. It won't be hard to stage a mutiny then—he did it to Chapelle, after all. We can't keep blindly following a captain who puts his desires before everyone else's. We need to be strong again—without him."

The idea of a mutiny shook something deep in Jane's core. Had she climbed aboard the *Licorne*, supposing its captain would be lenient if he discovered her? If the men who spoke in secret supplanted his control, she would have no protection. She shuddered to imagine what might happen to her then.

A tickle sprung up in Jane's nose, perhaps from the dusty nature of her hideout. She squeezed her eyes shut, willing the sensation to flee her. Her teeth clenched, her hands flying over her face. But she failed to quench the sudden urge, and a choked sneeze still shot from her nose.

"Who's there?" the first man demanded, his boots crashing toward her.

Jane could barely breathe as one fist grabbed hold of her hair at the nape of her neck and yanked her into the sunlight. His face materialized before her—plump, whiskered cheeks that dented as his mouth broke into a full smile.

He shook her excitedly. "How is it I found you here? Did the captain sneak you aboard?"

Jane swallowed, aware of the increasing number of men pooling at the sight of her discovery. Her eyes narrowed. "I came aboard myself."

The man whooped, setting off a chain of hollers around them. His eyes shone bright with glee as they skittered down her plain dress. "I never would have guessed." He whistled low, shaking his head. "You certainly came to the right place, mademoiselle."

Misgiving broke through her fear as she stood trapped in a sea of ogling stares. They didn't look at her with the air of victory the first pirate she'd met had. They were anxious, like children waiting outside a candy shop for it to open. Some of them tidied up their ragged clothes and began to slick back their hair, as if they might impress her. Jane glanced around confusedly before looking back at the man whose hand had relaxed on her neck.

"I'm first," he announced proudly. "It's only fair since I found her." The group around him grumbled but only weakly protested.

"Don't worry, you'll get your turn." His fingers lowered to Jane's back, one hand sweeping in front of him as if he expected her to follow his lead.

Jane blinked, unsure what he meant, before reality hit her like a punch to the gut. After overhearing his brash conversation, she had expected they might try to assault her, but this—did they all expect her to perform for them? To just let them defile her? Panic seized her as the group pressed closer, the licentious looks on their faces leaving no doubt. Nobody here would treat her like a lady. She'd doomed herself the moment she'd stepped foot on this ship.

T he wind worked in their favor as the *Licorne* pulled away from the ship they'd ambushed. Christophe peered up at the strategically placed sails, their bold white faces billowing against each gust. Good. The quicker they escaped her, the better. If another ship came to their aid, it could mean the death of his entire crew.

On his command, several sailors hoisted the bronze falcon back into place on the masthead. The last time they'd worn this face, they had taken Madeleine from Traitor Island to Marseilles. It seemed so long ago now, and yet her face on that voyage still burned in his memory—her curious, vulnerable expression, her clear attraction to him. Christophe had abandoned all good sense when his study of her converted to love. He'd only meant to gain her secrets, but unlike his predecessor, he possessed not the skill to woo a woman simply to deceive her.

He pivoted away from his men and sauntered across the forecastle deck. He couldn't let them see the raw emotions still plaguing him. Setting his hands atop the bulwark, he stared after the ship getting farther away with every blast of the wind. Never again would he fall prey to a woman's affections. Never again would he put his command in jeopardy to chase an ill-fated relationship. The sea was his love—he'd known that from the start. He *must* rebuild his crew's trust in him so he wouldn't lose her, too.

The Atlantic peppered his skin in her invigorating spray. Christophe closed his eyes for a moment, simply savoring the feel of her. Then, almost without thought, his hand drifted to the satchel still slung around his shoulder. He lifted the flap, digging until he produced the trinket which had caused so much turmoil during their attack. The ruby teardrop and diamonds winked in the morning sunlight, driving bizarre guilt into his chest. What room did he have for guilt? What care did he have for a woman foolish enough to defy skilled fighters in order to keep it?

Yet still, her green eyes blazed in his memory. Her blonde hair had fallen about her shoulders in a stunning way that stirred his interest despite his very best efforts. He sighed, leaning against the ship's side. Perhaps he'd lived too long without companionship, or maybe his lingering feelings for Madeleine had compelled his heart to race at the sight of her. Though he could not deny—she was beautiful in every sense of the word.

Christophe had allowed himself to peruse her face perhaps too long. She had a curved, slightly freckled nose, pink bowed lips, porcelain skin, and an abundance of lashes that leant her luminous eyes the air of innocence. Indeed, everything about her had looked innocent, even with the fire that raged from her stubborn will. He found he wanted to know more in spite of himself.

The woman had worn obviously fine clothes, though they were too plain for an aristocrat. He'd wondered at first if she was a well-dressed servant. Then she'd opened her mouth and left no doubt as to her station. A woman like that hadn't worked a day in her life. She wasn't used to relinquishing anything she didn't want to, least of all a treasured piece of her family's history.

A smile crept over the captain's lips as he slipped the necklace back into his bag. He couldn't forget the way she'd quivered in his presence yet stood her ground. Every muscle in her body had betrayed her fear. She'd hardly been able to look at him. Yet relent, she would not. She would have defended that necklace with her life if he'd let her.

Shouting arose from the quarterdeck, no doubt his crew celebrating their victory at sea. Christophe leaned on his elbows and gazed at the ship, now barely visible in the drifting mist. A strange ache erupted inside when he realized that brief encounter would be their only one, yet perhaps it was best that way. How badly he'd wanted to let her keep her cherished jewelry. The pleading in her eyes had torn at him. But he couldn't let a woman dictate his actions again—not with his men watching. He hadn't been given a choice.

The sailors' revelry transformed into what sounded like angry bellows. Christophe frowned, pushing off the ship and aiming himself toward the commotion. A large group had assembled below, near the quarterdeck steps. He couldn't make out what they were doing from this distance, but it appeared as if they were jostling something between them. Christophe started off slowly toward the ruckus before a woman's scream propelled his boots into a run.

Sprinting down the steps from the forecastle, Christophe felt his limbs go numb. With every step, emerging details quickened his thudding heart. Familiar blonde tresses flew on the wind. Patches of her simple dress were visible from within the moving crowd. He saw Blanc chortling merrily as he seized a handful of her gown at the back and shoved her toward another sailor who waited with hands extended.

Christophe's vision went white as he thundered up to the group and began pawing his way to their middle. "Stop! Stop it right now! What is the meaning of this?"

Their laughter gradually died, replaced by hushed warnings. When Christophe reached the man who had her about the waist, he ripped his arms away and thrust him into the crowd behind him. The woman wrapped her arms around her surging bodice, her tear-stained face directed ashamedly to the deck at her feet.

Gulping a breath of briny air, Christophe's accusing stare flew around him. "Who did this? Who brought her aboard ship?" How mindless and utterly out of control had his company become, to steal a woman from a rival ship?

Blanc stepped forward, his mirth turned to irritation. "We didn't bring her. She came herself." He gestured at his companions, who nodded vehemently in agreement. "We were just having a bit of fun, Captain. She's a—"

"A bit of fun?" Christophe stomped toward him, ire flaming up his ruddy neck. "How many times must I state my rules before you abide by them? You are *never* to touch a woman who boards this ship. *Never.*"

Blanc's lips pursed, clearly holding back what he wanted to say. "But Captain, we planned to pay her. We aren't forcing her."

Heartbeat hammering in his ears, Christophe swiveled toward the woman who still shivered despite managing to quell her tears. "Does this look like a woman who wants to play any part in your games?" He gentled as he approached her, feeling as if he'd come upon an injured rabbit trapped in hunting snares. How could their story be true? She'd have to be an utter fool to have climbed aboard his ship, and he'd seen it in her eyes—this woman was no fool.

"Is what he says true?" he asked incredulously. "Did you really come here of your own free will?"

She hesitated a moment, her gaze darting around her feet before flickering up to meet his eyes. Inhaling, she nodded and fixed Christophe with that same determined stare he'd encountered beneath the decks of their rival ship.

He wagged his head, swearing beneath his breath. What manner of woman was this, and how much destruction had she just brought on his ship?

"See Captain, I told you—"

Roux silenced him with an upraised hand, his livid gaze still locked on her. "I don't care what she is. You know my rules. This isn't some back-alley brothel where you may behave as you please. We have a code aboard this ship." Female blood on his vessel presented a problem he'd fought all too hard when he'd invited Madeleine to sail with them. He had no desire to combat it yet again.

With a snap of his wrist, he summoned two sailors who hadn't taken part in this treachery. "Bring her to my office—*now.*" His hawkish stare pinned on the impossibly large group who'd already flouted his orders. "And from this point, if I find out that any of you has stepped within arm's reach of her, I will flog you myself."

Six

C hristophe's office sparkled with sunlight when he burst into it, his boots bashing a hasty trail over the floorboards. Situated at the ship's stern, the room was the brightest and most majestic of any below decks. Most captains chose such quarters for their cabin, but Christophe preferred it as a sacred space for work alone. Besides, he'd never find sleep with the moon pouring in through its colossal wall of windows.

With hardly a glance to the woman who'd been deposited into a chair before his desk, he strode around the massive mahogany piece and clamped his arms behind his back. Outside the row of domed windows, a flock of gulls flapped past on the wind. Their strident caws hardly touched his ears as he began to pace, the fury of this recent discovery ramming through his veins.

Between his angered steps, he allowed himself glances at her. She sat with the air of a polished aristocrat, her hands folded neatly in her lap, her legs tucked under the chair. Despite her obvious transgression, she held her head high, her gaze fixed on the far windows toward the endless sea. Did this woman have no shame? She'd stolen aboard his ship and now she didn't even have the decency to look remorseful about it.

Grunting in exasperation, Christophe spun away from her. "What, pray tell, could possibly have possessed you when you climbed onto my decks?" His voice was steady despite his every instinct to scream at her. "Are you insane? At least if you are touched, I might grant you clemency for the outright stupidity you've displayed today."

Silence engulfed them before her voice emerged, clear and confident. "Passion and insanity are two different beasts. Had I not possessed the first, I could never have acted as the second."

His face screwed up as he revolved to face her from his spot between the windows and the desk. Was she defending her perilous actions? Christophe dragged in the cedar odor of his beloved office and rubbed the bridge of his nose. "Passion. You would risk your life on a whim."

"I would risk my life for the heirloom you stole from me." Her jaw hardened, her green eyes displaying no fear as her gaze entwined with his. "You have no right to keep it. That necklace was my grandmother's, handed down from her mother and so forth for generations. I'd rather die than let you have it."

Christophe released a disbelieving chuckle, the absurdity of her statement unnerving him. "This necklace?" He lifted the satchel over his head, holding it out on display. "I have half a mind to chuck it into the Atlantic after what you've done." Clenching one fist, he slammed the satchel into the floorboards with a loud crash.

The woman leaned forward, her eyelids fluttering rapidly. She appeared as if ready to launch off her chair to retrieve the stolen item, but something held her in place. "Please, monsieur, I beg you." Her earnest gaze lifted, entreating him.

The backs of his teeth clenched together, rage heating his blood. What power did this woman think she possessed to come aboard without invitation and then ask him for anything? She was beautiful, no doubt. So beautiful a part of him wanted to easily forgive her. But beneath the angelic flowing hair and emerald eyes begging for him to relent, surely a devil resided.

"You know what would have happened had I not intervened out there, do you not?" Perhaps she'd never been schooled on the nature of men. Well, she would find out now.

She pinkened, her eyes drifting to the hands working in her lap. "I have an inkling, Captain."

"Oh, I doubt you understand the full weight of it." He sighed, sickened by the very thought. "Though I can hardly blame them, considering the actions you took today. You know what they think you are, don't you?"

She sat in silence a long moment before her horrified stare flew back to him. "I am not a prostitute, if that is what you're implying."

"I know you are not, but that is what every sailor out there who accosted you believes." One finger speared toward the decks they'd just abandoned. "What kind of a woman comes willingly aboard a ship like this one unless she's looking to capitalize on her feminine gifts?"

She flushed a deeper shade of red. "I—I hadn't—" Her palm rose to shelter her glowing cheek. "I suppose I hadn't imagined the possibility. My whole life, everyone has known who I am and respected it. This is the first time in my twenty-one years that I've left the cocoon into which I was born."

Christophe's steely face relaxed, his arms knotting over his broad chest. For the first time, he sensed a glimmer of humility in her. "And who are you, if you don't mind my asking? What is your name?"

Her lithe figure straightened in her chair. "Jane. My name is Jane Whitecliffe." Her chin lifted proudly with the name. "And your name is Roux. The papers call you Danglar, but your men call you Roux."

Despite his best effort, Christophe's mouth fell slightly open. Was she always this bold with everyone? "Indeed, I am Christophe Roux," he said finally. No sense in withholding a truth she already knew. "You have heard of me, as I have heard of you." At her questioning brows, he hooked his own. "Well, your father. Assuming you are the daughter of George Whitecliffe, Earl of Brambleshire."

Her shoulders squared. "I am. My father's reputation reaches even the high seas, I take it."

Christophe nodded. How could it not, with the amount of illegal trade the earl was engaged in? Deciding against exposing the man's covert affairs to his clearly proud daughter, he thumped his knuckles on the desk. "There are no limits to the reach of such an esteemed man."

The hint of a smile touched her lips. The idea passed briefly through Christophe's mind that her presence here might benefit him if he treated her well. How grateful might the Earl of Brambleshire be to have his lost daughter returned to him unharmed? Then, reality brought him back to earth. She had climbed aboard a mercenary ship. Surely the stories would paint him as the villain who had captured her. How long did he have before the authorities began sniffing him out in search of her?

"Tell me," he said, "what is the daughter of an English earl doing this far south, traveling aboard a cargo vessel? It seems very strange, indeed."

She hesitated, her eyes scanning the distant horizon. "Running away," she said, voice thin. Her gaze flickered up at him. "Running away from that life forever."

Though curiosity urged him to ask more, Christophe menacingly strode forward until he stood only steps from her. "And you think the *Licorne* is the ship to help you? You expect me to transport you wherever you desire?"

Her nostrils flared, vexation rising again on her pallid skin. "I expect no help from you. I only want what is rightfully mine."

"And then what?" Christophe leaned over her, setting his hands on the arms of her chair. "Let's imagine I give you the necklace at this very moment. What am I to do with you then? Throw you into the sea? By your logic, you will have what you came for. I owe you nothing after that, do I?"

51

Jane didn't flinch in the face of his nearness. Her bright eyes searched him, her chest surging despite the calm she forced over her features. "That is your prerogative, Captain. I hope very much that you will choose to take me with you to shore—any shore upon which I might find the means to continue my journey."

His head shook slightly. "Unless you brought money with you, I don't see how that is possible—short of selling the necklace you risked your life to retrieve."

She swallowed, her eyes never faltering from his. "I will find a way."

Christophe let his gaze drift over her face, her skin that emanated a soft glow in the sunny cabin. Her doe-like lashes blinked as he took in her proud cheekbones and feminine mouth. Her warm breath mingled with his. He hadn't imagined coming so close to any woman but Madeleine ever again, the knowledge that he meant to intimidate her with his nearness pummeling him with guilt. But what guilt should he harbor for this foolish woman he'd only just met? She'd chosen to come aboard, endangering his life and those of his entire crew by her haphazard actions.

"You realize you are nothing but a liability, don't you?" His eyes narrowed. "Now I must house you, feed you—"

"I will repay you for all of it. You have my word."

"And my men? How do I keep them from breaking down your door? You're among only a handful of women they've seen in months." He was weary of keeping them at bay after Madeleine had weakened their resolve to obey his orders.

She looked into his eyes with a solemn resiliency that drove beneath his skin. "You are the captain. Are your men so cavalier as to thwart your lead? Have you no control over their behavior?"

A low growl rumbled in his throat. She had no idea the precarious ice on which she walked. The crew of the *Licorne* teetered on the brink of overthrowing him, of ordering him to his death. If she upset their journey to France in the smallest of ways, the consequences might decimate them both.

Christophe stared back at her one more intense moment before abruptly pushing off the chair to a stand. He couldn't reveal the dangerous position she'd put him in. Now he'd have to find a solution with this new weight tethered to his ankle. His mother's gentle face flashed through his mind, stilling his hammering heart. He had to protect this new woman, as much as he hated the corner she'd backed him into.

"Come along." He twisted toward the door. "I'll show you where you can sleep until I can dump you on the nearest shore."

The chair scraped beneath her as she bolted to her feet. "But wait, what about my necklace? Aren't you going to give it back?"

Christophe set his jaw, not bothering to look back as he shoved the door on its hinges. "No." Any remorse he had once harbored for taking her treasured jewelry was gone, replaced with raw disdain for her. Jane Whitecliffe would never touch her necklace again.

J ane trailed the dogged captain across the deck and down a narrow flight of stairs. She couldn't miss the attention their interruption garnered. Leering stares aimed at her from every corner of the ship, many interested and others hostile. Captain Roux paid them no heed, his long strides pounding the deck at a pace she could barely match.

The stairs creaked as they descended into a passageway so dark, she couldn't see the hand in front of her face. She wanted to reach out a hand to Roux's shirt in order to guide her but thought better of it. She'd already kindled enough fury simply by climbing aboard. Instead, she followed the sound of his furious footfalls until they breached a cabin at the end of a long hall.

The room surprised Jane. It held a narrow bed with fine linens, a round table and chairs, and several bookshelves strategically placed on the walls. Did he keep this place for guests? The space was tidy, though a chest at the end of the bed with cloth peeping out and a discarded cup on the table suggested recent occupancy. As she gazed at the porthole shedding light over the small space, the scents of pipe tobacco and myrrh seeped into her senses.

"This is my cabin," Roux said, prompting her immediate attention. "It may not look like much, but it's where I rest my head between bouts of the insanity that transpires upstairs."

Jane glanced around at the sparse furnishings, shocked that a pirate captain would live in such simplicity. Hadn't she read accounts of their excessive extravagance, the papers painting Danglar especially as a hoarder of all things fine and unnecessary? This cabin told the story of a neat, quiet man who preferred books to people.

"I couldn't part you from your personal space, Captain." Her eyes landed on the bed that looked so much more comfortable than her previous bunk aboard ship. "Where will you sleep?"

At his protracted silence, Jane swung her gaze back to him. The captain stood with hands on his hips, his blue eyes incredulous beneath one arched brow. "I plan to sleep in my own bed, thank you." His finger speared toward a door she hadn't noticed. "You'll sleep there."

She reddened. "You expect me to sleep in a closet off your room?"

With an exasperated sigh, he strode to the door and pushed it open. "It's a separate cabin with everything you'll need. Nothing but the finest for our stowaway." He rolled his eyes with a shake of his head.

Jane peered past his extended arm to a bed and washstand crammed into a tiny room. Despite its diminutive size, the space radiated feminine refinement. A rose-adorned bedspread trimmed in lace covered the bed. The porcelain chamber set was beautifully scrolled, sitting atop a small, sturdy bureau. Why did such an elegant place exist attached to his cabin? Jane recalled talk of a baroness, but hadn't they said she slept in the captain's bed?

Aware of his eyes on her, Jane looked back at him. "This is lovely, but—" Did she dare to voice the concern on her mind? He was liable to toss her off the ship if she caused him too much trouble.

"But what?" The captain folded his arms over his chest, leaning on the doorjamb.

"I don't mean to sound ungrateful, it's just that—" Jane's gaze slid from the cotton shirt swathing his muscular shoulders to the leather pants tucked into his knee-high boots. Men like him were utterly absent from her world. How could she explain her misgivings to someone who had never been to court, never been penned in by the expectations of high society?

Rising up on the balls of her feet, she inhaled through her nose. "Well, I cannot rest so near a person of the opposite sex. It isn't decent, and I surely won't be able to sleep knowing you're in such close proximity—a man I hardly know."

His brow wrinkled slightly, a quizzical expression commanding his face before his nostrils flared in a humorless laugh. "You may share the berth with my crew if you're so inclined. I'm sure they'd be happy with the arrangement." He shoved off the doorjamb. "Beyond that, I have an unused deck or perhaps even a prison cell that will accommodate you nicely."

Jane huffed. "That isn't fair. I am only one woman amid dozens of men. I must try to preserve my dignity somehow. What will my father think when he finds out I slept alone with a man, practically in his own cabin?"

Roux stepped toward her, face ruddy. "Perhaps he'll think you should have stayed aboard your own ship, or better yet, never run away in the first place. You threw the word *fair* to the wind when you forced this situation on me."

Fire lit inside despite her better judgment. "*You* forced the situation when you insisted on taking my grandmother's necklace, which you have yet to return." How dare he place all the blame on her? She was simply retrieving what he'd taken.

He was so near she could smell the salt on his clothes, the foreign spices that must have laced his cedar chest. Jane's breath hitched as he leaned over her, his jaw working in self-restraint. "These are your quarters," he growled, his breath warming her cheek. "Take them or leave them, but I'll not hear another word."

Before she could protest, he spun on his heel and tramped to the door. "You'll not leave this room, do you hear?" he said without looking back. "There is a water jug beneath the table. I'll bring you food later."

At the thought of being trapped here alone, Jane lurched forward. "But—"

"I said, 'don't leave this room.'" Without glancing back, he stormed through the door and slammed it behind him.

Jane stood in the wake of his exit, unsure what to say or do to improve her lot. With a pang of guilt, she realized the validity of his anger. If she had behaved as Mrs. Byrd had begged her to, she would still be safely on her way to Barbados. But that possibility had flown the moment that necklace left her neck, taking all reason with it.

She turned slowly toward the room he'd offered her. Could she expect a more dignified arrangement after the stunt she'd executed? Reminding herself of God's hand on her, she whispered a prayer of thanks and passed through the open door. Without his intervention, perhaps she would be at the bottom of the sea now, or prey to a slew of sailors.

Seating herself on the bed, she swept one hand over the downy quilt. She frowned, leaning down to sniff the feathery pillow atop it. The scents of lilac and lavender lifted from the silk pillowcase. Curious, she bent to open the bureau. Inside lay two gowns of obviously fine craftsmanship—one of crêpe and the other silk. Beneath them, a cotton nightdress still bore several raven strands of hair. Stockings and a pair of slippers rested beside them.

Jane bit her lip, closing the bureau drawer. Everything about this modest space was designed for a woman, from the silver mirror to the floral-embroidered towels. What kind of a woman would leave her husband to sail across the world with this mercenary captain? He was handsome, certainly, but who would choose a rough life at sea over the comfort of a barony? She cringed, realizing she'd run from the very same kind of existence. Perhaps this baroness had more layers than she'd imagined. Perhaps the captain did, too.

Gazing back at the door through which he'd disappeared, Jane couldn't squelch the questions bubbling inside of her. She couldn't wait to uncover more about the peculiar captain who'd rescued her from his crew—and why her interest stirred more every time he was near.

Seven

All night long, the winds whistled and threw the *Licorne* into waves so tumultuous, Jane thought her stomach would never settle. Within the confines of her little cabin, she clung to her blankets and prayed for the ruthless weather to let up, but no relief came. Instead, she stared at the black ceiling, dreaming of home, wishing she'd never dared to step foot outside its protective confines.

As a little girl, she'd heard stories like *Gulliver's Travels* and dreamed of such adventure. What must it be like to roam about the world's massive seas, never knowing what lay in wait on the next shore, she'd wondered. She and Edward had played pirates and captives in the salon of her family's estate, their imaginations occupying them until her nanny awoke and chided her for unladylike behavior. Oh, what she wouldn't give to have those days back, with nothing ahead of her but the thrill of the unknown.

Jane rolled to her side, catching sounds of Captain Roux sleeping without care. How could a person relax in such a tempestuous environment? The very fact that a man slept within earshot could keep her awake for hours. She heaved her blankets under her chin, painfully conscious of her thin chemise. Perhaps she should have donned the night shift the mysterious baroness had left in the drawer, but the very idea felt wrong. The captain wouldn't dare barge in and risk seeing her in her undergarments, would he?

She huffed, sitting up and dragging her knees against her chest. Somehow, she felt safer this way, more shielded. Never mind the fact that every man on this ship could easily overpower her if they so desired. Their actions had left no doubt—they would gladly assail her the moment their captain stepped out of the way.

He was such a vexatious man, yet kind in a manner she hadn't expected. He'd brought her beans and a hardtack biscuit for dinner, served with a chunk of dry jerky. The tough meat paled when compared to her usual fare, but satisfied the grumbling of a stomach that had survived without sustenance all day. As far back as she could think, she couldn't remember a day she'd gone with so little food, save perhaps for times she'd fallen ill.

The captain had spoken no words as he plunked the meal in front of her on the table. When she opened her mouth to ask for salt, he'd fixed her with a look so fierce, she'd prudently remained silent. She could stomach bland beans for the sake of their peace, or so she hoped. Snatching up her spoon, she'd thanked him in a mouse-like voice before he retreated from the room in a succession of irritated thuds. So much for finding out more about him.

Dawn announced itself not in sunlight as Jane was accustomed, but with stirrings from the adjoining room and the bash of boots on the floorboards. Jane snapped to attention, afraid the captain might burst into her room and order her up, but the slam of his door eased her fraught nerves. With a yawn, she drifted back into the wondrous delirium that had coasted over her only in the morning's wee hours.

When she finally arose, a thin strand of sunlight peeking under her door announced the late hour. Jane sat up and stretched, her back sore despite the rather comfortable mattress Roux had provided her with. She dismally pulled on the beige calico gown she'd worn the previous day and did her best to comb her hair with her fingers.

The dress already felt sticky below the arms as she stood. On mornings at home, her faithful maid Wilhelmina would bathe her and twist her fair hair into a stylish design. She'd have a gown of silk and lace ready to drape over her, the perfect accent to whatever mood Jane found herself in that day. Nostalgia reigned over her as she poured water into the porcelain bowl and splashed it on her face. She would likely never see Wilhelmina again or feel the soft sweep of expensive silk on her skin.

Deciding to braid her hair rather than attempt anything more elaborate, Jane finished the last of her new modified routine and yanked the door open. She half expected the captain to be waiting on the other side ready to ridicule her, but his cabin was empty. Only the whistles and shouts of the crew overhead filled the abandoned room.

Her gaze darted to the table, where a new meal occupied the space taken up by her dinner the night before. As she came closer, she spied sausage and boiled potatoes, an array of freshly cut orange wedges surprising her. Captain Roux had even left her a cup of black coffee and another filled with milk beside it. If this was his idea of punishing her for boarding his ship, he needed help with the concept.

Loneliness swamped her as she sat at his table and partook of the surprisingly tasty food cooked in the ship's galley. Solitude had never suited her, but she felt its sting more keenly as she chewed her potatoes and sipped her coffee, contemplating her uncertain future. What would she do with herself at this journey's end, if indeed, she survived it at all?

The hours ticked by ever-so-slowly, each passing minute dribbling through the hourglass Roux kept beside his bed. Jane wandered the room countless times, snooping where she shouldn't have, prying into a life so unlike her own. The clothes in his chest were neatly folded—several shirts and pants like the ones she'd seen him wear, plus a navy-blue formal outfit complete with a jacket. He had ties for his hair, cravats, vests, stockings, and a pair of formal shoes. When her hand unwittingly brushed his drawers, she bolted to a stand and clumsily settled the lid back in place.

Sighing, she turned in a circle. There was nothing of entertainment value here except the rows upon rows of books neatly lining the walls. Jane perused them half-interestedly, realizing quickly that she'd read most of these works before. He had a mixture of French and English editions, with a smattering of languages from around the world. She wondered with a frown how many distinctive tongues he'd acquired from his life at sea.

Finally, her rumbling stomach signaled the fact that it was far past noon. Jane tried to glimpse the sun from the little porthole on the wall, but the celestial body stood somewhere out of sight, illuminating the brilliant blue sky. She couldn't stand this isolation a moment longer. She had to break free, if only for the moment, to feel the fresh air on her skin again. Surely, Roux couldn't object to that.

The deck swarmed with busy men as Jane reticently stepped from the stairwell, gripping the rail in a moment of indecision. A few of them had already noticed her, jabbing each other in the ribs and pointing her way. She angled her chin up, determined not to show her fear. She had a right to walk in the sunlight like everybody else. The cathartic sea air already funneled through her lungs, lending new life to her stifled chest.

Willing her legs not to wobble, Jane walked through the midst of them. Everywhere she looked, men climbed the rigging or fixed a torn sail. A group of younger boys regarded her with a snicker, pausing over their mops until she had passed. Jane noticed the burly man who'd accosted her before watching from beneath bushy brows, and directed her path away from him.

As she approached the ship's side, a sharp wind wafted over her face, nearly undoing the braid she'd fashioned. Jane smiled against the chilling blast, enjoying the first bit of freedom she'd tasted since sneaking on board. As far as the eye could see, white-capped waves of shimmering blue lapped over one another like dancers capering about a ballroom. No wonder some people loved this life. The infinite waters called to her, urging her into their outstretched hands.

"What do you think you're doing?" a harsh voice ripped her from her daydreams.

Jane whipped around to find Captain Roux already at her side, grabbing her wrist in one swift tug. "I told you to remain below decks. What part of my instructions were unclear?"

Incensed, she attempted to tear her hand away, but found it solidly locked in his grip. "You may think you own me, Captain Roux, but I can assure you that you don't. I may walk wherever I please."

His brows dove in consternation. "It isn't safe up here for you. I tried to warn you." He glanced warily around at the host of stares she'd already attracted.

"Fine." Jane managed to rip her hand away. "I'll go back down. I only wanted a bit of fresh air." A sudden sensation rose in her body, causing her to waver. "It's only that...well..." Color swamped her cheeks, her eyes darting to the distant edge of the sea. "I drank quite a bit of coffee this morning. Where might I go to—" The words refused to wet her tongue. What an uncivilized matter to discuss, especially out in the open like this.

When met with silence, Jane reluctantly raised her humiliated gaze and found the captain actually smiling. The look suited him, though at her expense, she didn't appreciate it—no matter how becoming she found the dimple in his cheek. "Did you not notice the closet just off my cabin?" he asked, glancing at her uncomfortable stance. "Have you been holding it in all this time?"

Jane turned a furious shade of red, already marching back the way she'd come. "Well, I was too unsettled yesterday to even think of such things. You could have just told me." She wouldn't mention the spare basin she'd used as a chamber pot in desperation overnight.

"I'd planned to, but you wouldn't stop calling me a thief long enough to hear it." The captain jogged after her to taunt her, surely. "If you'd rather use the head with my men, it's up in the bow." He pointed toward the ship's end, inciting chortles from the crew members close enough to hear.

Eyes flashing his way, Jane lifted her skirts and trounced back down the stairs. Good riddance to this uncouth captain *and* his men. The sooner they docked, wherever it may be, the better.

C hristophe stared down the stairwell at the flurry of skirts and windblown hair descending it like a cannonball. Amused as her embarrassment made him, he was glad to have confronted her false sense of self-sufficiency. Perhaps now she'd stay out of sight and keep herself out of harm's way.

At least a dozen pairs of eyes had witnessed their interaction. Christophe turned toward a group of young swabbies still tittering at her misfortune, his look stern. The boys resumed their work of pushing their mopheads over the deck, stealing smirks at one another. Blanc grunted as if he knew a most telling secret before returning to the knots he was untying.

Brushing him off, Christophe looked down on the darkened corridor into which Jane had disappeared. Blanc had nothing up his sleeve but a loud bark, and his sailors— including Cavaretta's men—knew he was liable to kill them if they came near her. Still, the possibility sent his stomach roiling. He could only protect her if she let him.

His lips moved upward in spite of himself. She had such spirit, such fire in her blood. Part of him wanted to toss her overboard, while the other felt bizarrely drawn to her. He waited until she had ample time to answer nature's call before he indulged the urge to march down the stairs himself. Perhaps he only missed Madeleine's company, but the prospect of spending time with a woman lured him—even a woman he found as utterly contemptible at times as her.

When Christophe tentatively swung the door to his cabin open, he found Jane seated at the table with a book open before her, strategically sitting so what little sunlight she had spilled across the pages. She didn't acknowledge him as he sauntered into the room, her disinterested eyes fixed to the book. Without a word, he snatched a bottle of rum from a bookshelf and sank into the chair opposite her.

In silence, she kept on reading, her hand rising now and then to flip a page. Christophe brought the bottle to his lips as he watched her, relishing the sweet, earthy flavor as it slid down his gullet. There was something strangely relaxing about sitting with a woman, even when no conversation flowed between them.

"Do you always drink straight out of the bottle like that?" Jane peered over the top of her book, judging him with her eyes. "You're next door to a perfect barbarian."

Christophe grinned, taking another slug of his drink before wiping a hand over his mouth. "I only do it when there are elegant ladies nearby to offend."

Her brows wrinkled, but she returned to her reading without another word. The action appeared to take effort this time, Jane softly exhaling and rereading the page several times.

"Which of my books are you reading?" Christophe asked, squinting at the gold embossed title.

"*Tom Jones.*" She turned another page. "The squire's just discovered a baby in his bed."

Christophe nodded, familiar with the story. He'd read every book in his collection at least twice. "Why don't you read me a passage?" He told himself he was merely bored, thrusting back the notion that he may just want to hear her voice.

With a sigh, she covered his view of her face with the book. "For my own part, if it was an honest man's child, indeed—but for my own part, it goes against me to touch these misbegotten wretches, whom I don't look upon as my fellow-creatures. Faugh! how it stinks! It doth not smell like a Christian!"

The line's absurdity launched Christophe into a full-on laugh. Jane lowered the book, her eyes sparkling despite the unaffected mask she wore. Finally, she allowed herself a giggle behind her wrist.

"I had forgotten how funny Fielding could be," Christophe said. "It's been some time since I read that book."

Jane cocked her head, curiosity livening her face before she set the book on the table. "Yes, well—my mother would call this trash. I've managed to read it behind closed doors, but illegitimate children and unbridled debauchery? She'd be aghast if she knew."

"You have quite the streak of rebellion in you, I see."

She rolled her eyes to the ceiling. "You don't have to watch me, you know. I promise I won't go out again." Her gaze roamed the books lined up on a high shelf fixed to the wall. "I suppose I'll read as many as I can before we land. It's as good a pastime as any."

Leaning back, Christophe set his foot on the table and teetered precariously on two chair legs. "I didn't come here to watch you, I just—" How could he explain his desperate need for human contact? "I just wanted to know more, is all."

She shot him a questioning look. "About what?"

"About you, I suppose." Christophe inwardly laughed as she bristled up at his words. "Beyond your deranged need to protect your ancestors' jewelry at the expense of your life."

Her lips pressed together, but she quelled whatever words sat ready on her tongue. Her gaze ricocheted about the room as if looking for a distraction before landing on a basket sitting on his bedside table. "What is all this?" she asked, rising and retrieving it.

Christophe shrugged. "Just a bit of mending I have to do." He'd let it pile up since before their trip to Rome, somehow wishing it would vanish if he ignored it.

Jane lifted a half-sewn sock from the mix, a giggle bubbling on her lips. "You, the mighty Danglar, vicious Thief of the Seas, darn your own stockings?" Her brows lifted. "Surely, you could call on one of your lackeys to do it."

"I don't like them touching my things. Besides"—he glanced up at the ceiling, where footsteps stomped above their heads—"not one of them would be any good at it."

"And neither are you." Jane seized the basket handle and glee-fully plunked it on the table between them.

"What are you doing?" Christophe watched as she reseated her-self demurely and began stitching where he had left off. "Am I to believe the daughter of an earl can sew better than I?"

"It appears so," she said with a mischievous smile. "I do plenty of needlepoint, and I've sewn for the poor on many occasions." Her fingers nimbly worked, the needle darting in and out of the sock in her grasp. "You would think a seasoned sailor would need to know how to mend a torn sail."

He sighed, weary of discussing his shortcomings. "It was never my strong suit." Using his hand for balance, Christophe let his chair legs thud on the solid floor. "Forgive me for defying your expectations. I had similar qualms about you."

Jane's brows quirked, though her eyes never left her work. "Such as?"

"The captain of the ship you were sailing on said you were headed to the West Indies. What business does the Earl of Bram-bleshire's daughter have in such a wild place?"

Her skin pinkened. "I told you—I was running away."

Christophe drummed his fingers on the table. "Running away from what?" Would she lie to him simply to have him leave her alone?

"If you must know, I was escaping an arranged marriage. It's an antiquated practice, and I won't have any part in it."

"And your only escape was to travel to the West Indies?" It seemed a rather drastic step, even to a man who sailed the globe for a living.

Jane focused on a particularly intricate stitch, pausing until she'd broken through the wool. "There is an Anglican mission in Barbados. I've vowed to join their ranks as a nun."

A laugh burst from his lungs before he could stop it. Christophe stared disbelievingly back at the wide eyes now fixed upon him. "You, a nun?" Somehow, the idea put a lump in his throat.

"Yes, a nun." A bit of humor lit her face before she returned to her work. "It's the rage among daughters of the aristocracy, didn't you know? We train for it in our youth."

"Oh, indeed." Christophe lifted his bottle high, then took another swig. "Well, they have quite the surprise awaiting them at that mission. A nun who can sew *and* stand up to privateers."

Jane appeared to fight the smile on her lips. "It takes all sorts," she said, her eyes flashing briefly to his before diving back to her mending.

The captain took her in a quiet moment—the golden hair barely clinging to her braid, the determined cheekbones and focused expression. Even in dirtied calico, she somehow managed to appear elegant. He wondered at the man she'd run away from, then perhaps if her devotion to God would have ripped her from any man. A woman like her would find a way to get exactly what she wanted from life. Yet knowing her only these past two days, Christophe doubted she would enjoy the existence she'd sailed across the seas to find.

Eight

The slow succession of minutes trickling through the captain's hourglass amassed into hours and then into days. Jane combated her boredom with frequent journeys in time, her mind wandering to the home of her childhood. What might her mother be doing this time of day, her sisters and her little brother? How had they received the news from Edward that she had abandoned them forever?

Losing herself in another of Roux's books, she tried to submerge her growing worry. No doubt her mother was heartbroken over her betrayal, her father characteristically angry. What would they think when news reached them that pirates had overtaken her ship and she had disappeared with them? Would they deem her an evil-doer or simply suppose her dead?

Groaning, she tossed Roux's book on the table and leaned back in her chair. She couldn't concentrate on it, anyway. Voltaire's philosophies on religion couldn't conjure enough of her interest to pull her from thoughts of home. The grand estate seated on the outskirts of London still burned in her mind, its marble halls and expansive lawns taunting her. How had she left it behind for this?

Jane glanced at the empty basket atop the captain's bedside table. She'd already mended his holey stockings and torn shirts.

One had even been stained in blood, but he insisted on keeping it. A memento of victory, perhaps. There was nothing left to do but wait—for a foreign shore she had no clue how to navigate, a plan she had foiled in execution.

Her own stench assaulted her. Despite frequent washings, she couldn't help it. The only dress she'd brought aboard had seen enough wear, clinging to her like a child desperate for attention. Roux never said a word, though on one rare occasion when they'd occupied the same space, he'd mentioned she could use the gowns tucked into her bureau.

The idea had never seemed so tempting. Her skin perspired, her armpits chafing beneath the rough, dirty fabric. "Fine," she said to herself, bolting to her feet. "But only until I can wash the dress I brought." She refused to be beholden to Captain Roux any more than she already was.

Her heart pattered as she lifted the cornflower blue silk dress from the drawer. Her fingertips grazed the soft material, admiring its elegant detailing. It looked just like something one would find in her wardrobe back home, a gown befitting a proper lady. Jane couldn't help wondering about the woman who owned it as she set to undressing and bathing herself at the chamber set.

Captain Roux had never mentioned her—the mysterious baroness who undoubtedly held a place in his heart. What man would decorate this space so lavishly without loving the person meant to fill it? She'd returned to her husband, or so his sailors had murmured when they thought no one could hear. Jane wanted to ask him about her so badly, but guessed it would only kindle his fury. She preferred the silent indifference he now greeted her with than the outright hostility she'd met her first day aboard ship.

Satisfied with her makeshift bath, Jane reached for the lovely dress on her bed and lifted it over her head. The gown had sewn-in stays in the bodice, lending her a graceful shape. After she'd tied the back and adjusted her petticoats, she sat down to don the stockings and slippers. How amazing it felt to wear fine clothes again.

Sighing, she tried to forget the plain frock she would undoubtedly wear for the rest of her days once she reached the mission.

The gown's flowing skirts fluttered about her knees and ankles as she walked, delighting her. Jane twisted her freshly washed hair up in the best style she could, using one of the captain's hair ties to keep it in place. She smiled to herself in the mirror as she adjusted the black ribbon peeking out from her blonde tresses. Would he notice that she'd borrowed his ribbon to style her hair? Would he notice anything about her?

The door to his cabin squealed open, inciting Jane to duck behind her own door. She'd kept it open while fixing her hair so she might see with the light from his window. Now, her heartbeat pulsed in her throat, her fingers grappling the wood. Somehow, it rattled her nerves to imagine stepping out in front of him, clothed in the vestments of a former lover.

"Jane?" he called, his boots thumping across the floor. "Jane, are you in there? I certainly hope you are."

The tinge of irritation in his voice flung her into motion. Jane begrudgingly dragged the door open, appearing from behind it. "I am, Captain. I was only tidying my appearance."

Christophe's lips parted slightly on sight of her, his eyes descending her and returning to her face. Jane's cheeks flushed the longer he stared at her, seemingly dumbfounded. Would he be cross with her for wearing the clothes, even though he'd offered them?

"Forgive me, Captain. I thought you'd said it would be all right." She gestured behind her to the soiled dress crumpled on the bed. "My dress was so dirty—"

"No." He raised a hand to silence her. "That's perfectly fine. Please, wear what you'd like." He gazed at her a moment longer before brushing a hand through his loose hair and diverting his eyes to the porthole.

"I thank you." Jane pressed a hand over her stomach. Perhaps this was the natural time to broach the questions raging inside her. "These clothes belonged to a woman you once knew, did they not?"

Christophe blinked as if looking for her through a fog. "What? Oh, yes." He cleared his throat. "A friend who sailed with us not long ago."

A friend. Jane fingered the soft crêpe of her skirts, unable to stop her next words. "I overheard your sailors saying she is a baroness."

He gave her a trite laugh. "I see my crew has nothing more fruitful to talk about than women." His head shook, a few sandy strands of hair falling into his eyes. "Yes, if you must know, she is a baroness of an estate near Paris. A *married* baroness. So you can squelch whatever romantic ideas are floating about that head of yours."

Jane simpered knowingly. "But she is beautiful, no doubt."

"Yes, she is beautiful." He took a breath, a far-off look clouding his gaze. "She is beautiful and intelligent and brave. She is exactly what a woman should be."

Jane couldn't miss the obvious esteem he still harbored for her, whether or not the bit about romance was true. "Your face said as much when you saw me wearing her clothes," she said, proud to be wearing the dress of such a woman.

Silence drifted over them for a few beats. The captain inhaled, as if swallowing his next words. Then his head shook. "On the contrary, I saw nothing but the way *you* look in those clothes."

Crossing an arm protectively over her body, Jane smiled shyly. "Oh." A curious warmth sprouted up from her toes, winding through her body like the branches of a climbing rose. Of course, she had admirers in London—suitors, even. Yet none of them stirred the thrilling apprehension that the look in Roux's eyes did now.

As if coming forth from a trance, he shook himself. "Anyway, I came here with good news. My navigator says we're only days away from shore. We should be in France before the week is out."

Jane clapped her hands together. "France?" He'd never revealed their destination to her before. "Why, that's ideal. I know people in France. Perhaps I might call upon them to help me get to Barbados."

Christophe regarded her a second longer, silent judgment twisting his lips. "You should go back home to your family. Go back where you belong."

Her brows knit. "Excuse me, sir, but you know nothing about my family. I will decide where I do and do not belong."

A smirk edged his mouth. "I know enough about you to know you'd make a terrible nun. You're far too headstrong and proud. You'll never make it in that life."

Jane straightened her back, affronted by his sudden shift in attitude. "Who are you to judge what kind of nun I will make? You—a man who has squandered his life racing around the seas, stealing what he cannot earn himself? Thank you very much for the advice, but I would be daft to take it from the likes of you." Her fingers dug into her skirts, grasping two handfuls of the delicate fabric.

"So I'm a pirate. I still have eyes." Christophe strode deliberately toward her, his bold stare pinning her in place. "I can still see when a woman's basest desires contradict everything she espouses to hold dear." His gaze slid down her neck, where her pulse hammered violently.

Shielding it in one hand, Jane sneered in disgust. "How dare you. Just when I thought you might actually be different from the men upstairs, you accuse me of—of—" She blushed, fully aware that she *had* been considering her attraction to him only moments before. "I am a woman of God, Captain. Perhaps you've met few in your treacherous life at sea, but you will not lessen my value by demeaning me in such a manner."

The humor in Christophe's eyes mingled with ire. "Believe me, mademoiselle. If I were anything like the men upstairs, you could no longer call yourself a woman of God."

Her breath hitched, his face so near she could see every whisker peppering his strong jaw. His fiery gaze told her he might strike her or kiss her at any moment—she couldn't be certain which. Sickened to her core, she wanted to spit in that presumptuous face. Remembering her breeding, she stuck up her chin.

"You are nothing but an animal," she hissed through gritted teeth. "You deserve your ignorant band of dirty reprobates. I hope you're caught up in a storm and the sea drowns you all together."

Christophe started. In truth, Jane had surprised even herself with the level of vitriol in her words. She couldn't remember speaking to anyone in such a manner in her entire life. Perhaps he was right about her ability to serve God properly. She had a great deal of pride to atone for.

Seeming to recover, he cast her a thin smile. "If I'm just like all of them, perhaps you'd feel more comfortable in their midst." He glanced at the ceiling. "It won't be long before they convene for supper."

Jane's hands began to quiver against her will. The very thought of going anywhere near that group of vile men launched icy chills down her spine. The captain had been so determined to keep her locked up before. Why did he challenge her now? She gulped back her fear, telling herself she could survive anything thrown her way with God on her side.

"Perhaps I shall," she heard herself say. When Roux only stepped aside with a sweep of his hand, Jane huffed and thundered past him. If he no longer wished to shelter her, fine. She could still thrive on her own. It wasn't like she hadn't snuck up top all week, stealing a breath of fresh air when she knew he wouldn't catch her. Last night, she'd been so bold as to creep past him as he slept, eager to see the vast black sky hovering over a nocturnal ocean. No one had bothered her then.

Her skirts rustled as she blasted toward the door, her slippers pounding the wooden floorboards. If he wanted to test her will, so be it. She wouldn't falter. At first, she wondered if he might follow her, but he simply ambled to his bed and stretched out languidly. Jane caught one last glimpse of him before she tramped into the hall.

The air in the narrow corridor chilled her, sprinkling gooseflesh over her skin. Jane buffed her forearms, unsure where to go next. At the end of the hall, the stairs led up to the main deck. The idea of mingling with his men repulsed her, so she turned aside into another darkened corridor. Perhaps she could find a new place to hide until they reached France. Roux had said it lay only days away. She could survive at least without food until then.

Trying not to think, she stole deeper into the corridor. She couldn't see through the dark. Using her fingertips to guide her, she stepped carefully over the uneven wood. On either side, the walls stood like sentries, firm to her touch. Every so often, they were punctuated by what felt like a door, or perhaps the entrance to a storage room. A dank odor increased the farther she went until it encapsulated her every sense.

When she'd traversed what must have been half the ship's length, the rumble of voices reached her. Jane strained toward the sound, curious where her venture had led. Carefully, she tiptoed over the creaking wood, following the sound of men's conversation growing more distinct. Then, before she could take another step, a hand shot out of the dark and clamped on her forearm.

Jane desperately writhed within the clenching grip as another hand seized her free arm. Gasping for breath in the cramped quarters, she realized with dread that two separate men had captured her. Their hot, foul breath swept her neck, their wicked laughter echoing in her ears. How had they known she was in the blackened hallway? Had they seen her come this way?

"Come on," one of them ordered, yanking her toward the voices she'd discovered.

"You let me go." She didn't expect that they would, but she *had* to assert her will in the matter.

A cold laugh skittered across her skin. "I'm not about to let you go this time, *cherie.*"

Jane wrestled with the two men, attempting to wrench herself free of their vise-like hands. She tried to scream, but a hand clamped over her mouth. The corridor sounded with the bumps and thrashes of their struggle, the two men's fingers only pressing tighter into her skin with every movement. Out of breath, Jane felt herself being dragged despite the wild fight she put up.

A door at the end of the hallway swung open and collided with the wall when one of her attackers kicked it in. The sight beyond it froze her blood. Seven or eight men were scattered around the dark room—their sleeping quarters, she presumed. They all stared at her in awe as her captors forced her inside, lantern light emanating off their white, rounded eyes.

Lifting her chin, Jane's glaring eyes took each of them in before glancing about for a means of escape. Even with her thrashing heart and wobbling legs, she must appear unmoved. Her brief look revealed a long room with linen hammocks suspended from the rafters. A few lanterns swung from the beams nearest them, but beyond that stretched only muddled dark.

"What's this, then?" a lanky man with unkempt blond hair asked, his licentious gaze descending her approvingly.

"We found her snooping around in the hall outside," one of her assailants said, shaking her. "Seems she couldn't stay away for long."

The gathered men chortled at her expense, prompting even more to turn in their hammocks to investigate the sound. Jane shivered, aware that she faced nearly a dozen men now. She couldn't hope to prevail without Christophe's help, yet she'd left his quarters of her own will, fueled by the righteous anger he'd ignited inside of her.

That anger converted to fear as several men began to approach, their focused stares leaving no doubt as to their intent. "Well, what are we waiting for?" one of them asked. "The captain can't be far behind. We ought to have our fun before he spoils it." Jane flinched as he reached out to cup her cheek.

The man on her right tugged her backward. "Wait your turn. We found her."

Jane's stomach roiled as she listened to them banter about who would defile her first. Tears sprang to her eyes despite her desperate attempts to swallow them. At home, she had always been revered and protected as a delicate creature designed by God. The worst treatment she'd faced was the prospect of being treated like a pawn in a game of matrimony. Now, with a dozen men closing in on her, all wanting to know her carnally, reality crippled her. Her beauty, her femininity, her spirit—it all meant nothing outside of the sheltered life she'd abandoned. She was nothing but a body to these men.

The group must have come to an agreement, because one of them released her and the other began fumbling with her skirts. Springing back to consciousness, Jane jerked away from him and launched a kick to his knee. The pirate swore, yanking her to his sweat-stained form, the reek of his odor drowning her.

"Wait a moment," a deep voice said in broken French with an Italian lilt. They all turned their sights on a man with dark hair flowing about his shoulders. "*Mi scusi,* I haven't been on this ship long, the captain—he said not to touch her, no?"

The strong man who held her laughed mockingly. "Who cares what the captain says? He just wants to keep her for himself." His dark eyes glimmered in the lamplight as they perused her face. "You boarded the ship of your own accord, then you escaped to find us, didn't you?"

Quaking with rage and fear, Jane squeezed her teeth together. "I am not a harlot," she hissed.

His head wagged, his tongue clicking. "That's too bad for you, then. You will be soon."

The one who'd defended her stepped up. "*Please,* signore." He extended a hand in supplication. "I must return home to my family. They need me."

"Then you should have sailed home with Bertrand instead of thinking you'd get rich riding with us," her captor growled.

"He's right." A new voice, steady and calm. A young man rose from the crate he'd been perched on, playing cards in his right hand. "Roux will beat us if he finds out what's going on here—probably worse. I'm not about to risk my place on board this ship just to satisfy an urge."

"She's a lady," an unseen voice shouted. "Let her go."

Jane's taut nerves began to relax with each dissenting opinion. If enough of them fought on her side, those who sought her harm would have to release her. Through blurry vision, she saw a scattered few approaching now, their fists preparing for battle.

"If you don't like it, you can leave," her attacker said. "You won't be punished for what you weren't here to witness."

The dissenters exchanged dubious looks but didn't retreat. The Italian cast her a sad look, as if he already mourned what would happen to her.

"Here, I'll forgo my rights." The man whirled her toward the pack of men eyeing her like hungry wolves. "Who wants her?" Without warning, he shoved her toward them, causing Jane to stumble over the uneven floorboards. She tried to scramble away, but one of them pulled her up by the hair. Her breath pressed painfully from her lungs as Jane met cruel, snake-like eyes.

"I believe we'll have a go." His impassioned gaze swept her neck, a similar looking man behind him licking his lips and nodding eagerly. Before she could make sense of what was happening, he thrust her against a beam and began pawing at his clothes.

Jane's back ached at the sudden assault. She thought perhaps she could escape him while he was distracted, but one solid hand on her middle pinned her in place. Her wild eyes flew to the three who'd tried to advocate for her, their tortured gazes burning back.

Even if they attempted to defend her, the number willing to harm her would easily overpower them.

Two of them sprang to action, stomping toward the man now reaching for the hem of her dress. Before they could lay hands on him, his comrade confronted them and a scuffle ensued behind his head. Hot tears rained down Jane's cheeks as her hope dwindled. It was too late. Nothing could save her now. The foolishness of her choices rang all too clear as her attacker laughed in wicked delight.

Then the door burst open again, and Christophe Roux's face stilled her hammering heart.

Nine

Uncomfortable silence enveloped the sailors' berth for several moments. Christophe's narrowed eyes shifted quietly over the assembly. Three of his men stood with chests heaving, seemingly prepared to fight. One of his deckhands faced them with fists clenched, his brother behind him pressing Jane to a beam. The look on her face twisted his stomach. He had seen the traces of fear in her eyes before, but now outright panic tremored through her entire body. Guilt assailed him as his gaze swept the six or so other men watching the exchange.

Without a word, he rushed toward the round-eyed sailor who had Jane and ripped him away from her. Blood channeled furiously through his veins as he held the offender up by his shirt collar, his muscles bulging in the effort.

"Captain, please." His lips trembled. "We thought she was a—"

But Roux's fist to his jaw silenced him. The man called Moreau stumbled backward, losing his footing and tumbling to the floor. Christophe stood over him, glaring through the hazy lantern light, silently promising a lashing he'd never forget. "You knew exactly what she was this time. I heard her tell you through the door."

Moreau sputtered but had no reply. When Christophe latched his stern gaze with Moreau's brother, the man jumped backward.

They could say nothing to avoid the just penalty awaiting them for their actions, nothing to calm the rage stampeding through his chest and up his taut throat.

He'd hardly managed to contain himself as he waited behind the door, listening to their foul words and the scuffle of feet as they squared off against each other. Jane's breath still wheezed from her throat. Her arms wound tightly around her surging torso. It tortured him to know he'd designed and executed the plan that caused her distress, but it had proven necessary for her safety.

The rest of the group stood motionless, waiting for a word from their captain. Christophe looked to Bassett and La Rue, the two who had captured Jane in the corridor. "Well?" His brows raised.

La Rue's pointed finger lifted. "Just these two." He indicated the Moreau brothers, who glanced at each other in confusion. "The rest of them didn't have a hand in it. These three over here tried to prevent it."

The man still licking his wound on the floor sat up. "But you had a hand in it, too, La Rue. You brought her here and offered her to us. You were set to take her first." His brother nodded shakily, as did several others sprinkled around the berth.

Christophe took a moment to answer, fearful of Jane's reaction. "La Rue and Bassett acted upon my orders." He pivoted his head away from her dismayed eyes. "I instructed them to take her from the corridor into your berth."

Lashes batting in bemusement, Moreau twisted up his face before bursting from the floor. "You tricked us. You used her as bait."

"Yes, and I'd say it worked rather well." The captain motioned with his head. "Take these two to the holding cell next to Vivianno. They will be punished for their crimes tomorrow."

Moreau struggled within the hands already clasping his arms. "You won't get away with this, Roux. It isn't fair, sending a woman like that down here to tempt us. What kind of a captain are you? I'll remember this when your rivals are coming after you. Don't expect me to defend you."

The sounds of his protests trailed behind as Moreau was led from the berth. Christophe's jaw clenched, but he left the threats and accusations unanswered. The deeper Moreau dug his own grave, the better. Right now, he needed to divide sheep from goats and reward the loyal among his company.

Christophe turned to the trio La Rue had indicated. "As for you three," he said, meeting each of their confident gazes, "because of your courage in standing against these traitors and your adherence to our ship's code, you are hereby promoted to chief officers. Only Monsieur Simon and I have the authority to trump your decisions, both at sea and on land."

The Italian stepped forward, his eyebrows working as if he searched for the right words in French. "Even me, Captain?"

Christophe smiled. "Even you, my friend." He clapped a hand on his shoulder. "You haven't sailed with us long, but you proved yourself today when you stood up for this fine lady."

Murmurs rumbled through the group. His newly promoted sailor beamed with joy. Perhaps this display of camaraderie would help carry them through until they reached French soil. With growing fear, Christophe knew he had to unite them somehow. Any day now, Blanc and his friends might wage war on him and take the treasure for themselves.

Inhaling the dank air, Christophe finally garnered the courage to look at Jane. She studied him for a quiet moment, her brows gathered and lips quivering. A dirty handprint tainted her gown on her stomach. Her hair fell about her, remnants of her earlier style barely clinging to her head. The look in her eye bespoke betrayal. Had he alienated her just as she had begun to trust him?

"Jane." Somehow, the word singed his throat.

She walked forward, her chin tilted upward, her emerald eyes fixed to his face. Keenly aware of the handful of men still watching their interaction, Christophe stood tall. How desperately he wanted to apologize, but not in the company of his crew. He must remain stoic, even as his instincts begged him to comfort the vulnerable soul peering out through her eyes.

"You—you did this?" Her chin trembled with her voice. "You sent those men to drag me in here and suggest that the others—" The thought suspended in the air, her strangled throat unable to voice it.

Christophe hardened his jaw. "I did. And I deliberately picked a fight with you to drive you out of my cabin. I needed to discern their loyalty."

Her forehead scrunched. "You used me." She looked on the verge of tears, but instead she flattened her mouth into a thin line, her sorrow usurped by rage. Her hand jutted up to slap him, but Christophe caught her wrist before her fingers could make contact. Their eyes locked, his touch gentle where he held her arm.

"Mademoiselle, I do not suggest violence on board my ship. You can be easily locked away, too."

Jane glanced at the men still gawking at them as if witnessing a circus act. Her nostrils flared, humiliation seeping over every surface of her reddened face. Then with a whimper she almost suppressed, she spun and raced back into the corridor, her skirts rustling madly.

One of Roux's newly appointed chiefs grimaced. "They scared her, Captain. I don't begrudge her response."

Christophe nodded, hoping his emotions didn't show. "We'll have her on the European continent soon. Until then, keep a watchful eye on her *and* the treasure. There are rats aboard this ship, I'm afraid. We must be ever vigilant."

The walk back to his cabin had never felt so lonely. He could have navigated the narrow passageways in his sleep, but he traversed them with deliberate slowness, giving Jane the chance to get there first. He owed her a shred of dignity after what he'd put her through.

When at last he pushed the door to his room open, he found her standing in a lone strand of sunlight, her back to him. She held one hand to her face as if chewing on a thumbnail. Christophe eased the door closed with an audible click, wishing to announce his presence without startling her.

His boots ruptured the silence, tapping the floorboards until he stood several strides from her. Jane protectively hugged her arms around herself, her breathing still labored. He fought the bizarre urge to fit her within his own and cradle her against his chest. Inwardly, he cursed himself. His impulses only arose because she looked and smelled like Madeleine in that gown.

"Jane, I'm sorry. I have no wish to see you suffer."

She slowly revolved to look at him, the shy interest she'd regarded him with earlier absent. Only an hour ago, she had stood in the doorway of her room, stealing the very breath from his chest with her beauty. Now, a cold resignation shone from her bright eyes as they settled on him.

"I see what I am now—why you kept me aboard." She shivered. "I was useful to you. Who else could provide the bait you needed to trick your men? It all makes so much sense."

Christophe stepped forward. "Jane, that isn't why I've sheltered you and fed you all this time. My plan only formed this morning. I protected you because you are a woman and you deserve that much."

Her lips pursed distrustfully. "A woman you would throw to lions for your own purposes."

Despite his attempts to remain unmoved, the chest beneath his linen shirt began to surge. "There is more to this than you know. I needed you to realize how dangerous this ship is for you if you don't obey my instructions. You can't survive on your own."

She scowled. "So you angered me on purpose in order to assert your dominance? I'm a woman, Captain Roux. You need not remind me that your sex overpowers mine in every way."

"I do not wish to control you. You're contorting my words."

"Am I?" Jane's skin reddened from her cheeks to her throat and down the length of her willowy arms. "The woman who just endured the threat of rape so you could look powerful in the eyes of your men? Forgive me for not cowering in your presence, oh mighty Captain."

Her furious words stirred a fire in Christophe's belly. "The woman who has accepted my hospitality, then sought to deceive me at every turn?" He laughed mirthlessly at the question on her face. "Do you think I don't hear you when you sneak out at night? That my sailors don't inform me when they see you on deck, lurking about despite my distinct orders to stay here?"

Jane angled her chin up, though guilt trickled through her every incensed feature. "I'm not allowed my own will, I see. I'm to be a well-fed prisoner until I've outlived my purpose."

"Prisoner?" Christophe brought one balled fist to his forehead. "You *chose* to come aboard. I never forced you to do anything."

"No, you simply commanded me, then tricked me when I showed any will in the matter."

"They were going to attack you anyway." His proclamation stilled her. Christophe looked into the wide eyes staring disbelievingly back, compassion seizing him. "Jane, those men had already hatched a plan. My quartermaster caught wind of it and brought the information back to me this morning."

Turning away, he strode several steps with his hands on his hips. He couldn't look at her any longer with her palpable fear shining through despite the anger she attempted to conceal it with. "There was talk of breaking in here when I wasn't around to stop it—perhaps tomorrow or quite possibly this evening while the crew takes their supper. What you experienced in their berth was only a small taste of the atrocities you would have faced, I'm afraid."

Wind swept over the *Licorne*, its aging boards groaning as it tumbled on the lapping waves. Christophe stood fixed in place, his head throbbing and breath tight. Her silence only drove the guilt deeper, stirred his already aching heart. Seeing her trapped in his subordinate's hold, panic gripping her every lovely feature, had only conjured pictures of his mother that last day in their quiet village. What he wouldn't give to go back and rescue her as he had Jane today. If only he had the power over death.

"How can—" Her voice choked. "How can you have such little say over what your men do? You're their captain, are you not? Why would they ever risk angering you over something so trivial?"

Christophe's eyes slipped shut. How badly he wanted her ideals to be true. "We're mercenaries," he said quietly. "I can spout my rules to them all day long, but in the end it only matters what the majority thinks. Right now, they still accept me as their leader. But that could change at any time if enough of them decide they want to abide by a different code of conduct."

Another long pause, pregnant with the odors of sandalwood and myrrh infusing his cabin. "So this isn't just your ship?" Her voice quivered faintly. "I mean, they can take it from you if they so desire?" From the corner of his eye, Christophe watched her fall limply into a chair at his table. She must have never considered the possibility before.

"They can if they band together." He turned to face her, fixing his solid gaze on her frightened eyes. "That's why I need you to follow my instructions. I'm not trying to dominate you; I'm trying to protect you."

Jane searched his gaze for a few beats before nodding. "I see." Her fingertips nervously tapped the tabletop. "Well, I needn't trouble you for long. You said France is only days away, isn't that right? I can keep myself hidden until then."

A sharp pain stabbed Christophe's chest. These last few days could prove the most precarious. The closer they got to shore, the better chances Blanc and his cronies had to upend the status quo. If they could convince enough of his crew to side with them, they could divide Clement's treasure and abscond to French soil as wealthy men. The thought of it kept him worrying through many sleepless nights.

"Now that you can see the perilous position we're both in, I hope you will take heed of my warnings." Christophe strutted to the table and snatched his bottle of rum from beneath it. "It's already difficult enough to control these men. Now I have the added displeasure of punishing their insubordination." In one swift movement, he threw back the bottle and let the warming liquor inside flood his gullet.

Jane hugged one arm around herself. For a moment, she looked like a child, vulnerable to a world that would certainly hurt her. Christophe could almost forget the headstrong spirit in her that set his pulse pounding in rage. She reminded him of Madeleine when he'd first met her on the island—attempting to cover her fear in stubborn wit. But Madeleine had carried a clearly jaded soul beneath the surface. This woman was pure—so pure, he sometimes had to fight the urge to wrap her in his protective arms.

"What will you do?" she asked finally, one brow raising in curiosity. "How do you plan to punish those two men for what they did—or planned to do, rather?" She swallowed, the very mention of it making her jaw clench.

"What I promised to do if they ever broke my rules." Christophe took one last swig of rum before recorking his bottle and pushing the cork down with his thumb. "They will be brought on deck tomorrow and flogged before the entire crew. Every last man will watch what happens to anyone who disregards my command."

Jane's gaze flew to him. "Flog them? With your whip?" As if on springs, she popped up from her chair. "But Captain, is that not the most brutal of penalties?"

His mouth pursed sardonically. "Clearly, you've never heard of keelhauling." Christophe had vomited off the ship's side the first time he'd witnessed the gruesome torture method as a youth.

"But surely you won't hurt them on account of me." Her hand shielded her chest, sincerity teeming from her eyes.

"They hurt themselves the moment they decided to disrespect our way of life aboard this ship. They are only reaping the harvest they chose to sow." He bent to plunk his liquor on the floor again, wedging it safely at the table's base. When he straightened, he found her a mere hair's breadth from him.

Jane reached out warm fingers to his wrist. The action sprouted a bizarre feeling within—misgiving mingling with want. Christophe looked from the delicate fingers laying atop his skin to the desperate eyes fixed on his. Beauty radiated from every plane of her innocent face—dangerous beauty. If he didn't quell his natural gravitation toward her now, she would inevitably cloud his better judgment. When Monsieur Simon had brought the brothers' plan to rape her to his door, Christophe had seen stars. It took every bit of strength in his soul not to kill them with his bare hands.

Her fingers tensed, causing his breath to thicken. "*Please*, Captain Roux. You must listen. No matter what a man has done to me, I cannot be the source of their pain. I cannot watch them suffer when God has called me to forgive them."

Christophe considered her words. How valiant they sounded, how beautifully merciful. In a utopian world, he might agree. But here, mercy only brought death. It only gave a man the chance to stick his knife in one's back the second they looked away. Mercy would send a man to the bottom of the sea perhaps quicker than his own stupidity.

"God may forgive them. *You* may forgive them." His gaze brushed her face one last time before he forced his hand away from hers and reeled toward the door. "But I, mademoiselle, never will. Those two will face the end of my whip if it's the last thing I do." He glanced over his shoulder, his gaze squaring on her as he reached for the doorknob. "As will any other man who tries to hurt you on board this ship. I will kill them all if I must."

Ten

J ane spent the night on her knees, her hands clasped together, her face buried in her blankets. Tears unexpectedly sprouted from her eyes, staining her cheeks and dribbling to her quilts. She had never been one to cry over ordinary matters, but every time she imagined the captain's whip, her heart ached. How could she watch him hurt another of God's creations?

The clammy feel of the men's hands still lingered on her arms. She could smell their feral sweat, see the hunger burning in their eyes. Their laughter echoed in her ears, conjuring a deep fear that wracked her body and mixed with guilt, only escaping her in choking sobs. Still, she didn't want to see them suffer. Had the Almighty not called her to this moment? Had he not asked her to turn the other cheek, to love her enemy despite the wrong they committed against her?

In the quiet hours before dawn, she drifted in and out of consciousness, curled in a ball on the floor. Her tears had shed until she had none left, her body weak with fatigue despite her every intention to weather the night in prayer. Nightmares plagued her mind—terrible visions of sea monsters and other mythical beasts rising from the ocean to clamp her in their powerful jaws. She'd never dreamed like this at home.

A gentle scuffling in the room beyond barely roused Jane from her fitful sleep. Blinking and vision bleary, she peered through the dark. It came again, footsteps tapping the floorboards outside her door. Jane tucked herself against the edge of the bed, imagining her attackers returning to finish what they'd started. Then, the hushed movements began to sound familiar. She recognized Christophe's gait treading about as he prepared himself for the day.

Scrambling off the floor, Jane resolved to be brave. Memories of her attack the day before still threatened to cripple her, but she refused to let them. In the dark, she grappled with the wardrobe until she laid hands on the beautiful crêpe gown she had worn the day before. She'd meant to wash her own dress, but after the tumult that had transpired, she'd possessed not the energy nor the courage to do so.

Navigating her tiny cabin in the dark proved easier than expected. She'd grown adept at knowing where things lay now. After shedding the cotton nightdress she'd found in the bureau, she took mere moments to wash her underarms and put on the baroness's still reasonably fresh gown. Her hair still smelled like rosewater from her wash the day before, and she had no time to waste. Jane quickly combed through it, letting it flow freely over her shoulders.

When she burst from her cabin, the captain stood near the door to the hallway, a cat o' nine tails clasped in one hand. His solemn stare shifted from it to her, his eyes wandering her form a placid moment before he twisted toward the door.

"Captain, wait." Jane surged forward, her hand outstretched. "Please. I beg you to reconsider." Her heart thudded against her ribcage as she caught him by the back of his shirt, halting him.

"Mademoiselle, I would ask that you unhand me," he said without turning back. The muscles in his forearm clenched and released. Calm indignation cloaked every surface of his stalwart body.

Jane gritted her teeth, tugging him back in spite of his warning. "No." She cried the single word, tears dribbling to her chin. "*I* am the one these men have wronged. *I* should be the one who decides their fate. And I choose to forgive. I choose to absolve them of their crimes."

Christophe released a weighty sigh. "Jane, it's not that simple." Gently, he pulled himself out of her grip and revolved to look at her. Compassion lit his gaze as it tumbled down her tear-stained face. "If I could, I would choose mercy each time I'm faced with a task like the one I have today. Like you, I don't have the desire to see anyone suffer."

Against her better judgment, she covered his hand holding the whip with her fingers. "But why can't you?" Her head shook. "Why can't you show the crew that you are a man of strength *and* clemency, like the Lord himself? He looks down on each of us in our sinful state and still he chooses grace over our just penalty for breaking his commandments."

A crease dented the skin between his eyes. Christophe was silent for a long moment, something deep in his soul escaping his hard exterior. Then his fist tightened around the handle of his whip. "If I had the power of God himself, perhaps I wouldn't have to worry so much about keeping my men in line. Perhaps I could choose mercy." He looked back at her with sad resignation. "So God may choose to forgive these men if they repent of their deeds, but I do not have the luxury."

Panic stiffened Jane's frame as the captain turned to leave. "Wait. Please don't go. Listen to me, *please.*"

In response to her pleas, Roux only pushed the door open. "Come if you'd like. This is the only time I will allow you on deck. It will be good for my men to see you in association with the just consequences that await them if they touch you."

Jane could barely breathe as she scampered after him out the door and up the staircase leading to the deck. The higher they ascended, the brighter her world became. When they reached the deck, Jane found herself clothed in the colors of dawn, a brilliant array of orange and pink spilling over the eastern horizon. Sparkling clouds trundled over the sky, their bushy forms rolling atop each other. What an agonizingly gorgeous picture to backdrop the horror about to take place.

Awareness jolted through her as she noticed two men already tied to the main mast. The one who'd held her wore a face of impenetrable anger, his helper quaking in visible fear. Jane glanced around at the host of men drawing near, many still ogling her with interest, others full of vitriol in her presence. Surely they wouldn't approach her with the captain so near, but still their leering gazes planted nausea in her stomach.

A briny wind swept over them, blowing Jane's hair into her eyes. She did her best to tuck it behind her ears, then hugged her torso. If only she had a shawl to bring with her. The chilling winds skittered up her arms, raising her skin and driving deep into her anxious body.

Captain Roux's boots rattled the deck floor as he approached the offenders with a look so stern, Jane almost couldn't see the man who'd regarded her with sympathy only moments before. His white shirt flapped loosely in the wind, his long hair blowing wildly about his face. She had seen conflict in his eyes every time she implored him to show mercy, yet he let not a glimpse of it mar his confident stance now.

"Gentlemen," he began, his steely gaze roaming the crowd of his gathered men. "The task I must perform today is a most serious and distasteful one. I take no pleasure in its delivery, just as I have no wish to see my crew disjointed in such a manner."

He whirled around, marching past the three men who had attempted her rescue, each standing proudly with their hands clasped behind their backs. "As some of you bore witness to yesterday, we had an outright infringement of our code of conduct in the sleeping berth. Two men attacked the woman you see here"—he pointed to Jane, directing their eyes to her—"and attempted to take her by force."

"We were tricked!" her assailant shouted from the mast. "He used LaRue and Bassett to deceive us into touching her."

Against scattered whispers, Christophe charged toward the tied man. "Speak another word and I'll throw you into the sea myself," he barked, his muscular body flexing with the threat.

The man called Moreau retreated into silence, though his snarled lip and fuming nostrils spoke for him. Jane shuddered to notice a handful of similar expressions peppering the listening crowd.

Christophe leveled his gaze on his men again. "This vile traitor speaks only half the truth, of course. Yes, I used La Rue and Bassett, but only to discern the truth. I tricked nobody. When I received word that they planned to break into my cabin to defile her, I walked them into a trap of their own devising."

Another wave of scattered whispers settled over the assembly. Some of Roux's men appeared skeptical, others bobbing their heads in agreement. Jane couldn't miss the man with bushy hair who'd found her that first day, taking in the captain's every word with narrowed, beady eyes.

"Now, we have a strict code on board this ship, gentlemen." Christophe stood tall, addressing them as esteemed peers. "We comport ourselves not as vandals and madmen, but as dignified men of the seas. Men who command respect. Men who have a higher purpose in life than to take whatever we desire, pretending it leaves no consequences."

He turned his eyes on Jane, the admiration in them halting her trembling breaths. "A woman is not an object, gentlemen. She is not just another piece of goods to steal when the urge arises." His look softened. "She is the finest of God's creation and she should be protected from villains like the ones you see here, who possess not the control to rein in their foul imaginations." He shouted the last words, inciting applause and shouts from his crew.

"Now you tell me, gentlemen." He pointed his whip toward the pair strapped to the mast. "These two have not only transgressed my laws, but ours. We wrote our code together, long ago when we freed ourselves of Chapelle's treacherous reign. How would you have me respond to the flagrant disregard for our rules? Should I show mercy, or should I deliver the retribution that awaits anyone who flouts our ways?"

"Beat them!" someone shouted.

"Show them how we treat traitors!" another said.

All around her, the cry of violence rose, plummeting Jane's heart. She glanced around at their enraged faces, spying only a few who seemed to disagree but judiciously held their tongues. An icy chill overtook her, even as she comprehended this mentality would provide her safety. Who would disobey the captain's orders now, with an entire ship primed to defend her honor?

Jane swung her gaze back to Christophe, who still looked at her through the morning mists. His chest heaved, his solemn stare piercing through her. How desperately she wanted to ask for his mercy yet again, but understanding passed between them now. He couldn't stop the stampede she'd begun when she boarded his ship without making the consequences of hurting her plain.

Moreau tried to spit at the sailor who approached and stripped him of his shirt. Next, they disrobed his brother, who begged for reprieve like a child caught stealing his supper. Christophe stood steadily against the baying wind, waiting for his moment to perform. Through his whirling blond hair, Jane saw the turmoil churning in his narrowed gaze. He allowed himself one last look into her eyes before spinning away and pointing himself at his target.

The whip's crack unnerved Jane as Christophe took a few practice swings through the air. Both of the men awaiting punishment quaked in terror now, one watching with rounded eyes, the other mumbling prayers to Heaven. The first strike upon his bare back sent a bone-chilling holler through the air. Jane shut her eyes, sheltering her face with one hand as the blows came again and again. Cheers bounded all around her, men's fists rising up, their foul breath combined into a united, dizzying sound.

Jane tried to block them out, her breath heavy in her aching throat. With each slam of the whip, her body shuddered. The cat o' nine tails lashed through the air, its knotted ends colliding with injured skin, producing screams of agony that stirred her angry stomach. She tried to take even breaths of the algae-laden air, but found them rising in uncontrollable waves, faster with every snap of the merciless whip.

When the penalty for attacking her had ceased, she dared to peek at the aftermath. Two bodies were slumped against the mast, their bloodied backs shimmering in the rising sun. Jane tasted bile. Surely the captain hadn't whipped them enough to fatally wound them, but the gaping lacerations on their backs would heal into scars they'd carry forever. They would never forget her.

Without a glance to the out-of-breath captain, Jane wound her way through the crowd and ducked into the stairwell. Her slippers battered the stairs, unable to carry her fast enough to safe quarters. Stumbling into Roux's cabin on wobbly legs, she shut the door and leaned against it. She inhaled through her nose, but the deepest breath she could take wouldn't erase the horror she'd just witnessed.

Feet slipping from beneath her, Jane eased down the door and crumpled to the floor. She tried to kneel, but her legs protested with surges of pain. Bringing her knees up, she buried her tear-stained face in her skirts and let her tears flow. That distant moment she'd decided running from England and her father would solve her problems seemed like a lifetime ago. How little she'd understood of the world.

The captain's humble cabin smelled of sand and pipe tobacco, though she'd never seen him smoke it. Inhaling the pleasing mixture, her breaths began to slow. What kind of a man occupied these walls? From the time they'd spent together, she had come to know a gentle, thoughtful person. Yet he was a man who made his living stealing from others, intimidating them with threats of violence, carrying out such acts like the one she'd seen today. The very idea shook her core.

She tried to pray silently, but the words seemed to bounce back from the ceiling. How could she petition a God she had failed to trust? Had she stayed in England, he might have provided a way for her to marry as she pleased. Instead, she'd blazed her own path against the advice of those she cherished most.

Was God punishing her for unbelief? Or perhaps for the belief that her power alone might protect her when she'd foolishly come aboard the *Licorne*? Or perhaps there was more to it. Her skin flushed as she remembered the look in the captain's eyes when he'd first beheld her in this gown. Warmth had trickled through her—a delightful anxiety that she wanted more of. Would God forsake her for her attraction to a sinful man?

Sobs still wracked her body when the door groaned open. Two feet shuffled in, stopping for a few seconds behind her before the door snapped shut. "Jane." He said her name almost reverently. Christophe's exotic scent touched her nose as he knelt on the floor and laid a gentle hand on the back of her neck.

Even through her hair, warmth radiated from his fingers. Jane kept her bleary gaze to the floor, trying to ignore the effect his simple touch had on her. Surely she harbored sin in her heart if a man like him could pique her interest. Already, her skin tingled and pulse had quickened in his presence.

"I wish there had been another way—truly I do." His fingers stroked her loose hair. "I am a pirate captain, but I am a man above all. I bleed just as everyone else. I feel the pain of what I've just done in my own body." He exhaled heavily. "I lived under a blood-thirsty captain, and I have no desire to become him."

Jane shook her head. "This was all a mistake. I should never have left home. If I'd never have climbed on board your ship, you would have no one to punish."

A short, humorless laugh escaped him. "Oh, I'm afraid I would still have my troubles. Someone was getting that lashing whether you were here or not."

She turned bemused eyes up at him. "What do you mean?"

A troubled look passed through his gaze before he swallowed. "Nothing. I mean nothing. It's just that"—he pulled his hand away, propping himself on the floor with it—"there was unrest on this ship long before you encountered us. If anything, you've made my burden more bearable."

Jane tried to stop her skin from coloring, but still her cheeks flushed as his steady gaze held hers. She'd known this truth from the beginning—that the man called Blanc and his comrade planned some sort of insurrection against the captain. She had hoped for whatever scheme they'd concocted to transpire after she was safely off the ship. But now the thought of them hurting him roused a bizarre foreboding within her.

"I heard them talking," she said finally, deciding to trust her gut. "On the day you attacked our ship. That large man with the curly hair—Blanc, I heard him called—he told another sailor that they would mutiny against you when the time was right."

His expression unreadable, Christophe studied her a moment before his gaze lifted to the window. "Yes, I know what they plan to do. The Moreaus' punishment serves two purposes. I needed them to know what happens to anyone who raises their hand against me."

Her stomach knotted. "So you're expecting an attack at any time? What will you do?"

A soft smile edged his lips when he looked back at her. His broad shoulders lifted. "There is always a way to outsmart men like that, especially with allies willing to bring me information like what you just told me."

Jane swiped at her wet face with one hand. She'd never imagined being an ally of a pirate captain, but what choice did she have in the matter? If they overthrew him, the future awaiting her was far grimmer than the reality she'd stepped out of. She would rather marry Davenport a million times than succumb to these reprobates' twisted desires.

"You're in the game now, Jane Whitecliffe." The captain cast her a sly smile despite the worry still plaguing his eyes. "Stick with me and I won't let harm come to you, I promise."

Somehow, in the raging midst of tumult, Jane believed him. She nodded, wiping away the last of her tears. She would try to follow his command, even when it hurt to relinquish control. Soon she would be on French soil, this ship and its captain merely a memory.

Eleven

"We'll be in Brest by nightfall." Monsieur Simon scratched his shaven chin as he paced Christophe's office.

Seated behind his mahogany desk, the captain set his elbows on the wood. "I know that."

Monsieur Simon's boots bashed the floorboards some more, drumming a nervous rhythm. "If we reach shore and try to take the treasure from the men, they'll kill us."

Christophe sighed. "I know that, too." How keenly he knew it. He'd imagined this day every waking moment since leaving Traitor Isle and many of his sleeping ones, as well. "Jane says Blanc is planning a mutiny. It wouldn't serve him to wait until the treasure is already dispersed."

Stopping before the desk, Monsieur Simon launched him an incredulous look. "Jane told you? That woman hiding out in your cabin? What does she know about Blanc's motives?"

"She overheard him talking with someone the day she snuck aboard." Christophe tented his fingers. "She said he was waiting until he could get as many of our men to his side as possible before attempting it."

Monsieur Simon swore under his breath. "He's probably rallying them this very moment, while we sit here trying to make a plan like a couple of confused jackrabbits."

"That's what we always were, isn't it?" Christophe managed a weak smile. "We've been fighting for our lives ever since we took this ship from Jacques Chapelle—and if we hadn't, we would already be dead."

"Yes, but never with priceless cargo stowed away." His quartermaster released a puff of air from billowed cheeks. "Never with the enemy we fought only weeks ago sailing amongst us, their leader in our holding cell."

Christophe leaned back in his velvet stuffed chair. "Has Vivianno been talking? What has he been saying to the men who feed him?"

"Not much of anything as far as they've told me. If anyone has snuck down there to speak with him, I haven't gotten wind."

"We must keep it that way." Inhaling the odors of cedar and cinnamon, Christophe tapped his fingers on the gold trim of his chair. "We can't have his hatred poisoning the men before we reach shore."

Monsieur Simon scoffed. "As if Blanc and his accomplices haven't poisoned them enough already. They could spring an attack at any moment."

The thought twisted Christophe's stomach. He leaned forward, slapping his palms on his desk, disturbing the neat stacks of papers piled there. "Well, then. You must return to them. Keep yourself in the midst of their every conversation. Tell our three new officers to do the same. They can't talk if we're present to catch their every word."

"And what if they've formed a plan already?" Monsieur Simon's fingers splayed on either side of him.

Christophe avoided his penetrating gaze. "Then we'll deal with it."

"Deal with it?" The quartermaster's voice rose. "You're telling me there very well could be a mutiny *today*, while we have untold riches stored beneath our decks, and your advice is to deal with it?"

"Jacob, listen." Christophe took a cathartic breath, his eyes roaming the quill and ink pot adorning his desk. "I will devise a plan that will solve this. I promise. Just manage our crew until it comes to me. I know it will come." *It had to come.*

Long after the sound of Monsieur Simon's footsteps faded in the hall, Christophe sat with his head cradled in his open hands. He racked his brain, the possibilities raging through his mind, scattering like a chaotic hive of bees. How could he possibly follow through on his promise to Madeleine? How could he sneak the priceless treasure they'd wanted so long out from under them, expecting no retaliation? He felt as if teetering on the edge of a cliff with no one able to pull him back.

He rubbed his eyes with the heels of his hands. If only he hadn't allowed a woman into his heart, he wouldn't be in this predicament. Without Madeleine, he could have easily claimed the treasure for himself and never had a care for the rest of his days. But without Madeleine, he never would have found it in the first place.

Something stirred within him, a strange emotion he thought he'd buried when Madeleine told him once and for all that she'd chosen Gabriel Clement over him. His thoughts flew to Jane, how she'd looked as she cried into her skirts on his floor, the vulnerability glinting from her eyes. Surely his affections for her only stemmed from a heart desperate to forget the woman who'd trampled it.

Yet the longer he considered it, the less certain he was. The image of Madeleine in love with her husband no longer summoned a raw ache inside of him, but the idea of Jane leaving his ship—that constricted his very breath. Against his better sense, he wanted to know more about her. He craved it. He longed for it even as he lay upon his bed at night, wishing he could spend it in quiet conversation with her.

Christophe seized two handfuls of his hair. How could he be thinking of a woman at a time like this, when his life was at stake? He had to come up with a plan. But the harder he tried, the more her allure called to him. He would not be able to think until he'd satisfied the need to see her, to find out what she'd say this morning.

Pushing off his chair, Christophe stood and tidied himself. He'd never given much thought to his appearance before now, but he found himself pulling at the wrinkles of his shirt and combing his hair with his fingers. Jane was used to sophisticated men. No doubt, they lined the streets of London for her.

His cabin was quiet and still when he wandered into it, pushing the door closed with his hip. Jane's door stood open beyond his room, the food he'd left her earlier clearly eaten. He craned his neck, his gentle footsteps approaching her tiny room. He didn't want to catch her in an indecent state of dress as much as the idea sent his heart racing.

"Jane?" he called softly, stepping up to her darkened cabin. "Jane, are you in there?" His heart jumped to his throat as he imagined that she'd left the room yet again, until he made out her lithe silhouette lying atop the bed.

Jane started, her eyes popping open and peering through the dim light. "Captain, I—" She sat up and bolted from the bed, standing before him with shame filling her cheeks. "Forgive me, I didn't expect you." Her fingers knit before her, nervously twisting around one another.

"There is nothing to forgive." Christophe tried to squelch his smile, but felt it still, radiating from his eyes. "Were you napping? I don't wish to disturb you—"

"Oh no, no." Her hand shot out to detain him. "Please don't go. I was only praying. There isn't a lot to do other than read around here, and it helps to pass the time."

Christophe nodded, pleased with her reaction. But did she want him to stay because she enjoyed his company, or simply out of loneliness? Either way, he would seize the opportunity to bask in her presence.

"Was there something you needed, Captain?" Her green eyes rounded in the dim light, nothing but innocence filling them.

"No"—the word caught in his throat—"no, I just—" Could he say he just wanted to see her without frightening the poor woman? "I just wanted to check how you are. After that grizzly experience yesterday, I imagine it can't be easy."

She looked down, smoothing her skirts with both hands. She wore another of Madeleine's dresses, a lovely gown of lilac crêpe that accentuated her peach-toned skin and bright eyes. "It isn't, but I'm managing. Thank you, Captain."

The sincerity of her words couldn't escape him. In all his years of life, his experience with the gentry had painted a starkly different picture than the one she displayed. He had never expected such humility, such care for her fellow man, especially ones who had tried to hurt her. She was nothing like the spoiled and entitled girl he'd pegged her as that first day.

Suddenly aware he still stared at her, gaping like an unpracticed schoolboy, Christophe rubbed the back of his neck. "I'm glad to hear it." He cleared his throat, glancing away. "Your solitude won't last for much longer. We will be in France before the sun sets."

Her gaze leaped into his, the joy he expected to see there clouded with doubt. "Well, that's"—her hand clamped on her throat—"that's wonderful, isn't it? I will be able to continue my journey to Barbados." She batted her eyelashes quickly, and Christophe thought he spied tears sprouting beneath them.

The desire to keep her with him swelled in his chest. Did she feel the same magnetic force binding them together? He gazed into her eyes, the honest purity in her face urging him to take that chance. He had to, before it proved too late. "Jane, I—"

A sudden knock on the door shattered the moment. Christophe twisted toward the incessant sound, irritation biting at him. "Yes, what is it?" His heart still smashed against his ribs, the prospect of pouring his soul out setting his entire body on edge.

The door swung open, revealing Bassett's blanched face. "Pardon the intrusion, Captain, but you must come immediately."

His pulse quickened. Had Vivianno escaped his confines? Had Blanc succeeded in rallying the men? With endless possibilities torturing him, Christophe blasted toward his waiting comrade. "What is it? What's happened?"

Bassett swallowed, his eyes brimming with fear. "There's a ship on the horizon, sir. An enemy ship."

Christophe's stomach tightened. He had fought off enemy ships often enough, but not while transporting a load like the one they carried now. It would weigh them down, and paint an irresistible target on their backs if their rivals discovered its existence.

"Stay here, Jane," he commanded over his shoulder, praying she would listen. "Don't come out until I retrieve you personally."

The upper deck streamed with dashing sailors as Christophe emerged from the stairwell and darted through them. Shouted orders reverberated from side to side, scuffling footsteps lighting the air. Even the tangy scent of ocean water couldn't relieve his tense muscles as Christophe rushed toward the source of distress.

Monsieur Simon stood on the forecastle deck, staring off in the distance with his brows drawn. As Christophe approached, the quartermaster silently handed his spyglass to the captain. Pressing the cold metal to his eye, Christophe searched the horizon until he spotted the vessel in question.

"Dominguez," he said, the name bitter on his tongue. Fernando Dominguez had plagued his life at sea for as long as he could remember. The rival pirate's sloop danced over the distant waves, pointed their way.

"Normally I'd say we could outrun him," Monsieur Simon said, "but not with Clement's treasure weighing us down. He'll be on top of us in an hour or two."

"I doubt we even have that long." Christophe watched his speedy approach a minute longer before lowering the spyglass. "If he has a full crew on board his ship, we might be finished. Our numbers are weak since losing so many on the island."

Monsieur Simon nodded. "We need everyone, including the Moreaus." Already, he descended the steps toward the imprisoned brothers.

"*Not* Vivianno," Christophe shouted after him. At least the Moreau brothers would have enough sense to fight off the enemy before they turned their sights on him. Diego Vivianno would surely shoot him at the first opportunity.

Christophe squinted through the spyglass once more, dread permeating his body. The enemy sloop sailed toward them with impressive speed, her black flag with its skull and crossbones flapping wildly in the wind. Most other pirates on the Atlantic respected their class, but *not* Dominguez. The Spanish privateer would attack anybody he thought might turn him a profit. How correct he was this day.

The captain turned to Bassett, who waited patiently for instructions. "Make sure the store room is well secured. If they board our ship, we can't have them finding out what's inside. And change out the masthead before somebody sees it."

Bassett nodded, then dashed off to complete the task at hand.

Taking the steps two at a time, Christophe surged toward the main deck. Everywhere he looked, men scampered to and fro, some expertly preparing their vessel for war, others floundering with inexperience. This chaos would make it easy for someone to cause mischief. He glanced quickly around before spotting Blanc working the sails. If ever an opportunity rose for vengeance, this was it.

"Gunners, make ready!" Christophe shouted over the assembly. "I need every man to his station. Do not fire prematurely. We wait until they are close enough to hit, but do not let them hit us first.

We need them to know we're in control, and we *won't* be trifled with."

"Aye, aye, captain." A band of men trained in the art of cannon fire whipped around and disappeared down the stairs. They would convene below decks, where the ship's guns stood ready for enemy invasions like this one.

Christophe looked up at the sailor manning the ship's wheel. "Do not let them see our broadside until they show us theirs," he called. He pivoted toward the group preparing pistols under the masts. "Remember to aim high first. Give them a chance to change their minds once they see the damage we'll do to their sails."

Most of Cavaretta's men appeared lost as they frightfully glanced around in the chaos. They hadn't seen much war under the Italian diplomat's employment, he guessed. Cavaretta was more the type of man who settled his disputes behind closed doors, where nobody could witness his atrocious deeds.

Approaching the new recruit who he'd recently promoted to chief officer, Christophe slapped a hand on his back. "I'm counting on you to lead the rest of Cavaretta's men," he said in broken Italian. "I need you to keep them calm and in line. Go where your skills direct you. If you are a practiced sailor, keep us afloat. If you know how to fight, grab a weapon. We will only survive this if every man works together as one."

The Italian eyed him apprehensively before nodding. *"Ci, signore."* He began issuing orders before Christophe stepped away to oversee the rest of his ship. These fresh recruits needed to take part in the action, needed to feel like part of the crew. But still, the prospect of arming them injected fear low in his gut. If just one valued revenge over his own life, Christophe could consider himself dead already.

He took up his spyglass again and peered through the hole. Dominguez's ship had gained considerable ground, the bejeweled depiction of Poseidon on its masthead gleaming in the midday sun. Dominguez had a smaller ship; with a full crew, the *Licorne* could easily overpower them. But his crazed Spanish rival had never employed logic to make his decisions, choosing instead to rely on his fanatical whims. Or perhaps he'd somehow heard that Roux's ship was severely understaffed.

Thoughts of Jane plagued his mind. What would they do to her if they succeeded in taking his ship? How could he keep her safe? The idea of harm coming to her volleyed a panic through his extremities that defied his expert calm. Curse the woman for ever boarding his ship, for distracting him from the grave job ahead. Christophe tried to bury all thoughts of her as he marched around his ship, preparing his men for the attack that would ensue before any of them were prepared.

Twelve

T he attack came at half past noon, when the golden sun sat straight overhead, casting its blinding rays over the tossing waters. Dominguez's sloop, the *Poseidon*, cut through the waves with the grace of a dancer, her sails billowing proudly and her sleek wood glittering. Christophe could almost admire her beauty if her nearing presence didn't signal utter destruction for his crew.

"Make ready, men! She's nearly upon us!" He stood on the forecastle deck, steadying himself with one hand on the ropes. "Aim your guns at their sails! Fire on my command!" He waited, the sea lapping at the sides of the *Licorne*, the ship riding the waves. "Fire!"

On his command, his men began to fire their pistols into the intricate system of ropes and sails commandeering the *Poseidon*. He doubted it would cause Dominguez to change his course, but at least it showed they wouldn't cower at his threats. Many ship captains would surrender at the thought of their rigging being ripped apart, but not Dominguez. He wouldn't turn back even with cannonball holes peppering his ship's hull.

After a round of exchanged gunfire, the sea air hung thick with acrid powder. Christophe squinted through it, examining the *Po-*

seidon's deck. Fewer sailors than he expected darted across it. Perhaps they did stand a chance against Dominguez's advance.

When the *Licorne* refused to surrender, the rival ship moved into a fighting stance, displaying its broadside their way. Christophe's stomach turned, his muscles clenching in preparation for the cannons' blast. His gunners would spare no ammunition. They had been ordered to strike the first moment they could, and he had no doubt in their initiative. At least his cabin rested on the starboard side, keeping Jane out of the cannons' reach.

The first blast shook the *Licorne*, its rails shuddering long after the cannonball launched from its belly toward the *Poseidon*. A barrage of cannon fire followed, many of their expert shots puncturing the enemy sloop and tearing through the wood with merciless force. Christophe braced himself, aware of what came next. While his gunners reloaded, Dominguez's ship returned fire, sending cannonballs blasting into the sides of his beloved ship.

The *Licorne* rattled with every explosion. The air clouded with noxious smoke. Pain-filled screams saturated the once calm sea, spearing Christophe's gut. The thought of losing more men tormented him, but even more, it carried him straight back to his childhood. Staring into the raging battle, he couldn't help seeing his village going up in smoke, his neighbors hanging from the trees, his family—

Thrusting his pain forcefully aside, he snatched the cutlass fixed to his waist. The enemy had come too close for cannon fire now. They dotted the edge of their deck, preparing to swing grappling hooks the *Licorne's* way. Many of them clutched grenades they would toss over the water to clear her decks. Christophe's men put on a mighty show of retaliation, ceaseless gunfire bursting toward the offenders.

Christophe ducked low as grenades pummeled the main deck, hissing and sparking before exploding in clouds of gunpowder. Dominguez's men climbed over the bulwark, yelling in unison and scattering over his ship. With a guttural roar, Christophe rose up with his cutlass posed. He couldn't let them capture this ship—not with the Moon King's treasure in her holds. Not with an innocent woman depending on him.

After racing across the forecastle deck, he quickly met an opponent on the stairs. The Spaniard looked him over with a laugh, his gnarled teeth twisting. Steel clashed with steel as their elegant swords collided. Christophe faced the man's every assault with expert precision—swinging when necessary, reserving as much strength as he could. The dance continued for several minutes, a blinding jumble of bashing and sweat, until his sword knocked his opponent to his knees.

He pushed on, fighting his way to the main deck, putting down man after man who stood in his way. Sweat slicked his skin and hair, his linen shirt clinging to his working muscles. His arms and calves ached with the constant motion of dodging and striking. Even after all these years of fighting, fatigue crept over his body, reminding him that he was no longer the youth who had learned these moves with ease. One day he would find himself no longer spry enough to command this ship.

The battle raged on, the men locked in desperate swordplay, grenades still occasionally exploding in random places. From the corner of his eye, Christophe spied several of them stealing down the stairs. He would have to wrestle his way out of this mess if he had any hope of saving Jane. His heart pounded with fear just as a sword swiped near his ear.

Christophe dove just in time to evade the whirling object. He spun around, coming face to face with Fernando Dominguez. The man's beady eyes raked him coolly, his lips parting to reveal several teeth capped in gold. His thick, curly hair fell in a dark wave around his crazed face, wet with exertion beneath the high sun.

"Capitan Danglar," he said, using Christophe's privateer pseudonym. Most of the men who roamed the seas didn't know his true identity. "It has been some time since we've had the pleasure of crossing paths."

Seething, Christophe gripped his sword. "Not long enough. The last time we fought, I let you stumble back to Spain like the injured dog you were. I will not make that mistake again."

Dominguez laughed, a bone-chilling sound. "You expect to prevail against me with the pathetic amount of men you have?" He glanced haughtily at the brawl raging around them. "What happened? Malaria? A tidal wave?" He tittered again, his decorated chest inflating.

Christophe's lip snarled. "Even with superior numbers, your untrained lackeys could never hope to defeat my men." Indeed, it appeared as if the pirate's band lessened with every blow of his crew's weapons. Christophe's men had always proven themselves skilled warriors in the heat of battle, a fact that had mysteriously eluded Dominguez thus far.

"Defeat you is exactly what we'll do." Anger wound up the Spaniard's reddened neck until it spilled over his face. He never liked to be insulted, especially when confronted with the truth. "I told you I would stop you if you ever tried to sail through these waters again."

Lifting his cutlass before his face, Christophe set his stance wide and angled his chin up. Only one thing could end this battle without more bloodshed. His sailors depended on him now to stand firm rather than to cower, to take up the sword where they could not. "Then fight me, Dominguez. The winner takes what he wants. The loser"—his nostrils flared, determination fueling his every word—"the loser dies today."

J ane knelt on the bed in her tiny berth, her hands pressed to her ears. All around her roared a battle she couldn't take part in, a fight not hers to win or lose. She detested feeling so worthless, so utterly incapable of protecting herself. Her fate rested in the ability of a group of strangers to kill harder and faster than their adversaries. The thought curdled bile at the base of her throat.

Glancing at the blackened ceiling, she tried to pray but couldn't form the words. Her hands trembled, her skin beading with cold sweat. Above her head blared an appalling cacophony of men's voices—swearing, screaming, pleading for their lives. Desperate footfalls pounded the wood. Swords scraped one another, bashing in ceaseless violence. How a fight like this could end in anything but death for all bemused her.

Tucking herself into the fetal position, Jane let her mind drift to images of home. She saw her mother seated before the marble fireplace, instructing her and her sisters on the art of needlepoint. Her father sat nearby, sipping tea from a hand-painted cup, one shoe perched on his knee. The parlor smelled of clove tea and hyacinth, sprigs of the purple flower adorning the mantel in crystal vases. What a lovely picture it made. But Jane only remembered hating it.

Her fingers had ached with every wayward prick of her needle. Her mother had reminded her to sit up for the hundredth time, even though Jane's lower back smarted with the effort. She had gazed out the pristine sash window at her brother engaged in wild play about the grassy yard and wished to be a boy. At least they were allowed to have a little fun. She would spend her life bent over needlework she didn't want to do, learning a fortepiano that howled in protest every time she tried to pound out an awkward tune.

Her petty concerns that day seemed ridiculous now, with war raging outside her very door. How destructively confident had she been to step out of that life and into this brutish world where her survival teetered on the brink of extinction every day? She had stood in front of her dressing mirror seeing a woman who could do anything she decided. How naive she'd been—a foolish little girl who had never struggled for anything in her life.

The agonizing truth tortured her as she lay upon her bed, willing the fight to stop. At least the cannon fire had ceased. When the first blow had rocked the ship, she'd thought for certain it would rip through the wood straight for her. If not that, certainly it would sink them. Then boom after terrifying boom had given way to gunfire and the frightening reality that these rival sailors had breached the ship.

Jane gazed through the dark, the idea gripping her that perhaps she needn't fear the enemy ship. What if they were the British Navy coming to rescue her? Could word of her disappearance off the merchant ship have traveled so fast? They could prove her redeemers, yet even that thought funneled horror through her. What would they do to Captain Roux if they prevailed? Could she say anything to save him from the authorities?

With her mind wandering and the skirmish still resounding overhead, she hardly heard the door to Christophe's cabin squeal open. Jane whipped her head toward the sound, unsure at first if it was real. When the tapping of footsteps ensued, she pressed her face into her pillow and prayed they wouldn't find her. With her door shut, they might not even notice it.

Two pairs of boots battered the floorboards in the cabin beyond. Ice tore through Jane's veins as she quietly listened, her body rigid. They sounded to be scouring the berth for valuables, upending tables and flinging Christophe's books across the floor. Would the British Navy care for such matters? Surely not.

Just when she thought they might leave her be, two solid footsteps halted before her door. Jane could see nothing through the dark, but couldn't mistake the rattling and turning of her doorknob. Her breath arrested as the door swung inward, revealing the bold silhouette of a man outlined against the porthole's scant light.

He pivoted halfway back to his companion, beckoning him in Spanish. The man perked up, dropping the box in his hand and joining his friend at the door. They both squinted into the small space, conversing with one another. Jane didn't speak Spanish, but with her fluency in French and Italian, she understood enough to know they were discussing the odd room's existence. Then, as if their eyes suddenly adjusted enough to see her, they excitedly yelped at one another.

One of them advanced into the room and lifted her off the bed. Jane stiffened up like an opossum, forcing the man to yank her into the captain's cabin. They appraised her in unison, their eyes curiously descending her braided hair to the lilac crêpe dress clothing her. The two nodded, the bits of conversation she could catch indicating their approval of her appearance. She froze as one of them reached out to run his fingertip down her cheekbone as if she were a doll to be examined.

"Don't touch me." She wrenched her head away, inciting a blank stare from the intruders. Then they erupted in laughter, chattering amongst themselves about how she'd make a fine prize to bring back to their captain. *Mujer hermosa*, they said. Is this how a lovely woman was treated at sea?

Despite her protests, the pair clamped a hand on each of her forearms and dragged her toward the door. Jane fought with all her might, but she couldn't match the strength of either one, let alone the two men combined. Her slippered feet bumped the stairs as they ascended, her arms flailing in hopeless dissent. Fear engulfed her to realize that her fate rested in the hands of two strangers intent on giving her like an object to their commander.

The scene above decks shocked her. Once Jane's eyes recovered from the blinding sunlight, she scanned the murderous frenzy with hope waning. Everywhere she looked, men lay dead or injured, wounds marring their bodies, blood pooling on the boards. Many were still engaged in the fight, swords tangled in the air, slashing ruthlessly at one another. She screamed as one pirate shot another at close range mere steps from her. Death and chaos reigned supreme on this once beautiful deck, making her miss the solace of home that much more.

Through the harsh fog of gunpowder, Jane spied Christophe locked in a strenuous engagement with a well-dressed man. *At least he isn't dead.* Her heart raced to watch them, stabbing without hesitation at one another, whirling their swords around and plunging them toward each other's spinning bodies. "Capitan," one of her captors said with a nod of his head toward Christophe's opponent. Her breath hastened to realize he fought the rival captain. The man had to be skilled.

Christophe's muscles flexed, his teeth gritting as he charged at his adversary. The Spanish captain ducked at the last minute, his blade slicing low. Christophe jumped, narrowly escaping his rival's trap. Jane gasped as the enemy captain followed up his assault with a thrust toward Christophe's torso. Leaning back, Christophe deflected his blade and returned a few blows of his own.

One of her kidnappers tightened his grip on her arm when Jane unconsciously leaned toward the fray. She snarled, trying to rip free of him. "Let me go!" Her arm burned with pain where he touched her. "I said, 'let me go!'" She struggled against him, twisting her arm until she thought it might fall off. "I am Jane Whitecliffe, daughter of George Whitecliffe, the esteemed Earl of Brambleshire. You will *let me go!*"

"Jane!" Christophe's voice touched her ears.

Jane ceased her struggle, suddenly aware that her antics might cause a fatal distraction. Christophe managed to dodge the next hit, but his eyes darted back to her time and again. He was trying to work out a way to save her, even as his life rested in a precarious position.

Rather than heed her warning, her captor pulled a knife from his belt and passed the blade before her eyes. Jane stilled, the knife's sinister gleam sickening her core. The man angled it near her face and let the blood-stained metal's scent infuse with her nostrils. It menacingly scraped her skin, drawing the lightest of trails, before he dragged it over her shoulder blade.

A sudden burst of pain shot through her. Jane cried out, hor-rified at the warm trickle oozing from her skin at the back of her shoulder. She couldn't angle her head far enough to see it, but her pulsing wound told her the knife had cut deep. Lips quivering, she tried to temper her reaction to the injury. Christophe had heard it, no doubt. His body had assumed urgent motions, as if ending the fight mattered more than winning it.

Jane watched his struggle, wishing she knew how to fight like he did, wishing she possessed the bravery to face their enemy with such prowess. Her attacker held his blade a breath from her throat, awaiting the result of his captain's fight. Would his captain keep her if he won against Christophe? If he lost, would the man hold-ing her kill her rather than release her?

The questions whirred in Jane's mind, their answers dizzying and elusive. Baring their teeth like rabid wolves, the two captains battled one another until sweat poured from beneath their sticky hair. Their chests surged, the ceaseless dance between them ob-viously weakening both bodies. Finally, the rival captain paused to take a needed breath, and Christophe seized the gap in his assaults. Diving in with blade pointed downward, he knocked the Spaniard's sword from his hand and wrapped an arm around his neck like a coiled snake.

The Spanish captain's eyes went wide, trained on the knife at his throat. Christophe breathed heavily against him, his muscled arm flexing as if it wanted nothing more than to drop the weapon he'd pressed to his opponent.

"Let her—let her go," Roux addressed the man holding Jane between gasps for air. "If you want your captain to live, let her go."

Jane couldn't see her captor from her vantage point, but she supposed him silently questioning his leader. A long pause ensued, the enemy captain appearing as if weighing his options. The battle around them continued, but not with the zeal and fervency it had started with.

"Blast it, Dominguez, you're already beat." Christophe shook the Spaniard, clutching his filth-ridden shirt. "My offer expires in one minute. If you don't tell your man to release her, I will slit your throat and kill the rest of your crew myself."

Dominguez blinked, his pride melting to reticent defeat. At last, he nodded. The fingers grasping a handful of Jane's dress unfurled, allowing her to lurch forward. Roux let go of the other captain, but kept his sword aimed straight for him. The Spaniard reluctantly whistled to his men and flung an arm toward their ship. His hawkish eyes took one last look at Jane before he whipped around and headed for the *Poseidon*.

Jane's hammering heart and rattled nerves begged for comfort. Without thought, she stumbled forward, straight into the arms of Captain Roux.

Thirteen

Life on board the *Licorne* felt eerily quiet after the boom of cannons had rocked her ancient shell. Jane sat atop a chair in Christophe's cabin, unable to pass the time as she normally would. Every time she tried to pray, her mind wandered to the sights she'd beheld upstairs. Reading proved no easier. So she sat, listening to the waves gently caressing the ship's hull until night slipped over the sea and bathed the room in blackness.

How inviting the captain's arms had felt that day, securely coiled around her trembling body. She had buried her face in his sweat-stained shirt, letting her tears meld with his skin, letting her rushing heart touch his. His fingertips had tightened on her ribcage, the muscular arm around her expanding as he protectively cradled her against him. For the first time in a good while, she had felt truly safe. He would fight off anyone who threatened to bring her harm.

Jane covered her face in splayed fingers, attempting to forget how good she'd felt in his warm embrace. She had never wanted to depart from it. Aside from the security it provided, the feel of his strong arms around her awakened a yearning she had little experience with. A few boys here and there had piqued her cursory interest, but never before had her heart felt entwined with another person's. Never had she longed for a man to kiss her out in the open and declare his undying love for her.

Her face burned beneath her palms to remember. Jane let her hands fall to her lap, steadying her anxious breathing. It didn't matter what she felt. Christophe Roux was a man of the seas, and a pirate to boot. She could never entertain true intentions with him, a criminal wanted by his own government. Shame seeped over her just to acknowledge the fact that she wanted him. Was this a test from God to determine her fidelity?

As if he could read her thoughts, Christophe's shadowed figure appeared in the doorway. He held a lantern in one hand, its rays barely reaching her wilted form at the table. His gaze ambled the cabin before resting on her, worried lines creasing around his eyes. "You are sitting alone in the dark?"

Jane took a quivering breath. "I was merely thinking. I'm not as crazy as I appear—yet." She tried to laugh, but it faded miserably into a choked sob.

Christophe stepped into the room and shut the door. Stooping, he set his lantern on the table beside his bed. His shirt was torn and splotched with blood. Gunpowder mottled his neck and cheeks. His sturdy form sagged with exhaustion. If she had the gumption, she would offer to rub his shoulders, but the very notion prickled her arms like needles on a pincushion.

"Have you eaten?" He strode around his bed and began restocking the shelves Dominguez's men had disturbed.

"No, I'm not hungry." Her stomach turned at the mention of food.

Christophe collected the scattered contents of a wooden box, then set it on a high shelf fixed to the wall. "I can never eat after a sea battle, either. Death has a way of disrupting a body's natural functions."

His brows creased as he turned to her. "How is your wound? I'm sorry to have neglected it thus far. There was much to do upstairs after the attack."

Jane self-consciously lifted one shoulder, as if the motion could hide it from him. "It's fine. The bleeding stopped long ago." Her cheeks filled with color when he moved around her, examining the injury in the weak light. "Really, I will survive. I don't need your attention."

Ignoring her, Christophe touched a thumb to the skin below her wound, angling her toward the light. "You most certainly do need my attention. This laceration will leave an ugly scar if you ignore it. Worse, it could get dirt inside and make you sick, even kill you."

Her throat constricted. "Kill me? A little cut like that?" As much as she tried to make light of it, she knew how much blood had drained from her cut. It had only stopped because Christophe had held a handkerchief to the opening.

"You would be surprised how much death I have seen from 'little cuts'." He bent to retrieve another box tucked under his bed. "A man slices his finger while trimming a rope or steps on a rusty nail that pierces his boot, and I lose a stubborn sailor who refuses to seek help. It's senseless, and I won't let it happen to you." He opened the box to reveal a collection of balled strips of cloth, medicines, needles, and twine.

Jane's heart thudded in her throat. "You don't mean to stitch me up, do you?"

"That is the general idea"—he lifted one brow—"unless you think you can do it yourself."

One look at those needles shelled her in panic. "But surely there is another way. You're only a ship captain, and I've seen your poorly mended socks. What do you know about sewing up wounds?"

Christophe didn't hamper his smile as he washed and dried his hands at the chamber set. "I assure you, I've fixed many a wound in my time at sea." He strode to his bed with his box in hand. "You're welcome to wait for the surgeon if you'd prefer, but he's a little preoccupied at the moment."

Heat rushed over her clammy skin. She watched in horror as he calmly organized his supplies on the bed, seating himself just below his pillow. "You want me to come there?" she asked. It was bad enough that they had to sleep in such close proximity.

He sent her a placid, self-assured look. "I can't reach you properly if seated in one of those chairs. Please, Jane. Forget who you are for one brief second and join me on the bed. It won't take long, I promise."

After a moment's hesitation, she nodded. She could hardly believe herself as she stood and followed his directive. What would her mother say to her situating herself on the bed of a man like Christophe Roux, preparing to let him touch her? At home, she'd never even been permitted to sit in a room alone with a man.

Tingles raced over her body as he gently gathered her long hair and laid it over her opposing shoulder. He pulled down the collar of her dress to fully expose the wound, resting the fabric around her upper arm beneath her exposed shoulder. Jane trembled, more from fear of him touching her than the prospect of a needle puncturing her skin.

"Try to relax." His warm breath tickled her ear, signaling his nearness. Jane tried to obey, but as he washed away the clotted blood with a wet towel, her angst only intensified. The masculine combination of sweat and sea air emanating off him made it that much harder to unwind.

A bottle appeared in her peripheral vision. "Drink this," he said, depositing it into her hands.

Jane peered through the quaking lamplight at a label indicating whiskey. "Thank you, but I don't drink. Not even at social functions."

"It's for the pain. Trust me, you'll need it."

Blood rushed in her ears as Jane uncorked the bottle and brought it to her lips. How bad would this experience be that she'd require substances to dull the sting? The amber liquid gushed over her lips and warmed her throat in a curious way. Her diaphragm threatened to regurgitate the unfamiliar beverage, but she managed to keep it in her rolling stomach. How mortifying it would be to vomit all over the captain's bed.

"Here. You shouldn't drink on an empty stomach." He shoved a tin of hardtack at her that Jane hadn't noticed before.

She quietly drank and chewed the unappetizing meal, angering her stomach with every bite. The first poke of Christophe's needle drove electric surges through her. Jane clutched the blanket in whitened knuckles, breathing against the increasing pain. The needle drilled through one side of her wound and into the other, drawing them together. Over her rapid breaths, she felt Christophe's fingertips massage the nape of her neck, a tender comfort amid the grueling task at hand.

Every push of his needle launched painful arrows through her body, but soon the whiskey began to have a calming effect. Jane grew used to the unfamiliar feel of twine tugging at her skin, suturing it together. She relaxed into the sensation of his fingers on her upper back, steadying her as one hand stitched her laceration shut.

"I suppose we won't be in France as early as you expected," she said, eager to distract her mind.

"We would be there already if Dominguez hadn't chased us down." Christophe continued working, a sigh from his nose misting her skin. "We sailed off course for miles trying to delay his attack, but that sloop was so much faster without—"

His words suspended in the quiet air for a moment, unfinished. Jane wondered what had caused his abrupt pause until his deep voice filled her ear again. "Anyway, we're much farther south than we were this morning. It will take at least two days to recover and turn around."

"We can't land in a French port farther south?"

"No, it has to be Brest." He offered no further explanation, just kept on with his work against the gentle lap of the sea outside.

"Well, at least we'll be there soon." Jane tried to ignore the hard sensation that coiled in her stomach to imagine it.

"Possibly." He prodded the needle into her shoulder blade again, producing a little whimper from her lips. "I plan to stick more closely to shore on our way north. I would rather face the patrols we might encounter there than Dominguez again. I know how to convince a naval ship of our legitimacy enough to prefer that over another battle."

Jane's brows gathered. "You think Dominguez will attack us again even after you defeated his men?"

Christophe's fingers tensed. "I know he will. He's a proud lunatic who can't stomach the taste of losing." He was silent for a few beats. "And then, of course, there's you."

"Me?" Contemplating his words, Jane lifted the bottle and took another swig to temper her throbbing shoulder. "Because I'm a woman? Certainly, there are easier ways of finding another than attacking a ship—" The moment she'd stood on deck in her captor's grasp flashed in her mind's eye. A sickening ache blossomed within her. "I shouldn't have told them my name, should I?"

An affirmative grunt growled low in his throat. "Dominguez couldn't contain the look on his face when you said it. He was so distracted, it allowed me to win the match that much quicker." His hand stretched above her shoulder, pulling the twine high in a taut line. "I fear he will see you as an easy ransom, if he can gather the reinforcements to face us again."

The thought sent tingles racing down her arms. "Surely he couldn't manage such a feat in time. He's on a fool's errand if he tries."

"I wouldn't put it past him. He may be mad, but he commands much clout in these waters. He considers this stretch of the Atlantic to be his territory for good reason. Many pirate captains support him."

Jane tried not to quiver as she imagined what life would look like on board a ship like Dominguez's. She doubted she would enjoy care and protection like she did from Captain Roux. Perhaps they would treat her better than Blanc planned to, though, if they expected to exchange her for money. Then she'd be forced to return home and wed Lionel Davenport. She feared that more than the prospect of sailing with Dominguez.

"I can only hope we reach Brest before he finds us again, then." Jane stared at the liquor bottle in her grip, its glass surface reflecting waves of lamplight. "I'm sorry I said anything. I wasn't thinking. At home, my name demands respect. Here, I suppose it only puts a target on me. Nobody in your world cares about titles or land, except for the wealth it might bring them."

Christophe laughed lightly. "On the contrary, I care. It isn't every day that I get to transport the daughter of an earl."

The corners of Jane's mouth lifted. "Isn't it, though? You had a baroness on board this ship recently, didn't you? Is this not her dress I've now ruined with blood?" She uttered the comment casually, but now her heartbeat sped at his silence. How fervently she wanted to discover more of the woman who'd captured his affection and if she still had it.

After what felt like an hour of dismal quiet, Christophe spoke. "You needn't worry about the dress; she has plenty. I don't expect to see her ever again, so it's safe to dispose of."

Jane should have felt relief at his declaration, but a sadness in his voice gave her pause. "I know you said she is married, that you have no romantic attachment." She inhaled, afraid she might cross a line if not careful. "But you love her, don't you?"

Christophe's hands stilled on her shoulder blade. The sound of his breath whirred in her ear, heavier than a moment ago. Then, ever so slowly, his work resumed. "I did love her. A part of me still does—the destructive part, I suppose."

Her fingers gripped the bottle as she contemplated asking more. She couldn't help herself. "How did that come about, if I may ask? Did you fall in love with her before she was married or after?"

He released an exasperated sigh. "If you must know, it was before. Apparently, I have a bad habit of giving rides to stranded women. She spent weeks on board this ship and I got to know her well. Then she went home to France."

Jane frowned. That couldn't be the end of the story. The way his sailors spoke, it sounded as if the baroness had traveled with them recently. "Is that when she got married? After she left your ship?"

"Yes, well—no. I saw her once in Paris before she married the baron, but it was too late by then. She was already in love with him."

"But you tried to win her back." Jane could barely feel the pain in her shoulder with the interest his story roused in her.

Christophe grunted, his irritation clearly rising. "Yes, I tried to convince her to run away with me, but she chose the other man. It's that simple."

"But it can't be." Jane shook her head. "Your men said her husband *returned* for her. That indicates she traveled on board this ship *after* she was married."

The captain gruffly seized her shoulders and straightened them. "Would you hold still? I can't sew with you wiggling around." Once she'd settled back into place, he placed another stitch. "Yes, she rode with me again, but not to be with me. The truth is—complicated."

Jane peered through the lamplight at the open door to her room. "So, you had a woman you loved on board all that time and you never came near her? That takes strength, even for a man like you." Color bloomed on her cheeks. Had she really just voiced such a suggestive thought?

"I hate to blight your picture of me, but it's distorted." Christophe pressed his thumb to her shoulder as he pulled another stitch through. "I *did* try to win her over, even after she was married."

Shock ripped through her, causing Jane to twist his direction. Only solemn calm met her rounded eyes. "You pursued a married woman?" Of course, she knew of such rakes among the society in which she lived, but her father had always done his best to keep her clear of them.

With a gentle nudge to her chin, Christophe positioned her head away. "Is it so hard to believe a pirate like me might try to seduce someone who is married? I don't exactly abide by the moral code you're used to."

Jane swallowed. "No, but I've spent enough time with you to know you respect women. You would rather sacrifice your life than let your crew touch me."

"Women are distracting. Our rule to avoid consorting with your sex while on board is in place to avoid fighting among my men. They may enjoy themselves as much as they please when we dock."

He kept up his work against Jane's blazing skin. "As for rape, I will never condone the practice, and I will indeed defend any woman with my life whom I find in such straits. Sex and rape are two very different things."

Grateful he couldn't see her face, Jane blushed furiously at the open way he talked. Nobody had ever spoken to her of such things, let alone a man she sat alone with so far from the society that had always dictated her rules. She didn't know whether to feel appalled or frightened, but somehow, she experienced neither in his strong yet gentle presence.

"My father would brain you for saying those words to me," she said finally, a nostalgic ache prickling her.

Christophe's laugh tickled her bare shoulder. "So I shouldn't expect an invitation to dinner anytime soon?"

Mirth bounded between them in the lamplit air. Jane laughed, perhaps more than she ever had, basking in the freedom that came with it. She could be herself with Christophe—ask questions, let go of her proper airs—without worry over him taking offense.

Pivoting far enough to look his way, she let her poignant gaze settle into his. Christophe paused, his look meaningful as his light eyes met hers. So much lay beneath the depths of his sturdy exterior. She wanted to know more, and yet, with a twinge of sadness she realized her attraction for him could go nowhere. His standing in society, she cared little about. But a man with his lifestyle and morality could never truly understand a woman like her—the love for God that fueled her, the desire to live a pious existence.

Despite her ponderings, her lips curled gently. "I've never met another person like you." And against every voice in her head, she never wanted to leave him.

Christophe smiled back, eyes twinkling. "I could say the same of you, Jane Whitecliffe."

Fourteen

T he ship's mess buzzed with energy that morning. The *Licorne's* crew had defeated its longtime foe and suffered little as a result. Several had died and others still convalesced in the infirmary, but such was life aboard a pirate ship. The cannonball holes dotting the hull would not sink them. With shot plugs and a fothered sail clogging the holes until they could reach shore for repairs, the ship should easily carry them home.

To the sound of crude laughter and jovial conversation, Christophe retreated into his breakfast. He preferred to take his meals in the mess amongst his sailors rather than below decks, alone in his cabin as many other captains did. He had first stepped foot on this ship as a boy of sixteen. No matter how much power the years brought, he would always be one of them.

Today, their revelry lifted his dismal spirit. His gaze darted to each face, searching for the hidden vitriol surely living somewhere below their amiable facade, but he couldn't find it. Even Blanc looked happy as he chugged a steinful of milk and relayed his fresh tale of gutting their enemy. Surely he hadn't abandoned his quest to end Roux's reign, but a threat to their lives would always bind them together in a mystical sort of way.

Christophe took another bite of hardtack, then washed it down with black coffee. A flock of hens kept on deck provided the eggs on his plate. Beside them rested chunks of exotic fruit they had acquired on Traitor Isle. As he took a bite of sweet papaya, Christophe thought of how much Jane would like it.

Jane. All night long, he'd tried to put her out of his mind, but the effort proved futile. How he'd kept steady hands to mend her wound, he'd never know. The way she'd looked in the wavering lamplight had only stirred the growing passion inside him—her soft, pink skin glowing beneath the flames, her angelic hair draped over one shoulder. The task at hand had prodded him onward, but he'd nearly lost himself in her feminine scent.

His fingers trembled to remember how they'd felt on her bare shoulder. Her smooth skin had sent his heart pummeling against his ribcage. The lithe curve of her collarbone had distracted his most concerted efforts to finish his grave assignment. Then she'd looked at him—those wide, innocent eyes speaking to his soul, asking to connect with the parts of himself he kept concealed from the world. It had taken every fiber of strength in his being not to pull her against him and kiss her, to end the torture plaguing him more every day.

Summoning his willpower, Christophe had respectfully returned to his work and finished the last few stitches. After tying off the twine and snipping it with a knife, he'd brushed his thumb over the row of stitches and regained his good sense. Jane had likely never even kissed a man before. He couldn't shatter her innocence, no matter how much that contradicted every instinct he possessed.

Sighing, he bit off another chunk of hardtack and hardly chewed it. For days, he'd wondered if his burgeoning affection for Jane stemmed from true feelings for Madeleine, even when thoughts of the baroness had faded. But seeing Jane on that deck in the hands of Dominguez's men, watching them cut her—something inside of him had snapped. It felt as though his very existence revolved around protecting her and only her.

Christophe rubbed his weary face. In spite of his blaring feelings, he couldn't entertain ideas of her—not real ones. Jane was raised in high society, a woman of breeding and morality. She would never be content to spend her life aboard a ship crammed with odorous men searching for the next target to ambush. He'd somehow convinced himself that such a wretched life might make Madeleine happy, but not Jane. A day would come when she'd surely resent him.

If no hope existed for their future, then he must temper the reaction he had every time she looked at him with those luminous eyes. Although he'd never fancied brothels or hopping from bed to bed as so many of his comrades, Christophe had not restrained his desires when it came to the female sex. An unchaste man like him would never merit the unblemished embrace of someone like Jane. She deserved a man who had known only her and could love her properly, not someone who lived a haunted existence, barely clinging to a false sense of decency.

"You're awfully contemplative." Christophe barely heard the voice above him, beckoning him from his spiraling thoughts. He cleared his vision, gazing up to find Monsieur Simon standing above his table. "I'm not interrupting the formation of a grand scheme, am I?"

"What? No, no." The captain shook his head, grateful for the reprieve from his musings. "Please, sit. I was only working out how we might reach Brest without tangling with Dominguez again." *Not pining after yet another woman I'll never have.*

Monsieur Simon lifted one leg over the opposing bench and sat with a thud. "That might prove a tall order, depending on how much support he can muster."

Christophe grumbled an affirmative. If Dominguez could rally a stronger ship against them, it would mean all their deaths, rendering his worry over Jane moot. His own crew was only the first of his mounting problems.

"The way I see it, we go as fast as we can northward," Christophe said. "The farther north we get, the less likely he'll be to follow. He knows he loses power and safety the farther he gets from Spain."

Monsieur Simon's head bobbed. "I agree. I think he'll risk himself only as far as it makes financial sense for him. At a certain point, assuaging his pride won't be worth exposing his ship to capture."

Christophe gazed over the rows of rough oak tables at a portion of his crew playing faro in the corner. "Now it's just a game for us—staying close enough to the coastal patrol to call for help if we need it, yet far enough to avoid any questions. We can't have them poking around our holds."

"And the sooner we unload the woman, the better." Monsieur Simon's words sent Christophe's eyes swiftly back to him. "She's a liability for all of us."

The captain hooked one irritated brow. "I can't exactly dump her in the middle of the Atlantic."

"No, but we could sneak into a quieter port on our way to Brest. It would certainly be less risky than carting her around after what she told Dominguez's men."

The idea soured Christophe's stomach. He wouldn't leave her in some random place to fend for herself. "Dominguez will chase us whether or not she's on board. He has no way of knowing if we still have her or not."

"Perhaps." His quartermaster stroked his shaven chin with two fingers. "But her mere presence causes more issues than one on this ship. It's already estranged a good number of your crew."

Christophe cleared his throat, trying to look unmoved. "I made a promise to take her to Brest, and I will." And he would savor the few moments he had left in her company.

"You promised that to the vagabond who stowed away on our ship?" Monsieur Simon eyed him warily before understanding dawned in his brown eyes. "Tell me this isn't another case of your imprudent affections—that you're not going to let another woman cloud your decisions."

Christophe glared in return. "I am in perfect control of my decisions. What I lack is the indecency to see a woman suffer, even if she did unwisely steal aboard my ship."

The glint in the quartermaster's eyes bespoke his doubt. "I watched your relationship with Madeleine unfold. I know first-hand how she influenced everything you did, to the point of self-destruction—"

"And it *won't* happen again," Christophe nearly shouted. He glanced around to ensure no one had heard. Leaning closer, he met the quartermaster's dubious gaze head-on. "Have faith in me, Jacob. I know what I am doing. I'm going to protect the both of us, but I can't do it without you by my side."

Monsieur Simon's worried expression softened as he finally nodded. "Okay." His head cocked compassionately. "You know it isn't a question of loyalty. I will fight next to you to my death if it comes to that."

Touched, Christophe grasped his arm. "I know, Jacob. Thank you." His thoughts shifted from Jane to the battle they'd just endured. "Do we have an official count of our losses?"

Sobriety cloaked Monsieur Simon's face. "We have four to send to sea today—Rochette, Lafaille, Dieulafoy, and Poulin. Two more in the sick bay are questionable. The surgeon says Stuart should keep his arm if he has sufficient rest and does not move it."

Christophe closed his eyes, raking both hands through his abundant hair. "A glimmer of hope in the midst of pain." His head shook woefully. "Let us hope there won't be another battle. I don't see how we'll survive it."

"We'll survive. We always do."

The pair sat in silence a few moments amid the din of the roaring sailors. Christophe opened his bleary eyes to the lamp swinging over the room on rusty hinges, its yellow light splintering over the assembly. He breathed in the scents of coffee and papaya, trying to press down his agony. Cannonballs proved useful in their trade, but they left an ugly mark. He would never grow used to losing his valued men.

"Have you heard any more stirrings among Blanc and the others?" Christophe finally dared to ask. He'd noticed Blanc glancing their way more than his comfort would allow.

Monsieur Simon shook his head. "Not a thing. I think the battle stalled their plans, at least for the moment."

"Good." Christophe sighed, unable to think beyond their present troubles. If Blanc or any of Vivianno's men had done anything perfidious during the battle, he was thus far unaware of it. Maybe they would put off their aspirations after what happened with Dominguez.

"Do you know what we're going to do," Monsieur Simon asked, "if we do get to Brest in one piece? Have you decided how you're going to get the treasure off this ship?"

With a hard look at the men beyond them to make sure no one heard, Christophe leaned in and splayed his hands on the table. He'd considered this question for days, the puzzle's pieces drifting ever so slowly into place until the picture snapped together. He looked back at the quartermaster with confidence beaming from his face. "I have a plan."

Tiny beads of perspiration dotted Jane's face. She felt warm all over, flushed—as if submerged in a tub of boiling water. A delightful, dizzying sensation engulfed her. She could float amid this dream forever, weightless and unbound. Then her eyes popped open, slamming her back to earth. The dark silence of the little cabin solidified reality.

Groaning, she rolled to her side and laid her cheek on her balmy hand. Her visions had felt so real in the moment, so torturously vivid. She'd just been seated on a wicker chair in the gardens of her family's estate, the warm sun on her face and a breeze fluttering her lacy gown. All around her, roses and azaleas basked in the spring afternoon, their bright petals announcing their beauty. The smell of their sweet nectar charmed her senses as she twisted a parasol over her head and gazed back at the enormous brick Tudor-style house her family called home.

In the distance, a figure approached. Jane supposed at first it was Edward, bringing news of his amusing adventures in school. They loved to titter over the latest guffaws of a stuffy professor or his classmates' wild antics. Yet as the man's form strolled through the gate and over the lawn, she frowned. Edward was not so powerfully built. He did not walk with such authority.

Jane couldn't stop her legs from trembling as she rose to meet whoever came near. With his every confident stride, details sharpened. He had on a well-fitting silk suit with long trousers and a double-breasted jacket. A top hat graced his head, though it couldn't hide a shock of blond hair tethered in a queue at the nape of his neck. His clothes declared the presence of a gentleman, but she'd never before seen a man who ran in her circles with such a strong physique.

Her breath hitched as his face emerged from beneath his hat. *Christophe.* How had he gotten here? Why did he look so much like the other men in her life, clean-shaven and dressed to perfection? Before she could think, he fixed his gaze on her like an eagle eyeing its prey. In two easy strides, he snatched her up in his arms and pressed her to him, his mouth crashing with hers, his presence overpowering. Jane lost every sense and melted against him, her heart hammering in her throat, her body tingling in response to his fervent kisses. She never wanted to let go, never wanted freedom from the brawny arms wrapped around her waist.

Bolting to a sitting position, Jane threw back her quilt and huffed. What was wrong with her? How could a woman who dedicated her life to the Church harbor such immoral thoughts? Her lips still burned with the fiery kisses Christophe had planted there, real to her body despite being a concoction of her mind. She could not deny how glorious his affection had felt, even as she chastised herself for the notion.

Her bare feet shuddered on the cold floor as she retrieved her newly washed dress for the day. The night before, Christophe had hauled in a tub for her to wash it, along with the baroness's spare gown not ruined with blood. Jane had never faced the task of laundering her own clothes before. Though it daunted her at first, with Christophe's help, she quickly took to plunging the fabric beneath the soapy water and scrubbing it on the washboard he provided. Warmth spread anew to remember his strong hands guiding hers through the water, and Jane shook off the recollection like drops of rain.

The cabin's darkness accentuated her every bump and shuffle. Jane dressed quickly, trying fruitlessly to put the captain out of her mind. After all, her carnal desires mattered not. He was an undeniably handsome man who had shown kindness to her. What woman wouldn't swoon at such treatment? The fact remained that nothing could transpire between them. Even if she hadn't decided on a life of service to the Church, this life would never befit her.

It took her only moments to brush through her hair and braid it before pinning it to the crown of her head. Jane had grown used to the routine of readying herself in the dark. Against her will, she pondered how many women had filled the captain's bed, then flushed and chided herself again for entertaining such thoughts. Just thinking on it soured her stomach. She could never fall in love with a man of such moral low ground, who would try to seduce a married woman and had undoubtedly known many more intimately.

Thrusting back the idea, Jane reached for the door. Something rattled against the wood as she pulled it open, causing her to stoop to inspect it. Her heart stopped. Through the dark, she reached for the unseen item and pulled it into the light from the little porthole.

Her grandmother's ruby necklace winked from atop her palm, as if happy to be home. Jane couldn't help the smile that lifted her lips as she tucked the precious item beside the baroness's dress in the wardrobe. She wouldn't be foolish enough to wear it again.

A breakfast of eggs, hardtack, and wild fruits awaited her on the table. Jane always looked forward to the morning meal, even as part of her wished Christophe would join her. Reminding herself this way was best, she sat down and quickly demolished the food. No need for a ladylike show of restraint with no one around to see her eat.

Christophe's cabin felt lonelier today. Sunlight filtered in as it always did, streaming over the tidy shelves and books, the bed he barely slept in. Jane often heard him tossing in the night and had to restrain herself from coming in to speak with him. Nights felt loneliest of all amid the trundling sea, and the comfort of a friend would pacify her. Yet how indecent she would be to approach his bed in the dead of night, clothed in nothing but a thin nightdress. Surely it would arouse ideas she couldn't have him thinking of her.

Slumping in her chair, she closed her eyes and listened to the gulls' distant cry. They must have been nearing shore. The cabin's cinnamon and sweet pipe tobacco scent drifted through her, mingling with the spicy odor of its cedar furnishings. How desperately she wanted to relax, but the stuffy air stifled her. She longed for a moment on deck, with the wind in her hair and the salty spray on her cheeks. One more moment alone in this tiny space might drive her mad.

Ever since Dominguez's assault on the *Licorne*, her mind had whirled with possibilities. The Spaniard could return at any moment, rip her from Christophe, steal her away. A man like George Whitecliffe would surely pay handsomely for the return of his daughter. With growing resentment, she realized she might actually be safer if Dominguez *did* kidnap her. But the thought of returning home paralyzed her.

Determination fueling her, Jane pushed off her chair and started for the door. She couldn't sit another moment in this isolation, Christophe's rules be cursed. Surely no one would dare to approach her after witnessing the Moreau brothers' punishment. Chills skittered up her spine to remember their hands on her, but she ascended the stairs anyway. She would avoid the narrow, confined passageways and search for Christophe in the open.

The deck swirled with delightful wind when Jane stepped from the staircase into the sunlight. Fewer crewmembers dotted the ship than she'd noticed before. The sails overhead billowed proudly, their clean white faces smiling down at her. Jane tucked rogue strands of hair whipping from her braided bun behind her ears and shielded her eyes with a flattened hand. She didn't see Christophe anywhere.

Ignoring the half dozen pairs of eyes now ogling her curiously, Jane bustled over the deck toward the opposing staircase. She had to speak to the captain, even if it meant wandering far from safety. Beneath her pounding shoes, she spied bloodstains still spotting the floorboards, remnants of a battle that could have proven her end.

Nobody attempted to stop her as Jane slipped through the doorway beneath the quarterdeck and flew down the stairs. The air chilled her skin as she reached the bottom, unsure which way to turn to locate the office Christophe had first interrogated her within. She knew it sat at the ship's stern, but couldn't decipher which passage would send her that way in the dark.

Deciding to go left, she used the walls to guide her. The smooth wood glided beneath her fingertips as she wandered deeper, hoping this hall would lead to the grand office she'd once visited. Abruptly confronted with another door, Jane turned the knob and stepped through it, unsure what she would find on the other side.

Nothing but blackness shrouded the space beyond. Jane squinted, hoping her eyes would adjust, but not a single shred of light touched whatever lay inside. A shuffling sound stilled her. The offensive smell of body odor reached her nose. Trembling, she began to back away from the unseen person. Who would inhabit this dark, abysmal place? Then a deep voice from the void froze her.

Fifteen

"Have you finally decided to hang me?" a gravelly, masculine voice asked.

Jane gripped the doorway, staring into a cavern of pure black and unable to move. "I—" Any words she might conjure died in her arid throat. What could she say to an unseen voice speaking of his own demise?

"Who are you?" he asked. Jane vaguely realized his words were Italian, yet her mind refused to put together a coherent answer. "Did you abandon your husband again, Antoinette?" He laughed—a frightful, eerie sound. "I'm not surprised."

Managing to unhinge her jaw, Jane wet her lips. "I—I'm not Antoinette. My name is Jane." Why would she reveal such information to a man she couldn't even see? Somehow, his mysterious presence intrigued her as much as it filled her with fear.

"Ah, yes. I've heard about you." His words echoed through the dark space, the blend of a growl and a purr. "You've caused quite the stir, haven't you? I had two cellmates for a short while because of you."

Despite her quaking dread, the accusation annoyed her. "I didn't *cause* anything. If a man can't keep his hands to himself,

138

that is his own condition. Those two suffered from depravity long before I came along."

The man laughed again, steel rattling with the action. "There's a candle by the door. Why don't you light it and let me have a look at what I'm missing?" At her hesitance, he clicked his tongue. "No need to fret, my dear. I have no means with which to hurt you. I'm locked behind an iron grate."

Gulping back her trepidation, Jane felt through the dark until she located the candlestand he spoke of. Her fingers quivered as she manipulated the tinderbox by feel. A voice inside warned her not to proceed, but a stronger one urged her onward. She had to find out who Christophe had locked away in the belly of his ship, and why. It took her unpracticed fingers several minutes to scratch a spark with the flint and get a flame going, but soon quivering candlelight brightened the dismal room.

Jane blew out the tinderbox and tossed it aside, afraid to look at the eyes staring back at her. When she did, her heart beat madly in her chest. Before her stood a row of black bars, stretching from floor to ceiling. Fingers curled around them, dirty but refined, hands that hadn't seen toil as she might expect. Her gaze drifted upward to the face looking down on her, the dark eyes pinned to her every move.

The man had the beginnings of a mustache and a beard, but underneath stood a chiseled, handsome face. His unwashed hair glistened in the candlelight, slightly shaggy and black as a moonless night. Eyes that said they could dissect a person's soul scoured her face, as if looking for something unseen. Behind the lattice of bars separating them, she noticed his clothes—soiled and smelling of filth, but constructed of finely woven silk. His finery and the proper way in which he spoke revealed the first man of her class she'd met since leaving England.

"Yes," he said, his lips curling approvingly beneath his stubble. "They were right about you. *Molto bellisima.*" Unlike most of the men aboard the *Licorne*, he didn't ogle her with lust as he said it.

Jane forced her unsteady legs to tread forward until she stood face to face with him, studying him through the bars. "Who are you? Why are you down here?"

He snickered lightly. "I'm surprised the captain hasn't warned you of my presence—told you to steer clear of my evil influence."

Her head shook almost imperceptibly. "He hasn't said a word."

"He would rather forget I exist, I'd wager." Sinister rage darkened his eyes. "I am Diego Vivianno, a diplomat from Venice. I am pleased to make your acquaintance, *signorina*."

"Jane Whitecliffe," she said instinctively, the automatic response she had acquired throughout a lifetime of practicing social graces. "Tell me, Signore Vivianno, how did a diplomat from Venice end up locked away on a privateer ship?" Her stomach knotted. Could she trust anything a man like this would say?

His mouth tipped. "Your Italian is very good."

"*Grazie.*"

Breath whistled from his nose. "I am here because I clashed with the captain. We couldn't see eye to eye—not after he killed my brother."

Her breath caught. "He killed your brother? Whatever for?" Jane's mind reeled to imagine Christophe killing anyone, then recalled with vivid force the times she had witnessed his violence when provoked.

"They tussled over a woman, of all things." Diego's eyes rolled. "The captain couldn't stand that she'd chosen my brother over him. He challenged him to fight—a fight my brother lost. Roux gutted him through with no mercy before my very eyes."

Jane's hand touched the bars, compassion stirring within her. "I'm so sorry." The sorrow in his gaze tunneled its way to her heart. "She chose him? You mean your brother is the baron she married?"

He blinked, then wagged his head. "There is much you haven't been told, I see. No, Antoinette was with my brother long before she knew the captain or the baron. I always knew she could be the death of him." His lip snarled as he looked at the cell's dark corner into a memory Jane wished she could see.

Pressing a hand to her middle, she breathed in the dank air. It smelled of rotting wood and tar down here—the majestic *Licorne's* forgotten underbelly. None of what she heard made sense. A part of her wondered if this Antoinette woman had tricked Christophe, another doubting the captain she'd known less than a fortnight. And then, of course, every word this man spewed could prove an outright lie.

"I know not what he's told you," Diego said, reeling her back to the present. His ink-like shimmering eyes hooked hers. "The captain of this ship is a liar and a murderer. He takes whatever he can from whomever he can with no thought to who might get hurt. If you help me, I promise I will get you safely to wherever you need."

Jane's brow scrunched. "What do you want me to do? I have no sway with the captain."

Diego's laugh echoed through the small space. "He cannot resist you. Everyone who comes down here says as much, and I see why." His face hovered near the bars, imploring her. "*Please.* You have no reason to trust me, but what I say is true. Here, look for yourself. See if there aren't more secrets on board this ship that he hasn't told you about."

From the depths of the lurid darkness, his hand extended through the bars. In it rested a small object, glinting in the candle's glow.

"What is it?" Jane could barely hear her own voice above her quickening breath.

His dirt-caked fingers extended toward her, bringing the item before her eyes. "Find out for yourself. Take it."

Jane hesitantly reached up, her fingers shivering. Her skin brushed his briefly as he slipped it into her grasp. Holding her palm open, she stared at the silver key, its teeth extending to the bends of her fingers.

"Just down this hallway, you will come to a locked door." Diego speared one finger toward the threshold beyond them. "Open it. See what's behind it. Find out for yourself just how virtuous this captain of yours is."

Jane's head throbbed, her chest feeling as if it might explode from the pressure built inside. She glanced back at the prisoner before shakily turning the direction he indicated. Did she want to see whatever lay beyond a door meant to stay locked? Her feet shuffled beneath her, every movement a betrayal to the man who had shown her such kindness. Yet how could she hear such accusations and not investigate them?

Diego was right. She walked straight on and found a locked door of solid wood and steel at the end of it. Sweat seeped into the folds of her dress. A voice whispered to stop. Shoving it down, she clumsily found the lock and thrust the key inside. It clattered and turned with a click, the door swinging inward beneath her palm.

A large storeroom lay beyond. At first, Jane's candle revealed little. She wandered inside, fearful she might have stepped into another trap. But no one waited for her on the other side. Her footsteps shattered the petrifying silence, carrying her toward a wall lined in various mastheads. Jane gazed up at the mighty unicorn she'd spied on the ship's bow that first day, its sinewy head and pointed horn invoking the fear and excitement she'd known that day.

After a quick glance at the other beautifully carved mastheads, she turned toward the center of the room. A bunch of huddled shadows lay beyond her candle's reach, beckoning her forward. Jane gripped the candlestand, the hair raising on her arms as she approached. What could possibly live in this room that might destroy her image of Captain Roux?

The candle's rays caught a wooden chest and then another. Jane lifted the light, its golden spray illuminating dozens of similar chests. A string of jewels peeped from beneath one of the lids. Breath hard, Jane knelt down and tossed it back. Inside, a collection of rubies and sapphires beyond anything she'd ever seen glittered back. She moved to another, finding gold doubloons. Still another had diamonds the size of pall-mall balls. A disbelieving squeal squeezed from her throat as she searched them all—emeralds, silver, tanzanite, and beryl, even crowns with jade and alexandrite fixed to their glorious faces.

Jane's chest pumped as she sat back and stared in wonder at the collection. How could such wealth exist in one place, let alone a ship floating amid the wild waves of the Atlantic? She had always viewed Christophe as a working man, but with this much opulence at his fingertips, he was far richer than she could ever dream to be. The sudden thought chilled her. She was in greater danger than she had realized, with a treasure like this at her feet.

Footsteps pummeled the hall outside. Jane spun around, her candle gusting out. There, face stern in the glow of his lantern, stood Christophe Roux.

C hristophe held his lantern high, casting a warming glow over the shadowy storeroom. After informing Monsieur Simon of his plan and agreeing on a course of action, he'd felt renewed vigor. They would be on French soil soon. They would work together to get the treasure to the priests, and he would see Jane safely to a hired coach home. Even as he detested the thought, it conveyed comfort. She belonged with her family.

Yet when he'd gone to his cabin, eager to inform her of his idea, it stood empty. He wondered with a fluster of panic if a member of his crew had dared to attack her again, but nothing seemed disturbed or out of place. The door had been shut. If someone unwelcome had breached those walls, surely she would have left signs of struggle behind.

A quick interview with the men up top revealed that she'd hurried across the deck toward the stern and vanished into the stairwell. Perhaps she'd gone to speak with him, perhaps not. In any case, his swift steps into the *Licorne's* underbelly had landed him at an open door outside Vivianno's cell and a trail of her scent in the other direction. It took little imagination to understand what had transpired.

Now, with his lantern shedding orange light on her startled face, he wished he'd told her about the treasure sooner. What harm could it have done? Had he been afraid she would disclose the information to Dominguez's men as she had her identity? That if the rest of his ship got wind that she knew of the treasure's existence, their vitriol for him might erupt into something he couldn't contain?

"I'm not supposed to leave your quarters, I know," she said, her mouth still agape as her astounded eyes stared widely at the glittering assembly at her feet. "I'm not supposed to be down here."

"Jane, I'm not vexed with you." He strode into the room, stopping short when he noticed her flinch. "I'm not going to hurt you." Did he still have to explain that, after all this time?

She blinked, folding both arms across her stomach. "I'm sorry, I don't know what to think. The things that man said—"

"What, Vivianno?" Christophe scoffed. "He's a criminal and a liar. He'll say whatever he can to disrupt the order we practice on this ship. He wants not only to see my downfall, but to orchestrate it."

Jane was silent for a dreadful moment, her face condemning Christophe to the terms he described Vivianno with. Then she spread her fingers in the dark. "What is all of this? Why didn't you tell me there was a trove of wealth just lurking on the other side of the ship?"

"Because it isn't mine to tell you about." Christophe sighed, stepping closer and setting his lantern on the floor as he sat on an overturned crate. "I didn't want to complicate your life, Jane. You already have worry enough without concerning yourself with treasure and the men who fight over it."

She nodded, seeming to understand. Awkwardly fumbling her candlestand, she found a flat-topped chest and sunk down atop it. "I'd like to hear now, if you don't mind. I'd like to decide that for myself." The sincere gaze she lobbed over the quiet space told him she would listen, even if she harbored doubts.

Christophe inhaled the musty air, collecting his thoughts. How much could he tell her about this cache of gems? How much did she want to know? Rubbing his hands together, he made up his mind to trust her, a leap his heart had already made.

"What you see has been my dream ever since I first heard about it as a boy of sixteen." A tilted smile crept onto his face, his eyes full of wonder to look around at the once elusive treasure. "I came aboard this ship to a captain who lived and breathed the vision of finding it, and I was caught so fast in his dream that I knew I would never escape it until I found it for myself."

Dipping his hand into a nearby chest, he returned it with a sapphire glowing blue in the lamplight. "This is called the Moon King's bounty, a collection of riches hidden away for centuries by a French baron who served in the court of King Louis XIV. The place he chose to hide this beautiful secret was a deserted island in the Atlantic—the very island from which we just sailed."

At her interested silence, he looked into the yawning darkness. "The baroness you're so curious about—her husband is a descendant of the baron who stashed it there. Everything you see belongs to them."

From the corner of his eye, he saw Jane cock her head. "So you stole it from them?"

Christophe laughed gently. "A fair assumption considering my occupation, but no. We found it together. The three of us worked together." The memory of that frustrating venture still irked him sometimes. Or perhaps it was just the knowledge that another man had usurped his attempts to woo Madeleine.

Jane simply frowned, an endearing crease denting the skin between her radiant eyes. It took everything in Christophe's power not to cross the short space between them and show her how her sweet expressions made him feel.

Closing his fingers around the sapphire in his hand, he refocused his mind. "A year ago, I found Madeleine on that island and took her back to France. Men had abducted her, left her there as a convenient place to keep her until they needed her again. I thought she might become the key to finding the Moon King's treasure, and I was right."

The sapphire slid smoothly beneath his fingertips, leaving indentations in his hand. "After she married the baron, after my failed attempt at convincing her otherwise, she came to me in Rome during Carnevale. She had a past she needed escaping, and I had the means to help her. I agreed, but I used the information she gave me against her."

Pain swelled in his chest to acknowledge it. Jane stared back, spellbound, and Christophe had to look away from her innocent eyes. She deserved the truth—all of it, not fractured pieces of a shattered picture as he'd given to Madeleine.

He cleared his throat. "Years before I met her, Madeleine lived with a man in Venice—a powerful diplomat by the name of Stefano Cavaretta. She was not the pure sort of woman you're used to. She used Cavaretta to gain information and sell it to his rivals. When he found her out, she stabbed him to escape. This is the woman I fell in love with—a broken woman I saw a piece of myself in."

Madeleine's face emerged in his memories, stunning despite her faults. Her beauty had captured him that first day on the beach, but his heart no longer yearned at its fading image. She would remain a part of him, always. But he'd finally let her go.

"Anyway," he said with a sigh, "I deceived her despite loving her. I conspired with Cavaretta to get her back on my ship and take her to Traitor Isle, as they call it. She had information on the treasure's location, and I used her desperation to trap her. I thought if we spent more time together, she would fall in love with me too. We could defeat Cavaretta and take the treasure for ourselves, settle somewhere and live like royalty."

Jane's lips parted, her eyes thoughtful. "So, even the idea of you and endless riches combined didn't appease her?"

Christophe chuckled sorrowfully. "She is not that kind of woman. Hardened by adversity, yes. But she didn't care a whit for the money. She wanted only the man she loved—a man who wasn't me."

Admitting the truth freed his shoulders of their enormous weight, but it also brought memories he would rather cast to the sea. He gazed across the flickering shadows into Jane's incredulous stare, realizing she would never see him the same, either. Whatever ground they had crossed toward one another had fallen away. Perhaps it was better this way.

Her face contemplative, she picked up a string of pearls forgotten on the ground and sifted it through her fingers. "If you found all this together, and it belongs to Madeleine and her husband"—her brows dove downward—"then why is it here? Why do you have it?"

The ship creaked and groaned as it crested a wave, protesting like a child awakened from sleep. Christophe was silent for a few moments, glancing warily at the door. Could he tell her everything without putting her at more risk? He had to.

"This must stay between the two of us." His eyes shifted back to hers. Jane nodded, her swan-like throat swallowing as she waited. "I made a promise to Madeleine before we left the island. We both grew up alone, robbed of our parents. She wished for all of these riches to be donated to the Church in France. She wanted them to help children like we once were—hungry and alone."

Christophe's nostrils flared. He hadn't expected the freedom that came with sharing this weighty burden. "My crew thinks we will split the treasure once we get to France. I have a plan, but I—" His voice broke, the vision of her with both hands positioned over her heart agitating the longing within him. "I need to get you off this ship before it can work. I won't have you caught up in the middle of our dispute."

Jane bit her lip, mulling over his words while he waited, hoping with everything in him that she would believe him. He had nothing left to tell her. Unlike with Madeleine, he had poured his heart at her feet, letting her see all sides of him. The fact that she could now whirl around and betray him didn't scare him, but the thought of her hating him slicked his hands with sweat.

At last, Jane rose and sauntered the few steps between them, extending her hand. "Here." Their hands met as she transferred something into his palm. Christophe held her there a moment longer, savoring the feel of her skin against his. When he pulled away, a silver key glistened in his grasp. "I don't know how he got it, but that man in there gave me this key. There are people on board this ship you cannot trust."

Closing the key in his fist, Christophe nodded. "Indeed, there are. Thank you, Jane." He had suspected someone might sneak below decks to help Vivianno during the fight. This key only confirmed his fears.

Eyes thoughtful, Jane looked down at him for several seconds. Christophe matched her gaze, wondering if she could see the restraint it took not to pull her to him. Wondering if his desire to hold her leaked from every surface of his body. Then she pouted, her soft lips billowing. "I only have one question."

"What is it?" Christophe inhaled, preparing himself. "I'll tell you anything."

Jane regarded him a few more uncomfortable beats before she unhinged her pursed mouth. "I understand that she's an unusual woman, this baroness of yours. But why does your prisoner call her Antoinette, while you call her Madeleine?"

Relief flooded Christophe, warmth spreading. The two shared a mirthful grin. "There is much left to tell you. Let's go back to the cabin. I won't leave anything out."

Sixteen

Butterflies fluttered in Jane's middle as she stood back to admire what she'd just spent the last two hours creating. At home, the meals were delivered on hand-painted china, a servant ever-present to put more on her plate or clear away her used dishes. She dined on caviar and roasted pheasant, pickled vegetables, potato soufflé, and chestnut soup. Dessert would arrive to the flow of champagne in crystal flutes, an array of mint jellies, fruit, and marzipan to appease her refined taste buds. Remembering the decadence, the frivolity and careless laughter of those faraway nights, she missed none of it. She would rather dine on hardtack for the rest of her life than go back.

The captain's cabin glowed in tremoring candlelight, infusing the air with romance. Jane had located a chest with extra candles and stands tucked away in the corner. She'd lit a few and scattered them over the room, deciding she'd send him more once she was settled and had a little money. Another night gnawing her dinner alone in the dim light of a single candle simply wouldn't do.

Despite her previous encounters outside his quarters, she had braved sneaking out once more. She knew where the galley was from her first trip through the ship's interior, and she could easily navigate the passages and back without being seen. In the galley, she had met a short man with a rounded belly and bushy hair sticking out on the sides named Hugo. The shy yet jovial cook had welcomed her presence, especially when she told him she wanted to learn something. Jane had never cooked a day in her life; the prospect both frightened and exhilarated her.

With Hugo's patient help, Jane had taken part in his dinner preparations that night. Together they made a stew of salted pork and vegetables, the rich scents of butter and thyme filling the tiny kitchen. Hugo showed her how he baked his biscuits on a stove suspended from beams overhead. He had barrels of salted meats and cured vegetables, fresh eggs from chickens kept on deck, and even some cheese that hadn't yet molded. Jane tried to poke her head in a few barrels in the corner, and Hugo waved her away. It was bad luck to make friends with maggots, he said.

Now, Jane surveyed her work with a sense of pride. The same pork stew that all the sailors were eating that night sat in two pewter bowls on the table, but somehow it felt more special knowing she'd helped it come to life. Hugo said the captain usually ate the hard biscuits brought from land, but that Christophe had asked the cook to make her special ones of his own creation. Her heart swelled to brush a hand over one now—a special gift Christophe had provided for her that she could give back.

The sweet cedar odor of his cabin mingled with bay leaves and thyme. Jane breathed it in, clutching a chairback, her eyes sweeping the plates and folded napkins, the simple forks that looked like silver to her imagination. Perhaps her inexperience with life made her silly, but she didn't care. Crafting a meal with her own hands for the very first time felt like giving him a piece of her heart.

That day had changed her—how she thought of Christophe, what she wanted for her future. Weeks at sea had shown his kindness and generosity, but never the depths of him. In that storeroom, surrounded by unimaginable wealth, the soul he buried beneath his hard exterior had peered back at her, unfettered. He existed, not to steal and to conquer, as she had often assumed, but to fulfill a passion raging in him since childhood. Suddenly, he was no longer just a pirate, but a man living out a dream.

Jane smiled, thinking of the newspaper accounts she had read of him—the dreaded Thief of the Atlantic, a savage who ripped out men's hearts and laughed while taking their widows for himself. How many people would buy a paper depicting a strong man with a kind heart, she wondered. Reality didn't tantalize the way overblown fabrications did.

Truth, as she'd seen it in his fathomless eyes today, altered people. So much of the world spun to the tune of greed, the ceaseless quest for extravagance far beyond one's needs. Today she'd sat with a privateer, a man feared and reviled by society, who had chosen to keep a promise at the threat to his own life. Chosen to help abandoned children rather than feed his own avarice. Jane took in a quivering breath, the seeds of affection sprouting into love. But how could she love a man who would never leave his beloved sea?

The door swung inward, revealing his flushed face. Christophe stumbled through it, eyes round. "Jane, are you all right? My cook said—" He stopped short at the sight of her, his eyes meandering briefly over the table. "He said you needed my help."

As he ambled forward, the captain's gaze swung around the room to the candles flickering from various tables and shelves, the perfectly arranged place settings and spread of food. "What is all this?"

A clever smile dented Jane's mouth. "I know I'm not supposed to go out. Luckily for me, Hugo is much friendlier than the Moreau brothers." She meant it as a joke, but still the mention of them twisted her gut.

Christophe nodded, still spellbound. "I am lucky to have him. He used to be a chef in the home of a marquis, if you can believe that."

"Oh, I believe it." Jane chuckled at her memories of the little man bustling around the kitchen like a whirlwind. "He is obviously skilled at his profession. And he didn't mind an interloper. He let me work right alongside him and showed me what to do."

His eyes caught hers in question. "You made this?"

Something inside her leaped, yearning for his approval. She nodded. "I hope it isn't the last meal I make. I just thought after so many days of you bringing me food, you deserved the favor returned." Color pinkened her cheeks. "And perhaps I didn't want to dine alone again."

For hours, Jane had wrestled with the fear that Christophe would reject her offer to dine together. What would she do if he simply walked away? Seeing light spread over his handsome features gave her hope. At least if they had nothing else, she would carry this night with her wherever she went.

Quick to react, Christophe moved toward her and pulled out her chair. Tingles raced up Jane's arms as she demurely took a seat and watched him do the same. His blond hair fell around his face as it usually did, his jaw peppered with a week's worth of whiskers. Did he always go unshaven, or was he avoiding his cabin because of her? His white linen shirt hung loosely off his commanding shoulders, this time sheathed in a leather vest. For all her effort, Jane couldn't stop her heart from pounding at the sight of him.

Christophe picked up his spoon and began eating while Jane smoothed her hands over the linen napkin in her lap. Somehow, jitters had immobilized her. She wanted to enjoy this moment, to savor perhaps the only meal they'd ever share together, but her nerves had the best of her.

"Will you not eat what you've worked so hard to make?" Christophe gave her a meaningful smile, lifting his spoon. "The soup is delicious."

Jane forced her lips upward and hastily grabbed her spoon. "I'm glad you enjoy it." Pushing through her stiffness, she compelled her spoon into the soup. "I suppose it's been a considerable time since I've dined with a man, and never alone, mind you."

Candlelight sparkled in the captain's blue eyes as he lifted his glass of rum and drank. "I promise to behave as a perfect gentleman—even if I'm less than the men you've dined with before."

"On the contrary, you are so much more." Her own words stilled her, uttered without thought. Jane halted with her spoon hovering above her soup, barely able to meet his amused gaze. "I mean to say you would fit alongside them just fine—perhaps with a shave." Though she supposed he likely knew what she had truly meant—that his strength and good manners, his careful protection of her, outrivaled any man she'd ever known in her life.

Not mentioning her faux pas, Christophe returned to his supper. "I can't say they would all agree with you on that. Especially your father. What would he say to you sharing company with a dastardly pirate like myself?"

Jane blushed, a fresh bite of soup warm on her lips. "Perhaps if he knew of the treasure, he wouldn't mind so much. The man he wants me to marry has no redeeming qualities *except* money, and title, of course." Had she really just expressed one of her heart's deepest burdens?

Christophe paused with a chunk of biscuit in one hand. "Well, that isn't heartening news. Who does he want you to marry?"

"Lionel Davenport, Earl of Westwick." Her stomach groaned at the mention of his name.

Redness seeped over the captain's face. His lips pinched, appearing to barely hold a string of uncouth words at bay. "Lionel Davenport? It's no wonder you ran away."

"Precisely." Jane's head angled. "Pray tell, how does a man like you who lives at sea know of someone like Davenport? Surely his antics don't stretch across the Atlantic. He keeps mostly to casinos and high-end brothels, I'm told." With any other man, she might have flushed to mention the sinful establishments.

"Davenport is too cowardly for the sea and if he ever came aboard my ship, I'd throw him over." Christophe's eyes narrowed in disgust. "I've never met the man in person, but I've had plenty of interaction with those he employs. He makes his money on ille-gal trade—hallucinogenic substances, stolen goods, slaves, mostly. He's a dangerous man, Jane, and you should have no association with him."

Jane's mouth fell open, her stomach feeling as if it had been punched. "And here I thought he was only a rake who bedded whatever woman suited him that day. He was never kind to me when we met at parties or he courted me at the estate. He looked at me like another piece of my father's property."

Christophe's eyes had softened, grown serious. They looked back at her as if peering beneath her refined layers and finding her soul. "How is such a thing possible?"

Heat rushed up her throat, spilling across her face. Jane held his affectionate gaze for a prolonged moment, the candlelight dancing between them, the air thick with spices. Then her gaze plummeted to the bare table, running along its weathered veins. "I cannot be wed to a man like that—never. I would rather die."

A few moments lingered, the tinkle of light rain peppering the deck overhead. The sailors must have cleared out as much as they could, for only a few scattered footsteps battered the wood above them. Jane took another bite, but the expert blend of pork and thyme did nothing to ease her agitated nerves.

"Is that the only reason you're running away—to escape Daven-port?" Christophe finally asked. "Would you still desire to join the Church if you had your choice in marriage?"

Despite her fear, Jane's gaze wandered into his. She saw accep-tance there, and urgency. Would he offer an alternative if she said no? "No, Davenport is not the only reason." She pressed a hand to her surging bodice. "I desire to do good with my life and to serve the Lord, even if the Church was not my original dream."

Christophe's brow lifted. "What was your original dream, if I may ask?"

Her skin warmed, surely turning her a darker shade of red. One didn't discuss such matters in polite society, but maybe she could say the words here if nowhere else. "Well, marriage—a real marriage, not a lifetime of waiting for an unfaithful husband to stagger home intoxicated. A family, perhaps a home I can make my own and raise children in."

He smiled kindly. "It's a lovely dream, Jane. You shouldn't let it go."

Their eyes locked in the candle's glow, a thousand unspoken words drifting about the sultry air. Her heart hammered, drawing her toward him, begging her to unveil her blossoming affections. Yet what a burden to lay at a man's feet when he already had life and death to contend with. Her thoughts must remain unuttered, even when everything in her yearned for him.

She cleared her throat, dropping her gaze to her lap. "Yes, well—if God wanted to make me a wife and a mother, I'm sure he would provide a way. In the meantime, I'm going to honor him by dedicating my life. It's the very least I can give him."

Christophe studied her a moment, his eyes exploring her face. "Your dedication is admirable, but I fear you may regret your choice if it is not what you truly desire. Vowing yourself to nunhood is a lifelong commitment."

His words only shoved her existing fears deeper. When Jane had first answered the solicitation for women of the cloth, she'd been so sure, so ready to throw off her life of excess and walk the path of Christ's servant. But every day since then, she'd wondered if it was merely the frivolity she wanted to cast aside. No matter how hard she tried, she couldn't squelch the desire for a husband and children of her own.

Throwing off the notion once again, she met Christophe's imploring gaze. "It might not matter, anyway. If Dominguez ensnares us once again, he'll send me back to my father and I will be the Countess of Westwick whether I like it or not."

Christophe's jaw tightened. "Jane, I won't let that happen. I'll stand in front of the sword if I have to."

"And what good would that do?" Her brows lifted. "Then you would be dead, I would be on a ship back to England, and who knows where the treasure would fall." A hard lump materialized in her throat at the sorrow in his eyes. "I must accept that it may happen, as should you. I refuse to bring about your death, as I refuse to stand in the way of distributing your treasure to the poor. You should get me off this ship as soon as you possibly can."

The captain's hands balled into fists, then released again, as if grasping for an answer elusive as snow in summer. He hated to relinquish control. Jane could see it written all over his burdened face. The sea tossed beneath them as he sat still with jaw fixed and nostrils flared before at last his broad shoulders relaxed.

Peering down at their empty bowls, Christophe's face lightened. He appeared to need a change of topic as greatly as she did. "Say I did come to one of those elaborate dinner parties you speak of. Say I was a guest. What would we do after the meal ended?"

A smile dented the corner of her mouth. "Well, I would probably retire to the drawing room to chat with the ladies and you would join the men for cigars, talk of war, politics. Nothing a woman should hear, of course."

Humor lit his eyes despite his grimace. "Too dull. What man in his right mind would spend an evening discussing world powers with someone like you in the next room?"

Jane tried to keep her cheeks from flushing, sure she failed miserably. "If it were a true party, there might be dancing. We aristocrats love our dancing."

Without a word, Christophe rose from the table and discarded his napkin over his used bowl. His eyes twinkled as he held one hand out to Jane, a placid smile pulling at his lips. Jane gracefully sat her napkin aside and set her hand in his. Warmth spread from her fingers up the length of her arm as he gently helped her stand.

His other hand came around her, settling on her hip. Jane marveled at the feel of his large hands, the commanding way he propelled her in a circular pattern. She must have entertained hundreds of dance partners over the years since making her debut, yet none led her with the fluid grace and quiet authority of this man.

She wanted to comment on his surprising skill, but instead she found herself caught beneath his gaze. Throwing off her fear, she latched her stare with his. It looked so calm and assured, like he could gaze into her future and had determined she would survive the challenges ahead. Jane found herself staring, swimming through the depths of him.

The hand on her back urged her closer. She didn't resist, coiling her arm around his trim waist. His heartbeat thudded through his leather vest, comforting her. Could he possibly feel as nervous as she did beneath his bold exterior? She hoped so. She hoped his chest hardly took in air—the way hers did when she looked at him.

No music needed to play for Jane to sway to its rhythm. A perfect concerto floated through her mind, notes from an invisible violin dazzling her. Suddenly, she was back in the halls of her grand estate, swept up in the dance she'd always longed for. Except no man had ever held her this close. Her father would never have allowed it.

Christophe's hand pulsed on her lower back. His stunning warmth encompassed her. The smell of the sea lifted from his clothes, swirling through her senses. Jane let her gaze wander his proud brow, his eyes that shimmered like pools of tropical water, the whiskers sprinkling his jaw. Any childhood crush or boy who had caught her eye in youth faded away, as if he were the first man she'd ever beheld. Indeed, he was unlike any she'd ever known before.

His chest swelled. "Jane, I—" But she held up one hand, her fingertips gently brushing his lips.

"Please don't." If he voiced the concern in his eyes, she would have to face it. "Let's just keep dancing." Snuggling closer, she set her cheek on his brawny chest and closed her eyes. The world and all of its dangers could spin on without them. For one blissful moment, she wanted to forget it all existed, and simply fall into the arms of the man she couldn't help but love.

Seventeen

The brilliant hues of sunset tumbled into a dark night, painting the skies in ebony brushstrokes. When the stars emerged, they dotted the vast canvas above in twinkling wonder, shimmering off the turbid waves. Christophe peered up at them, searching for the moon, but it stubbornly hid behind patches of wispy clouds. He must have wandered the deck a thousand times, drawing in the cathartic sea air, avoiding the inevitable. Surely after all these useless hours, Jane would be asleep.

His cabin was shrouded in silence when he finally ambled into it, his wary eyes locked on her door. The wind still clung to his clothes, chilling them as they slid off his tired body. Christophe undressed quickly, finding the loose-fitting slacks he usually wore to bed in his trunk before stepping into them and diving beneath his covers. Suddenly, a task he'd performed every night since Jane had come aboard took on more urgency. He couldn't let her catch him standing bare-chested in the midst of his cabin, staring listlessly toward her door.

The minutes piled on top of each other, none bringing the sleep he so ardently sought. His bare skin felt clammy within his satin sheets, his eyes unburdened and trained on the ceiling despite the late hour. He'd seen a change in her that night that scared him. Jane had always looked at him with curiosity, yet reservation. Tonight, her honest eyes had entreated him, her actions inviting him into the secret caverns of her soul. She had made clear for the first time that she reciprocated Christophe's feelings.

Just thinking about it made him want to scream. How long had he suppressed his natural impulses and the growing affections she planted in him? Knowing she wanted him too made keeping her at arm's length that much harder. The fact that his ship would reach Brest before sunup tortured him. *It's for the best. She needs to get off this ship, for her own safety as well as ours.* Yet no matter how hard he tried to convince himself, he wanted her to stay.

Whatever plan Blanc and company had hatched seemed to have dissipated by now. Christophe had noticed an uptick in Blanc's work effort and a lightening of his spirits. Perhaps they had decided to trust him after Dominguez's attack. War often brought men together. Maybe they realized they would be better off collecting their share of the treasure and finding their own ship to purchase in Brest. His stomach roiled. How would they react when they discovered the treasure had vanished?

Lost in his musings, Christophe barely heard the door to Jane's cabin squeal open. When soft candlelight flickered against his cabin's walls, he took notice and sat up, his blankets falling away from his bare chest. Jane stood in the space beyond her open door, blushing and glancing away at the sight of him.

Christophe's breath hastened. She looked beautiful in every-thing she wore—even the plain smock she had crawled onto his ship wearing. But nothing compared to the sight of her clothed in Madeleine's white cotton nightdress, the fabric falling grace-fully off her lithe frame, the hem dangling above her bare toes. Her flushed face glowed in the capering light of the candle in her hand. The loose hair tumbling over her shoulders created a halo, shrouding her in angelic beauty. For a brief moment, he wondered if her entire existence was but a figment of an imagination longing for the perfect being he saw before him.

"I can't sleep," she said, managing to swing her eyes back to him.

Christophe shook his head slowly. "Neither can I." He swallowed, aware of how easy it would be to invite her into his bed. But Jane deserved so much more than a single night of passion. He found his discarded shirt in the dark and pulled it over his head. "We should try, though. You should go back to your room." Before he had no control left.

Her head angled, the innocence on her face breathtaking. Did she not understand the implications of her presence in his cabin this time of night? Did she think because he behaved as a gentleman during the day that he didn't have natural compulsions? Had she even learned of such matters?

"Can't we talk?" Her bare feet trod across the floor until she stood over him. Christophe could hardly keep his body from trembling as she dropped to the edge of his bed and looked into his eyes. "I want to know you better before it's too late. We don't have much time."

"Oh, Jane. Dear Jane." Christophe released a held-in breath and let his fingertips brush away the hair framing her forehead. "Of course we can talk, but not here." Not with the powerful emotions surging through him at her nearness. Taking her candle, he reached for her hand and pulled her away from the bed. He had a better idea, one that might preserve his sanity and her innocence.

"Where are we going?" she asked, brows knitting as he opened the door and led her into the dark corridor. "Surely your men will be angered if they see you with me on the deck in the middle of the night."

Christophe lifted a finger over his lips, indicating silence. "We're not going up on deck," he whispered. "Come on, there's a path through these hallways that doesn't lead to the sailors' berth."

Gently tugging her along, he navigated through the narrow passages with only the candle's short rays to illuminate their footsteps. Christophe let his thumb stroke her hand as they walked, the warm feel of her fingers in his spreading a joy through him that he hadn't experienced in some time. They traveled on in silence until a doorway led to the mess with row after row of tables sitting lonely in the rocking ship. Hugo slept in the galley, but if he heard them, he didn't stir.

Their feet thumped the uneven floorboards, carrying them through another dank hallway leading to the ship's stern. A sharp wind blew from the east, tossing the *Licorne* this way and that, knocking them against the walls and each other. Christophe tightened his grip on Jane's hand and expertly led her the last few feet to a door etched in ornate, gilded carvings of sea creatures and kelp.

His office gleamed with ethereal beauty when the pair stepped into it. The clouds had parted overhead, no longer hiding the moon, but allowing her to radiate her beauty on the sleeping world. Streams of white moonlight showered over the playing waves, illuminating the broad wall of windows with a bluish tint. One could almost see well enough to read in the soft luster. Christophe strode forward and set the candlestand on the desk, knowing he wouldn't need it until they ventured back to his cabin.

Mouth agape, Jane wandered toward the wide expanse of windows. "This is incredible." She gazed out at the moon a moment before whirling around and exploring the office itself. Her outstretched hand brushed his mahogany desk, the ornate chair behind it, bookshelves lined in ledgers and maps, the globe stationed beside a case containing navigator tools. "Did it look this beautiful when I saw it before, or did I simply miss the fact?"

Christophe smiled, wondering the same about her. "It's the grandest place this ship has to offer, but it's always loveliest when the moon shines her face in."

A placid look covered her visage as she gazed on her surroundings with awed approval. "Why don't you sleep in this room? Don't most captains use the finest space for their personal quarters?"

He gestured toward the windows. "Who could sleep with all this light pouring in?"

"Have you never heard of curtains?" She laughed, the moonlight defining her teeth.

Cruel memories squeezed his stomach. Christophe rapped his knuckles on the desk as if to banish them. "Evil slept in this room before I became captain. I would rather forget. Besides, work and leisure shouldn't interact."

She stared at him thoughtfully, her green eyes asking for more. At his silence, she turned, skipped to the windows, and settled atop the bench lining the wall. Pulling a decorative pillow into her lap, she gazed out on the ocean as it dipped and swelled across the black night. How lovely a picture she made, framed in the windows' celestial glow. Christophe couldn't keep his feet from shuffling toward her, drawn inevitably to her captivating presence.

Her mouth tilted when he took a seat beside her, her eyes sweeping the array of silk pillows before landing on his. "I never dreamed I would be in a place like this with someone like you. It's strange how life harbors surprises."

He chuckled. "Indeed, I never expected a daughter of an earl to climb aboard my ship in the Atlantic's midst."

Jane's brow hooked. "Well, you should never have taken my necklace, then." Her clever simper melted into a thankful smile. "Thank you for giving it back, by the way. My grandmother was gifted that necklace by her mother, and her mother before her. She always said it brought luck and love to the wearer. I just wanted a piece of her with me."

Luck and love. Wasn't that exactly what it had delivered to his door? Christophe leaned his back against the windows so he could take in every curve of her beautiful face. "You must love your grandmother very much."

Her eyes lit at his mention of the old woman. "She is the kindest, feistiest soul I know. She doesn't live to please others as so many people in my world. She speaks the truth exactly as she sees it." Jane paused, her eyelashes batting playfully. "She would certainly have a few choice words for you."

"Oh, really?" Christophe grinned, imagining the old woman in all of her gusto, saying what mighty ship captains wouldn't dare in his presence. "She wouldn't approve of my crooked ways, would she? She'd tell me to get a new profession."

Jane's eyes glistened in the moonlight. "Perhaps." Her gaze softened, roving his face. "More likely, she would tell you to quit running from your pain and face it."

A sudden lump rose in his throat. Was he really so transparent? "You think I'm running from something?"

"Your chosen profession doesn't suit you." Her shoulders lifted. "You must be leaving something behind."

Christophe chuckled mirthlessly, a hard blow delivered to his chest. "Doesn't suit me? You're not one to mince words, are you? Do I not fight well? Command my men with authority? Know how to sail perhaps better than any of them?"

Her fingers touched his arm lightly. "That isn't what I meant, Christophe. You're a good captain." Her head wagged. "But you have too much compassion, too much care for your fellow man. I could see you at the helm of any merchant vessel in the world, commanding bravely and effectively. How you ever ended up on a ship like this, I can't even picture."

Christophe exhaled a pent-up breath, relaxing. "Some facets of our lives are more complicated than others." Even when he tried to remember, the images of his past appeared hazy, like peering into a smudged mirror. All except those early, horrifying memories of his childhood.

"Tell me," she urged softly. "Where did you come from? How did you wind up here?"

Chest aching, Christophe tried to take another breath and couldn't. Had so many years failed to subdue the raw pain that remembering invoked? He could still hear the screaming, smell the smoke of his burning village. He could still see his mother's desperate eyes gazing on approaching death.

"I grew up in the Vendée," he finally said, leaning on the windows for support. "It's a lovely region of the Loire Valley, so picturesque one might think they've stepped into a painting. I remember long days exploring the forests and rivers, the sandy beaches, cliffs of pampas grass up to my waist."

He glanced up at the naive smile on her lips. Could he really tell her what had happened in that wonderful place—how the earth had rumbled beneath them at the stomp of soldiers' feet, how his very world had shattered that blissful day in the chestnut tree?

Looking away, he propped his chin up. "We lived a simple life in a cottage there. My father was a farmer, and he provided for us despite difficult times. I had a whole brood of brothers and sisters, but we never went hungry. We were happy."

Christophe suppressed the tears threatening to flood his eyes. "Then war came. The entire region, the people of our village, my parents, even—detested the idea of our nation splintering. They were staunch royalists who clung to the Crown even in the face of danger. They refused to back down, and they paid for it."

From the corner of his eye, he saw Jane cover her cheeks with her hands. He couldn't stop now, though remembering set his chest on fire.

"The people of my region fought hard against the revolutionary forces. They fought for their king, for what they thought was right. They fought for us, their children—" His voice broke, and Christophe raked a hand through his loose hair. "In the end, the Republican army won. They marched through our towns, killing everyone they could—women, children—it didn't matter. We were all useless traitors in their eyes."

Jane gasped, her eyes round with horror. "What about your family? Did any of them survive?"

Sorrow drenched him as he forced himself to look back at her. "I honestly don't know. I ran through the woods as fast as I could before my legs gave out. I never saw any of them again, but"—he swallowed back the bile high in his throat—"I did find a friend who was there. He hid in a well while the massacre took place. He told me they killed everyone in our village, that they raped the women. My mother and older sisters—" The words refused to dislodge from his throat, emotion grabbing hold like a vulture's claws.

"Oh, Christophe." Jane found his hand, her fingers intertwining with his. Plump tears sprouted in her eyes, spilling down her face without restraint. "I'm *so* sorry. I can't imagine what that must have been like to endure, especially for a child."

He nodded, clenching his jaw to subdue the tears prickling behind his eyes. He had cried enough over the actions of those cowards. His mother's legacy deserved more than a few scattered tears. If only he'd possessed the strength to avenge it.

"I was nine years old at the time. I did what I had to in order to survive—apprenticing in a cobbler's shop for several years, learning the art of pickpocketing. But I never forgot that day, and it fueled me with rage. I joined the army at fourteen, determined to rise within its ranks and find the men who slaughtered my village. They couldn't be hard to find. Cowards who rape women for sport and murder children love to brag about it. By then, I supposed I would be powerful enough to walk right up and exterminate them, one by one."

Jane's fingers tightened against his. "But you never did?"

"No, I barely survived a year in the army." Christophe sighed. "My commander was a brute who starved us, made us run naked in the frigid snow even with men losing toes to frostbite. I knew I had to desert if I wanted to survive, and my revenge would just have to take a back shelf."

One side of his mouth lifted as he thought of the ship when he'd first laid eyes on her—sides glistening under a yellow sun and sails billowing. The falcon at her bow had cinched his decision, but he had fallen instantly in love with all of her. The call of the sea meant freedom, adventure, escape from his haunting past.

"I knew not what would happen when I snuck aboard this ship, but I took a chance. I figured I could stow away unnoticed if I was lucky. When the captain found me, he threatened to throw me into the sea, but instead he showed mercy. He gave me a job as a swabbie, taught me to fight and to sail. He mesmerized me with tales of hidden treasure. From that day on, I was hopelessly addicted."

Jane smiled, laying her cheek against his upper arm. "And now you'll never leave her—the sea you love so dearly."

"No, I suppose I won't." His stomach tensed at the notion, even though it brought familiar comfort.

Silence lingered over them for several moments. Christophe listened to the waves sloshing against the *Licorne's* hull, enjoying the feel of Jane snuggled against him. At first, he'd figured he was so lonely that anyone's presence would do. But each new day he spent with her, learning her curious ways, he understood more clearly that she alone had captured his heart and mind. When she left, his heart would split in the shape of her.

"I won't leave you alone, Jane." He could scarcely believe he'd uttered what he'd already vowed to himself. "I won't drop you in Brest with no one. I'll make sure you get wherever you want to go. You won't have to return home and marry Davenport, I swear it."

Jane rose and searched his eyes, a myriad of questions lacing her moonlit face. "You can't promise me that. If it's meant to be, no one can stop it."

His hand gripped her arm. "I won't let that happen to you." But what could he do if Dominguez overpowered them? How could he keep her father from tracking her down and forcing her to wed the rake? Short of marrying her himself, he couldn't follow through on his promise. But staying with him would only endanger her more.

Her charming lilac scent touched his nose, driving his need for her deeper. Christophe gazed into her crystal eyes, his breath heavy and heart gaining speed. How hard he had fought the urge to pull her into his arms, and now—now the effort felt useless. Like searching for water in a desert with a lake at his back. He needed to hold her, to feel her against him, to show her his true and unbridled feelings.

Leaning down, he brushed his lips with hers—lightly at first, the pressure increasing with the thud of his heart. Jane spread her fingers on his chest, pushing him gently away, but not enough to separate them. Would she refuse him? It was the sensible thing, and she had every right. Then, after a moment of indecision, her fingers curled around his shirt and she pulled him closer. Her balmy lips moved over his, supple and sweet. Christophe wove his fingers into her silky hair, losing himself in her wondrous kisses. Whatever lay ahead, he would live in this moment, wrapped in her arms beneath the luminous glow of the moon, for the rest of his life.

Eighteen

C hristophe woke before the sun rose and pulled on his clothes
as quietly as he could. The night had afforded him little
sleep, but he didn't care. He would endure a thousand sleepless
nights for the energy pulsing through his frame now. The wee
hours had roused conversation between him and Jane, their walls
shattering, their affections reciprocated in each other. Part of him
wanted to wake her, the more prudent half warning him to let her
sleep.

A quiet whistle blew through his lips as he bent to yank his boots
over his feet. The remembered feel of her slender frame in his arms
warmed his body. Her soft lips, her unbound hair, the brush of her
skin on his—he would carry their stolen kisses with him forever.
The realization that today would bring their parting filled his chest
with an aching sadness.

He had always known he would see Madeleine again when she
strutted down the pier and disappeared into his carriage. Their
fates had intertwined, his love for her tangled in deception. The
quest for Henri Clement's treasure would drive them together,
again and again, like waves in the same ocean. With Jane, he had
no such assurance. If he could successfully garner her passage to
Barbados, she would don the robes of nunhood and shun any

interaction with men like the one they'd shared last night. The very thought nauseated him.

Christophe pushed off the bed, determined to shake off his dismal thoughts. His navigator had assured him they would reach Brest this morning, and all his efforts must focus on the treasure's safe transfer. He would deal with his feelings for Jane later.

Just as he strode toward the hall and reached for the handle, Jane's door groaned open. Christophe twisted around to see her standing sheepishly in the doorframe, still garbed in her night clothes with her blonde hair tumbling over her lithe shoulders. The sight of her took his breath away.

"It's early," he said, altering his course her way.

"I heard you leaving." Jane smiled shyly. "I just wanted to say good morning."

Her wholesome goodness drove his feet onward. How could he resist loving a creature who woke to his sounds, her first inclination carrying her to his cabin in her bare feet just to see him? He reached her in a few strides, hooking an arm around her waist and hauling her to him. Jane blushed but didn't stop him. Instead, her timid gaze ascended his chest until it landed on his face, a smile spreading to her eyes.

"Good morning," he said in a husky tone, bending close until their lips nearly met. "Good morning, my dear Jane." He kissed her tenderly, his every emotion poured into the action. She tasted so devastatingly sweet. How could he ever let her go?

Jane returned his kiss, her arms lifting to wind around his neck. Her fingertips pressed softly against his skin as his kisses deepened, his ardor grew. Even in the morning, her scent intoxicated him. When he pulled away, Christophe prayed it wouldn't be their last embrace. He would give up the ship and buy another if he had to, a respectable vessel upon which she wouldn't have to fear for her life. Would she be content to live at sea her whole life? To raise a family under such uncertain conditions?

"We're nearly to Brest." He pressed his forehead to hers, settling her into a snug embrace. "Land might be in sight already."

She sighed, her thumb stroking his jaw. "I know. I couldn't sleep these last few hours, my stomach was so tied up in knots about it."

"This is a good thing, Jane. I will get you to safety. You won't have to worry about Dominguez or Davenport or any of the wretches on this ship again." Oh, but how his heart crumbled to imagine her sailing away from him.

Jane pulled back enough to look at him, her eyes posing a question he wasn't yet sure he could answer. "This journey has been the most dangerous, terrifying experience of my life." She laughed, her face brightening with beauty. "But it's brought the best days, too. I wouldn't trade them for anything."

He cradled her face in one hand, his thumb brushing her chin. "For me, too. I never imagined how I would feel now when I first saw you on that ship. Is it wrong of me to say I'm glad I robbed it?" Guilt bit his gut. If he hadn't, she would be safely in Barbados by now, serving God as she wanted.

Her head shook, a giggle escaping her lips. "No. You were meant to. We were supposed to meet, even with all the trouble it caused."

Christophe's chest swelled at her words. "Tell me it doesn't have to end here." Could he truly utter his heart's longings? Could he say he wanted to marry her, to sweep her around the world and ask her to leave the existence she'd always known behind? His courage heightened. "Jane, I—"

The strident ring of a bell pealed overhead. Christophe froze, glancing at the ceiling, where boots had begun to pound the wood. "The emergency bell." His hand on her waist gripped her tightly. "Jane, get dressed. Don't leave this room unless you have to. Lock the door."

She nodded shakily, her hands sheltering her surging chest.

Four swift steps brought Christophe to his door, which he yanked open. Frantic shouts tunneled down the stairwell, howling over his sailors' thrashing footsteps. Christophe took the stairs two at a time, catapulting to the deck into a scene of utter panic. Men dashed everywhere he looked, lowering the sails, preparing weaponry.

Monsieur Simon emerged from the melee, a look of relief flooding his face as he spotted Christophe and sprinted up to him. "It's Dominguez again. He's nearly upon us."

Christophe nearly asked for a spyglass, but whipped around and saw the imposing sloop approaching from port side. "How did he get so close without someone ringing the warning bell?"

Out of breath, the quartermaster wagged his head. "The mists have been so thick this morning. He managed to get in range without anyone spotting him." His finger speared through the morning fog to the open space beyond Dominguez's ship. "He's brought reinforcements this time."

Squinting, Christophe angled toward the indicated spot and made out the rough shape of a man-of-war at Dominguez's back. He swore, swinging his gaze to their starboard side. The sun barely peeped over the horizon, coloring the sky in orange and purple hues. Under its sparkling rays, the jagged coastline of France was barely visible to the naked eye. Close enough to see but not enough to protect them. Someone on shore might spy their impending clash, but not in time to help them.

Dominguez's sloop cut sharply through the water, close enough now that he could decimate them with cannon fire if he desired. Christophe knew his gunners would be primed to fight at his order, but with Dominguez's proximity and the man-of-war accompanying him, they had no hope to prevail. He swallowed, uncomfortable with feeling vulnerable and exposed. They couldn't even change the masthead to disguise themselves, and he would never don the unicorn so close to shore.

"Run up the white flag," he said finally, his lips pained to say it.

"You're sure?"

Nausea churned in his stomach to imagine the consequences, but he had no other choice. "Run up the white flag."

As the flag of surrender ascended their mast and beat in the wet breeze, the mad crew around him fell silent. At once jarred from the task at hand, they simply stared at the looming sloop through solemn eyes, their bodies still hopping like they wanted to do more and couldn't. The white flag had never seen daylight on this ship. Christophe cursed himself for needing it. He should have anticipated Dominguez's next move. Had he not been so distracted by his feelings for Jane, he could have saved her and his crew.

Dominguez wore a smug look of satisfaction when he alighted from his ship and descended on the *Licorne* with a bevy of bulky privateers at his back. He swaggered over the deck, his scathing eyes raking Christophe's crew until they landed on the captain himself. The lips below his thin mustache curled, his dark brows narrowed.

"The mighty Captain Phillipe Danglar at last brought down by a superior show of strength." He spoke French with a thick Spanish accent, every word a caustic reminder that he'd won. "Only"—one finger aimed toward the masthead—"what is this on your bow? Surely you haven't replaced your entire ship in so short a time. I see deception at play here."

When he stood a stone's throw from Christophe's solid stance, Dominguez's eyes wandered him mockingly. "I've heard of a ship that travels these seas with a falcon at its head, captained by a man named—what was it?" His lips contorted. "Christophe Roux, I believe." He cocked his dark head. "You wouldn't happen to know him, would you?"

Christophe squeezed his teeth together but said nothing. Since the days of Chapelle, the success of their operation depended on hiding and changing identities, confusing their enemies. Now that Dominguez had connected the name Danglar with Roux, he would spread the word. Their dealings at sea could never be the same.

"What do you want, Dominguez?" Roux's forearms flexed, the Spaniard's arrogance driving his hands into fists.

Dominguez chuckled, revealing a row of gold teeth. "We've come for the girl, of course. Unless you have something else you'd like to offer us." He spread his spidery fingers wide on either side, indicating the *Licorne's* vast deck where her crew patiently waited with concerned expressions.

Their penetrating stares bore into Christophe. He tried to steady his breathing, but it rammed against his chest, desperate to invoke panic. Dozens of lives depended on him now, on a decision that pained him to even consider. Could he release Jane into Dominguez's wicked hands, powerless to ensure her safety when he'd promised over and again that he would? He didn't have a choice. If Dominguez sniffed out the treasure below decks, he would kill them for it and take her anyway. They couldn't defeat a combined force of two ships.

Breathing through his nose, Christophe tilted his chin up and glared at his enemy. "I'll go and get her."

J ane paced the floor of Christophe's cabin while incessantly gnawing a thumbnail. Her shoes drummed a rhythmic pattern, echoing the frantic thud of her heart. The same calico dress she'd come aboard in sheathed her slender body, a comfort from home. Her palms, slippery with sweat, shook as she attempted to brush back her untethered hair.

Every once in a while, she stopped her frenzied pacing to listen. She heard no boom of cannons or fighting like before. Distant strains of voices filtered in, the sound too thin to decipher a word being said. Would Christophe negotiate terms with Dominguez to keep her safe? Could he? More importantly, would the Spanish captain hurt Christophe? The idea launched chills down her arms. She preferred her own capture a million times over harm coming to him.

When the door swung open, she jumped. A split second existed when she wondered if the enemy had arrived to take her. Then Christophe's face on the other side flung relief through her. She scampered into his arms, burying her face in his chest and inhaling his exotic scent.

"What's happened?" Jane pressed her cheek to his loose shirt, unable to look at his face. "Is Dominguez still here? What did he say?"

Christophe wove his fingers into her hair, cradling her head a moment in tender hands. Then he angled it backward, compelling her face toward his. Her reluctant gaze had nowhere to go but the grave eyes staring down at her. She knew in an instant what had to happen. His deep blue eyes already mourned her.

Jane nodded, gripping his muscular arms. "I can be brave. God will go with me." Even though the picture of Dominguez having complete power rattled her deep within.

His fingers clenched a fistful of her hair. Gone was the privateer who had pointedly interrogated her that first day, all confidence and bravado. Before her stood a broken man, raw emotions teeming from his tortured face. He gazed at her, his heart open in his eyes, before he drew her against him.

"I can't let you go." His chest surged, tears mingling with her hair. "How can I live wondering if you're safe, knowing I couldn't protect you?" His warm breath brushed her ear in sobbing gasps for air.

Jane held him tighter, aware she must be strong in the face of his emotion. "You have to. Dominguez will kill your entire crew if you don't. You know that." Her heart ached as his arm wound around her waist as if to anchor her. "Think of all the children like you once were who will benefit from that money. They'll have food, water, shelter, a warm place to sleep. You *must* follow through on your promise and give that to them."

His head bobbing, Christophe embraced her a moment longer before pulling back to search her face. "You are brave, Jane Whitecliffe. Brave enough to defeat anyone who stands against you." He swept several strands of hair behind her ear, wet with his tears.

"Dominguez won't hurt me. You've said as much yourself. He needs to keep me alive and unharmed in order to ransom me back to my father."

"This is true." Yet still his eyes radiated worry. They both knew what would happen even if Dominguez managed to safely transport her across the channel to England. Marriage to Davenport presented a more fearful scenario than the threat of pirates.

Her hands lifted to his face, nesting his square jaw in her palms. "I'll be fine, I promise you. Do what you must to secure that treasure. I have a will of my own that no one can break. Not Dominguez, not my father or even Davenport. I'll write my own story."

Despite his worry, a sad smile broke over his face. "That you will. I have no doubt."

The gentle kiss he planted on her lips encapsulated every moment they'd spent together aboard ship. Jane savored his warmth, his scent, his salty tears melding with hers. This might prove the last time he ever held her. She tried to memorize the feel of his solid arms, the cadence of his heart. She would carry it with her a lifetime.

When he led her up the steps and onto a deck riddled with crewmembers, Christophe didn't unlatch his hand from hers. Jane supposed he didn't care who knew of his affections for her now that her presence would no longer cause strife among his men. They wound their way through the gaping onlookers, toward the familiar man dressed in a red jacket with gold buttons, standing proudly like a king among peasants.

"Ah, there she is." Dominguez eyed her languidly, his probing gaze pausing on their intertwined hands. "I hate to break up whatever this is, but you have a father waiting for you at home, sitting atop a pile of cash."

Jane forced her head up, willing her body not to tremble. *Don't show your fear. Don't give your hand away.* If Dominguez only knew the riches stashed just below his feet, he wouldn't bother with a small fish like her.

As if reading her thoughts, Dominguez girded his brows and glanced around. Could he sense that he had missed something? That the *Licorne's* entire crew stared at him with bated breath, praying he would leave with only Jane? *Please, God.* If he decided to go digging, all of their lives hung precariously over the void.

"Capitan!" one of his sailors shouted. Dominguez whirled toward the sound, where his subordinate stood with spyglass pointed toward the east. "Another ship, Capitan. It appears to be a shore guard."

Jane understood enough of his Spanish to glance warily at Christophe. Would this help them or hurt them? Christophe stood motionless, staring ahead as if weighing the circumstances himself.

Grunting, Dominguez rushed forward and seized Jane's other hand. "Back to the ship. We must be away," he told his group of brawny sailors. Before Jane could think, he tugged her away from Christophe like a ragdoll to be tossed on the floor. One moment, his hand still held hers squarely. The next, their fingers pulled apart, the feel of his skin lingering against hers long after they parted.

As Dominguez dragged her away, Jane kept her gaze steady on Christophe. His eyes promised he would find her again, on a day free of death and danger. Jane clung to that silent promise, steeling herself for the trial ahead.

Nineteen

The sun had broken free of the horizon and climbed the misty skies as Christophe stood motionless, staring after the *Poseidon*. His heart crumbled. His breaths came tight, each a concentrated effort. He clutched the bulwark with white knuckles, fear grabbing hold. Dominguez surely wouldn't injure Jane, but what else would he attempt?

His crew, frozen like a menagerie of statues, gradually quit staring his way for instruction and began milling about once more. A voice screamed in his head to turn and face them, to motivate them after such a humiliation. Yet his dry tongue and weary body refused. The world must spin on without him, if only for a few stolen moments.

A hand soon squeezed his shoulder, Monsieur Simon's face filling the space at his side. "The ship approaching is a coastal guard," he said gently. "What do you want us to do?"

Brushing off his remorse, Christophe cast an irritated scowl on the brig now within easy sight of the naked eye. "We wait for them. Try and pass us off as a cargo vessel. Our numbers are small enough to make the story believable." His eyes lifted to the flag atop their mast, fluttering next to the white banner of surrender. "Thank God we're flying the colors of France."

Monsieur Simon nodded and set off to marshal the crew. Hiding in plain sight had become a game for them, a challenge. Yet whenever Christophe stepped upon a beach as himself, with the falcon standing guard over his vessel, he used the utmost precaution. He avoided authorities like the one nearly upon them now. He never stayed in one place long in case someone recognized him or his crew caused trouble in town. His guard didn't come down until he reached the open sea and could breathe its cathartic air once more.

Dominguez had left them no choice this time, attacking so near the shore. With weighted legs, Christophe turned and made his way toward the approaching brig. He must put on his best show or every last man aboard his ship was doomed. Concern for Jane would just have to wait its turn.

When the newcomers eased their ship beside the *Licorne*, Christophe ordered his sailors to help assist their envoy in boarding. Two men dressed in rich blue, finely woven jackets accepted the outstretched hands and climbed over the bulwark. *A good sign.* If they distrusted the deceptive image he'd painted, they would never send only two to face his crew alone.

"*Bonjour, Capitaine,*" the tallest one said, nodding toward Christophe.

"*Bonjour.*" Christophe tipped his head, summoning his most welcoming smile.

"We saw your encounter in the distance and noticed your flag," the stouter one said, peering through the lifting fog at the two retreating ships. "They are pirates, no? They usually don't come so near our shores."

"Yes, it is Fernando Dominguez." Christophe watched the way they glanced at each other with rounded eyes. "He had been after us all week. He brought reinforcements before we could reach the city." He nodded toward shore, where the aforementioned metropolis glistened under the morning sun.

"We heard he was in these waters," the first man said, "that several pirates were." The glint of suspicion passed through his eyes as they darted around the deck. "What kind of a vessel is this, Captain?"

Christophe straightened. It would do no good to give them false information too weak to fool them. But with too many details, they could easily sniff out his falsehoods. "We're a cargo ship en route to Brest to pick up a load of household goods. They are to be transported to America."

They both nodded, the operation a common one. "Why would a privateer have interest in an empty ship?"

"We had some goods brought from the Caribbean, where we just sailed from—sugar, coffee, timber, some gold. With land in sight, I instructed my men to bring the items on deck to prepare for their transfer. Dominguez used the thick fog to ambush us."

The stout man squinted through the murky air, still clouded but improving. "Oui, it was like a swamp this morning. You're lucky we even saw you." He nudged the man beside him. "The mist is clearing. We should go after them. It's not every day we get a shot at someone like Dominguez."

Christophe's Adam's apple bobbed involuntarily. If only they knew who stood at their mercy this very moment. "He has a man-of-war with him that I'm sure is fully loaded with sailors. I wouldn't chase him unless you have more ships to back you up." As much as he wanted Dominguez caught, that result would imperil his ship, too.

"He's right." The tall man woefully wagged his head. "We're not prepared to fight that many men. They would crush us." He set his arms akimbo. "We will just have to keep a vigilant watch on every ship coming in and out of the city, and warn the ports around us. He's bound to look for a buyer before too long. It would be foolish for an instigator like Dominguez to sail a long stretch with gold aboard."

Both men looked around them again, their shrewd gazes examining Christophe's men. The captain held his breath. One wrong word from any of them could rip their ruse asunder. Vivianno had but to scream out from his holding cell, and they'd certainly send a group to investigate. If they found the treasure, his body would be hanging from the gallows of Brest before sunset.

"Very well, then." The stout man looked up at Christophe. "Would you like our assistance sailing into port? Your crew must be shaken after such a rude encounter."

The urge to laugh bubbled inside him, but Christophe held it at bay and simply bobbed his head. "Thank you, monsieurs. That is very kind." Better to keep them occupied and feeling needed than to let their minds wander. If they had only performed a precautionary sweep of the *Licorne*, they would have exposed his lies and claimed riches beyond imagining. Surely the French government would award and promote two such brave officials. If only.

After the men returned to their ship, the *Licorne's* crew guided her into port behind their friendly helpers. The rounded stone battements of the ancient city rose into view, majestically towering over the churning waters. The wharf, dotted with various ships and sailors dashing over the pier, eased his troubled nerves. A difficult task lay ahead, but at least they'd safely traversed the Atlantic with Clement's treasure. At least his feet could carry him away if trouble erupted. He could run away like he always did.

"Are you still certain of our plan?" Monsieur Simon's voice hummed in his ear.

Christophe pivoted toward the man, his face hardening. "We will do exactly what we discussed. When night falls, our plan goes into motion." He clenched his jaw, preparing to pull off his greatest deception on the men he called his own.

T he *Poseidon's* interior reeked of rotting wood and dust. Its hull groaned against each hit of the frolicking waves, the rafters creaking and shuddering. Jane shivered from her crouched position on the floor, afraid the ceiling might cave in on her head. Around her, nothing but blackness showed its face to her wandering eyes. *He will not hurt me,* she reminded herself again, though every minute in solitude chipped away at her surety.

Dominguez's guttural laughter still howled in her ears, the feel of his men's hands on her arms burned into her skin. With a few no doubt vulgar words she couldn't understand, they had swiftly marched her below decks and tossed her in this empty cabin—a prison cell without the bars and chains. Jane had tried in vain to get out the door, but found it locked. Besides, what could she do if she did escape—swim the impossible distance to shore?

Resigned to her fate, she found a wall and slipped down its length, plopping on the floor and resting her shaken frame. Closing her eyes, she pretended she was back in Christophe Roux's office, in the secure shelter of his arms. The memory of his kisses, so gentle yet passionate, warmed her dejected spirit. Christophe Roux—the first man she had ever kissed, the only man she ever wanted to again. *Keep him safe. Please let him get the treasure to the priests and live to tell about it. Bring him back to me when the time is right.* Could a future even exist for them now? Would God and fate allow such an unlikely pairing?

The door screeched open on rusty hinges, making Jane's body go rigid. A single orb of candlelight bobbed toward her, its bearer unseen. Only his footsteps and something dragging behind announced his approach, rattling the floorboards under her hand. Then the odor of sweat and bay rum clouded the air. Dominguez's haughty face emerged from the dark. The candlelight illuminated his face with an eerie glow, accentuating the hollow curves beneath his eyes.

His shimmering eyes raked her before he plunked down on the wooden chair he'd brought with him. He set his candle on the floor near her feet and studied her in the orange light. The idea tempted her to kick it over and set fire to his ship, but as much as she wanted to thwart his endeavors, she didn't fancy suicide.

"How are you finding your accommodations aboard my ship, *mi querida?*" The curled lips beneath his thick mustache mocked her.

Jane pressed her lips together and looked away. She wouldn't give this lout the satisfaction of seeing her suffer. Despite her unwelcome presence, Christophe had given her a bed and clothes to wear. She wondered if Dominguez would even provide her food.

He laughed, the haunting sound reverberating off the tight walls. "I see you are not much for talking. No matter. I didn't abduct you for your speaking skills." He leaned down and hooked her chin, lifting her face in the candlelight. "Lovely, yes. I can see why Roux kept you aboard his ship."

Her eyes flashed toward him. "He didn't *keep* me. I came aboard of my own free will." Realizing how that made her sound, her cheeks heated. She didn't need another shipful of men believing her a prostitute.

His thumb stroked her chin, volleying chills down her back. "Why would a fine woman such as yourself keep company with a dirty privateer like Roux?"

"That is none of your concern." Jane whipped her face away from him, freeing herself of his ghoulish touch.

Dominguez's hand froze in midair a few seconds before jutting out to coil around her throat. "It is my concern if I so choose. You belong to me now." His fingers constricted, not enough to hurt her, but enough to warn her.

Jane clenched her teeth. "If you want ransom from my father, you will not touch me. He will never pay you if I'm injured."

"Oh, I believe he will pay as long as you're alive." His glare skittered down her crumpled form. "There are other activities in which we may engage that involve no injury whatsoever."

A hard knot formed in her stomach. "Touch me and you die." She had already prepared herself to put up such a fight that any attempt at stealing her virtue would leave obvious bruising.

Amusement swam in his eyes before he released her head forcefully against the wall. "You aren't as much fun with everyone, I see. I do believe your father will pay more if you are left untouched, as you say."

Relief sank over her, but she wouldn't let it show on her face. She would rather go home to deal with Davenport than let any of these smarmy pirates near her.

"I sent an envoy as soon as I saw you aboard Roux's ship," he said, leaning back in his chair. "My sources tell me your father has already set across the channel with the money I asked for. I thought briefly about simply ambushing them. Then I could keep you both." He sighed, straightening his legs and crossing them at the ankle. "Alas, it will be cleaner this way. You are not worth the gunpowder."

Her anxiety shifted from concern over her future with Davenport to her father's safety. It had never occurred to her that Dominguez may seek his bodily harm. If running away put her father in danger, she must return home as quickly as possible.

"I thank you," she said quietly. It took her every last bit of strength to utter such words to this vile creature.

Dominguez smiled, though it looked more like the leer of a wolf. "I'll have you some food and water brought. It's the least I can do until we reach shore this evening."

"Where are we going?" Maybe if she had an inkling, she might somehow signal Christophe to her location.

He wagged one finger in the air. "Now, that is not something to concern yourself over. Don't worry; you'll be quite safe. The authorities have yet to discover any of our strongholds along the coast. Our hideout in Brest is perhaps our finest. You'll be very comfortable."

The sarcastic lilt in his voice caused Jane to question whether he was serious or meant his words as a joke. Perhaps they would throw her in someplace worse than this—a dungeon, maybe. Against her every desire, she found herself praying to go home—away from the wicked hands of pirates, away from the capricious sea.

As she sat considering it, the legs of Dominguez's chair scraped backward. Jane looked up to see him stooping to collect his candle. His ominous smile flared over his candle's glow one last time. "I do loathe to leave you in the dark, *mija*. Remember, I have quite comfortable accommodations in my room if you wish to join me. Your father never has to know." He pressed one finger over his lips, like he held the most amusing secret.

Jane balled her legs up so her knees touched her chin and wound her arms protectively around herself. Her eyes flashed a warning his way before her gaze flew to the corner of the blackened room. He may find enjoyment in treating her like a harlot, but she would never answer as one. More of her longed for home every second, where even if she didn't have a say regarding her future, at least people respected her. At least her femininity was revered rather than regarded as another prize to be won.

She barely heard Dominguez's confident stride exit the tiny room. The dinner he had mentioned consisted of cold slop and a wedge of sourdough bread that unsettled her stomach. Jane laid on the uneven floor, resting her face on the backs of her hands and retreating into her memories. Christophe would come for her. He had to. If he didn't, she would simply go home, explain to her father why she couldn't wed Davenport, make him understand.

Her body shivered, the chilly air and disquieting thoughts raising the hair on her skin. Somehow, even as she tried to convince herself otherwise, she knew a peaceful resolution would never come so easily.

Twenty

T he sun hung low in the afternoon sky as the *Licorne's* crew anchored her near the beach, where a dock jutted out through the tossing waves. Christophe had directed them toward a secluded section of coastline, still close enough to access the ancient city, but far enough away to perform the task ahead without detection. He skimmed the row of tethered ships bobbing along the docks, satisfied with his selection. A hill covered in pampas grass partially hid them from the city's watchmen. He would need as much secrecy as they could accomplish.

Glancing at the fading sun, he knew he didn't have much time before darkness cloaked the city. Christophe ducked down the stairwell and strode the hallway to his cabin. The ache of losing Jane crushed him again as he moved about the room, gathering his belongings. It had never felt so quiet and lonely now that her face no longer brightened his dreary quarters.

Opening his knapsack, he set it on the bed. In went an array of items he might need in case of emergency—candles, flint, a canteen of water, medicinal vials, bullets and gunpowder. One never knew what lay in store in a foreign city, especially with the nefarious scene he planned to orchestrate tonight. He stretched high and removed his secret box from behind the books on his tallest shelf, not bothering to rearrange them. Something inside warned him to take everything of value, just in case.

He had a silk purse folded in the drawer of his bedside table. Christophe retrieved it and loosened the drawstring, holding it open to pour the contents of his box inside. Another purse stuffed with money hid beneath a floorboard beside the bed. Kneeling, he pulled it from its cocoon and crammed it into his pack alongside his emergency items and nostalgic mementos. A quick sweep of Jane's room produced nothing, until he yanked the bureau drawer open and spied her grandmother's ruby necklace sitting atop one of Madeleine's gowns. Had she meant to leave it behind? It was the smartest move, considering Dominguez would probably search her. Gently, he reached in and grabbed it, settling it among the other treasures in his pack.

With the pistol on his hip loaded and his knapsack slung over one shoulder, Christophe climbed the stairs and looked for Monsieur Simon. The quartermaster stood amid a group of sailors with his finger pointed, directing them toward various jobs throughout the ship. When Christophe ambled up to them, they quietly dispersed like a colony of ants scurrying back to their hill.

Christophe motioned him toward the stern, where no one could overhear their conversation. "I made certain Hugo left plenty of ale on the tables downstairs for celebrating." He dipped his head to look into Monsieur Simon's eyes. "Are you sure you're up for this task?"

The quartermaster chuckled, though misgiving still played behind his gaze. "Getting a group of men like this drunk? I think I can manage my end of the assignment. Just give me enough time for the alcohol to take effect."

"Good man." Christophe clapped his shoulder. "Remember, every last one of them. I can't have one sailor sober enough to realize what's going on. If they find out I sent a group of thieves to attack the ship, they will kill you and me both."

"I won't fail you." Determination fueled Jacob Simon's dark eyes. "We have sailed together most of my adult life. I trust you. If you say you can pull this off, you will."

A hard lump rose in Christophe's throat. Monsieur Simon had much faith in him, as did so many of his crew. He couldn't fail the ones who stayed loyal. The thought of deceiving them created a cold, sickening ache in his belly. But this had to be done—for Madeleine, for the orphaned children of France, for himself. After so many dishonest deeds, he would perform one more to achieve what was right.

"Godspeed, my friend." Christophe tried to smile but only accomplished a frightened swallow. Turning slightly, he spoke so the others could hear. "Now I must go into Brest to find a buyer for our goods."

Christophe ignored the distrusting scowl Blanc launched his way as he alighted from the ship and strutted the dock toward the beach. Several others had joined the rebellious sailor, nudging Blanc and whispering once Christophe had left hearing distance. Whatever their plan, he would put an end to it tonight.

The medieval city of Brest welcomed him as Christophe ambled into the heart of its ancient streets. Winding cobbled passages opened into charming squares, stone buildings rising against the sky on every side. A market bustled along one street, with vendors hawking fresh fruit and women holding out colorful homespun cloth for their perusal. *Jane would love this.* Casting the notion aside, Christophe tipped his head respectfully and kept on climbing the street. He had a mission to fulfill if he ever wanted to see Jane again.

Past the timber-framed houses with thatched roofs he traveled, through the enticing aroma of chickens roasting for dinner. A row of business establishments up ahead kept him marching onward. Christophe passed shop after shop, selling everything from furniture to firearms, before the swinging sign he remembered came into view.

As he approached, the mingling of bourbon and whiskey teemed from the rowdy establishment. Beyond the heavy oak door, laughter and shouting rumbled, streams of it pouring out of the diamond-paned windows into the street. One side of Christophe's mouth lifted. How many times had he passed through that door as a youth, learning the ways of a sailor?

Christophe strode up to the door and hauled it open, allowing several people to pass through before he followed. He had learned long ago not to step over a threshold with someone at his back. Once inside, the din of revelry transported him straight back to his adolescence. Not much had changed about the Shaggy Dog, except perhaps a fresh coat of paint and new glasses.

Everywhere he looked, men sat around circular tables, gambling and drinking, bragging about their adventures at sea. A giant swordfish adorned one wall, a proud reminder of the owner's best day on the water. With a hint of sadness, Christophe wondered what had become of Old Joe. He was probably dead by now—of old age or disease, unless someone's bullet had done him in first.

Pushing his way through the crowd, Christophe headed past the bar toward the room's back corner. Heady cigar smoke clouded his path, the clink of tankards resonating through the air. Would Ambroise still inhabit the same spot he did every night those many years ago? A tall form bent over a journal at the far back table provided the answer he needed.

"I see you're still a recluse, my old friend." Christophe sidled up to the table, tossing his knapsack beside the man's book.

Ambroise started, his quill frozen in mid-sentence. He cocked his head toward the intruding knapsack before swinging a befuddled gaze up at Christophe. "Roux!" His face brightened as he sprang up and captured him in a tight embrace.

Laughing, Christophe slapped his back. "It's good to see you, too. It's been a long while."

"Too long." René Ambroise leaned back, breathless. The years had added a few gray sprinkles to his jet-black hair and trim mustache, as well as matured his gentle features, but he still looked like the young adventurer who had spent every waking moment teaching Christophe how to sail.

"Please, have a seat." Ambroise swept a hand toward an empty chair beside his, and both men sat. "You look good. The sea is treating you well, I see."

Christophe bobbed his head. "As well as ever. I'm happy to have my feet on solid ground again, though."

"And you are the captain now. After Chapelle's—accident." Ambroise's dark eyes glinted, revealing he knew the truth of the matter. They had both sailed under Chapelle's iron rule. Ambroise had warned Christophe when he fled the ship beneath the cloak of darkness that upheaval was inevitable with their cruel captain.

"I am, indeed." Christophe shifted in his chair. "Though for how long, I can't be certain."

A crease formed between Ambroise's eyes. "Are you in trouble, my friend? I'll do anything in my power to help you."

Christophe waved off a barmaid, leery of anyone hearing. "I am, in fact, in serious trouble." He shifted his gaze back to Ambroise. "I hate to bring trouble to your door after so many years apart."

A solid hand reached out to clamp his shoulder. "That's why good friends exist. It matters not how many years have passed since we last spoke. I am here—for whatever you need."

A cleansing sigh settled through Christophe. How good it felt to hear those words after relying on merely himself for so long. He leaned closer, tucking his loose hair behind his ears. "What I'm about to say must stay between the two of us. Promise me, René."

"Of course." Ambroise nodded, then paused, his eyes widening. "You found it, didn't you? I can see it in your eyes."

Christophe tried to keep his smile at bay, but it broke over his face. "We did. In a hidden cave behind the island's waterfall. It's more spectacular than you can ever imagine."

Ambroise had a dreamy look in his far-off gaze. How many years had he sacrificed in search of the Moon King's bounty? "Might I see it?" He bit his lip, unable to suppress the childish giggle that erupted there.

"Of course you may. But I need to get it to safety first." Christophe's stomach knotted to imagine it in the care of his wayward crew. "That's why I need your help. Do you have a group of men you can trust—men who are sordid enough to participate in an illegal endeavor but won't attempt to keep the money themselves?"

His friend thought, brows girded. "*Oui*, I believe my brothers-in-law would suit you perfectly. If you paid them handsomely."

"I will pay them whatever they ask and then some. I need them to stage a robbery and transport it for me to a place in the city waiting for its arrival."

Ambroise looked dumbstruck. "You want me to have it stolen off your own ship? Whatever for?"

"I can't explain here. I don't have enough time." Christophe glanced over his shoulder again. "I know what I'm asking is dangerous, to go up against a group of skilled fighters to retrieve a hoard they would give their lives for. It won't be so difficult, though. My quartermaster is getting them drunk as we speak. If we time the attack right, they won't present a threat to your men."

Ambroise nodded, twirling his glass of *chouchen* in two fingers. "Then, of course. I'll gather them immediately and we'll go to the docks together." He replaced his quill and slammed his book shut. "My poetry can wait for another day."

Before he could rise, Christophe laid a hand on his shoulder. "There is one more thing." When Ambroise merely looked back expectantly, he swallowed. "You remember Dominguez, don't you?"

He received a scowl in return. Ambroise pivoted away and spit on the floor. "How could I forget the madman who killed so many of my comrades? It's a good thing I'm not in the business of killing anymore."

"He attacked us just before we reached the bay. He's here in Brest." Christophe gripped the table, his next question dominating his mind more than worries over the treasure. "I need to find out where he hides out in this city. Do you know where his stronghold is? I need to get there—tonight."

J ane teetered unsteadily as she stepped into the rowboat from the ladder precariously dangling off the *Poseidon's* side. One man reached out a strong hand to help her into the boat, and Jane settled uncomfortably between two solid forms. Dominguez grinned devilishly from the rowboat's bow as the oars dipped into the water and propelled them to shore.

The fading light of oncoming dusk lit the horizon, still a yellow glow beneath an unblemished sky. Jane surveyed the coastline, hoping to gain a better understanding of their position. Just over the treetops, the city of Brest sat nestled against the rolling tides. Up ahead, what looked like remnants of a castle jutted out of the sand, a tall tower with a pointed top rising from a series of crumbling battlements.

As if inside her mind, Dominguez followed her gaze proudly. "It used to be a military fort, back in the days when the city needed a strong defense against its enemies. It was abandoned long ago. Nobody bothers us here. Think of it as your own private castle while we await your father's arrival."

Ripping her gaze away from his repelling presence, Jane looked across the expansive sea. Gulls bellowed over the sparkling sky, soaring and diving through the mists. She took a quivering breath through her nose, but even the salty ocean air couldn't calm her rampant thoughts.

The rowboat settled with a gentle thud against the sandy beach. Dominguez climbed out and extended a hand to Jane, but she shouldered past him, avoiding his touch. An icy chill grabbed hold as she stepped into the shallows, not bothering to keep the hem of her skirt out of the frigid water.

A short climb up the beach brought them to the decaying structure. It looked grander up close, its stony walls covered in moss telling the story of a once great edifice brought down by years of neglect. The inside possessed the same aged beauty, though it stunk of mud and mildew.

"Take her up to the tower," Dominguez ordered casually before his haughty form disappeared down a hallway. His boots echoed after him on the broad stone floor.

Perhaps he has comfortable quarters set up among these ruins, Jane thought as the hand gripping her tugged her toward a set of stairs. She surely wouldn't see them. "The tower", as ominous as it sounded, would at least provide her distance from the disgusting pirate. Jane could only hope it bore no similarities to the tower she knew in London.

She shuffled up the steps in front of her captor, every step a chore in drenched slippers. No decoration adorned the landing upstairs, beyond which a narrow hallway extended. The man pushed her down it, piloting her toward an imposing wooden studded door at its end. Jane's desperate eyes glanced in every direction, but no escape existed up here. She would have to sneak past the guards upstairs if she had any hope of getting away.

The tower beyond the impressive door consisted of a single circular room with a window facing the ocean. Its exposed stone walls held nothing save an empty chair that the man promptly shoved her into. Jane gasped as he yanked her hands behind her back and began tying them to the chair with a length of rope hanging from his belt.

"A room with a view," he said mockingly before depositing her in front of the window and leaving the room. The door slammed shut, the sound of his retreating footsteps both relieving and terrifying her.

Jane blinked back a stray tear, feeling more alone than she'd ever been. Through the open window, the sea sparkled beneath a pinkening sky, its tranquil beauty reaching out as if to bring comfort. She craned her neck to steal a glance at the harbor, but it lay out of sight. If only she could see the *Licorne* from here, know Christophe was safe, have hope of him coming for her.

Snapping out of her self-pity, Jane squared her shoulders. She couldn't wait for rescue. She couldn't sit by while men wrote a life for her she didn't want. Praying for courage, Jane scanned the room again in search of a means of escape. The scant space answered back with a howl as wind funneled through it. *I must be brave and self-sufficient. I must prove my father wrong.* Yet the harder she strained her mind, the more an answer eluded her.

Twenty One

T he streets of Brest came alive with activity as the sun set and
darkness settled over the old stone structures. Christophe
wound through the maze of buzzing citizens, all intent on a drink
at the local watering hole or chattering while out for an evening
stroll. He had two missions in mind and would not be deterred.
Secure the treasure. Find Jane.

The Catholic church he had agreed upon with Madeleine lay
on a tranquil street not far from the flurry of the city. Christophe
hoped it would prove far enough away not to attract attention as
he spotted its high stone spire rising above the buildings. With a
furtive glance around him, he crossed the street and hurried toward
it, dodging a wagon trundling up the cobblestone.

Three solid knocks on the church's door brought an aged priest
garbed in silk robes to his call. The old man's white bushy eyebrows
rose in question, awaiting an explanation.

"I am Christophe Roux." Relief flooded him as the priest nodded in recognition and stepped aside to admit him. At least part of
this harebrained plan had gone right.

Christophe passed beneath the doorframe and circular
stained-glass windows into a foyer aglow with candlelight. He
briefly stole a glance inside the chapel, its polished wooden floor

and stone carvings trapped in dancing light, before the priest waved toward a hallway to their right. Christophe followed, eager to put an end to this perilous adventure once and for all.

A long hallway flanked in windows and streaming with moonlight led them to an archway with an open door. What lay beyond looked like a rectory with the comfortable furnishings of a home, but the priest's demeanor didn't invite questions, so Christophe obediently trailed him into what appeared to be a parlor.

Immediately, two heads swiveled his way. "Christophe!" a woman's voice shouted before Madeleine's face materialized from behind a high-backed chair. She sprang from her seat and greeted him with a tight embrace.

Hesitant at first, Christophe returned her gesture with a gentle hug, his eyes never leaving the baron who had risen from his spot beside her. They both looked healthier than their last meeting on Traitor Isle, like they'd gotten food in their bellies. When he pulled away from Madeleine, he noticed her skin had healed of its sunburnt hue. She appeared happier than he'd ever seen her, a fact that would have twisted his gut weeks ago. Now, he relished the comforting knowledge that his love had tempered to the affection of a friend.

"We landed in Brest over a week ago." She lightly squeezed his forearm. "We were so worried something had happened to you."

Christophe raked a hand through his loose hair. "Something did happen." He glanced from Madeleine to Gabriel, who now stood at her side. "We were attacked by a rival pirate ship—twice."

Madeleine gasped, her hand flying to her mouth. "The treasure, is it—"

"Don't worry, it's safe." He watched her visibly relax. "We fought them off the first time. The second time, we managed an exchange."

The baron frowned. "An exchange of what?"

"It doesn't matter now," Christophe said with a sigh. He couldn't discuss Jane's existence without losing his wits. "The fact is that every bit of your ancestor's treasure is now on the beach and will be delivered here soon."

Madeleine clapped her hands together. "Oh, thank you, Christophe. I knew you could pull off the impossible."

Knotting his arms over his chest, Gabriel looked less convinced. "How did your men react when you told them you were distributing the money to charity? Can you trust them to bring it here untouched?"

Christophe heaved a weighty sigh. "I didn't tell them, actually. They would never have agreed to such terms." When he received only dumbfounded stares, he raised both hands. "The treasure is safe, I can assure you. I have an old friend here in Brest who has agreed to get it here safely."

"By what means?" Gabriel asked.

Another hesitation, accentuated by pops and fizzles from the fireplace. "By robbery." Before Madeleine could protest, Christophe rushed on. "There was no other way. A group of my crew members are set to overthrow me, anyway. If I told them I lied to them, they would have killed me. Monsieur Simon was tasked with getting them drunk tonight so the plan will go smoothly. No one needs to be injured. My friend's men will easily take the money."

Madeleine's brow wrinkled. "You're sure this will work?"

"I think it will, yes. We have the element of surprise on our side. Most of the men are not astute enough to see something like this coming."

"And you trust the man who is supposed to perform this robbery?" Gabriel asked.

"With my life." Christophe rubbed the back of his neck. "Look, I know this arrangement isn't ideal, but it's the best I could do given the circumstances. Anyone who encounters that much wealth is going to want to take it for themselves. It was always a risk to take it off that island, and a bigger risk to let a ship full of privateers transport it."

Nodding, Madeleine paced to the chairs sitting around the fire. "You're right. You did what you had to." She sank into a slipper chair, gesturing to the empty one beside her. "All that's left to do is wait. You deserve a rest after all you've been through."

Christophe waited for a nod of approval from the baron before he took the chair beside Madeleine. Gabriel sat on the opposing side of the hearth, no longer eyeing the two of them warily as he had on Traitor Isle. Christophe supposed their marriage had mended after he sought to rip it apart. Guilt wrenched at his soul like never before to acknowledge it.

"You look different." Madeleine's face glowed in orange fire-light, her eyes studying him closely. "I've never seen you so tense before."

Christophe rested his elbows on the chair arms and let his legs extend toward the fire's warmth. "I'm worried about delivering on my promise to get the treasure here safely."

She bit her lip, her brows working a moment before she shook her head. "That isn't it. I've seen you face the impossible amid those men. You never once had the fear in your eyes I see now."

His chest expanded with painful air. Could she really see that far into him? They had always shared an uncanny connection. Perhaps he'd mistaken this bond for love.

"If you must know, there is a woman," he said quietly. "Her name is Jane, and a captain named Dominguez has her. I had to give her up to save my crew. It's something I might never forgive myself for."

Madeleine shot him a quizzical look. "A woman? How could you have possibly met a woman en route from Traitor Isle to Brest?"

Christophe sighed. "It's a long story, and one I don't fancy relaying at the moment. Suffice to say, she didn't deserve to be taken captive by Dominguez. She is pure of heart, and I can't help worrying for her safety."

A few moments drifted past, the wind moaning through the trees and smashing against the ancient stone. At last, Madeleine smiled gently. "You love her."

He swung his gaze back sharply. "Why would you say such a thing?" He'd never uttered the words himself, yet they stung his chest to hear.

"Because I see honest devotion in your eyes—a look of adoration I've never seen before." She angled her head. "Not even with me."

Christophe swallowed. As much as he wanted to cast them aside, his feelings for Jane remained. The idea of her in fear or pain drove an urgency through his body, begging him to find her at once. To sit and wait felt like a torture he wouldn't wish on his fiercest enemy.

"She has become rather important to me." To admit more felt like tempting fate.

"Then you should get her back from Dominguez." Her eyes sparkled in the firelight. "I could help, you know."

Christophe raised one brow in question.

Tossing her head back, Madeleine laughed. "Oh, come now. You know I'm capable."

A smile erupted on his lips. Indeed, he had seen her impressive swordplay skills in action. "That may be, but I don't need anyone fighting my battles for me. Dominguez is mine to take down and nobody else's." The folly in his words occurred to him before it reflected back in Madeleine's dark eyes. If he really loved Jane, he should swallow his pride and bring along as much help as he could muster.

Before Christophe could think on it further, the priest shuffled back into the room. "They have arrived," he announced, gesturing toward another hallway. "I've sent them around to the back entrance to unload the cargo."

All three people seated around the fire jumped up and headed toward the indicated hall. Madeleine and Gabriel joined hands, their shoes tapping the stone floor as Christophe trailed them.

When they reached the outer door, two wagonloads covered in burlap sat in the grass outside.

Spotting Ambroise jumping down from one of the rigs, Christophe jogged toward him. "How did it go? Did everyone get out safely?"

Ambroise nodded, wiping his gloved hands on his trousers. "We did. Your plan worked. We have all of the treasure, and your men are unharmed, as well as ours."

Relief flooded Christophe. He hadn't realized how tense his muscles were until this moment. "Thank you, René. I couldn't have managed such a feat without you." He clapped his friend's shoulder.

The wary look on Ambroise's face gave him pause. Ambroise looked to the ground before meeting his gaze, concern lurking behind his normally tranquil eyes. He shook his head before sighing. "There's something you should know."

S weat leaked from Jane's hairline, her teeth gritted and jaw tight. Her body burned from the energy of wriggling this way and that. Her fingers stretched as far as they could, but no matter what she did, she couldn't free herself of her bonds. She inhaled wearily. How long had she been about trying to escape her restraints? One hour? Two? The minutes had begun to blur together.

The evening tides washed over the beach outside her little window, like music to accompany her flailing attempts to acquire freedom. The thin, luminous strand of moonlight playing over the waves and shining in her window would have charmed her in any other condition. Tonight, it only reminded her that time was running out.

The stones around the window gleamed under the white light, accentuating a ledge at the window's bottom that Jane had paid little attention to. Now, with a fresh idea in her mind, she gently shifted her chair around and sidled up to the wall with her back facing it. Finding the ledge with her fingers, she began sawing the rope between her tied hands against its solid edge. Her efforts might take a while, but perhaps she could loosen her ties with time.

Little sound came from outside her door as Jane repeatedly moved her hands up and down, working at the rope's fibers. More than once, she wondered if they had abandoned her, the idea of being tied up alone with no food or water more frightening than their presence. An occasional voice drifting up the stairs reminded her that Dominguez would never be so careless. Perhaps they were arranging her transfer. Had her father already made it to France's shores?

Lost in thought, she barely heard the batter of approaching footsteps. Jane gasped, lurching herself away from the window and rotating back to the position the guard had left her in. Her hands twisted, attempting to cover the fraying rope, but her fingers wouldn't contort that way. Would her visitor see the result of her escape efforts through the dim moonlight? She held her breath as the door groaned inward.

Two booted feet stopped in the doorway. Jane's heart hammered in her throat, the feeling of eyes on her back launching skitters up her spine. After a moment, the footsteps advanced. A familiar face materialized beside her—the muscular guard who had tied her. Without a word, he held out a ladleful of water.

Grateful, Jane leaned forward and gulped down his offering. The water was tepid and tasted of brine, but she didn't care. Hours had passed since her last drink of water. Her tongue had dried even more with the desperate attempts she'd made to break free.

The guard stood back, not seeming to notice the frazzled rope between her hands. "I'll bring you some bread when Perez gets back with it. Shouldn't take long."

With that, he disappeared, the door smashing shut behind him. Jane waited until his footsteps descended the stairs before spinning around again. She had little time to work before they interrupted her again. She *had* to move quickly.

Every stroke of her furious hands broke through the rope more. The tension on her wrists decreased until a few thin strands remained. Out of breath, Jane severed the last of the rope and swung her arms to her front. How freeing the motion felt after hours of muscle cramping, unable to move. Quickly, she bent to untie her feet and remove the ropes still tied around her wrists.

At last unfettered, Jane sprang from her chair and started for the door. She'd heard the guard vacate the hall. If she could quietly get down the stairs, maybe she stood a chance of sneaking past whoever remained downstairs. But when she pressed her thumb to the lock, the door refused to budge. Jane's shoulders slumped. Of course. Had she simply ignored the sound of his key twisting the lock?

Breathless, she scurried to the window. Poking her head out, she squinted to make out the darkened beach below. It sat a good distance down, no more than two stories, but certainly not close enough to jump to. Jane reached out to run her fingers over the stone wall outside. She hoped to find it uneven enough to climb, but the smooth stones had few imperfections. It would be foolish to attempt such a feat.

Jane glanced furiously around the room, unwilling to admit defeat. With each moment that passed, she became increasingly aware of her precarious position. If her guard found her free of constraints, they would certainly fashion a worse way to confine her, perhaps even punish her. She had to leave this place before he returned to bring her food. Already, she heard wagon wheels nearing the front door.

Her gaze settled on the rope she had cast upon the floor. She had split it at one end, but perhaps enough remained to use. Seizing it from the floor, she unraveled all of its knots before tying one end securely to the chair. Jane tossed the rope out the window, delighted to find it dangled perhaps seven feet from the ground. Her briefly elevated hopes fell again when she eyed the chair and knew something so lightweight would never hold her.

The front door opened, its squeal echoing through the structure. Voices mingled from down the stairs. It didn't matter now; she had to move. Jane snatched up the chair and wedged it beneath the window ledge before climbing into the open air. Her stomach churned and her vision swayed, but she set her jaw with confidence. She could be brave like Christophe, like the woman who had captured his heart before her. She would not wilt away in the corner, watching her future be determined by somebody else.

Jane's first step on the stone sent her foot slipping madly down the wall. Huffing, she sat on the ledge and removed her waterlogged slippers. Next came her stockings, all tossed behind her into the room she'd just abandoned. With her bare toes curled around the building's cold stone exterior, Jane gingerly began to shimmy down its side. Her hands turned white, gripping the rope with everything she had. *God, make this work. Don't let me fall.* The chair above her squeaked, but stayed jammed beneath the window ledge as she repelled lower.

When she neared the rope's end, Jane took one last breath and let go. Her skirts fluttered around her as she plummeted toward the beach, heart in her throat. The soft sand caught her feet first, then the rest of her body as she fell with the impact. Jane's ankles stung in protest, but as she rolled to a sitting position, she found no injuries to her body.

Exhaling in her relief, it transformed to a shuddering laugh. Her shoulders shook. The nocturnal beach and swirling wind seemed to gather her up in a comforting embrace. She had seized freedom for herself without help from anyone else. Glancing up at the window and dangling rope, she wondered how long it would take Dominguez's men to find her gone. Though exhausted, Jane pushed off the beach and ran toward the city's lights, kicking chilly sand under her bare feet.

Her sides ached and the soles of her feet screamed for relief by the time she stumbled up the first cobblestone street leading from the beach. Beneath the moon's faint light, she couldn't tell if the *Licorne* bobbed among the other ships anchored near shore. Had Christophe stayed or been forced to sail elsewhere? She shivered to imagine trying to evade recapture without money or the skills to make any.

Ahead of her, a form emerged from an alleyway. At first, her instincts led her to shrink back against the buildings, fearful of the approaching man. Then, as his form began to take shape, hope leaped inside of her. She couldn't mistake that tall frame or those brawny shoulders and arms.

"Christophe." It came out as a half-cry, half-laugh. Jane sprinted over the cobbled street without thought to her unprotected feet.

He paused, brows gathering, before thundering toward her with broad steps, the cape he wore over his clothes billowing behind him. "Jane?" When they met, he swung his strong arms around her body and pressed her tight against him. "Oh, Jane." His face nestled in the nape of her neck, wonderfully lost in her disheveled hair.

Tears flooded her eyes, trickling down her cheeks and wetting his loose hair. His arms had never felt so warm, his sea-drenched scent so welcoming. Swept up, Jane couldn't tell when their embrace converted to a drawn-out kiss or where she began and he ended. The space of his presence felt so natural, shared freely with hers, the promise of an eternal bond that would not shatter.

"I was just on my way to scout out Dominguez's stronghold," he said, cradling her face lovingly in his hands. "I have several friends who agreed to help me rescue you, but you're free." He shook his head, dumbstruck. "How did you accomplish it?"

Jane grinned, proud of herself. "With some quick thinking and a little luck." She glanced furtively behind her, half expecting an attack at any moment. "Dominguez might know I'm gone already. We should get out of the street before he finds us."

Christophe nodded and found her hand in the dark. Hand in hand, they scampered up the street and through a confounding maze of alleyways. Christophe must have known the city well, because he expertly navigated them past rows of thatched-roof houses until they reached lively squares of people gathered around public houses and dance halls. The pulse of his hand against hers soothed her agitated nerves. They were together again. No matter what happened, they had each other.

Halting in a busy square with a fountain at its center, Christophe peered over the buildings to a spire rising above them, then swung toward the docks. "I should take you to the church," he said, still working the problem out on his face. "We successfully moved the treasure, but I had to deceive my crew. It might not be safe for you there."

Jane moved to his side, squeezing his hand. "Please, Christophe. Don't leave me. I'm not afraid of your men. I won't be without you again."

Deliberating, he searched her pleading eyes. Perhaps she was foolish to ask him something so risky, but the need for his presence compelled her. Every moment on Dominguez's ship and locked in that forsaken tower had taught her that Christophe mattered above anything else this world could offer. She would stick with him, even in the face of danger.

"All right." At last he nodded, then leaned in to place a gentle kiss on her cheek. "I may live to regret this, but come along. We'll find out what happened when the men I hired stole the treasure from my men. They should all be so drunk, it won't matter anyway."

Pulling her between two buildings, he charged toward the beach. "My plan was to get them so intoxicated that they couldn't resist the robbery," he threw over his shoulder. "But my friend who led the mission told me that several were not, including Blanc.

They tried to warn the others and get them to see reason, but they couldn't hope to prevail against the number facing them. Blanc could stir up trouble, since he witnessed the entire event while sober."

Jane hopped onto the sandy shore behind Christophe. "Do you think he will suspect you?"

"He might." Christophe carefully watched his step as they trampled the dark beach. "Ambroise sailed aboard our ship long ago, before Blanc's time. Still, Blanc might recognize him from previous trips to Brest. I've never hidden my friendship with Ambroise from my men."

Before she could open her mouth, Christophe's sudden stop caused Jane to collide with him. Confused, she looked up to find him staring off toward the *Licorne*, which sat a stone's throw from their position, shimmering under an orange, raging glow. Blanc's rotund figure stood at the bow, the blazing torch in his hand mesmerizing her. Beside him, the prisoner named Vivianno stood proudly, unfettered. A crowd had gathered around them, staring up at them. Beyond them, something swung in and out of the torchlight, creaking with every jostle. Jane gasped as she discerned the silhouette of a hanging man. *Monsieur Simon.*

"Get down," Christophe ordered in a whisper. When Jane obeyed, he lay next to her and draped his cloak over her trembling body. His frame shook just as violently—from fear or anger, she didn't know.

"We have been deceived, gentlemen," Blanc roared over his crowd of attendants. "Roux claims to be our advocate, but he's done nothing save to lie to us for his own gain. He puts the wishes of the women he beds above ours. He selfishly seeks what he wants when our needs are overlooked."

With every word, the frenzy of agreement built, men shouting with their fists in the air, their heads bobbing and glassy eyes fixed as if in a trance. It couldn't have been hard to convince a crowd of drunken fools—fools who would have to live with their ruthless actions in the morning.

"We rejected the rule of a tyrant when we cast off Chapelle," Blanc said, violence ablaze in his rounded eyes. "But Roux is ten times worse. He orchestrated this robbery tonight to steal the money for himself, using this traitor here as an accomplice." He gestured toward poor Monsieur Simon. "He expects us to blindly follow him, to behave as imbeciles, while he rolls around in our hard-earned wealth."

Blanc's chubby finger rose to the black sky. "I say 'no more', gentlemen. We've taken the *Licorne* for ourselves now. If Roux shows his duplicitous face, he will meet the same fate as his cowardly quartermaster."

At the pirates' angered shouts of agreement, Jane's stomach lurched. If they were discovered, they would both hang with Monsieur Simon. Her fingers tingled as Christophe snatched them up without a word and pointed toward the city. Together, they slinked silently over the sand in a crouched position. Heart hammering like an anvil, Jane could barely breathe as they absconded the beach and broke into a run. Her chest ached. Her soul cried out for the dead man who had only shown her kindness the few times they had interacted. Holding tightly to Christophe's hand, she prayed he wouldn't meet the same end.

Twenty Two

The first breakfast with fresh ingredients he'd been offered in months sat steaming on the table before Christophe, and still he had no desire to touch it. Ambroise's wife Elise had lovingly prepared a feast—crêpes and fresh fruit, eggs en cocotte, and grilled sausage. Any man who had just spent months at sea would welcome the aromatic array—any man but him. Stomach reeling, he gazed with glossy vision out the second-story window, where the *Licorne* no longer graced the coastline.

"I still don't see how anyone could kill Jacob Simon," Ambroise said from beside him. "He was a kind soul. He would never have dreamed of such a vicious attack."

Christophe listlessly turned back to the table, hardly seeing the two women or group of children crowding the tiny kitchen. "You don't know Blanc." His lip snarled. "Blanc would kill anyone he could to seize an opportunity at power. He's wanted to be rid of me since we sailed from Traitor Island."

Elise Ambroise fluffed her auburn hair and glanced warily at her gaping children, but said nothing. Her husband comforted her with a gentle pat to her wrist. The nutty odor of his hazelnut coffee drifted about the air as he shook his head and lifted the mug to his whiskered lips.

"At least the treasure is safe," Ambroise said. "It could have caused an all-out war."

"Father Enzo said they had already begun transporting parts of it to its intended destinations," Jane offered. "They didn't want to attract attention, of course, but it won't be safe staying together in one place forever."

In the humble kitchen of an ordinary home with average, working-class people, she looked like a dahlia among daisies. Although Elise Ambroise had outfitted Jane in a simple homespun day dress of pale-yellow cotton, her etiquette and mannerisms gave her away. Her rigid back never faltered, her elbows keeping clear of the table as she daintily took bites of her sausage. How Christophe would ever please a woman like that, he hadn't worked out.

"The treasure is safe and so are you," Ambroise said. "That's all one can ask for, especially from the life you've chosen. Perhaps this is an opportunity to begin again with a clean slate. There's nothing to hold you back now."

Christophe's gaze flitted from Jane's hopeful smile to the simple kitchen around them with its hand-carved furnishings and terracotta floor. He could make a good life with Jane, turning aside from pirating and learning a new trade as Ambroise had done. Something inside begged him to consider trading his sea legs for a peaceful existence with a quiet home and loving family. Then the image of Jacob Simon, hanging from a yard of the *Licorne*, flashed through his mind again. He could not let his death go unpunished.

He shook his head emphatically. "I can't move on from this. They stole my ship. They killed my quartermaster. I will make Blanc and his conspirators suffer for what they did." Suffer for killing his best friend of so many years. Unbearable pain swelled in his chest, Monsieur Simon's words tolling again and again in his mind. *I trust you. If you say you can pull this off, you can.* How greatly he had failed the most faithful sailor he'd ever known.

Ambroise exchanged a worried look with his wife. "You should get some rest before you go charging ahead on that front," he said gently. "You have just experienced unimaginable loss. You won't be thinking clearly."

"No. It must be now." Christophe's nostrils flared. "I must find out where they've gone and exact my revenge. They won't expect it so soon."

"How do you expect to achieve such a feat on your own?" Ambroise's fingers spread in question. "You are one man, and they are an army. You know this; you've stood at their helm for years."

Christophe's fingers coiled around his warm coffee cup. "Many of them will come back to my side once they wake from their drunken stupor and realize what they've done. The majority are loyal. We bonded under Chapelle's rule. We came together to overthrow him."

"But how will you know which ones you can trust and who will only betray you again?"

"I'll know." Christophe took a swig of his steaming coffee, the bitter liquid nearly scalding his tongue as it slid down his aching gullet.

Ambroise sighed again, then lifted his shoulders in defeat. "I don't think it's a good idea, but I won't tell a grown man what to do." He hesitated, drumming his knuckles on the table. "I inquired down at the docks. Several people I know overheard your sailors mentioning Barbados. I believe that's where they headed early this morning."

Barbados. Of course they would flee to the West Indies. Their ship had always enjoyed a good relationship with the merchants and authorities there. The governor often dined with Christophe personally, believing him to be an honest captain of a French cargo vessel. His errant crew could easily sell what they had stolen from Jane's ship without many questions.

The fact that Barbados also housed the mission Jane had pledged her life to didn't escape Christophe's notice. He allowed himself to look into her searching green eyes a moment, hoping to find an answer to the questions plaguing him. Would she still want him when she witnessed the lengths he would travel to avenge Jacob Simon's death? The purity in her honest gaze assailed him with guilt.

Swallowing back the solid lump in his throat, Christophe swung his gaze to Ambroise. "Will you help me? I have money for a ship passage and supplies. We'll need clothes and food, weaponry—"

A reassuring hand on his forearm halted his mad frenzy of words. Ambroise gave him a pointed look. "I will aid you in any way I can if this is what you really want." His fingertips pressed harder. "Remember, revenge won't bring you happiness. It will only bring a moment of euphoria that will fade. Your pain will remain."

Christophe considered his words briefly before casting them aside. Forget happiness, joy, the future. He wanted nothing more than to gut Blanc and Vivianno for stealing the life of his innocent quartermaster. The rest he would think about only after he'd completed the mission ahead.

Ignoring the silent pleading in Jane's eyes, Christophe fixed his steely gaze on Ambroise. "I'll take what I can get."

Elise Ambroise showed Jane and Christophe to a small bedroom off their townhouse's living space. In other circumstances, Jane might have asked for separate rooms, but she knew from counting both the children dwelling within the home and the bedrooms that they already deprived at least two of their beds. As the door clicked shut and she found herself alone with Christophe for the first time since his crew's attack, she pressed a hand to her middle. Whatever they had to say, it wouldn't be easy.

A single candle stationed on the nightstand illuminated a quaint yet beautifully decorated room. A floral patchwork quilt covered a bed designed for two, plump white pillows propped against the oak headboard. In the corner, she noticed a miniature table and chairs with a cracked teapot painted in rosebuds. Even the chest at the foot of the girls' bed bore an etching of a rose.

Christophe stood in silence, vacantly staring at the wall as he had done for much of the day. Unsure how to talk to him, Jane moved past him with her skirts swishing and sank onto the bed. Her body ached as if she'd worked all day, though she had merely bidden her time as Christophe mourned his beloved friend and stewed about seeking revenge. In a moment she wanted to bring him comfort, she felt utter fear.

Last night when they'd snuck from the beach, he had taken her first to the church. Father Enzo had provided them with a hot dinner and a place to sleep. Happy to be free of danger, Jane had sought to soothe her frenzied nerves in the calm and confident man she loved, but found instead a hysterical ball of wrath. Despite the anguish in his eyes, he never cried. Instead, he feverishly paced the church halls, vowing death on his men for their wicked deeds. In the quiet moments, he stared into the fire as if in a trance. Jane couldn't have consoled him if she tried.

Ironically, she had found peace spending the night in the nuns' quarters with the baroness she had heard so much about. Jane recognized her immediately. Her raven hair and striking beauty would have given her instantly away, but the way she smiled spoke even louder. The baroness had kindness and pain behind her eyes, a gentleness and a ferocity Christophe had described so well. No wonder he had loved her. Jane wanted to be her friend from that one night alone.

As Christophe refused the company of others, Madeleine had taken her gently aside and asked what she needed. Jane had to ashamedly admit that she had already been wearing her clothes aboard ship, to which Madeleine merely laughed. The baroness had seen to getting her a warm bath poured into a copper tub and had given Jane a nightdress from her collection.

In the yellow glow of candlelight, they had sat up like two sisters and chatted about the events that had led to this night. It felt good to share her burdens with another person, someone who listened with genuine care and helped her understand the enigmatic man she'd fallen in love with. Jane hadn't realized until then just how deeply she missed her friends back home. Would she make new ones in this new, bizarre life she lived? She hoped so.

Now, trapped in the company of a wounded man, Jane wished she could have the safety of Madeleine's friendship back. A shiver racked her body. She saw nothing of the warm and gentle soul who had tenderly provided for her those many days aboard ship. His blue eyes blazed with fury, fixed on an unseen foe as if the imagined creature stood before him.

Sighing, she pushed off the slippers Elise had given her, lifted the quilt and sheets, and lounged against a pillow. She wanted to change into Madeleine's nightdress, but not with him standing there with that menacing expression. The day dress Elise had provided would just have to do. It felt comfortable enough to sleep in.

Snapping out of his stupor, Christophe blinked a few times before raking a hand through his abundant hair. "I'll sleep on the floor." His gaze darted fruitlessly around. "There must be an extra blanket around here somewhere."

"There's no need." Jane's simple words stilled him. He gazed questioningly across the bedroom at her. "Christophe, we've seen death together. There is no need for niceties between us now. Besides, I won't have you losing sleep because I banished you to the floor."

Christophe nodded, though he stood frozen in place a long while as if he didn't believe her. She couldn't blame him after the fuss she'd put up about sleeping in a room next to his. Slowly, he sauntered around the bed and removed his boots before crawling beneath the covers next to her.

Skitters traveled her extremities to feel his warmth, his nearness. How badly she wanted to ask him to hold her, to subdue her fears with his strength. But he was broken. He had no power left to give her. Jane thought about embracing him instead, in hopes that she could somehow comfort him. Her trembling hands refused to budge. Instead, she rolled away from him and tucked her knees high. It was better in such a scandalous position that they didn't touch anyway.

The sea sat near enough to the townhouse for the sound of its sloshing waves to carry from the beach. Nocturnal breeze gusted through the window, fluttering the curtains and blanketing the room in a refreshing chill. Laughter and violin music drifted up from the streets, the scents of ale and food mingling with it. The world went on as normal while the two of them lay contemplating its weight on their shoulders.

Soon, Christophe drew near and draped an arm over her body. She hadn't expected it, but the action kindled a sense of belonging. Almost without thought, she snuggled against him, letting his face nestle at the back of her neck, fitting them together like puzzle pieces.

"Oh, Jane," he whispered into her hair. "Jane, I'm so sorry." Every word swept warm breath over her neck, driving her affection deeper.

"What do you have to be sorry for?" She laced his fingers on her side with her own, marveling at their perfect fit despite their difference in size.

"I've failed you in so many ways. Pushing you away today is just the least of my offenses." His arm constricted around her, tucking her into a loving hold.

Every instruction from her upbringing screamed at her to spring from the bed at once, but instead she rotated in his arms to face him. Candlelight played over the robust lines of his face, illumining some and shadowing others. The unshakable poise she usually saw in him was supplanted by pain. His jaw clenched, fighting his emotions, biting back the agony buried beneath his rage.

"You haven't failed me," she said softly. Her hand rose to caress his cheek, where light stubble had sprouted. "Without you, I would be dead. It was the daftest act of my life to come aboard your ship."

Christophe smiled against his anguish. "It was rather daft." He laughed with her, the sound soothing to her ears. "But it's my duty to protect you now. I almost got you killed last night. I won't see that happen again." His fingers subconsciously tightened on her side with his words.

Jane watched him silently for a long moment, reading his face. "You're punishing yourself for what happened to Monsieur Simon, aren't you?"

Brows lifting, he swallowed. "How can I not? He trusted me, and I failed him. If I had only been there, I could have—" His voice choked, the tears he'd held so long at bay suddenly gushing in his eyes and spilling down his face.

Drawing him against her, Jane let Christophe sob in her arms. His hot tears soaked her dress; his quivering frame clung to her. How long had he stored up his grief inside, putting on a wrathful front for the world? She stroked his face and combed her fingers through his hair until his powerful cries melted to a whimper. How strongly she wished she could take away his sorrow, bring back his ship, restore Monsieur Simon. Somehow, he would have to find a way to live without them.

"I've never cried like that in front of anyone," he said, wiping the remaining moisture from his cheeks. "Truth be told, I can't remember the last time I even cried."

"It's good for the soul at times."

Christophe gazed back at her through the quivering lamplight, his affection deepening. Jane's heart lurched at the look he gave her—tranquil yet passionate, like her presence both put him at ease and fueled him. "I love you, Jane. You know that, don't you?"

She nodded, his words soaking into her like balmy rain. "And I love you."

His fingers lifted to softly brush away the loose hair from around her face. Jane closed her eyes at his touch, imagining them lying in a grassy field in summer, free of the pain that encircled them. In her dream, they shared a picnic lunch and drank lemonade, chatted about the social events of the season. But when she opened her eyes to the little bedroom her mind had left, reality snatched her in its claws.

He had another look on his face now—steely and determined. If only his tender love for her could erase the need for vengeance Blanc and his men had roused. Perhaps he might discard it if she tried to convince him.

"Christophe?" She cupped his jaw in her open hand, waiting for his gaze to drift into hers. "I know you purchased the tickets today, but"—her throat closed, suddenly sore—"I don't want to go to Barbados."

A crease formed between his eyes. "I can't leave you here alone. Your father could arrive any day and force you back to England to marry Davenport. Neither will I leave you unprotected in a place like this."

Her hand clutched his shirt. "I don't want you to go, either."

Understanding dawned in his eyes. Christophe rolled away from her and gazed at the ceiling. "They sailed away on my source of income, Jane. That ship was my livelihood."

"Can't you purchase another? I've seen how much you have saved. If it's not enough, surely the baroness could help—"

Christophe scoffed. "It's more complicated than that. One doesn't just buy a ship. You must hire a crew, build a reputation. If anyone got wind of my true identity, they would hang me."

A streak of anger bolted through her. He didn't *want* a better solution. "Captaining a ship isn't the only thing you could do. I'm sure you are qualified for a great many jobs."

His head shook, his nostrils widening. "The sea is my life. I won't leave it, no matter the dangers it might present. I'll never leave it."

"So then, I must watch helplessly as you run off and get yourself killed trying to fight an entire band of men with your bare hands?" Her chest pitched. "If you take me to Barbados and die, what protection do I have then—especially from the crew who murdered a man like Monsieur Simon without a second thought?"

Christophe rolled his gaze back to her, fire in his eyes. "I will not lose this time. I will kill anyone who stands in my way of that ship."

"You don't *know* that." Jane wrung her hands. "You hope to prevail, but what chance do you have against that many men? At some point, you're bound to slip up. Then I'll lose you." Her chest took on a hollow feeling just to imagine it.

"I see your faith in me has dwindled." His eyes flashed. "You think I don't know these men, that I can't anticipate their next move? They are as predictable as the sun. I know how to ensnare them, I promise you."

Jane resisted the urge to say that he hadn't predicted Monsieur Simon's death so effortlessly. Such words from her would break him. Instead, she clamped her lips into a thin line and waited until his face softened. How desperately she wanted to stand at his side and support him in whatever he set his mind to. Yet how could she play a part in the malice he planned?

"You have so much goodness in you." She reached out, laying a hand on his surging chest. "I don't want to see it destroyed by hate. It feels like you need vengeance now, but that path will only bring more pain. Please stay here with me. Choose love over revenge. Choose me."

Christophe laced his fingers with hers, his eyes gentle as he lifted her hand to his lips and kissed it. "Jane." Closing his eyes, he pressed the backs of her fingers to his face. "If only it were so simple." When he looked back at her, a certainty had grabbed hold that frightened her. "I *must* do this. It isn't about choosing revenge over you. I must fulfill my duty. Then I'll be free to love you as I should."

An enormous lump ballooned in Jane's gullet. He would never understand. The act he planned to perform would rend them apart. There would be no more love left for her. She doubted he would survive it. Her entire body ached, already mourning the loss of this man she would give her world for.

"If I can't stop you, then neither can I stand by and watch." Jane slipped her hand from between his, compelling the next words from her tongue. "When the ship docks in Barbados, I wish for you to take me straight to the mission. I shall join their ranks as I always planned."

Christophe looked like she'd struck him across the face. "Jane." He reached for her, but she scooted farther back on the bed.

"I'll not hear any arguments. If you travel the road you've chosen, then I cannot be a part of it. I can't let my heart break any more than it already has."

Bitter silence settled over them as he contemplated her words. His blue eyes, shimmering in the candlelight, begged her to reconsider. "We'll be at sea for at least a month before we arrive in Barbados. We'll have only each other."

Steeling herself, Jane sat up and blew out the candle, dousing the room in darkness. "Then we'll have plenty of time to say goodbye." Before he could protest, she rolled away from him and tucked her pillow beneath her head. She would not let him see her tears or the uncertainty plaguing her. Better to sever their attachment now than to spend a month pining after a man she knew she must let go of.

Twenty Three

T he mess of the *Intrepid* roared with voices as Jane sat down
to dinner. Her stomach growled. In any other environment, she might have excused herself and stewed in shame. Here,
she doubted anyone even heard the commotion within her middle. The host of sailors crowded around the long wooden tables
drowned her out, and nobody cared anyway.

After weeks at sea, many of her cultured mannerisms had
slipped. Jane sank without care beside Danielle and Anouk, two
women from Bordeaux traveling to the West Indies on the promise
of a job and the chance at finding a husband. She shivered to
imagine the prospects that awaited them, hoping for the best.

"We're having fine weather," Anouk said, already digging into
her bean stew. "The captain says we'll be in Barbados in a week."

Danielle sighed. "I can't wait. I hear the beaches have warm sand
as white as sugar. I hope we all find rich and handsome men and
live in villas overlooking the ocean."

"This one already has a man." Anouk elbowed Jane, her ebony
ringlets bouncing with her giggle.

Jane reddened, trying not to look Christophe's way, but failing.
"I told you—he is my brother." He had concocted the story to

protect her safety and her reputation, but Jane knew it appeared thin and suspicious.

"And I'm your Aunt Mabel," Danielle said with a snicker.

Anouk batted her lashes. "If that man is your brother, the way he looks at you is criminal." She patted Jane's wrist. "Don't worry, dear. Your secret is safe with us. We won't tell anyone he's your secret lover." The girls both retreated into shared laughter, their chatter blending with the clink of their spoons.

With a weighty breath, Jane picked up her spoon and attempted to take a bite, but the bland, lukewarm soup would barely slide down her gullet. The familiar sensation of being watched prompted her head up, her gaze meeting Christophe's across the crowded mess. Despite the rather large group of passengers convened for dinner, he took his meal with the sailors, as usual. Perhaps he felt more comfortable in their presence, or maybe he kept his distance to respect her wishes.

For weeks, they had shared little interaction. He slept in a berth with a group of single men, checking on her from time to time. Usually the exchanges came while she roamed about the ship's decks on an afternoon stroll, or just before a meal commenced. He inquired after her welfare, assuring she was comfortable in her own berth with the women, and asking if he could bring her anything. They had shared not a kiss or intimate touch since that night in René Ambroise's townhouse, only the pleasantries shared by two hardly acquainted with each other.

Jane's stomach protested again, this time from heartache rather than hunger. She attempted a small smile, but her lips remained frozen. The two just stared at each other across the lively room, a multitude of unspoken words hovering in the tepid air. If only he could let go of his pain, cease his quest for vengeance, they might have the future every fiber of her body longed for.

"If you want, we'll leave the berth empty for an hour or so." Anouk's words snapped Jane back to reality. "It appears the two of you have unfinished business." Her brow lifted, a suggestive simper pursing her lips.

"Certainly not." Jane ripped her stare away from Christophe's lonely eyes and snatched her spoon. "He is my brother, I said. Besides, I am a lady." Summoning her most practiced pose, she straightened her back and began gracefully eating her supper.

The two women exchanged a knowing look. "Whatever you say," Anouk put in, the gleam in her eyes alive with amusement.

Though hungry, Jane struggled through her watery soup. The tasteless concoction and rock-solid bread that accompanied it made her miss Hugo tremendously. She often worried after the kind cook's health, hoping he fared well aboard the *Licorne*. He could certainly teach the cook on board this ship a lesson or two.

When she had finally consumed enough to satisfy her aching belly, Jane rose and took her dishes to the galley. Never before had she needed to clear her own plates, and the experience made her grateful. A lifetime awaited her of not only cleaning after herself, but caring for others. She had much to learn.

Emerging from the galley, she stuck up her chin and refused to look Christophe's way. The scent of sweat and body odor followed her like a rabid dog as she wound through the array of cajoling seamen. By now, she'd grown used to the odd aromas she'd never faced at home, but they still remained unpleasant.

Just before she reached the door leading to the decks, a young sailor jumped in her path. He had long hair like Christophe's tied at the nape of his neck. A dimple dented his shaven skin, his eager smile denoting a man of twenty, maybe younger. Jane had seen him on her daily walks, often staring her way without reticence.

"Bon soir, mademoiselle. Might I walk you out?"

Covering her smile with her fingers, Jane resisted the urge to chuckle. The man put on every air she expected from the gentlemen at home, yet the sweat-stained arm he extended gave him away. Still, she appreciated the effort.

"No, but thank you, sir. I am very much in your debt." Jane watched his broad shoulders slump as she strolled past him out the door.

"Wait." The man chased after her, trailing her up the stairs to the main deck. "I've seen you on the ship. You're not like the other girls on board. You're—" He stopped when she turned to him, shyly tucking a chunk of hair behind his ear. "Well, you're an actual lady, aren't you? You carry yourself differently."

Jane cocked her head, studying him in the moonlight. He looked harmless, but what did she know about worldly men? He admitted his attraction to her arose from her breeding. What an utter disappointment he'd face to discover she had no wealth to accompany her practiced grace.

"I *was* a lady," she corrected. "Now I'm a woman bound for a life of servitude. I will be a nun in less than a fortnight."

His brow wrinkled. "Well, that's a shame. You are much too pretty to be a nun." He took two steps toward her, prompting Jane to cross her arms defensively. "Please, I mean you no harm. I just—" One shoulder lifted. "I just wanted to get to know you better."

A mirthless laugh escaped her throat. "Sir, I assure you, there is nothing to know. I suggest you seek company with one of my bunkmates—perhaps Anouk. I'm sure she will welcome the distraction." With that, she turned to leave him with a shake of her head.

Before she took a step away, a hand hooked her elbow. Jane looked incredulously up into a determined face. "Mademoiselle, you haven't given me a chance. I'm sure you will like me once you get to know me." His words sounded innocent enough, but something more sinister lurked behind his already wandering eyes.

For the first time, Jane's skin prickled beneath the threat of danger. "I assure you, I will not." She tried to jerk her arm away, but his grasp held her firmly. "Sir, you will unhand me at once."

The man stepped closer, his taller frame swathing her in its shadow. "I just wanted to have a little fun." His lips curled innocently as if speaking of a game of checkers, his dark eyes telling a different story. Jane realized with great unease that she possessed no skills to defend herself. Unless she sought Christophe's instruction on the matter, she would have no means to fight off every rake who crossed her path outside of the mission.

"I believe the woman said to let her go." Another voice pierced the thick air between them. Jane and her companion both whirled to find Christophe standing an arm's length away with his pistol aimed at the man's head. "You have five seconds to abide by her wishes."

Swallowing, the man released her arm and stepped backward with his hands spread in the air. "Please, I meant no harm. I only wanted to talk."

Christophe rolled his eyes to the black sky. "I know what you were about." He flicked the barrel of his gun toward the mess. "Now go back to dinner and leave this woman alone. If I catch you so much as speaking with her again, I'll put a bullet between your eyes."

"Y—yes, monsieur." The young man nodded, shrinking back like a wilted flower and sending one more disbelieving glance Jane's way before scampering back the direction he'd come.

Releasing a shaky breath, Jane smoothed out her skirts. "Thank you." She watched thoughtfully as Christophe returned his pistol to its holster. "I must learn to shoot one of those. Perhaps I'll buy one when we land."

One corner of his mouth crimped. "A nun with a pistol. Sounds like a lethal combination."

She laughed, a bit of her anxiety releasing. "I shall prove myself a force to be reckoned with."

Moonlight shone on his square jaw, lighting the masculine lines of his face. He studied her for a quiet moment, his eyes soft. Then he held out his arm. "For now, would you allow me to walk you back to your cabin? I would hate to imagine you in harm's way again."

Jane grinned. "I think there's little threat of that with you mindfully keeping watch." Slipping her arm into his, she reveled in his familiar warmth. "But I accept your invitation, sir."

Their ramble across the deck and down the steps to the sleeping quarters felt natural despite the lack of conversation between them. Jane fell into step beside him, picturing them walking through the gardens of her estate or into a ballroom crammed with interested guests. How proud she would be to enter a party on his arm, this handsome mountain of a man who loved her. Remembering the doomed nature of her dream, her heart plummeted.

When they reached the door to her berth, the cramped hallway sat in abandoned silence. Jane turned to Christophe, unwilling to detach from him. His eyes swept her face in the winking light of a single lantern swinging from a beam. Their gentle glow converted to fire as they searched her gaze, wandering to her lips.

"Christophe—" The word barely escaped her mouth. Her heart rammed against her ribcage. His face hovered closer to hers until their noses brushed, his hastening breath hot on her skin. "Christophe."

But she didn't stop his lips from softly caressing hers, his sturdy frame pressing her gently to the wall. Her hands clung to his arms, her eyes closing, every piece of her delighting in the euphoria of his nearness. She missed his nautical scent, the tender way his fingertips swept her face. They stood together a beautiful moment, his butterfly of a kiss lingering on her lips.

"We can't," she finally said against his lips. "You're supposed to be my brother, remember?" Her eyes opened, determined to end this before it intensified, in spite of every instinct begging her to pull him close.

Christophe dipped his head and laughed against her neck. "Does anybody believe that?" When he pulled back, sad resolution had supplanted his desire. "Forgive me, Jane. I know how you feel. I promise to keep my distance." With one last squeeze of her arm, he stepped backward.

Heart in her throat, Jane managed to stumble forward and pull the door open. Stepping around it, she used it as a shield as she dared to look at him once more. His form, once so powerful and bold, looked defeated in the lonely hallway. He held her gaze a long moment before he rubbed the back of his neck and gave her a sad smile.

"Good night, Jane."

A lump materialized in her throat, and she had to swallow to answer. "Good night, Captain Roux." With one last flicker of her gaze, she closed the door to her cabin and her heart. It had to be this way.

A whisper of wind swept her face and lifted Jane's unbridled hair as she stared in wonder at the approaching island. She gripped the ship's rail, entranced by the white sand beaches and clear blue water, the lush palm trees fluttering in the breeze. She'd never seen or even imagined anything like it. The illustrations in her encyclopedia couldn't hope to encapsulate such wild beauty.

"It's quite something, isn't it?" Christophe watched her with a grin from her side. "I spent several days getting lost on the beaches the first time I visited the Caribbean. It's hard to imagine a place so incredible until you see it with your own eyes."

Jane nodded, the right words escaping her. Society and the papers described these waters as the most ruthless, dangerous place in the world. Yet as she took in the verdant undergrowth and cloudless sky, the horses roaming the beach, she remembered the pull on her heart when she'd first come across the mission's advertisement. As if her heart knew what her mind couldn't yet comprehend. This unusual place was meant to become her home.

The thought left her excited and lonely all at once. England, her estate at Brambleshire, the family she loved dearly despite their flaws—they would fade into her memories. One day, she might even forget the face of her beloved grandmother. Yet what an adventure lay ahead. A new life. A chance to start again, free as the birds swooping over their heads.

Her gaze latched with Christophe's thoughtful stare, her lips parting as if to speak but having nothing to say. The love she would always harbor for him reflected back at her in his tender face. He looked like an ordinary traveler in his gray double-breasted jacket and linen shirt, the plain trousers so unlike the leather he wore when captaining his ship. If only he could become that man for her, but she'd known the truth from the beginning. Christophe Roux would never truly love anyone but the sea. To compete with that would only rip her apart all the more.

When the ship settled against the docks with a thud and the sailors rushed around them to anchor her there, Jane tore her stare from Christophe's and bent to retrieve the valise the Ambroises had given her. Christophe followed suit, a valise in one hand and his knapsack slung over his back. His hand gripped hers to aid her in stepping off the ship, but never let go. The natural feel of his touch calmed her as his fingers wove with hers and they strode the length of the docks together.

Jane's stomach roiled and her heart begged her to reconsider her decision, but she kept walking. Barbados presented a chance to begin anew in service to the God she loved. Her temporal love for the man beside her would fade with time. She would grow used to an existence of solitude, the prospect of never having children of her own. It would become as natural as holding his hand—the hand of a man who had frightened her at first.

Reminding herself of this truth over and again, Jane walked closer to his side. For these last few stolen minutes, she would pretend she might hang on to him forever.

Twenty Four

J ane would never know what walking onto the familiar shores of Barbados with her hand in his meant to Christophe. Since his adolescence, he had loved this place. When Jacques Chapelle had first introduced him to the magical shores of the Caribbean, Christophe's heart had ever longed to return. Bringing her here felt like melding the two he loved above all else in glorious unity. The perfect land and the perfect woman, together at last. If only he could keep her by his side.

Delaying the task at hand, Christophe first walked her into the main square of Bridgeport. Careful to blend in with the crowds, he wove them toward the market with its whitewashed buildings and bustling activity. He had spotted the *Licorne* among the ships along the harbor. His double-crossing crew had to be around here somewhere, and he would rather meet them with Jane safely within the mission's walls.

Jane. The feel of her soft hand in his launched a thrill through him he wished he could control. She looked unearthly in the white muslin gown they'd purchased in Brest, her blonde hair flowing freely over her lithe shoulders. This trip had changed her. The airs she'd assumed when they first met had vanished, leaving behind a free and relaxed woman, confident in herself without the finery of home. Her transformation drew him to her even more strongly.

The colorful market sat within a lively square teeming with people. Jane's eyes lit as they passed women hawking homespun textiles of every pattern and color imaginable. Tables covered in vegetables of every variety greeted them—cabbage, beets, okras, peppers, and pumpkins. Jane stood over a table of bananas, mangos, and prickly jackfruit with her mouth agape. Christophe realized with a cheerful laugh that she'd likely never imagined all these fruits existed.

When his meticulous scan of the crowd turned up nothing, Christophe led her past sellers of beaded jewelry and ceramics, toward the road that would lead them out of town. As much as he wanted to savor this time amid the comforting scents of fresh-cut guava and exotic wildflowers, he had to take her to safety before Blanc or anyone else spotted them. He must deal with those traitors on his own.

Jane paused along a wall with chipping paint, beside which a group of men played various musical instruments. Christophe was about to explain the unusual sound rising from the steel drums when he noticed her attention diverted elsewhere. Seemingly oblivious to the vibrant music, she had narrowed her focus on a group of drawings tacked to the wall.

"Is this—" Her finger indicated a crude drawing of a vicious-looking man with a scar across his forehead and unkempt hair hanging around his face. Beneath the gruesome drawing read the name "Danglar" in red painted letters.

Christophe drew near, glancing uneasily around. "Yes, I'm a wanted man in many places," he said quietly into her ear. "Though you needn't worry. The local authorities have never connected me with Danglar. I'm in good standing with the governor. I've even dined at his home on occasion."

Her brows lifted. "You're worth a lot of money. Perhaps I should turn you in." She flicked an amused look his way, her playful expression making his urge to kiss her unbearable.

Instead, he leaned close enough for his lips to brush her ear. "I'm a dangerous man. I wouldn't suggest it."

Jane merely simpered, looking back at the over-exaggerated depictions of ghastly pirates adorning the wall. "There are lady pirates?" Her hand hovered over a drawing of a woman with light braided hair and a wide-brimmed hat pulled low across her steely brow.

"Aye, that's Bonnie Robbins." Christophe moved back, shaking off an involuntary shudder. "I've sailed with her before, and believe me, she is no lady. She has a fouler mouth than any man I know, and she finds no reason too small to fight. She tried to stab me once for beating her at whist."

Jane chuckled, the angelic sound delighting him. "She sounds like fun." Her head angled. "I think I look a little like her. If I wore a hat like that and tried to appear angry."

Christophe scoffed at the preposterous idea. "Besides your hair color, there is nothing alike about you. This woman breathes insanity."

Almost without thought, his hand sought hers again, and she willingly turned her palm to meet with his. Christophe tried to ignore the heavy weight pulling him down with every step they took toward the mission. Yet as the rumble of town and the odor of rum melted into wild grass, he knew he couldn't escape reality. He would never again hold her hand, never again relish her feminine scent or feel her silky hair beneath his fingertips. His thoughts spun in a dismal whirlwind until the Anglican mission at last rose into view above the blustery treetops.

In silence, Jane stared at the whitewashed walls and gray-capped roof with a cross affixed to the center. It felt more like a burial ground than a place of hope. At last, she inhaled deeply and pressed on, never letting go of his hand. They wandered up to the building until its shadows engulfed them, blocking any sunlight in their path. A studded door lay within an alcove, and Jane moved toward it without a word.

Flexing his forearm, Christophe pulled her backward. Jane stared at the ground, her nostrils flaring, every lovely feature of her face holding back tears. "Jane." His hand instinctively cupped her face, his fingertips brushing her cheekbone. "Please don't do this."

Her shimmering eyes reluctantly climbed to meet his, the pain in them agonizing. Why couldn't he let go of his pride and take this woman instead? She would bring him so much more joy than revenge ever could. Still, the fire of indignation burned in his center. He couldn't forget what Blanc had done. He couldn't forgive as Jane would.

"I—" Before she could utter another word, he eliminated the space between them and captured her in a passionate kiss. Her tears salted his lips. Her thundering heart matched his own. Jane returned his fiery kisses, her fervor unbridled, her love for him manifest in the way she clung to him.

But when he lifted his face from hers, the hope in her eyes crushed him. "Stay with me," she said. "Build a life for us. Don't chase after them, Christophe. Please. I can't watch you be killed."

His Adam's apple bobbed, his throat and chest on fire. "I wish that I could. I want to let go."

"Let go, Christophe." Her warm hands sheltered his. "I'm here to catch you."

Everything inside of him ached at her words. How much he wanted to let her, but the rage inside him refused to retreat. "I—I can't." It stung just to say.

Disillusionment clouded her eyes again. Jane stepped backward, letting him go and bending to retrieve her valise from the dust. "Then I must do this." She blinked back her tears, gazing at him sadly one final time before turning and advancing toward the door.

With a knock and a greeting to the nun who met her on the other side, she vanished into the stone walls and out of Christophe's life forever.

C hristophe waited for nightfall to enter the town again. By then, the streets had come alive with merriment and the blaze of torchlight. Navigating to an inn he had employed many times before, he checked in and left his belongings on the bed inside his room. After changing his shirt and tethering his hair at the nape of his neck, he pocketed a few bills and left for the task ahead.

The air outside the inn smelled of roasted nuts and grilling fish from the local eateries. Piano music jangled from an open door, its charming melody spilling into the unpaved street. Christophe scanned the people still milling about as the market closed down, recognizing no one. All of the town's activity seemed to dwell in the public house with the chipper music and several more businesses lining the street.

Setting his sights on a tavern he frequented often while in Bridgetown, Christophe crossed the street and eased through the swinging double doors. Immediately, the odors of sugared rum and heady cigar smoke greeted him. He carefully surveyed the crowd of men inside, some hardened sailors and others well-to-do businessmen looking to alleviate their stress with a game of cards. One's station in life mattered little in a place like this—only one's freedom to spend money. Christophe shivered to think of the myriad slaves chained to this beautiful island.

Relieved to find none of his former shipmates yet occupying the tavern, Christophe snaked between the tables and approached the bar. "A glass of rum," he told the barkeep, "and anything you have to eat." His rumbling stomach reminded him he hadn't eaten since morning, but watching Jane walk out of his life forever had soured his appetite.

The burly man returned with a glass of sloshing liquor and a plate containing a questionable looking meal of rice, stewed chicken, and breadfruit. Christophe paid him and accepted the meal with gratitude, then turned toward a table in the corner. He had already spied the man he wished to speak with, sitting alone amid the revelry with a book propped open in his hand.

Barnaby Wolton, as his British Christian mother had once named him several thousand miles from here, hadn't changed much in the years since Christophe had last seen him. He still wore a crooked powdered wig and spectacles that had gone out of fashion a decade ago. His rounded belly shook as he chortled at the book in his hand—a collection of satire, if Christophe had to guess—and took a swig of ale.

"Mind if I sit?" the captain asked, standing over his old friend.

Barnaby started, his wrinkled eyes jetting from the page. "Why, Christophe Roux." An infectious smile spread over his face. "I wondered when I might see you. I noticed your ship docked in the harbor several days ago. Please"—he gestured toward an empty chair opposite him—"rest your legs. I have been hoping you would show up."

Taking the indicated seat, Christophe watched with amusement as Barnaby fumbled for his napkin and dabbed at the ale puddling around his mouth. How such a clodhopper had achieved his high-ranking position, he often wondered. Perhaps his wealthy father had years ago found a way to distance him from the family without shaming them.

"Forgive me for taking so long," Christophe said, settling in and grabbing his fork. "I had business to attend to before making my usual rounds." He saw no need to expose the fact that he no longer captained the *Licorne*. He couldn't afford to arouse suspicion, even in a friend like Barnaby Wolton.

Barnaby's white head bobbed. "Now, that is something I can commiserate with. The governor has kept me quite busy these past few months with negotiations and the passing of new bills." He released a breath from ballooning cheeks. "The job of magistrate isn't what it used to be."

Christophe cocked his head, finishing his bite of surprisingly good pork before speaking. "What sorts of negotiations does he have you working on?"

Eyes widening, Barnaby glanced around before leaning inward. "With the land owners. They're bringing more slaves to our shores every day. The governor is afraid of an uprising if they can't keep their slaves happy."

"A happy slave?" Christophe laughed dryly. "Does such a person exist?"

"Precisely. They think because they let their slaves throw parties and give them extra rations at Christmas that they're content. We've had to double the number of soldiers in our streets for fear of a revolt." The magistrate slumped as if the very thought exhausted him.

Uneasy, Christophe took a drink of rum. Even more law enforcement crowding the town did not bode well for him. If somebody uncovered his true identity, he doubted even Barnaby or his weak association with the governor could save him. Besides, neither would have much desire to do so when they found out who he really was.

Just then, the tavern doors punched open and in strutted a group of familiar sailors. Christophe stealthily watched them, Barnaby's jawing a mere hum in his ear as Blanc and a handful of his cronies selected a table and plunked into the seats. Blanc hailed a barmaid, his brow haughty and nose snarling as if he owned her and this place. Already, the title of "captain" had gone to his head.

"Excuse me a moment, if you would, Barnaby." Christophe pushed off his chair, hardly able to contain the rage blazing down his arms. He could whip out his gun and put a bullet in the back of Blanc's head at this very moment. As much as this knowledge tempted him, he calmly strode to the table with all the control he could muster. The British authorities would have him at the gallows by sunrise if he committed cold-blooded murder in such a public place.

"Have room for another?" he asked the group already distributing cards for a round of commerce. Blanc's back stiffened at Christophe's voice, his narrowed eyes slowly ascending the newcomer.

Without waiting for a reply, Christophe slid into a chair beside him and opened his hands to receive his share of cards. The sailor dealing them hesitated for a brief moment, waiting for Blanc's nod. Christophe clenched his teeth to keep his anger at bay. How quickly his *loyal* crew would replace him.

The game passed like any other to the outside eye. Barnaby had returned to his book, seemingly unconcerned with the rude interruption. Blanc glared at his cards, his noxious scent quickly traveling in the confined space.

"What do you want?" he growled, not daring to shift his gaze Christophe's way.

"I believe you know what I want." Christophe leaned forward, setting several chips in the table's center. "A real man doesn't cower when bullies come to steal his possessions."

"*Your* possessions?" Blanc snorted. "The *Licorne* was never yours. You stole it, same as me. Chapelle probably stole it, too. It's our way."

Bile rose in Christophe's throat. He never *stole* that ship. He had always loved and cared for it, perhaps more than any of his human connections. "It was never our way to kill innocent men. It was never our way to murder our own."

"Tell that to Chapelle." Blanc tossed two cards down and picked up two more. "Besides, Simon was never innocent. He played a part in your scheme. The two of you plotted to get the crew drunk so you could take the treasure for yourselves." Anger blazed behind his eyes. "Did you come all this way because of your own pride? All that wealth wasn't enough for you?"

Christophe bit his tongue. Blanc had correctly disassembled his plan, but not his motive. It would do no one good to reveal the truth—that orphanages throughout France were now sharing the Moon King's treasure. Surely that would make them all targets for rogues like Blanc.

Glancing around the circle of his former crew, Christophe noticed both animosity and interest. Did enough of them still harbor loyalty in their hearts for him to stage a coup? Perhaps, but he couldn't take the chance. Not with Jane and people like Barnaby here, blameless people who could become unsuspecting victims in their power struggle.

"The government here still believes you run an upstanding business," Christophe said to Blanc. "I could easily dissolve that misconception, but I would have to expose myself in the process and watch from the gallows as they confiscate the *Licorne* for themselves."

Blanc grunted an affirmative, his whiskered jaw tensing. "So, what do you plan to do? You can't hope to fight all of us. You'll meet the same fate as Simon did, only most of us will enjoy its execution much more."

Christophe laid a winning hand on the table. "I have no wish to fight my crew. Just you." He watched Blanc's chubby fingers whiten around his cards. "If you're the brave captain you espouse to be now, meet me on the rocks in an hour. We'll settle this like men."

With that, he rose and sauntered back to Barnaby Wolton, leaving a ring of stunned expressions. Blanc couldn't refuse him now. He had put forth his offer loudly enough for the other men to hear. If Blanc didn't show, they would call him a coward. No one aboard a privateer vessel would respect a coward. And Christophe knew, with satisfying certainty, that he could win any battle Blanc brought to his door.

Twenty Five

T he wind whistled through the trees as Christophe trekked to the beach under a cloud-blotched sky. Even before he reached the shore, the scent of sand bathing in the briny sea pulled him onward. How many times had he walked this magical stretch of coastline, savoring the wild sounds and smells of primitive nature? Tonight, he would end Blanc's crusade to usurp him and take back what rightfully belonged to him.

Jane's eyes flashed in his mind again, and Christophe had to focus on his steps along the crude path to ignore their pleading. Seeking revenge and retaining his life of privateering meant letting her go forever. She wouldn't be content spending her days aboard a ship that fought and stole its way across the Atlantic. His chest ached. Was *he* content with it anymore? Hadn't he decided to give it up for her, for the withering soul within him that begged to live an honest life?

Emerging from the shelter of trees, Christophe set his sights on the beach's rocky section and forged onward. It didn't matter now what dreams Jane had kindled in him or the dissatisfaction plaguing his heart. The moment he'd seen Jacob Simon hanging from the *Licorne's* yards, everything had changed. The quartermaster's death would haunt him forever if he didn't avenge it.

The roving clouds prevented much light from seeping into the sultry air. Christophe peered through the muddled dark, making out the rough shape of boulders jutting up from the earth. The landscape here was referred to as "the rocks" by any seafarer who frequented these shores. They had long provided the natural cover necessary for nefarious deeds or those a man couldn't have the authorities notice. Christophe hoped they still turned a blind eye to what happened out here.

A hint of misgiving bit at his middle. He was, after all, one man facing what could become an entire crew. Would Blanc prove so cowardly as to ambush him? Christophe had to take that chance. If Blanc truly wanted to assert himself as their leader, he must meet any threat to his rule face to face. The men would never respect him otherwise. In a way, Christophe was merely giving the unseasoned captain an opportunity to authenticate his claim.

A slow smile lifted his lips as he charged along the rolling surf toward a figure standing atop one of the boulders. That rotund body with its arrogant stance could belong to none other than Blanc. Christophe drew his cutlass, his blood heating. How much he would relish making this false usurper pay for his crimes.

Blanc also drew his weapon, his sword flashing briefly in a strand of moonlight. He hopped inelegantly into the sand, his slow gait pointed Christophe's way. They stopped several paces from one another, eyes glaring through the dim light.

"I see you've come alone," Christophe said, scanning the rocks behind him. "That was wise on your part."

Blanc flicked his head toward a nearby dune, where a group of shadows milled in the darkness. "I brought enough to watch you fall—so there will be no doubt in my men's minds as to what transpired."

My men. Christophe's ire bubbled at the slob's impertinence. The *Licorne's* crew could never be Blanc's crew, and he would make sure of it.

"I hope they enjoy watching you die." Christophe's face scrunched into a scowl. "I know I will."

The insult was enough to propel Blanc forward. His giant feet plopped across the sand toward Christophe, his loose cotton shirt flapping in the breeze. Christophe stood tall to meet him, priming his sword, waiting for the precise opportunity to strike.

Within seconds, their swords clashed. Blanc wasted no time, advancing on Christophe like an unpracticed schoolboy with a stick in his hand. Christophe easily deflected the first few blows, noting the force behind each of Blanc's swings. What he lacked in grace, he made up for in sheer power. Christophe had often used him aboard ship to haul whatever he needed moved, as Blanc possessed the strength of two men.

Their dance continued on the tranquil beach, the clouds parting to expose the moon. Blanc was not the most skilled fighter among Christophe's men, but his swift movements never gave a moment's rest. Christophe whirled this way and that, defending his leaner frame, trying to get a blow in between Blanc's incessant hits. Their boots flung sand as they circled one another, a moving jumble of grunts and scraping steel.

At last, a weakness in Blanc's strategy presented itself. He could survive so long with brute force, but his stamina could never match Christophe's. The white moon revealed sweat emerging beneath his curly hair, slicking his hairy arms. Christophe had only to outlast him to win the match.

Summoning his fortitude, he escalated his attacks while Blanc's waned. Blanc's chest surged violently, his strikes growing weaker. When he left his side undefended, Christophe swooped in and nicked him in the arm. Blanc stumbled backward with a yelp, a small bloom of red spreading across his shirtsleeve.

Eyes round, Blanc tried to retreat, but Christophe pursued him with the point of his blade aimed at Blanc's rounded stomach. His opponent managed to thwart one last blow with a sweep of his sword, desperation seizing his face. "Now, men. Now. Attack!" He glanced wildly around at the blackened shadows behind him.

Christophe's blood went cold as three or four figures materialized from the sand. So Blanc possessed enough faith in his abilities to fight him, but not enough to face him alone? "You're a dastard, Blanc. You'll never be man enough to command my ship."

But it didn't matter now. Blanc's minions descended on him anyway, their shimmering blades pointed his direction, their dogged stares fixed on his weary form. Would any of Christophe's former sailors defend him after he'd exposed the utter fool they sailed under now? He didn't have time to wonder. Gritting his teeth, he lifted his cutlass, meeting each attack as it came.

None of these fighters matched his skill with a sword. Alone, he could have decimated them one by one. With each advancing from a different angle, Christophe found himself within a deadly trap, his every strike not a move to gain an upper hand, but a desperate attempt at survival. He fought them off for several minutes, slashing the air like a madman, the clang of steel reverberating over the quiet beach.

Cold sweat seeped into his brows, his hair coming untethered and flying around his face as he fought. Christophe's sword managed to connect with one man, the tip breaching flesh, a scream erupting into the night. He didn't have time to see where his blow had landed. Another sword came at his head, and Christophe pulled his weapon free to block the assault. Quick on his feet, he ducked another blow and struck his attacker in the thigh, buckling him.

Uncontrollable breaths rammed against Christophe's chest. His swollen muscles and aching legs pleaded with him to stop, but quitting at two men would mean certain death. Another blade flashed on his left, and he barely had the strength to subvert it. The assailant on his right lunged at his unprotected side, his blade diving into Christophe's torso. Blinding heat radiated from the spot where the sword split his skin. Christophe looked down to find a puddle of blood oozing through his shirt.

White spots blinked before his eyes, a dizzy sensation grabbing hold. Still he fought on, somehow injuring another of his foes. In a daze, Christophe weakly defended himself from his last adversary. Either the man possessed little skill and had kept back thus far, or he went easy on his former captain. Christophe couldn't even see who he fought through the blur. Backing across the bloody sand, he battled on until he found the opportunity to run.

Nobody gave chase. Perhaps his last weakling of a competitor had chosen instead to tend to his fallen comrades. Clutching his side, Christophe sprinted with all the force he could muster over the beach and into the cover of trees. Every fiber of his body screamed at him to stop and rest, but he hobbled on through the leaves and palm fronds, determined to escape anyone who might follow. The pain in his side built with every step.

With horror, Christophe dared to look down at his bloody hands, then the path behind him. Under the silvery moon shone a trail of dripping blood, tracking his every move. He would have to find a way to quell it and escape to shelter soon, or he would die in this jungle—one way or another.

*D*ear Father God—Uncomfortable, Jane repositioned herself on the bench. A groan echoed off the sanctuary walls with her every movement. *Our Father*—What? What did she want to ask him for? To tell him? Hadn't she flouted his every instruction by disobeying her parents and making a man the center of her thoughts these past few months? Would he even hear her after such flagrant disregard for his teachings?

Huffing, Jane opened her eyes to the church and slumped back against the pew. Four white-washed walls stared back at her, as if they could hear her silent self-censure. The air hung thick and moist, alive with the chirp of cicadas from the neighboring jungle. The mission's sanctuary held so little decoration compared to the churches at home—a domed roof with exposed wood over the altar, a row of clover-shaped windows, a chancel rail forged from iron. Every church should look like this, she mused, rather than man pouring senseless amounts of money into maintaining a lavish facade.

Jane leaned her elbows on the pew in front of her, pressed beneath her own guilt. Hadn't she spent her life enshrined in luxury, happy to let her father shell out ridiculous sums so she wouldn't want for anything? Hadn't she donned the silks and feathers a thousand times, traveling in velvet-lined carriages past people dying in the streets? The enormity of it weighed heavily on her chest. It shouldn't have taken the prospect of marriage to Lionel Davenport to wake her up.

She studied her hands in the church's dancing candlelight. The priest hadn't expected her to work that first day, but she volunteered her services anyway. Thanks to Christophe, she at least knew how to wash clothes. Now, her normally soft hands appeared a little more worn, rougher and drier from only one afternoon of toil. So much learning lay ahead. She would have to acquire the skills to cook, to clean, and to garden. Her rudimentary knowledge of mending would have to improve. A completely new person must emerge from within her.

Lifting her eyes to the wooden cross affixed to one wall, Jane found a prayer tangled somewhere within her thoughts. Not complete sentences, perhaps, but the rough formulation of a plea that only the Almighty would understand. If he had truly brought her to this point, he would guide her onward. He would piece together her splintered parts, mend her broken and battered soul.

But oh, how could she release the part of herself still yearning for the man she'd left behind at the church door? The part that desperately wanted to love him despite his flaws, to grow a family with him? How could she heal the wound he'd slashed open when he chose hate over the love she offered? She cradled her face in spread fingers, wondering if she could truly serve God as she pleased after what they had shared aboard the *Licorne*.

The priest had told her she had months before becoming a novice. Months to reconsider her plans, to become acquainted with daily life in the mission and decide if it truly suited her. Months to convince herself to leave her dreams behind. If only they would force her to take her vows this instant and lock her away without a say in the matter. The tiny inkling of hope still lingering in her heart brought torture.

Barbados had charmed her like no place before it—the stunning white sand beaches and exotic flowers, the colorful buildings and lively people. Jane had watched them dance and sing in town, awed by their happiness, their freedom of expression. More skin tones than she could have ever imagined graced the sun-soaked streets. This was truly a place of variety and untouched beauty. Jane couldn't help thinking God had truly led her here. If only she had stayed on the ship he put her on.

Footsteps pounding beyond the sanctuary's double doors directed her attention that way before one of them swung outward. A small, elderly nun dressed in a blue and white habit appeared beneath the doorframe, perspiration glistening on her dark skin. "Miss Whitecliffe, you should come quickly. You're needed in the rectory."

Frowning, Jane quickly rose and hastened down the center aisle. "What is it? Has something happened?"

Sister Agnes nodded rapidly. "A man is here. He says he knows you. He is injured—badly." With one sweeping hand, she directed Jane down a hallway lit with candles.

Jane's blood turned to ice. Snatching up her skirts, she didn't bother to wait for Sister Agnes's slow shuffle. Air blasted over her face and unsettled her hair as she ran, eager to reach her destination. She knew only one man in Barbados, and the thought of him in harm's way plunged her spirits so deep within her, she could barely breathe.

In seconds, she reached the church's stone entrance. A trail of droplets led from the door down a hallway leading to the rectory. Her stomach lurched at the sight of fresh blood. Jane ran without care over it, not worrying whether she would slip or dirty her shoes. She had only one thought in mind—get to him, help him, *save* him if she must.

Within the rectory's darkened hall, Jane found a chamber door open. Rushing inside, she first saw the priest and another nun bent over a bed, then a form writhing beneath their touch. Chest pumping, she flew around them to the foot of the bed. Her roiling stomach tightened. There, stretched across the sheets, was Christophe, his shirt stripped off his torso and a gaping wound on his side.

"What happened?" Jane steadied herself on the stone wall, suddenly dizzy.

The old priest glanced up from beneath bushy brows. "He won't tell us. It appears he's been stabbed, though." His eyes shifted warily back to the injured man. "He said he knows you. Are you not from England, Miss Whitecliffe?"

"I am." Jane's head bobbed desperately. "He brought me here. He is my—brother. He's my brother." She swallowed, chiding herself for lying, especially in God's very house.

Father Bryan exchanged a look with the nun beside him, but they kept whatever suspicions they harbored unspoken. "We do not condone violence here, but he clearly needs help. I've already sent for the surgeon. Perhaps you would like to tend to him until he gets here."

"Yes. Please." Jane swiped away a stray tear and accepted the bowl of warm water and cloth the nun extended. "I'll do whatever I can."

Sinking into a chair beside the bed, Jane let her frightened eyes roam Christophe's shaking frame. He had clearly engaged in a fight. He had cuts and purpling skin all over his exposed trunk and arms. His eyes fluttered deliriously, his skin sweaty and flushed. She doubted he even knew she was there.

Jane summoned her strength and wrung water from a cloth before pressing it firmly to his wound. It appeared someone had already stopped much of his bleeding, but still a steady trickle colored the mattress. Christophe cried out, his agony suffocating her. Suddenly, the words she had for God unscrambled. She knew exactly what she would pray for, plead for, and give her very life for if she must. *Save him, Lord. He is all that matters. I will do anything you ask, as long as you save him.*

Twenty Six

A light rain trickled over the lush Barbados countryside, battering the leaves outside the window and pinging the glass. Against the howl of wind, Jane tended Christophe's wounds by candlelight into the wee hours of morning. The surgeon had stitched him up hours ago, instructing Jane on properly cleaning the area. He didn't think the assault had breached any vital organs, but the captain would need monitoring and proper rest to heal.

Jane's shoulders ached and her eyelids drooped, but still she sat by his bedside, smoothing his fevered brow with a towel. His bandaged wound wouldn't need redressing for another few hours. Once, Sister Agnes shuffled in and offered to relieve her, but Jane insisted on staying. The elderly nun's wrinkled eyes said what the priest's had—that Jane had no hope of joining their ranks. They all saw through her lie about having a brother. But after being dismissed, Sister Agnes merely nodded and squeezed Jane's shoulder before disappearing into the hallway and closing the door.

Wearily blinking her way, Jane sighed. No civilized person had ever left her alone with a man before. Clearly, she and Christophe could be up to nothing indecent at a time like this, but still the action stung. Any dream she harbored of serving the Lord with her life had vanished the moment he stumbled through that door and her love gave itself away. When she peered through the muddled candlelight at his sleeping form, she ceased to care.

Despite her resolve, sleep overcame her several times. Jane woke with her head on the mattress beside his body or her arm draped gently over his legs. Each time, she tried to shake away her fatigue, but it wrapped around her like the sinister tendrils of a climbing weed. At last, her head found sanctuary nestled at his side, her hand softly rising and falling on his blanket-clad torso. The rhythm of his sleep overcame her, delving her into a foreign world with terrifying colors and sounds, all swirling incoherently about her.

After what must have been hours of delirious torture, a hand gently brushed her hair from her cheek. Jane smiled, imagining Christophe touching her, the two of them walking down a hallway of her father's estate. "Jane." His voice even sounded real. Her heart ached to know such a glorious vision only existed in her head, far from the island to which they'd journeyed.

"Jane." His voice came again, still weak but louder this time. Jane ripped herself from the dream, bolting up from the bed. Rubbing the lethargy from her eyes, she blinked several times before Christophe's face came into focus. He wore a placid smile, his hand gently rising to tuck a strand of hair behind her ear.

Her breath hastened, a smile overtaking her face. "You're awake." She glanced down at his bandaged wound. "How do you feel? Are you in pain?"

Christophe winced slightly, then masked any such involuntary actions. "Nothing I won't survive. I've been through worse a time or two."

Jane simpered. "That wasn't what I asked." Leaning down, she retrieved a bottle of rum from the floor. "Sister Agnes snuck this into the mission. Either that, or she had it on hand already."

Leaning forward, Jane sandwiched a hand beneath his pillows to prop his head up and held the bottle with the other. Slowly, she brought it to his lips, tipping it until the brown liquid could gush into his mouth. Christophe's eyes met hers over the bottle, the significance in his gaze unmistakable. This time, she held his meaningful stare, unshaken by the devotion she saw there. She wouldn't leave him again, no matter the consequence.

Once settled again, Christophe reached for her hand. Jane let her fingers entwine with his, enjoying their warmth and reassurance. How natural it felt for their palms to meet, for his thumb to brush her forefinger. Silently, she vowed to never take such simple touches for granted again.

"I was so scared," she finally said, gazing at their laced hands. "When you came in here bleeding like you were, I thought—" Her sentence faded into a choked sob.

"Oh, Jane." Christophe reached up to stroke her cheekbone. "I'm sorry. I didn't know where else to go. I knew I'd die if I stayed alone in the jungle. I never wanted to put you through that."

Her head shook vehemently. "No, I'm glad you came here. I'm glad I have the chance to tend your wounds. It will distract me from my worry."

He smiled sadly. "You will make a most excellent nun. Perhaps it truly is your calling after all."

Jane hesitated, her chest heavy. Could she tell him she didn't *want* to join the nunhood? That she wanted marriage, and family, and stability with *him?* Would he trample on her words and run back at his first chance to fight whoever had performed this grievous act? A leopard didn't change his spots. Hadn't scripture taught her that?

"How did you get this wound?" she asked, voice tremulous. "Did Blanc do this to you?"

A familiar ire flashed in his eyes. "Blanc couldn't hit me if I were standing still and unguarded, begging him." His lip snarled. "I challenged him to a fight and he lost. I had him. I was seconds away from ending his miserable existence."

Jane swallowed, her insides trembling. "What stopped you? How did this happen?" Her fingers curled around his. Was she grateful he hadn't added Blanc's murder to his list of indiscretions?

"He had a whole group waiting in the shadows, primed to ambush me." Christophe swore, his nostrils flaring. "The coward couldn't even face me alone."

"You fought off a whole group of them?"

He nodded. "Three of them. I had to run after one of them stabbed me. The fourth could have chased me down, I suppose. But he didn't." Bitterness plagued his eyes, shame over not beating them all.

Jane released a long-held breath. "I'm just glad you're here now. I hope Blanc doesn't follow you, hoping to finish what he started."

"He won't. Blanc is nothing but a worthless coward." His sorrowful eyes ascended to hers. "I wouldn't put you in that kind of danger. Blanc will run like he did before. Jump aboard my ship and sail off to God-only-knows-where, though he won't be captain for long. The crew will elect a new leader after his dastardly display tonight."

Her heart wrenched at the pain in his eyes. "I'm so sorry, Christophe. I know how much that ship means to you."

He stared at her for several seconds, his eyes bright in the frolicking light. Then his hand lifted to smooth her hair. "It means nothing to me now. Not with you in front of me."

Breath solid, Jane felt her heart flutter. Did he really mean it? Would he give up his life at sea for her? *Could* he? She had already promised God she would surrender anything to see Christophe live. She had believed their separation to be inevitable in the arrangement.

Jane tried to brush him off with a laugh. "That's the delirium talking." He had told her many times that the sea would forever hold his affection—nobody else.

"My mind is perfectly clear." Christophe cradled her face in his fingers. "When that sword pierced my flesh, my world turned upside down. I thought I was going to die." His head shook slightly. "I saw not the sea nor the *Licorne* in what I mourned to leave behind. I saw you. Only you."

Warmth and fear twisted around each other, sprouting in her middle and climbing upward. Jane held his steady gaze, wanting to believe him with everything in her. The vision of growing old with him, of creating new life together, tempted her beyond anything else this world could offer. But she'd witnessed the streak of hatred inside him, the hardness that arose from an existence built on a lie. He could not so easily abandon all he'd known for so many years. Her heart sat vulnerable, waiting to be crushed if she let too much of it go.

From down the hall, a clock struck four, its chimes echoing off the stucco walls. Coming forth from her trance, Jane let go of his hand and reached for the blanket sheltering his chest. "We'll talk about this tomorrow. It's time to redress your wound." Ignoring his affectionate gaze, she worked quietly, following the surgeon's instructions on keeping the newly stitched skin clean.

Proud of herself, Jane stood back and watched him succumb to sleep once more. She hadn't flinched at the sight of blood or at caring for a half-naked man, for that matter. She hadn't lost herself in his ocean-like eyes as they roamed her face in the candlelight. When first she had set sail over the Atlantic, she had doubted her abilities in every way. Months at sea had revealed her weaknesses, but taught her she could survive even when it seemed impossible.

A pounding from somewhere unseen swiftly sent her head that direction. Jane frowned, leaning toward the door, listening harder as it came again, more insistent this time. Sister Agnes must have been roused from her sleep, because moments later, her dragging footsteps scooted past down the hall. A squeal echoed through the vestibule, the front door creaking on its hinges. Sister Agnes's voice barely carried back to Jane, mingling with several men's.

Misgiving converted to fear, tightening Jane's throat. She glanced around the tiny room, envisioning their escape. Surely, she could force the little window open and crawl through, but she could never hope to carry Christophe with her. The surgeon had warned her not to move him, anyway. Sister Agnes's approaching footsteps escalated her fright to sheer panic.

A gentle knock sounded on the door before it opened and her face emerged from around the side. Her shining eyes first landed on Christophe before rising to Jane's pacing form. "There are men at the door."

Jane paused, summoning her most unaffected look. "What do they want?" As if she didn't know. Christophe thought Blanc and his men would run with their tails between their legs, but his very existence terrified them. Of course they would seek to finish the job they started.

"They're soldiers," Sister Agnes said, surprising Jane. "They've received word that a dangerous privateer by the name of Philippe Danglar is hiding out in our midst." Her eyes rounded, reeling to the sleeping man. "Is that who this is, Miss Whitecliffe?"

Blood boiling, Jane wrung her hands. Of course they would take the coward's way out, discovering Christophe's location, then sending the authorities to do the hard work for them. Blanc could reap all of the rewards without assuming any risk. He wouldn't get away with it this time. Jane knew what she must do.

"No." She stood tall and determined. "No, he is not Philippe Danglar. That is just a vicious rumor." Jane took a shaky breath, silently praying for courage. "I will take care of them, Sister Agnes. I will get them to leave."

Lingering at his bedside one last time, Jane softly touched Christophe's ankle. She tried to soak in the memory of his sleeping form—his quiet, gentle strength, the way his lips puffed with each breath. She never expected to look at him again.

Her footsteps clicked on the tile floor, ricocheting off the walls in the dead of night. Before she reached the vestibule, the angry orange flames of their torches guided her onward. A group of five men waited in the dirt outside the mission, their impatience growing each passing second. Jane sensed Sister Agnes somewhere behind her in the dark, but she marched up to the door with her head held high, determined to let the little nun hear what she needed to say. It didn't matter now, anyway.

"Good evening, gentlemen." Her eyes calmly swept the group of men garbed in red uniforms with white trim, the long guns strapped to their backs gleaming.

"Miss." One of them stepped forward, seemingly their leader. He tipped his bicorn hat.

"I hear you are looking for the famed Captain Philippe Danglar." She could say no more before emotion clamped her throat shut.

"We are looking for the *infidel* Philippe Danglar, yes." The man's probing gaze slipped past her into the mission's shadowed halls. "He attacked a group of sailors on the beach tonight, who told us we could find him hiding out here."

Attacked. The utter gall of these fools. Jane lifted her chin, vowing never to let them win. "I can assure you, no man named Philippe Danglar has breached these walls. Nor does anybody in this church know his whereabouts."

The man in charge studied her closely. "I appreciate your forthrightness, miss. However, I cannot take your word at face value. We *must* search the church and grounds for your safety as well as our citizens'. Philippe Danglar is a dangerous man."

He stepped up as if to move past her, but Jane set a hand on his arm. "Gentlemen, please. This is a house of God."

"All the more reason to rid it of sinners." Freeing his arm, the man strode into the vestibule with his comrades close behind.

Ice raged through Jane's blood, her gaze skittering past them and down the hall to Christophe's open door. She had no choice now. She must proceed, no matter the consequence. "Your informants are only correct on one account, sir."

The man frowned, turning her way. "And what is that?"

Jane glared at him in the flickering torchlight. "They didn't fight with Philippe Danglar. They fought with me."

He shared a glance with his men, his brows raised, before perusing her from her slippers to her swept-up hair. "And who might you be?"

Setting her jaw, she forced herself not to waver. "I am Bonnie Robbins, Terror of the Seas." Their confused expressions morphed to shock. "I am wanted for thievery, piracy, and the murder of two local lawmen." She recited the poster she'd read that day, conjuring the wrathful visage sketched on the paper.

The soldier drew his pistol, as did his men. "If you are Bonnie Robbins, why would you reveal such incriminating information about yourself? Certainly you know there is a bounty on your head."

She did, but the prospect of dying scared her so little when compared to watching the man she loved meet his end. "Because the good people of this church took me in, believing the false story I gave them." She looked at Sister Agnes, whose face was barely visible within the circle of torchlight. "They didn't know my true identity. They don't deserve to suffer on account of my sins. Leave them be and take me. I will go willingly."

In seconds, she was snatched up by two pairs of hands and led through the doorway. Jane peered back at Sister Agnes, whose lips were pursed and brows wrinkled. She knew the truth. *Please don't say a word. Please don't tell them.* Jane silently pleaded with the elderly nun, aware she could end Christophe's life with one wag of her tongue. Yet the old woman simply gripped the door and remained silent, a mournful look overtaking her as the officials led Jane away.

Relief flooded her, even as they marched her through the jungle toward the prison she'd spied in town earlier that day. Christophe had informed her that the gallows awaited anyone caught for the crime of piracy. The Crown had no mercy for such souls. Cold sweat broke over her brow to imagine a noose tied around her neck, a jeering crowd crying for her execution. When she had sat within her posh bedroom in England, free from danger, Barbados had looked like an exciting adventure. She'd never imagined this fate, let alone choosing it willingly.

Jane reminded herself over and again that Christophe would be safe. He could move on, find someone else to love, seek redemption for a soul long drifting through the murky waters of a dishonest life. He could be happy. As her feet plodded the grassy trail toward certain death, she held onto this hope and tried to forget what would become of her.

Twenty Seven

T he incessant chirp of a bird woke Christophe from his slumber. He blinked, his vision still fuzzy, his mind halfway between images of life aboard the *Licorne* and reality. A yellow slice of sunlight streamed through the window beside the bed, warming his skin. Christophe's gaze darted around the room to four plain, stucco walls, a table with a candle and a ceramic pitcher, an empty chair. Had he merely dreamed of Jane nursing him through the night?

His eyelids drooped and his head pounded. Christophe lifted the blanket covering his bare torso and spied the bandaged wound around him. The pain had subsided a little, but still it throbbed where the surgeon had stitched his skin together. Worse raged the ire inside him when he thought on Blanc's cowardly display last night. If he didn't have a better life to pursue, he would hunt him down and kill him—or perhaps die trying in his injured state.

A small knock tapped on the door before it crept inward. Christophe's heart leaped, expecting to see Jane on the other side. He had so much lost time to make up with her, so many sins to account for. But the kind face of an elderly nun startled him. Subconsciously tugging the blankets high on his chest, he watched her stooped form enter the room with a tray in her arms and deposit it on the table beside his bed.

"Good morning," Christophe said.

The old woman simply replied with a nod of her head, then turned to arrange the steaming food she'd brought. She wore a blue nun's habit that practically swallowed her tiny frame, her dark skin glowing in the morning sun as she worked. When she pivoted toward him with a bowl of what looked like porridge, Christophe smiled sheepishly.

"I suppose Jane is finally getting some rest," he said. "I'm glad of it. She needs it after tending to me all night." Though he'd have to quell his disappointment at sharing breakfast with this grandmotherly nun instead.

A small frown pulled at her mouth. "Miss Whitecliffe left the mission before dawn." She said it so matter-of-factly in her Caribbean accent that Christophe nearly missed her curious words.

"Left?" He sat up, heart thumping. Why would she have left after the conversation they'd shared? Had she run away again, knowing he'd never be enough for her?

The nun nodded. "The soldiers took her."

Christophe stiffened. "Soldiers? What soldiers?"

Sighing, the woman set the bowl on her tray and reeled back to him with black, sorrowful eyes. "The soldiers came looking for a pirate they were told was here—Philippe Danglar. Miss White-cliffe convinced them he wasn't here." She studied him, her shrewd gaze saying she knew every bit of the truth.

"If she convinced them, then why did they take her?" Panic seized him, gripping his throat in its ugly claws.

The woman's small shoulders lifted. "She convinced them she was another pirate named Bonnie Robbins, a woman wanted for theft and murder."

Her words funneled dread through him. "That's preposterous. She isn't Bonnie Robbins. Who would believe that?"

"I know she isn't." The nun pursed her lips, her hands folding in front of her. "The woman I met yesterday couldn't kill a housefly."

Christophe's mind raced with possibilities and upended plans. He threw the covers back, ignoring the screaming ache in his side as he sat up without concern and seized the bloodied shirt strung over his bedpost.

"The surgeon says you shouldn't go anywhere," the woman weakly protested. "He says you need rest to properly heal." She said it like a cursory rule she was compelled to, rather than something she expected him to do.

"I don't care what the surgeon says." Christophe's face emerged from the neck hole while his arms dove into the sleeves. "I'm going to get her."

Eyes emotionless, the hint of a smile crimped her lips. "I thought as much." She shuffled to the door, opening it wide for him. "I won't tell you there's an unattended wagon waiting outside the front door, either."

Christophe briefly touched her elbow as he rushed past. "Thank you."

When he attempted to run, his fatigued body and stinging side prevented him. Gritting his teeth, he hobbled down the corridor and into the dusty yard. A wagon with two horses waited just where the sister had indicated. Disregarding the flustered stare of a pair of nuns at work in the garden, Christophe climbed into the seat and released the brake.

The horses broke into a gallop beneath Christophe's prodding, dust clouding the air around their frenzied hooves. Air thick with vanilla-tinged durantas and bay leaves blasted over his skin as he drove, tossing his hair wildly behind him. He had no time to waste. They might have already taken her from the jail. The authorities liked to perform their executions early, when crowds gathered to trade at the market.

His stomach constricted as he rounded a bend and beheld a host of people already streaming toward the town square. They wouldn't rush like that without a spectacle. Imagining Jane paraded before them, a curiosity for their lurid amusement, drove him onward. Christophe nearly toppled the wagon as he sped down a hill, urging the horses into a breakneck speed.

Once he reached the crowd, Christophe had no choice but to hop down and dig his way through them. People of every variety crowded the stone square—old men, mothers, children whose eyes had opened too early to the dark realities of life. Their jostling launched bolts of unbelievable pain through him, but Christophe shouldered through the fog of body stench and tobacco until he neared the gallows.

Upon a raised platform strutted a man with burnished brown hair, wearing the red military uniform of the British Empire. He marched to and fro with his arms gesturing dramatically, rallying the excited crowd. Beside him, Jane stood with her arms tied behind her back, her blonde hair cascading over her shoulders. A thin trail of tears marred her cheek, but she comported herself with dignity, her chin up and shoulders pushed back. She looked like a warrior facing the enemy's blade.

"Good people of Barbados," her captor was saying, inciting a wave of shouts. "Before you stands the vilest of creatures. A woman known the world around for her nefarious deeds, her crimes against innocence, her complete disregard for the ways of civilized man."

The crowd answered back with a roar, whistles and jeers cast her way. Near the stage, someone tossed a tomato that splattered across her skirt. Christophe's hands clenched at his sides, fire burning down his arms. He wanted to decimate anyone who dared treat her in such a manner, yet he knew the blame rested on his shoulders alone. She only endured this wretched treatment for him.

"Bonnie Robbins has terrorized the Atlantic for decades," the man bellowed, his scathing eyes raking over Jane. "She has robbed countless ships, stolen priceless items that can never be replaced, even taken human life." His eyes turned somberly on the crowd.

"The soldiers she killed here last March were your kinsmen, men sworn to protect you at all costs. To some of you, they were friends, brothers, even sons."

Quiet now, the crowd listened with bated breath. Many bobbed their heads, some dabbing at tears. The man onstage whirled slowly, his hands clasped behind his back, his boots thumping the wood as he approached Jane. Behind him, the glorious beach with its white sand and frothing waves, its placid row of bobbing ships, contrasted bleakly with the gruesome scene onstage.

"This woman stole the lives of those brave men." His finger jabbed at her in accusation. "This woman, with her reckless behavior and flagrant contempt for law and the sanctity of human life. This woman, with her murderous assaults on innocent citizens of Barbados. The spirit of Satan leers from her eyes as if looking straight at us from Hell!"

The assembly shrieked, their eyes rounding in fevered madness, their fists rising to the sky. More items flew Jane's way—bits of lettuce, raw eggs, sludge scooped from the muddy street. Jane closed her eyes, absorbing every assault with a stoic face. The simple dress she'd worn when he met her, woven from the finest silks, was now blotched with filth, her beautiful hair drenched and dripping.

Christophe had but a few more paces left to conquer. He shoved his way through the infuriating mass, throwing civility to the wind. Something ripped at his side, a new stain of blood seeping through the dried one. All thought of his welfare vanished, his mind focused only on rescuing her. On atoning for his many wrongs.

"The choice is yours, my fine fellow citizens," the speaker said, his skin red and veins surging up his neck. "What would you have me do? How would you see her punished?"

A unanimous clamor boomed back, their shouts deafening. "Kill her! String her up and let the birds feast on her flesh!" Their frantic cry rose, their writhing bodies pressing toward the stage, nearly knocking Christophe over. Out of breath, he lurched toward the narrow staircase and gripped the rail.

"Enough!" he shouted, grabbing the immediate attention of the orator. He tried to scramble up the steps, but two soldiers blocked his path. Jane's eyes popped open, her tearful gaze finding him at the edge of the crowd and widening. Her head shook, her look mournful.

"You will let that woman go this very moment," Christophe said, frantically trying to paw his way past the guards. "You will loose her bonds."

An amused expression overtook her captor's face. "What's this sudden display of gallantry?" His eyebrow perked toward the crowd. "Does the pirate queen have a lover?"

The crowd chortled and jeered mockingly, shoving at his back. Christophe held his ground, his desperate attempts at reaching her failing as the two brawny guards seized his arms. Warning flashed in her eyes—the plea to turn and run while he still had the chance. But he would never leave her—not with breath still in his body.

"She's not a pirate." Christophe's skin flushed red from beneath his blood-stained shirt to his heated face. "Her name is Jane Whitecliffe, and she's the daughter of an English earl. She doesn't know the first thing about piracy."

The speaker stood to mock attention as if shocked, then bowed low before Jane. "The daughter of an earl? Forgive me, my lady." The gathered mass howled with laughter at his antics, its grating sound ringing in Christophe's ears.

"You can laugh all you want, but it won't change the facts." Christophe's eyes narrowed on the man. "If you execute her here today, Lord Whitecliffe will have your head. He isn't one to trifle with." Indeed, he would probably hunt down anyone involved in her capture, including Christophe.

Head wagging, the man clicked his tongue. "I will just have to take my chances, now won't I?" His leering eyes landed back on Jane. "Does *Lady* Jane Whitecliffe have anything to say for herself?"

Jane angled her chin up but said nothing. Madness rammed through Christophe's body. *Say something. Defend yourself.* But he knew why she wouldn't. She had intentionally let them drag her here like a lamb to the sacrifice.

"It seems our esteemed lady is a bit tongue-tied." The speaker puffed out his chest as the audience cackled louder. "Perhaps a noose around her neck might give her something to say." With a flick of his wrist, he signaled for a masked man standing nearby.

Panic surged up Christophe's chest. He tried to push past the soldiers again, but they held him at bay. With his injuries, he didn't have the strength to wrestle them both, and certainly the line of soldiers beyond the gallows would stop him if he did. Helplessly, he watched in horror as the enormous executioner led her to a spot beneath a dangling circle of rope and slipped it over her head. Jane uttered not a sound, her detached gaze fixed to the ground.

"You can't do this." Christophe's words sounded more like a plea than a command. "Where is the magistrate? Surely he doesn't allow you to execute whomever you please without his say in the matter." Barnaby would stop this. He had to when Christophe relayed Jane's true identity.

An unconcerned laugh flitted from the commander's rosy mouth. "The magistrate sleeps until noon most days. You won't see him in these parts, especially during an execution. He leaves such business to me. It proves too grizzly for his sunny disposition." He had somehow found a way to make Barnaby Wolton's humanity sound like a weakness.

"You will regret this, I promise you. I have the magistrate's ear *and* that of the governor. You will lose both your post and most likely your life if you kill this innocent girl."

The man shook his head with an exasperated sigh. "All this dramatic flair for nothing." His eyes rolled skyward. "The governor will commend me for what I'm about to do. There is no doubt in the matter, despite your groundless accusations. I have a signed confession stating that she is, in fact, the pirate Bonnie Robbins."

His words jolted Christophe, flooding his mind with memories. How many years had it been since he sailed with Bonnie Robbins? A woman that surly couldn't change too drastically in that span of time.

"You've already disproven your theory." Christophe looked straight at his opponent, clothed in surety. "I know Bonnie Robbins. She can't read or write a single word—not even her name. She signs an "x" to make her mark on papers."

The man's brows cinched slightly, though he covered his surprise with a cool smile. "And how might you know Bonnie Robbins? Does she often have you over for tea?" The crowd erupted in laughter again.

"Don't change the subject," Christophe growled. "That woman is not Bonnie Robbins, and I can prove it with her confession. I have samples of both women's writing in my keep." Or he would, if he could only get to the *Licorne*. He had assumed Blanc would run away like a frightened rabbit, but his beloved ship still graced the docks.

A change had come over the commander onstage. He must have sensed his folly in the matter, for he snapped his fingers toward the executioner. "Enough of this ridiculous exhibition. Let's be on with the task at hand." On his order, the masked man tightened the noose around Jane's neck, inciting the smallest of whimpers from her throat.

"No. You cannot do this. She is an innocent woman, I promise you." Christophe's muscular arms flexed in a last-ditch effort to push past the soldiers.

The commander turned to him, eyes aflame. "And why would an innocent woman offer herself up to be chained and imprisoned? Why would she sign a confession sure to bring a swift death her way?"

Christophe swallowed, knowing only the truth could fix this terrible moment. His gaze swung to Jane, who shook her head again, silently begging him to let her die in his stead. But he could never live knowing she'd taken the penalty for his sin on her blameless shoulders. Neither did he want to live without her. Ripping his gaze from hers, he set it firmly on her accuser. "She signed it to protect me."

A murmur rippled through the crowd. The man took a step toward him. "And who might you be, exactly?"

Lifting his chin, Christophe pushed off the guards and faced the crowd with his head high. "I am Christophe Roux. You know me better as Philippe Danglar, captain of the *Licorne*, dreaded Thief of the Atlantic."

Somewhere near him, a woman gasped. Whispers scattered through the crowd, their eyes turned up to him in fear and wonder. A sob issued from Jane's throat, wrenching his heart. He wanted a life with her more than anything now, but such a dream was doomed from the moment they met. Their worlds could never truly entangle. At least he might send her home, hoping she moved on from this dreadful chapter.

"Seize him." In a split second, two soldiers had clamped onto his arms and hauled him up the remaining steps. The crowd stood hushed now, waiting with bated breath to find out what would happen next. Christophe looked disdainfully toward the haughty commander, strutting around as if he'd conquered the mighty pirate who had walked willingly into his hands.

"You have me now. Let her go," Christophe said, unable to look at the crying woman beside him. "She never did anything wrong."

A clever smirk turned up the man's lips as he signaled for the executioner once again. "Oh, but she did. No matter if she is this Jane Whitecliffe you speak of, or Bonnie Robbins, or anyone else. She willingly attempted to abet a known privateer, and for that, the penalty is still death."

Christophe stared disbelievingly into the man's eyes, sickened by their victorious gleam. He would not only send an innocent woman to her death, but he would enjoy it. Ropes twisted around Christophe's hands before he could stop them, his fitful struggle useless as two more soldiers approached to hold him still so the others could tie him.

"Barnaby Wolton will have your head for this." His teeth clenched, every muscle in his body straining against their hands as another noose slid over his head. "You are skirting the due process of law, and you know it. There are hundreds of witnesses here. They will all see your misdeeds."

Against the excited shouts of the reanimated crowd, the commander merely laughed. "They see what they want to. And right now, what they want is both of your heads on a silver platter. I intend to give them just that."

He spun toward the crowd, stirring them up, his delighted cries regarding the combined deaths of Philippe Danglar and Bonnie Robbins whipping them into a fever pitch. The noose tightened around Christophe's neck, pressing his gullet. He began to shiver uncontrollably, not for himself, but for the woman at his side.

Lifting his traumatized eyes to her, he found her staring back. Her gaze—a more beautiful shade of emerald than he'd ever noticed—dove into his soul. Her compassion tunneled through his darkness, illuminating a soul he'd allowed to fester in misery too long. In his blackest moment, she brought him hope, just with the forgiveness written across her lovely face. How he wished he could reach out and touch her now, to pull her into his arms and promise that this nightmare would end in their reunion.

"I'm sorry, Jane." His voice shook out the whispered words, barely audible above the assembly. "I'm so sorry."

Her mouth lifted sadly, wisps of hair flying around her face in the wind. "I'm not. I met you, and that is enough for me."

Christophe stared helplessly at the woman he loved, the woman he would make his wife if given the chance. Everything else faded around him—the mocking crowd, the orator and his infuriating antics, even the call of his gleaming ship in the harbor. He saw only her, Jane Whitecliffe, the woman who had foolishly climbed aboard his ship and captured his wayward heart.

Almost without his knowledge, his thoughts melded into prayers. *She has served you faithfully all these years. Come through for her now. Save her in this most desperate hour. Not I, but her.* Would God even hear his prayers after a lifetime of running away? His pleas kept coming, rising unseen into the balmy air, begging a God he hadn't acknowledged since childhood to perform the impossible.

Peering at Jane's placid face, he suspected she did the same for him. The executioner stomped to the lever, rattling the boards beneath their feet. His hand rested calmly there, waiting for the speaker's instruction. Christophe reassured her with a tearful smile, savoring the impossible beauty of Jane's lips as they shakily lifted in return. Come what may, they would face the end together.

Twenty Eight

The terror had drained out of Jane as she stood beneath the gallows, waiting for her own death. Where once her body had trembled and her chest ached in painful gasps, now an inexplicable peace descended over her like a blanket of morning dew. She barely heard the soldier's animated talk of her execution, her eyes sweeping the trundling sea as it dumped onto shore in fizzling waves. The world went on despite her fear, the docks still swarming with activity, the birds cawing and diving through the air as if today were like all the others.

She turned to Christophe, his love for her evident in his tear-filled eyes. How strongly she wanted to free him of this moment. Perhaps, according to the law, he had earned it with his dishonest ways. All of England would celebrate the death of the infamous Captain Danglar. They would splash it across the headlines, whisper about it over their fancy suppers. But they would never know the man they spoke so flippantly about—a good man despite the sins he had committed.

Jane squared her shoulders, proud to die beside him. Let the record show that Jane Whitecliffe, not Bonnie Robbins, met her end trying to protect him. She didn't care who knew. Not a seed of doubt lingered in her mind now. The mission's advertisement had led her here, but she was meant to come for Christophe. In life or death, she would love him. She could harbor no regrets now, seconds away from her own demise. She could only gaze into his adoring eyes, happy to have known him.

A commotion stirred amid the listening crowd. Jane ignored it at first, used to the random eruptions that sprouted among them. Then a man's voice lifting above them snatched her attention. She knew that voice. Swinging her gaze to the source, she spied a small entourage of people weaving their way to the gallows from the docks. As the man at their head rose into focus, her breath stopped. "Father?"

"You will halt this execution immediately!" her father yelped over the bustling crowd. He frantically pushed through them, his velvet and lace clothes contrasting starkly with the homespun cottons around him. When he stumbled in front of the stage with his group of servants and advisors, Jane couldn't help her sudden surge of elation. He wore that familiar haggard expression, his white hair in uncommon disarray, his lips puckered beneath his trim mustache and beard. *Father.*

The commander froze his conceited swagger across the stage. One brow lifted, he regarded the intruder with a generous portion of skepticism. "And who might you be, to impede the just work of the law?"

Her father stepped forward with his hands planted on his hips, his elbows tented in his cloak. "I am George Whitecliffe of England, Earl of Brambleshire." The blood drained from the commander's face. "And this"—her father pointed up at her—"is my daughter, Lady Jane Whitecliffe, whom you've tied up like a worthless criminal and threatened with the noose."

Eyes darting between Jane and the earl, the commander appeared to weigh this new information. He could suppose her father was an actor sent to rescue her, but his details matched Christophe's too perfectly. Only a fool would disregard what he had to say, especially with his obviously fine attire and dedicated entourage.

"Lord Whitecliffe, if that is indeed who you truly are—" The man cleared his throat, plainly unsure of how to proceed. "Your daughter is not innocent in this matter. She stands accused of harboring a known pirate, of masquerading as a criminal herself to keep him out of the law's grip."

Lord Whitecliffe glared. "*Accused* is the operative word here. You have no proof. Even if she did claim a different identity, you cannot say for certain *why* she chose to do so."

The commander laughed mirthlessly. "Sir, why else would she assume the identity of a pirate woman already sentenced to death? It's quite obvious she was trying to shield her lover, here."

"Be careful what accusations you lay at the feet of a lady," her father spat through gritted teeth. "Now, you will release her bonds and hand my daughter over to me at once, or I will petition the king for your head on a spike, along with every person who contributed to her demise." His eyes narrowed darkly. "I warn you, sir, I have the power to do it, and swiftly. You will likely not see the end of the month if you proceed with your plans."

Face pale, the commander stared wide-eyed down at Jane's father a long moment before he swallowed and blinked toward the crowd. They all waited, craning their necks, eager to witness his next move. At last, he nodded toward the executioner. "Fine. Release her. Let the man have his scandalous daughter."

A buzzing murmur floated throughout the spectators again. Jane's hands quivered as the executioner untied her wrists and removed the rope cutting into her throat. Void of gentleness, he shoved her toward a soldier, who ushered her down the stairs without affectation and deposited her into her father's hands.

"Jane, are you all right? Are you hurt?" His hands hunted her dirtied face before he pulled her into a tight embrace. He had never held her with such unhindered affection before.

"Yes, Father. I'm fine. Thank you for saving my life." Her chest swelled with fresh sea air, at last able to breathe again.

"Let's get you into my hired carriage, shall we?" One hand pressed her upper back through her hair. "I brought a surprise with me—a friend I'm sure you'll be grateful to see again."

As if from thin air, a familiar face emerged from within his group. "Jane?" He looked the same as the day she had left him on the shores of England, his reddish-brown hair curling at the nape of his neck, his clothes perfectly pressed.

"Edward." Jane rushed into his arms, her filthy face pressing his pristine waistcoat without care. She clung to his tall, sturdy frame, grateful for the presence of a true friend. Who understood her better than the companion of her childhood?

"I thought I might die seeing you up there. Thank God you are safe now." His gloved hand swept her hair. "Let's get you out of here. Your father has made arrangements to rent a villa before we return to England."

"Wait." Jane resisted the hand that tugged her toward the street. Whirling, she saw with horror that the commander had resumed his spectacle and addressed the crowd again with fingers spread wide. Christophe peered down at her with sheer joy on his face despite his tethered hands and the rope still binding his neck.

Jane turned to her father. "I need to ask you a favor, Father. Please don't let them execute that man you see there. Can you force them to release him as you've done for me?"

The earl's brow scrunched as he glanced warily up at the accused prisoner. "Darling, he is a pirate. He deserves the penalty coming his way."

"You don't understand." She gripped his arm before he could turn away. "This man saved me, Father. That's why I said what I did. Without him, I would be dead. He doesn't deserve the punishment he's facing now."

Eyes tender, her father regarded her a quiet moment before looking again at Christophe. Then something steely and inhumane slid into his eyes. "I'm sorry, dear. A man like that is better off dead, no matter what he's done for you." Without another word, he spun and started toward his waiting coach.

"No." The word barely escaped her sore throat. "No, this can't be the end."

"I'm sorry, Jane." Edward offered a comforting hand to her shoulder, but she barely felt it.

Hot tears gushed from her eyes, streaking her dirt-caked cheeks. Jane looked again to Christophe, his stalwart form standing bravely, the wind beating his bloody shirt against his injured body. Hands rose to pull her away, but she fought their unseen grasp. "No. No!" Yanking her arms away, she staggered back toward the gallows, planting herself at the edge of the stage. She couldn't leave knowing he still stood under the executioner's grasp, but how could she watch him die?

In spite of his helpless position, Christophe looked like a man on his wedding day. He gazed down on her with such love, she could almost forget someone stood ready to end his life. Jane soaked in everything she could—the untamed hair blowing about his face, the fathomless blue of his eyes. "I love you," she whispered through her tears, her weight of emotion both agonizing and wonderful.

Hands again seized her arms and hauled her backward. Jane struggled at first, the fight inevitably yanking her away from him. The crowd's deafening plea to kill the man she loved merged into a confounded jumble to her ears. She saw only him—the brave captain of the *Licorne*, her protector and defender, the face she would carry with her always.

A streak of white flashed in the corner of Jane's vision. Curious, she turned her head to see a stocky old man with a crooked powdered wig running their way, waving a slip of parchment in his hand. "Wait." Jane's gaze flew back to the executioner, whose fingers coiled around the lever to release it. "Wait! There's someone coming."

The commander ignored her, lifting his hand to signal Christophe's hanging.

Jane's heart thumped under her ribs. "I said to wait. It appears someone has a message for you."

"The magistrate approaches!" someone behind her yelled.

With a flicker of irritation, the commander dropped his hand and spun toward the newcomer. "What now?" At the sight of the out-of-breath old man, he stood a little straighter. "Sir Wolton, what might we do for you today?"

Wolton stumbled past Jane and up the steps, glancing briefly at Christophe before addressing the tyrant on stage. "I have in my hand official orders from the government of France," he declared, igniting scattered whispers across the crowd.

"They came across my desk last night, but I didn't see them until this morning." He giggled slightly, then reached into his pocket for a pair of spectacles. "That's better now." Clearing his throat, he peered through the glasses teetering precariously on the end of his nose. "By order of Napoleon and the nation of France, Christophe Roux—otherwise known as Philippe Danglar—is officially absolved of his crimes against the Republic and free to live his life in peace from this day hence."

The commander's mouth hinged open, the breath momentarily punched from his chest. "Well, I—" He shook himself. "What manner of events brought such a bold declaration about?"

Wolton pivoted to Christophe with a smile. "It says here that he is responsible for finding the long-rumored treasure of Henri Clement and bringing it back to Europe."

The other man scoffed. "So he finds a fortune for himself and gets rewarded for it? Why would Napoleon issue an official pardon for that?"

"Aw, but he didn't keep it for himself." Wolton paced forward, gesturing the executioner away before clapping Christophe's shoulder. "He saw the treasure safely off his ship and into the hands of a local diocese. He was nearly killed for it, lost his quartermaster, and his ship."

Chaotic murmurs swelled among the crowd. The commander glanced nervously their way, as if still grasping for any type of vindication. "What does the government of France have to do with our fine island? We are under the rule of King George, not Napoleon. He has no say here. This man has committed the vilest of acts to *our* citizens."

Wolton reached into his jacket and pulled out a stack of parchment. Holding it up for the crowd, he grinned. "I have here orders from King George, Ferdinand, King of Spain, Frederick of Denmark, every political power in Europe. They have all agreed to renounce their claim on this man's life and grant him an official pardon for his heroic acts in service to the Church."

Stunned into silence, the commander watched dumbly as Wolton tucked his orders away and reached up to free Christophe. Jane had stood fixed in place, resisting the hands pulling on her arms, her blood like ice. Now, relief flooded her in trickling warmth. She beamed up at Christophe, joyful tears rushing down her face. His eyes never left her, even when the noose passed over his head.

The excited crowd drowned out what he said to the magistrate. Christophe appeared deathly serious a moment before his face brightened and the two embraced. Then, something changed in his face when he gazed across the mass of people. His joy dissolved to anger.

"There." Christophe aimed his finger toward the edge of the crowd near the market. Jane turned to see Blanc and a group of his closest companions. "Those are the men who murdered Monsieur Simon, who stole my ship and ambushed me last night. If anyone deserves death, it is they."

Blanc whitened, coming to attention as the commander signaled and a cluster of guards moved his way. Unable to escape, he whispered something to a small man beside him, who ducked into the crowd and disappeared. Blanc glared back at Christophe, letting the swift soldiers bind his hands behind him. "You won't get away with this, Roux!" he shouted. "You will regret this!"

Wolton shook his head, a frown on his face. "We'll not have any more of this spectacle today. Take them to the prison until I decide what to do with them." As a soldier nodded and rushed off with his orders, Wolton turned toward the commander. "And let's not perform any more executions without my say-so, hmmm? It doesn't sit well with me that men are dying without my knowledge."

Enraptured with the scene, Jane almost didn't notice Edward at her side again. "We should go," he said. His concerned gaze wandered her face before lifting to Christophe. "This isn't a safe place to be right now, Jane. I don't want you getting hurt again."

But she barely heard him. The corners of Jane's mouth tugged upward in response to the look of sheer adoration shining her way. What would her father say when she told him she wanted only this man—a pirate, a man without station or even moral ground to stand on? Somehow, she didn't care. When he descended the stairs toward her, she decided she would not hold back. She would display her love for all the world, Edward and her father included.

Just then, an explosion erupted along the water's edge. Gasps filled the air around her, women shrieking and pointing toward the harbor. Confused, Jane followed their pointed fingers as several more explosions rocked the beach. Her heart stopped. There, bobbing atop the shallows and engulfed in angry flames, sat the *Licorne*.

Christophe staggered forward, watching helplessly as the mast and sails fell, the remaining men on board diving into the ocean. Orange flames tinted the sky in acrid smoke, reflecting in the captain's horrified eyes. Jane's stomach turned. Blanc had no reason to burn the *Licorne*, except to punish Christophe. Utter sorrow teemed from his aghast frame as he dropped to the ground on his knees.

Jane instinctively started toward him, but a hand on her shoulder halted her. She looked up into Edward's hazel eyes, full of concern for her. "We should go," he said again. "Please, Jane. I *must* get you to safety."

Everything in her screamed to console Christophe, whose crumpled body knelt in the dirt, overtaken by sobs. She'd only ever seen him cry like this once, and never in public. Would he even acknowledge her in his present state? Her hand reached out but didn't touch him. Words failed her. At last she nodded, taking Edward's arm. Nothing could comfort Christophe now. Nothing could bring back his beloved ship.

Jane hadn't noticed her dirty and ragged condition until she stepped into her father's hired coach. The red velvet interior smelled of sweet pipe tobacco, its lush seats gliding beneath her fingertips as she sat beside the earl. Cleanliness and luxury enshrouded her, oddly familiar despite her months at sea. It felt like picking up a horse's reins after not riding in years. She intuitively knew what to do here.

Soon, the wheels began to spin and the carriage swayed past Christophe, still cloaked in inconsolable weeping. Jane stared after him as long as she could. Guilt bit low in her gut to leave him there alone. But as the coach hauled her farther from his dismal sight, his reaction replaced her guilt with fear. Christophe may love her, but would he ever care for her like he did the sea or the ship now crumbling beneath licking flames of fire? Could he leave it all behind without resenting her?

The answer terrified her. Jane endured the rest of the carriage ride in silence, praying she would prove enough for Christophe Roux.

Twenty Nine

D inner passed without Jane's notice. Though present in body, her mind drifted to the town square where she'd last seen Christophe pouring his heart out for his lost ship. Conversation hummed around her—the earl jawing about all the goings-on in London, Edward politely engaging him. Jane often felt her lifelong friend's eyes on her as she pushed her steak around her plate and barely ate a morsel. Somehow, she couldn't bring herself to eat knowing Christophe suffered.

She sighed against her stays, unaccustomed now to their constant presence. On board the ship, she had worn only necessary undergarments and whatever clean clothes she had. Now she sat within a rose-printed silk gown trimmed in lace with an elegant silhouette and a sweeping train. As soon as they'd reached the villa, her father had ordered her upstairs for a warm bath laced with milk and rosewater. A skilled maid had stood ready to style her hair into curls and pin them at the crown of her head. She had everything she could dream of again—fine clothes, delicious food, safety. Everything except him.

"This war with the United States will blow over before you know it—mark my words," her father was saying. "They are just being haughty because of their victory in the rebellion. We have a far superior navy. They will run back to their shores with their tails between their legs."

Edward retrieved his crystal goblet. "I wouldn't be so sure about that. They proved a formidable force in the Revolution. One mustn't discount them so quickly." He took a swig of claret.

"Ah, that was luck and a handful of bad decisions made by Cornwallis." The earl swiped his wrinkled hand through the air. "They're not established enough yet to take on a force like the British Navy. If they weren't still so reliant on trade with our great nation, we wouldn't be in this mess to begin with."

With a small shrug, Edward looked to Jane across the table. "What do you make of it, Jane? Does the United States stand a chance in their fated war with us?"

Jane blinked, color flooding her cheeks to notice both pairs of eyes pinned on her. She'd been immersed in rampant thoughts of the captain and his burning ship. "I—I don't have many thoughts on such matters, I'm afraid. I would rather stick to talk of the latest marriage at court."

Edward and her father shared a laugh. "Come now, we all know that's not true," Edward said. "You have never hampered your political opinions with me, even in the presence of ladies who do talk of nothing but the latest scandal."

Her father's seat groaned as he leaned inward with a sly grin. "You think I haven't noticed you sneaking my newspapers and reading them at your leisure? I'm quite aware I didn't raise a wilting flower, Jane Whitecliffe."

A tentative smile pinched her lips. "I suppose I'm not the most gifted actress, am I?" Her chest expanded. "The truth is, I'm not capable of pondering such matters at the moment. I have much weighing on my mind after what I've experienced." They had spoken little of her flight from England, but her father had managed to coax out pieces of her journey. He at least knew of Christophe's battle with Dominguez and how the captain had endangered himself to bring her here.

Edward's face turned compassionate. "That is understandable. You've been through a great deal."

Clearing his throat, Lord Whitecliffe tossed his napkin on the table. "I do believe supper is finished, unless anyone protests." When his raised brows elicited only silence, he pushed off his chair. "Why don't we have a chat in the parlor, Jane? There are some matters I wish to discuss."

A dizzy sensation showered over her as Jane rose and took his extended arm. Edward politely excused himself, apparently well aware of the talk that needed to be had. With great effort, Jane put one foot before the other, matching her father's calm walk out the door and down a hallway glittering with candelabras. The villa he had rented had a long corridor overlooking an impressive vestibule below. A residence fit for a king.

The parlor he led her to glowed with light from a marble hearth, even as open windows emitted the ocean breeze. The tangy scents of grapefruit and wild blossoms drifted in, mingling with refined mahogany and vanilla from inside. Jane took a seat in a green suede slipper chair, watching as he deposited himself onto a matching settee with a moan. Perhaps her clandestine journey had aged him beyond the natural consequence of years.

They both stared into the snapping fire for an expanse of minutes, neither willing to broach the uncomfortable topic lingering between them. When Jane managed to look into her father's eyes, the softness there startled her. She had expected censure for her actions, not the love she saw teaming from his wrinkled face.

"I'm sorry, Father." The words poured out like an unstoppable flood. "I didn't mean to hurt you when I left."

He held up a hand. "The fault lies with me, darling. You have nothing to apologize for." Inhaling through his nose, he shook his head. "I regret to admit that I was more worried about my business prospects than I was about my own daughter. I should never have chosen a man like Lionel Davenport for you to marry, let alone tried to force you into the arrangement."

Relief surged through her. "So you won't make me marry him?"

Her father laughed with a snort. "The cad is already married. As soon as you jilted him, he found an equally wealthy countess—a recent widow—and wed her instead."

"Oh Father, I am sorry. That must have caused you a terrible scandal."

"I'm not. The two already live in separate estates after news of several illegitimate children reached the ears of court. Davenport isn't even feigning a proper union with the poor woman. He's simply using her money to entertain more women and feed his gambling addiction."

Jane pressed a hand to her throat. "Oh my, that is unfortunate news."

Regret laced her father's tender eyes as they took her in. "It has become glaringly evident to me that my own wrongs have clouded my judgment in regard to my eldest daughter, and I will not have it. You are not a medium for negotiation, Jane, and I will never treat you as such again."

A single tear slipped down her cheek. "Thank you, Father."

He sighed, his lips compressing. "Now, I won't pretend that a life on an island like this one is what I dreamed for you, or that I want you to take on the mantle of nunhood as you planned."

Jane chuckled. "I doubt they would even have me after I claimed to be a pirate and was arrested on their doorstep."

An amused light brightened his eyes. "Assuredly not, but anything might be arranged if you wanted it." He paused, his face growing serious. "Is that what you want, Jane? To become a woman of the cloth?"

The question halted her. *Did* she want to throw off her earthly desires and devote herself wholly to God? The idea had felt so right under the threat of marriage to Davenport, but now it seemed rather like a death sentence. A world beyond the mission's walls waited to be explored, a world in which she could serve God *and* have the life she'd always dreamed of.

At long last, she shook her head. "No, Father. It's not what I want." Could she tell him she desired marriage to a privateer—one who might never be happy again, now that his ship had gone up in smoke? "I want to marry a man I love, a man of my choosing. I want to have a family."

A slow smile spread over her father's face. "I can give you that much. You needn't run from me again, I promise." He reached out, capturing her hand in his warm grip. "A man learns a lot about himself when he sees his beloved daughter on the brink of death. It makes him reevaluate his priorities."

"Standing on the brink of death does the same." Jane thought back to that moment, the unblemished devotion she had felt for Christophe. No doubts had plagued her mind, just pure and honest love.

The earl's fingers tensed on her arm, attracting her gaze. "That brings me to what else I wanted to tell you." His gaze swept to the closed door. "I will not compel you into any unwanted engagements this time. But I do believe there is a fine alternative waiting in the very next room."

Jane's mouth opened. "Edward? Surely you are jesting."

His head cocked knowingly. "Is the idea so hard to imagine? The two of you have gotten on like two chicks in a nest ever since you were babes. I can't believe I didn't see your obvious endearment before."

She swallowed. When first presented with marriage to Davenport, Jane had *wished* for Edward to propose instead. Perhaps there had never been love between them, but friendship trumped a life of inevitable misery. Yet after knowing Christophe, she could never settle for a lukewarm union.

"Edward and I are merely friends, Father." Uncomfortable, she fiddled with the pearl bracelet clasped around her wrist. "He is the best companion a woman could ask for, but he's never felt that way about me."

"Oh, I sincerely doubt that."

Jane's cheeks heated. "I know him. He needs a woman who is gentle and demure, who loves Beethoven as much as he does. He would never be content with me."

"Then why did he ask me for your hand?"

Her gaze flew up. "He—" Her breath stuck in her throat. "What did you say?"

Earl Whitecliffe chuckled. "He asked for permission to marry you, my dear. You don't think a man would cross an ocean into a foreign world for a woman he doesn't love, do you?"

"I—I thought he was merely being the good friend he always was." Her brows cinched. "He really asked for my hand in marriage?"

Her father patted her hand. "Why don't you discuss it with him, hmmm?" Rising, he disappeared before Jane could unravel her own thoughts, and a new face materialized at the door.

Edward quietly closed the door behind him, then turned to Jane, who had risen on unsteady legs. He looked more nervous than she'd ever seen him, his hands fidgeting and gaze darting about as if searching for an invisible source of comfort.

"Did you ask my father for my hand in marriage?" She had no use for pretense. Edward had been her best friend since as far back as memory would allow.

He took a breath, daring to entangle his gaze with hers. "I did."

The fireplace's heat flamed from her hands up the lengths of her arms. Jane studied him in the edge of the glowing firelight, fussing with his silk cravat, the chest beneath his cream-colored waistcoat surging. Had he taken such a bold step simply to rescue her, or had he developed genuine feelings for her?

At last, he trod her way until only an arm's length of sultry air separated them. "Look, Jane. I know this probably comes as a shock, especially after I let you get on that ship without ever saying a word. I didn't expect to feel the way I did when you left."

Jane searched his hazel eyes, looking for the love she saw in Christophe's. "Which was?"

"I honestly don't know." Edward rubbed the back of his neck. "I suppose I had never really thought seriously about the two of us. But when you left"—his brows knit—"I can't explain it. I felt like a part of me had gone, too. I missed you, Jane. More than I ever expected to. I never realized the emotional connection we shared until that moment."

Her mouth lifted. "I missed you, too. You're my best friend. But Edward, I think you're confusing the bond of good friends with romantic love." She might have, too, on that day they said goodbye. But the difference blared after having known Christophe.

"Perhaps I am." He sighed heavily. "All I know is that I worried every day for your safety. I couldn't get you out of my mind. I decided then that if ever given the opportunity, I would offer my hand to you. That I'd marry you before you slipped away from me again." He seized her hands, his fingers warm against hers.

Jane stared down at his hands for several beats. How easy a route lay before her. She could forget this place, the horrors of her journey, the pain of her near execution. A life with Edward would be comfortable and pleasant. He would never mistreat her, always support her. Yet why did her chest ache to consider it?

"Jane, look at me." At his bequest, she lifted her gaze to earnest eyes. "I know I should have done this years ago. I was foolish, thinking love came packaged in some sort of magical way."

"But it can, Edward—"

"But it doesn't have to." His raised brows implored her. "We already have what so many couples take years to build, if they ever acquire it at all. We love each other in a pure and honest way. You will never want for anything with me. We already know each other so well, there will be no surprises."

Jane tried to slip her hands from his, but he held her firm. "Edward." The hurt in his eyes tore through her soul. "I wish I could agree to this. I probably would have, had you asked before I boarded that ship."

A muscle in his jaw flinched. "But you fell in love on your journey here, didn't you?" His head angled. "It's that pirate—the one you nearly died for."

She swallowed back her tears, nodding. "I don't know if any hope exists for us, but I can't change my feelings." Even if it meant risking her future for a broken man who might never love her like she needed.

"I wish I could stop you." His fingers tensed. "Any life with a man like that will imperil you. I don't want that for you, Jane."

"Just as I can't let you spend your life tethered to a woman you don't truly love. You deserve more."

Edward cast her a sad smile. "I never could argue with you, even when you relayed your plans to cross the Atlantic and become a nun. I thought you were mad, but you couldn't be stopped."

Jane laughed wistfully. "I was mad, and I still am." Only a crazed person would choose a life of uncertainty over the comfort Edward offered.

"No." His head wagged playfully. "You are passionate and un-stoppable. I do believe you will get whatever you please out of life." Drawing her against him, he embraced her as the true brother he'd become in her life.

"Please don't tell my father," she said against his chest. "I'll have to find a gentle way to disappoint him yet again."

"I won't." Edward pulled away, smoothing down her hair before detaching himself and starting for the door. "I will skirt the subject when he asks me. And I'll remind him how lucky he is to have a daughter like you."

Jane stared at the closed door long after he'd left. Part of her wanted to run back and rescind her rejection of his proposal. It would greatly simplify her life ahead. But something stronger tugged at her—the way it had when she had first left England, and again when she'd boarded the *Licorne*. She could not deny the relentless pull drawing her toward the sea, and to the man who loved her.

A gust of tropical air blew through the open double doors, lifting the curtains and dancing up Jane's arms. She could hear the crash of ocean waves below even before she walked across the room and passed to a balcony overlooking the sea. The Atlantic appeared endless from here—its blackened waves stretching to the far reaches of the earth. Though her home rested thousands of miles north, it was difficult to imagine anything beyond this island, dropped into the sea by the hand of God.

The night's stillness enraptured her. Jane closed her eyes to the gentle sweep of the invigorating wind, knowing she was always meant to feel its subtle kiss. The trees around the villa rustled, their leaves brushing against one another. She pressed her hands to the carved stone rail, cold seeping into her skin. *Open your eyes.* A calming sensation touched her, like an unseen hand laid upon her shoulder.

Jane opened her eyes to the quiet night, drawn instantly to the wild beach below. There, a figure strode in solitude beneath the moon's vibrant rays, his mighty gait unmistakable.

Thirty

Christophe walked the beach that night, experiencing it as he never had before. Over the years, he had roamed this shoreline from time to time, falling more deeply in love with it on each journey. Yet now, with the stresses of a privateer's life lifted from his shoulders, he found himself immersed in unearthly beauty he'd never truly seen.

The wet sand squished beneath his bare feet. The evening tide sprinkled his skin in droplets of cool water. Above its lulling rhythm, a chorus of whistling frogs sang to the deep night. Christophe drank in the lovely medley of hibiscus and cherry flowers carrying on the breeze. How had he visited these shores so many times and never really looked at them?

Memories of the day wafted through him. His heart stung each time he pictured his ship succumbing to the ruthless tongues of fire that had devoured it whole. Blanc's malicious face sickened him. Yet he had lived through those hours, and Jane had, too. The miraculous nature of that outcome didn't escape him. Fate had set out to kill one or both of them today. What had held it at bay he feared as much as he longed to discover.

Lifting his eyes skyward, he peered into the black expanse overhead, winking back in speckled stars. Jane was so certain that a loving God ruled this earth. So sure, she had thrown her life into his hands and ventured into the unknown with only one comfort from home. If such a God did exist, and cared enough to save them that day, would he forgive someone like Christophe, who had spent a decade cheating and deceiving? Perhaps he'd find out.

The rolling surf pacified his agitated nerves, pulling his mind into focus. Every muscle in his body had shaken with sobs that day, an ache sheathing him that he hadn't felt since he'd fled his village in childhood. But he understood what mattered now. He felt it, as real as the cool wind feathering up his arms. For the first time in years, his life made sense.

"Hello, Captain Roux," a feminine voice lit the air.

Christophe turned to find Jane as he'd never seen her before, clothed in a floral gown with a frilly collar. Her hair was swept up in ringlets atop her head; pearls shone from a strand around her slender neck. She held the train of her gown in one hand, exposing bare toes wiggling amid the sand.

"Jane. You look—" Could words even describe it? The very sight of her made every last doubt lingering at the edge of his mind shatter into oblivion.

"Rich?" She arched a brow, self-consciously smoothing her exquisite gown with her free hand.

He chuckled. Her clothes *did* finally match the practiced poise with which she always carried herself. "No, you look beautiful." So beautiful, he had difficulty staying planted in the sand.

She cast him a shy smile, one shoulder shrugging. "Just a few gifts from home. Trappings of wealth I was apparently in dire need of."

"I see." His head cocked. "How did you find me?"

"I saw you from the window." Jane pointed toward a row of stately homes rising amid the trees. "My father rented a villa down the beach."

"Your father." A strange blend of emotions brewed within him. "Thank God for your father following you here. I don't know what I would have done if"—his voice broke, the memory of her with a noose around her neck still nauseatingly fresh—"if he hadn't."

Jane's shimmering eyes disclosed her fear. Did she doubt him after the day they'd endured? Had she beheld him pouring out his soul on his knees, knowing a far steadier world waited for her at home? He wouldn't blame her for returning. Earl Whitecliffe and her home country offered so much more than he could ever dream of.

"He wants you to go back," he finally dared to say. "To return to your estate and marry that man he brought with him." Christophe gestured toward the villas with windows aglow in candlelight.

Her chin tilted upward. "And what makes you think that?"

"Because he looks exactly like the type of man an earl would want his daughter to marry." His smile slanted. "And he looked like he might jump onstage and murder the executioner when he saw you on those gallows."

Jane nodded. "Edward has been my best friend for many years, and he is most definitely the type of man my father hopes I marry." She regarded him softly. "But he's not the man I want."

Her simple words made his chest surge. Could a woman like her, bred from the finest of high society, really love an abandoned creature like him? He felt his reality low in his gut—the sins he had committed, the hate he had harbored for so long. He'd spent a decade trying to run from it, chasing after happiness as elusive as the mythical beast adorning his ship's bow. But when he looked at her, inexplicable peace descended over him.

"I'm so sorry about your ship." Jane pressed a hand to her bodice. "You must be devastated after all the time you've spent together."

Christophe inhaled a quivering breath, dragging in the salty nocturnal wind. "I *am* devastated. But I'm also grateful." At the question in her eyes, he stepped toward her. "If I was bound to lose one love today, it should have been her."

Tears filled her eyes, her lips curling sweetly. "I thought—" Her curls bobbed as her head shook. "Never mind what I thought."

When Christophe stood close enough to touch her, he paused, his heartbeat suddenly picking up speed. He had one question left to ask, and her answer terrified him. "Your father wants you back in England, but what do you want, Jane?"

Lashes batting away her tears, she looked down a moment before gazing out at the moon-brushed surf. "I want to stay here—on this island. I love it here. The animals, the flowers"—she closed her eyes, inhaling the exotic, earthy scents around them—"the beaches and the sea air on my face. I was meant to find this place long before I understood it."

Christophe's heart bounded with love for her. "And you still want what you did when we came here? To spend your life at the mission?"

She opened her eyes to him, a playful smile on her lips. "Of course not. Even if they would accept me back after the show I put on for them." Her fingertips gently touched his chest. "I want to stay here with you."

Unhampered joy flooded him—the kind of joy he hadn't imagined possible again. "And I you." Hooking one arm around her waist, he pulled her to him.

"Truly?" Jane searched his face. "What about your life at sea? The reputation you've worked so hard to build? Can you so easily leave it behind?"

Christophe laughed, pressing his forehead to hers. "I have spent the last decade fleeing my pain, building an empire of falsehoods, burying myself so far beneath them that I forgot who I was." Their breath mingled, warming his cheeks. "You liberated me, Jane. You found me, still that lost little child, trying futilely to erase my pain. You saw who I was beneath it all."

She smiled against his skin. "I *love* who you are beneath it all."

Unable to restrain himself a moment longer, Christophe pressed his lips to hers. Jane returned his ardent kiss, her arms winding around his neck, her bare toes lifting her toward him. The rhythm of her heart pounded against his chest, the vanilla scent of her skin intoxicating him. He could stay in this kiss forever, loving her, promising himself to her eternally.

"Marry me," he said against her mouth, too enamored to let go.

The gentle laugh from Jane's throat vibrated on his lips. She pulled back enough to look at him, her eyes full of wonder. "Of course I'll marry you, Christophe Roux. I'll marry you every day for the rest of our lives."

The warm tides washed over their feet as they stood together beneath a cloudless sky, wrapped in each other's love. Christophe held tight to Jane as the cicadas struck up their nightly song, the beach coming alive with chirping. He couldn't help wondering if they celebrated, too. For after so many years of sailing the globe in search of his missing pieces, his soul had come home.

S treams of yellow sunlight showered the beach, heating Christophe's skin and producing tiny beads of sweat on his reddened face. He leaned far over the boat's edge, dipping his hands into the ocean and hauling the net up from her depths. A load he could barely lift emerged from the water, testing his straining forearms. Christophe gritted his teeth, grunting as he pulled the net over the bulwark and onto the deck.

Breathing heavily, he stood over the net filled with wiggling fish. It was a good haul—one which would bring him plenty at market. Perhaps Jane would have a new kerchief in the exchange, or whatever she desired.

A growl in his stomach reminded him of the time. Christophe glanced at the western horizon, where the sun had begun to descend on the water. Dusk would soon cover the ocean's face in deepening blues until night overtook it. He squinted toward the tiny cabin situated near the beach, barely visible in the distance. He should return home before Jane worried.

Navigating his little fishing vessel toward shore, Christophe arrived just as the last rays of sun flashed over the waves, painting a glimmering sunset across the sky. Its pinkish glow radiated around him as he bent to anchor his boat and hopped onto the beach with his fresh catch draped over his shoulder. Out of breath, he dropped onto the white sand and allowed himself a moment to rest.

Sailing a ship had never been an easy endeavor, but fishing required wear on his body that he'd never before experienced. Each night, he crawled into bed with newfound appreciation for men who devoted their lives to this endeavor. Christophe didn't mind the work, but with the store of gold he had saved, he imagined his days as a fisherman were numbered. Within months, perhaps a year, he would have enough for his own vessel and the starting wages for a crew.

He smiled at the fading sun, grateful for this time of restoration and reflection. So many years he'd spent fighting, stealing, deceiving for his next meal. Chasing a dream that only filled him with emptiness when realized. Jane was right; this island brought peace. A sense of belonging in a corrupt world. A chance to step back from it all and marvel at a unique, God-given sunset.

"I wondered if you were home yet." The voice at his back still excited him every time he heard it.

Christophe twisted around to see Jane under the open door of their cabin, one hand on her back, the other sheltering the rounded bump beneath her apron. For a woman raised in the house of an earl, she fit beautifully into Barbados's verdant landscape. Her blonde hair, tied up in a simple bun, framed her face in curly wisps. The blue gingham dress she'd stitched herself fell gracefully off her. Christophe couldn't help but gaze at her a moment longer, amazed by both the woman he'd married and the new life maturing inside of her.

"What are you staring at, silly?" Jane laughed, the most charming sound on earth. "Come in for dinner before it gets cold. I made lamb stew and fresh rolls."

Christophe couldn't help remembering the first meal she'd made for him aboard the *Licorne* with Hugo's help. Now, cooking was just one of many new skills she had acquired and practiced daily. They both had entered a different world full of foreign responsibilities. It was a good thing they had each other—and Hugo, of course. The old cook worked at the hotel in Bridgetown now, promising to join Christophe's future crew once they had assembled.

"I'm coming, my darling." After pushing off the beach, he bent to retrieve his discarded net. "Let me take care of these and wash up first. I wouldn't want the house smelling like fish."

Her grin reached his soul. She hated the stench of fish, but she never turned him away, especially after a grueling day's work. "I'll be waiting." With a wink, she disappeared into the house again, leaving Christophe wholly awestruck.

He collected his catch and carried it to a small shack outside their house, whistling the entire way. A man with more riches in life, he couldn't imagine.

Acknowledgments

As you can probably tell from the word "trilogy" in this series, I never expected to write a fourth book. The conclusion to Madeleine's story was supposed to end these books entirely. But low and behold, a character emerged who connected both with myself and readers more than I ever planned. I couldn't leave Christophe Roux sitting alone on that beach, gazing into his lost dreams. His story needed a proper ending.

So, thank you to the readers who voiced their love of the mysterious pirate captain, despite his flaws. Your bond with Christophe helped fuel me to write another book, one that resonates deeply in my heart. I hope you will enjoy joining the last chapter of this adventure as much as I enjoyed writing it. And who knows? Maybe we will see more of these characters' stories in the future.

Special thanks to members of my ARC team, especially those who have left such beautiful notes and reviews. Just knowing other people relate to my words is a big reason I keep writing. Thanks to every reader, friend, or family member who has supported me over my writing career and in life. Without you, I am just a lonely girl with a keyboard. You mean everything to me and the future worlds I hope to create.

Books by Laurie Sanford

The Winds of Freedom

November Rain
Moon Over Blazing Star Field
Midnight Road to Heaven

The Memory Chase

The Guardians' Plot
The Moon King's Bounty
Traitor Isle
To Capture a Unicorn

For exclusive scenes you can't get anywhere else, head to www.lauriesanford.com/signup.

About the Author

Laurie Sanford is a writer of historical Christian adventure and romance. Her first series, the *Winds of Freedom* trilogy, tells the story of a young woman whose experiences on an antebellum cotton plantation lead her on a journey of self-discovery and ultimate freedom. Her new series, entitled *The Memory Chase,* is an adventure through Napoleonic France and beyond, through the eyes of a woman devoid of memory.

Laurie attended Pacific Union College in Napa Valley, where she earned her Bachelor's Degree. She studied to become a teacher, but wound up as a dispatcher, a job she loves and finds fulfillment doing. Laurie is happily married with two small children.

When she's not at work or wrangling little ones, Laurie enjoys writing (her first love that now comes in fourth in line), reading or watching anything historical, traveling (32 states and counting), exploring nature, playing guitar, and studying genealogy. Having a family is the greatest blessing she has ever been bestowed, and everything she has she owes to Jesus Christ.